SURRENDER

the

HEART

MaryLu Tyndall

BARBOUR
PUBLISHING

Other books by MaryLu Tydall

CHARLES TOWNE BELLES
The Red Siren
The Blue Enchantress
The Raven Saint

THE LEGACY OF THE KING'S PIRATES
The Redemption
The Reliance
The Restitution

The Falcon and the Sparrow

© 2010 by MaryLu Tyndall

ISBN 978-1-60260-165-9

All scripture quotations are taken from the King James Version of the Bible.

Published by Barbour Publishing, Inc., P.O. Box 719, Uhrichsville, OH 44683, www.barbourbooks.com

Cover design: Faceout Studio, www.faceoutstudio.com

Our mission is to publish and distribute inspirational products offering exceptional value and biblical encouragement to the masses.

 Member of the Evangelical Christian Publishers Association

Printed in the United States of America.

❖ HISTORICAL NOTE ❖

Captain Issac Hull of the USS *Constitution* was a Connecticut Yankee and the son of a Revolutionary brigadier general. He went to sea at an early age, and by 1798 became a ship master. Known for his quick thinking and natural talent for leadership, he obtained a commission as a lieutenant in the then forming U.S. Navy on board the USS *Constitution*. In May of 1804, he was promoted to master commandant, and he received command of the *Constitution* by the time war broke out on June 19, 1812.

On August 19, 1812, he met HMS *Guerriere*, an enemy frigate. In a battle that lasted nearly four hours, Hull managed to outmaneuver and pound his foe to pieces. (No record is mentioned of the help he received from the privateer, *Defender*, or that a lone woman aboard a nearby enemy frigate saved the day. But we know what really happened—*wink*.)

This battle marked the first time an American ship had ever defeated a British man-of-war. American navy captains gained confidence from this victory and went on to win more victories at sea. There were celebrations in every American city, and Hull was hailed a hero. Congress awarded him a gold medal. Since then, five ships in the U.S. Navy have been named for Commodore Hull.

Across the Atlantic, the British were shocked and dismayed. The *London Times* reported, "The Loss of the *Guerriere* spreads a degree of gloom through the town which it was painful to observe." Later, the newspaper stated: "There is one object to which our most strenuous efforts should be directed—the entire annihilation of the American Navy."

❖ CASUALTIES ❖

The USS *Constitution*
Deaths: Lieutenant William Bush, Six seamen
Wounded: First Lieutenant Charles Morris, Master John C. Alwyn, four seaman and one marine

The HMS *Guerriere*
Killed: 23 sailors including 2nd Lieutenant Henry Ready
Wounded: 56 men, including Captain Dacres himself, 1st Lieutenant Bartholomew Kent, Master Robert Scott, two master's mates, and one midshipmen

❖ DEDICATION ❖

To everyone who has ever felt ordinary

*And who knoweth whether thou art come to
the kingdom for such a time as this?*

ESTHER 4:14

❖ CHAPTER 1 ❖

June 18, 1812, Baltimore, Maryland

I would rather boil in oil than marry Noah Brenin." Marianne tossed the silver brooch onto her vanity.

"Hold your breath and stay still," her friend Rose said from behind her. "Besides, it is only an engagement party, not a wedding."

"But it is one more step to that horrid destination." Marianne sucked in her breath as Rose threaded the laces through the eyelets on her stays. "Why must women wear these contraptions?"

"To look our best for the gentlemen in our lives." Cassandra appeared on Marianne's left, a lacy petticoat flung over one arm. With shimmering auburn hair and eyes the color of emeralds, Marianne's other friend, Cassandra, had no trouble looking her best for anyone.

Marianne huffed. "I don't care what any gentleman thinks of my appearance."

"Which is why you are still unmarried at five and twenty."

"Then what is your excuse at three and twenty?" Marianne arched a brow, to which Cassandra gave a shrug. "I have not yet met a man worthy of me." She grinned.

"Where on earth is your chambermaid?" Rose grunted as she squeezed Marianne's rounded figure into the stays and tied the final lace tight. "Shouldn't she be doing this?"

"I dismissed her." Marianne waved a hand through the air. "I prefer to dress myself." She hoped they didn't hear the slight quaver in her voice. She didn't want her friends to know that her mother had been forced to let the entire staff go and the ones here today were hired just for her betrothal party.

"There." Rose finished fastening the corset and stepped back.

Marianne took the petticoat from Cassandra and slipped it over her head. "Truth is, I do not wish to marry—ever." She squared her shoulders as Cassandra slid behind her and latched the petticoat hooks.

Rose put her hands on her waist. "Noah Brenin is a fine man and a good catch."

Marianne gazed at her friend. She couldn't help but smile at the motherly reprimand burning in her crystal blue eyes. Tall and slender, with honey-blond hair, Rose turned many a head in Baltimore. Just like Cassandra.

Marianne wished she had the same effect on men.

"He is a boor."

"Why so low an opinion of him? Haven't you and he been friends since childhood?" Rose cocked her head and gave Marianne a look of censure.

"I wouldn't call it friendship, more like forced acquaintance. And my knowledge of him is precisely why I know him for the churlish clod he is."

Gathering a cream-colored silk-embroidered gown from Marianne's bed, Rose and Cassandra tossed it over her head, assisting her as she wiggled into it. She adjusted the ruffled lace that bordered her neckline and circled her puffy sleeves. Cassandra handed her a jeweled belt, which Marianne strapped around her high waist and buckled in front. She pressed down the folds of her gown, admiring the pink lace that trailed down the front and trimmed the hemline. After slipping on her white satin slippers, Marianne moved to the full-length looking glass and paused to eye her reflection.

Plain. Despite the shimmering, glamorous dress, *plain* was the first word that came to her mind. That was how she had always been described. Brown hair, brown eyes, average height, a bit plump. Nothing remarkable, nothing to catch an eye.

Simply plain.

Which was precisely why, when the other girls her age were being courted, Marianne had chosen to spend her time caring for her ailing mother and younger sister, particularly after their father died. No whirlwind romances, no soirees, no grand adventures lit up the horizon for her. She had resigned herself to lead an ordinary life. An ordinary life for an ordinary girl.

"Come now, it won't be so bad." Rose brushed a lock of hair from Marianne's forehead and then straightened one of the curls dangling about her neck. "You look as though you were attending your own funeral."

"I daresay I feel as though I am." Tired of staring into the mirror hoping her reflection would transform into that of a beautiful woman, Marianne turned aside, picked up her silk gloves from the vanity, and sauntered toward the window.

"I, for one, cannot wait to get married," Rose said. "To the right man of course. He must be a good, honest, God-fearing man. A man who stays home, not a seaman. And he must be agreeable in all respects."

"What about handsome?" Cassandra asked. Marianne turned to see a blush creep up Rose's neck.

"Well, yes, I suppose I would not be opposed to that." Her blue eyes twinkled.

Facing the window, Marianne slid the white gloves onto her hands and tugged them up her arms. Shouts echoed from the street below, accompanied by the *clip-clop* of horse hooves and the grating of carriage wheels. She brushed aside the curtain to see people running to and fro darting between phaetons and wagons. A warm breeze, heavy with moisture and the smells of the sea, stirred the curtains. A bell rang in the distance, drawing Marianne's attention to the maze of ships' masts that thrust into the sky like iron bars of a prison. A prison that could not constrain the ravenous indigo waters from feeding upon the innocent—an innocent like her father.

Rose and Cassandra joined her at the window as more shouts blasted in with the wind. "What is all the commotion about?" Cassandra drew back the curtains.

"There have been rumors that President Madison will soon declare war on Britain," Marianne said.

"I hope it doesn't come to that." Rose peered over Marianne's shoulder. "War is such horrid business."

"But necessary if the British insist on stealing our men from land and sea and impressing them into their navy." Marianne said. "Not to mention how they rouse the Indians to attack us on the frontier."

"They want their colonies back, I suppose." Afternoon sunlight set Cassandra's red hair aflame in ribbons of liquid fire. "England never was good at losing."

"Well, they can't have them." Marianne's voice rose with a determination she felt building within. Though she'd been born after the Revolution, she had heard the stories of oppression and tyranny enforced upon America by a nation across the seas whose king thought he had the right to dictate laws and taxes without giving the people a voice. But no more. "We won our freedom from them. We are a nation now. A new nation that represents liberty to the entire world."

"I couldn't agree more." Cassandra nodded with a smile. "Perhaps you should run for mayor?"

"A woman in public office?" Marianne chuckled. "That will never happen."

The door creaked open, and Marianne turned to see her mother and younger sister slip inside.

Lizzie's eyes widened and she rushed toward Marianne. "You look so beautiful, Marianne!"

Kneeling, Marianne embraced her sister. She held her tight and took a big whiff of the lavender soap with which their mother always scrubbed the little girl. "Thank you, Lizzie. I can always count on you for a compliment."

"Now, Lizzie, don't wrinkle your sister's dress." Marianne's mother sank into one of the chairs by the fireplace and winced. The slight reminder of her mother's pain caused Marianne's heart to shrink. She squeezed her little sister again—the one beacon of joy in their house these past three years since Father died—and kissed her on the cheek. "You look very beautiful, too."

The little girl clutched her skirt and twirled around. "Do you really think so?" She drew her lips into a pout. "But when can I wear a dress like yours?"

"Come now, Lizzie," Mother said. "You are only six. When you are a grown woman like Marianne, you may wear more elaborate gowns." She gestured toward Rose and Cassandra. "Ladies, would you take Lizzie downstairs for a moment? I need a word with Marianne."

"Of course, Mrs. Denton." Rose took Lizzie's hand. "Come along, little one."

Cassandra followed after them, closing the door when she left.

Marianne sat in the chair beside her mother and gently grasped her hands. She flinched at how cold and moist they were. "How are you feeling, Mama?"

"Very well today, dear." She looked down as if hiding something.

But Marianne didn't need to look in her mother's eyes to know she was lying. The sprinkles of perspiration on her forehead, the paleness of her skin, and the tightening of her lips when the pains hit, spoke more clearly than any words.

Marianne squeezed her mother's hands. "The medicines are not working?"

"They will work. It takes time." Her mother attempted a smile. "But let us not talk of that now. I have something more important to discuss with you." She released a heavy sigh then lifted her gaze to Marianne's. Though illness had stolen the glimmer from her eyes, it could not hide the sweet kindness of her soul. "You don't have to do this, you know."

The truth of her words sliced through Marianne. She stared at the floral pattern woven into the carpet. "You know I do."

"It isn't fair of me to ask this of you." Her mother's voice rang with conviction and deep sorrow.

"You didn't ask, Mama. I want to do this." A truth followed by a lie. Marianne hoped the good canceled out the bad.

"Come now. You cannot fool me." Mama said. "I know this is not the match you would choose."

Releasing her mother's hands, Marianne rose from the chair and moved toward the window. The rustle of her gown joined the sounds of the city filtering in from outside. "In truth, I would choose no match ever." She turned and forced a smile. "So if I must marry, why not this man?"

Her mother gazed at her with such love and sorrow that Marianne felt her heart would burst. Once considered the most beautiful woman in Baltimore, Jane Denton, now withered away with sickness that robbed her of her glow and luster and stole the fat from her bones, leaving her but a frail skeleton of what she once had been. The physicians had no idea what ailed her; they only knew that without the medications they administered, she would die a quicker and more painful death.

Tearing her gaze from the tragic vision, Marianne glanced out the window where it seemed as though the approaching evening only heightened the citizens' agitation over the possibility of impending war. "Marrying Noah Brenin will save us. It will save you."

"But what of saving you?" Her mother's sweet plea caressed Marianne's ears, but she forced down the spark of hope that dared to rise at her mother's question. There was no room for hope now, only necessity.

"You know if we continue as is, all that is left of our fortune will be spent in one year on your prescriptions. Then what will we do? Without my dowry, no man will look my way, since that and our good name is all that has caught this particular fish upon the hook." And without a husband to unlock her inheritance, her father had ensured that the seven thousand dollars would remain as far from her reach as if she did not own it at all.

"Perhaps you will meet another man—someone you love?" her mother said.

"Mama, I am five and twenty." Marianne turned and waved her hands over herself. "And plain to look at." She gave a bitter laugh. "Do you see suitors lining up at our door?"

"You are too beautiful for words, dearest." Her mother's eyes beamed in adoration. "You just don't know it yet."

Shrugging off her mother's compliment, Marianne stiffened her back before she attempted to rekindle an argument long since put to death. "We could take what's left of our money and fund a privateer, Mama." Marianne glanced out the window at a mob that had formed down the street. "War is certain and our fledgling navy will need all the help it can get."

Her mother's nervous huff drew Marianne's gaze. "It is far too much of a gamble. And gambling destroys lives"—a glaze covered her mother's eyes as she turned from the window and stared, unseeing, into the room—"and families."

Marianne grimaced. "This is nothing like what Papa did. I have heard these privateers can make a fortune while helping to defend our country."

A breeze stirred a curled wisp of her mother's hair as she gazed at Marianne with concern.

Marianne twisted the ring on her finger. "Down at the docks, merchantmen are already outfitting their ships as privateers. The call for investors goes out daily." If only she could convince her mother, not only would Marianne not have to marry that clod, Noah, but also she could do something to help this great nation of hers.

Her mother's boney hands, perched in her lap, began to tremble. "We could lose everything. And what of Lizzie? I could not bear it."

Shame drummed upon Marianne's hopes. She had upset her mother when the doctor strictly instructed her to keep her calm.

"Perhaps you could take up a trade of some sort?" Mama offered.

"I hear that Mrs. Pickersgill makes a decent living sewing ensigns."

A blast of warm wind stirred the gauzy curtains and cooled the perspiration forming on Marianne's neck. "Mama you know I have no skills. I'm not like other ladies. The last gown I attempted to sew fell apart. My cooking would drive the hardiest frontiersman back to the woods, and the pianoforte runs when it sees me coming."

Mother chuckled. "You exaggerate, dearest."

But Marianne could tell by the look in her mother's eyes that despite the humorous delivery, her words rang true. Though a governess and her mother had strived to teach Marianne the skills every proper lady should acquire, she had found them nothing but tedious. She possessed no useful skills, no talents. As her father had so often declared before his death. Marianne had nothing to offer. If her mother would not agree to fund a privateer, Marianne would have to accept her fate in marriage.

"I must ensure you and Lizzie are cared for either by this marriage or by some other means." Mama said with a sigh. "I'm an old woman and will die soon anyway."

Marianne's heart sank at the words. Gathering her skirts, she dashed toward her mother and knelt at her feet. "You must never say such a thing."

"Do not soil your beautiful gown." Her mother smiled and wiped a tear from Marianne's cheek. "Perhaps we should simply trust God with my health and let His will prevail."

Marianne laid her head on her mother's lap like she used to do as a child. She had trusted her father, she had trusted God.

And they had both let her down—her and her mother.

"I will not let you die, Mother. I cannot." Her eyes burned with tears. "As long as I have my inheritance and a man who is willing to marry me, I promise you will be well cared for. And Lizzie, too. That is all that matters now." Marianne lifted her gaze to her mother's, feeling strength surge through her.

"And mark my words, Mama. Nothing will stand in my way. Especially not Noah Brenin."

❖ CHAPTER 2 ❖

Noah Brenin doffed his hat and wiped the sweat from his brow as he made his way down Hanover Street. He adjusted the purple ostrich plume attached to his bicorn. His first mate, Luke Heaton, walked beside him, nodding a greeting to every pretty lady who passed by. Plopping his hat back atop his head, Noah forced his feet to continue. He was late and he should hurry his pace, yet all he wanted to do was turn around and go back to his ship. He had work to do and no time for his father's absurd commitments. Not to mention he had been dreading the announcement of his engagement to Miss Denton ever since he'd agreed to the match several months ago.

Now that the night was upon him, he truly wondered what he'd been thinking. Miss Marianne Denton? Had he gone mad?

"You look more nervous than if we were caught in the sights of a broadside." Luke chuckled, but Noah offered no response. He found nothing humorous about the situation. They turned down Conway Street, trying to avoid the people and carriages crowding the narrow avenue. A blast of muggy June wind struck him as if an oven had been opened. Sweat slid down his back.

A man in top hat and coat stood on the corner handing out pamphlets and shouting, "War is coming. Join the militia!"

Skirting him while holding up a hand to ward off the pamphlet being thrust into his hand, Noah plodded onward.

"It appears war will indeed be upon us," Luke said.

"What is that to me? I don't care unless it interferes with my trade."

"I daresay, where is your patriotism, man?" Luke applied his most pompous tone to a statement devoid of enthusiasm.

An absence of which, Noah shared. "Where yours is. In the lining of my pockets." Noah grinned and halted to allow a horse and rider to pass before he crossed the street. A hot breeze wafted the smell of manure his way as if the city were unhappy with his diminutive allegiance. But who could blame him? England had always been good to Noah. His trade with Great Britain had enabled him to keep his father's merchant business afloat. Why would he wish to go to war against the nation that fed him?

Noah hesitated before a large brick house. Music and laughter bubbled from the windows, grating over his nerves. He steeled himself against another overwhelming desire to turn and bolt for his ship.

Luke studied him, a curious look on his face. "Scads, Noah, Miss Denton cannot be all that bad."

"Humph, you think not? She is a spoiled, silly girl. Let's get this over with. I want to set sail tonight."

"Aye, aye, Captain." Luke grinned as they took the few steps up to a wide front porch and rapped the front door's brass knocker.

A servant answered, took their names along with their hats, and escorted them inside to a parlor brimming with people. The smell of myriad perfumes mixed with the scent of wine tickled Noah's nose. He sneezed then scanned the room, searching for his father so they could proceed as soon as possible. To his left, a large mantel of polished black marble perched proudly against the wall. Around it stood a group of men—none of them his father—involved in a heated argument. From the few words that drifted his way, Noah surmised their conversation centered on the potential war. A serpentine serving table laden with sweet cakes, lemonade, and wine stretched nearly the entire length of the room. Around it hovered several guests, pecking and nibbling at the food like a flock of birds. Walnut wing-backed armchairs, along with two mahogany settees, provided the only seating—all taken by elderly women, their heads leaning together in gossip.

"Mr. Noah Brenin," the butler announced. "And Mr. Luke Heaton."

All eyes turned to the two men, and some of the women whispered to each other behind fans. How Noah hated being on display.

"It is about time." Staring at a pocket watch in his hand, Noah's father's portly frame emerged from a crowd on Noah's right. The scowl on his face made him look much older than his sixty-two years.

Luke murmured a hasty excuse and headed toward the buffet, leaving Noah to deal with his father's foul mood alone. "We were delayed with business aboard the ship," Noah said, hoping to belay the man's usual rebuke.

The frown on his father's face did not falter—a frown Noah had grown accustomed to over the years. His mother sashayed forward, a glass of wine in her hand. "Do not argue please, William. It is our son's engagement." The sting of alcohol from his mother's breath filled the air between them, and Noah cringed, hoping she would not embarrass him tonight.

Then, as if she saw him for the first time, his mother gasped. "What are you wearing? What of the dark silk suit Matton laid out for you in your chamber?" She eyed him up and down and clucked her tongue. "What will everyone think?"

"I haven't a care what they think, Mother." He glanced down at his tan breeches and black waistcoat and saw nothing wrong with his attire. At least he had donned an overcoat and a clean shirt. "I had no time to return home. I have been working all day, preparing the ship to sail. I must leave forthwith."

"Tonight? Why the rush?" His father's forehead wrinkled.

"I must sail my cargo to England as soon as possible before our trade is further restricted. Mr. Glover expects me in South Hampton in six weeks' time or he threatened to purchase his flour, rice, and iron from another merchant." Noah studied his father, searching for some sign of approval of his plan. "With all this talk of war, I dare not delay another day."

"Very well, by all means, leave as soon as you can." His father straightened his coat. "But I do not think it will come to war. We could never hope to win against a nation as powerful as England again. Madison knows that all too well."

"I am not so sure."

"Nonsense." His father chuckled. "What do you know of it, boy?"

At the word *boy*—the only endearment with which his father addressed him—Noah felt as though he were shrinking in size. At six and twenty he was hardly a boy anymore. Hadn't he proved that by now?

His mother sipped her wine and gazed over the crowd as if bored with the conversation.

"It was the American embargo that caused us the most damage." Noah shifted his stance as anger boiled within him at yet another circumstance that threatened his success. "Blasted Jefferson. Now with the threat of war, how do they expect us merchants to survive?"

"Ah, let us not trouble ourselves with it." His father leaned toward him as if sharing a grand secret. "Soon we will not have to worry overmuch." He leaned in and lowered his voice. "Miss Denton's inheritance will assure our merchant business stays afloat until all this trouble with England has blown over." He stretched his shoulders back. "That is, if you don't muck up the opportunity it presents, boy, to make the Brenin name successful and well known. You know your mother and I are depending on you."

Yes, Noah knew that all too well—was reminded of it often. "There is not much I can do if war is declared."

"War, indeed. Bunch of rubbish, if you ask me."

But Noah knew better. He had heard the talk down by the docks. The merchantmen were furious at Britain's impressments of American sailors into their navy, not to mention the trade restrictions. In fact, he knew several merchants who were already refitting their ships to be privateers. But he held his tongue. He had no time nor interest in another argument with his father.

Luke joined them, drink in hand and stuffing a piece of cake into his mouth. "You should try one of these. They are excellent."

Noah's mother finished her wine and gave Luke a lift of her nose. "William, please escort me to refill my glass." She stumbled slightly, and Noah closed his eyes.

"Very well." His father sighed, disappointment reflecting in his blues eyes. "We should make the announcement soon." He gave one last look of disapproval to Noah before he offered his elbow to his wife and led her to the buffet.

Noah took the opportunity to slip into the corner away from the crowds, his first mate following on his heels.

"So where is your beloved fiancée?" Luke surveyed the guests. "And why have you not greeted her?"

Noah gestured with his head toward a cluster of women to the right of the fireplace. "There, in the middle of those three women. And please refrain from calling her my beloved."

Luke's gaze shot in their direction and studied her for a moment. "The brunette? Hmm. Not so bad, Captain. Certainly not extraordinary, but she seems pleasant enough."

Noah had never thought of Marianne as pleasant. Spoiled, demanding, obnoxious, but never pleasant.

Luke blew out a soft whistle. "But the lady beside her is quite remarkable."

Noah followed his gaze. Fiery red hair framed the delicate features of a near-perfect face. Her emerald green eyes suddenly shot to his and he looked away. He tugged at his cravat. "The redhead? I suppose."

"Who is she?"

"Miss Cassandra Channing, I believe."

"You must introduce me, Captain."

"We haven't time. Besides, word about town is that she is hotheaded and independent."

Luke's blue eyes sparkled. "Ah, but you know how I love a challenge."

Noah chuckled, amazed at his friend's constant infatuation with the weaker gender.

Luke sipped his wine and lifted a brow toward Noah. "You did not answer my question. Why have you not greeted your intended?"

Noah stiffened his jaw. "Because, my good man, it is best I keep my distance from Miss Denton as much as possible." He leaned toward his friend. "For I have every intention of persuading her to break off this absurd engagement."

Luke's eyes widened. "Why would you wish such a thing? Don't you need her dowry?"

"Not if things go well on this next voyage. We stand to make a fortune if I can get to England on time."

"It seems cruel." Luke gazed across the room toward the woman.

Noah shrugged. "Why? Neither of us have affections for the other. I am sure she would welcome a reason to disengage herself from any association with me. And rather than cause her or her reputation any harm, I shall allow her the honor of making the split."

"And how do you plan to do that?"

Noah raised a brow. "Watch and see."

"I daresay, he does present a handsome figure, don't you agree, Marianne?" Cassandra plucked out her fan and fluttered it about her face.

Rose laughed. "Quit drooling, Cassandra. He is not your fiancé."

"Oh, that he were." Marianne sipped her lemonade and studied the man she would marry. Indeed, he had grown up quite nicely from the skinny jackanapes who used to pull her hair when no one was looking. His broad shoulders and thick chest stretched the fabric of his black coat. His light brown hair, streaked with gold by the sun, was combed back in a fashionable style, and not in the usual windblown disarray she'd grown accustomed to seeing among others of his profession. A recent shave revealed a strong jaw that, coupled with his dark eyebrows, gave him the appearance of a man in control of his destiny and determined to get what he wanted.

And Marianne was positive it could not be her. "You may have him, Cassandra. It is settled. I will go tell my mother at once." She took a step forward but Cassandra's strong grasp pulled her back. "You know you cannot do that. He is the only option you have. You must get used to the arrangement."

Marianne stepped back between the two ladies with a sigh and glanced over the gathering of people who were partaking of the cakes, lemonade, and the wine her mother had spent two weeks' of their food allowance on. Some dear friends, some acquaintances, and some she hardly knew but who had been invited because of their positions in society. Edward Johnson, the mayor, Mr. Wilson, the magistrate, two councilmen, and General Stricker. Her father had been an influential man.

Then her eyes met Noah's, and he winced as if he could not bear the sight of her. She lowered her gaze and took a sip of lemonade, wishing she could melt into the cup and disappear. She had not spoken to him in over a year. He was always at sea and when he was in town, he never called on her. Even during the arrangements of their betrothal—a meeting between Marianne's mother and Noah's parents in this very parlor—Noah had slipped out before she'd had a chance to speak to him, leaving her wondering how he felt about the match. But now after looking in his eyes, she had no doubt where his feelings lay.

The chime of silverware on glass filled the parlor, drawing all eyes to Marianne's mother who stood before the fireplace. She gestured for Marianne to join her.

Lizzie appeared out of nowhere, her face beaming. "It's time, Marianne." Her innocent enthusiasm tore at Marianne's heart, making her long to be young again, free from the fetters of adult responsibilities. Taking a deep breath, she pressed a hand over her roiling stomach and handed Rose her glass. "That is my cue."

Cassandra gave her a little nudge to get her moving as Lizzie tugged on her hand.

"Noah, Noah! Come here this instant." Noah's mother shouted across the room, pointing at Noah with her glass of wine. The dark red fluid sloshed over the rim and slid down the sides. Silence struck all tongues as reproachful glances shot to her and then swept to the corner where Noah stood. His jaw flexed and his face reddened.

Marianne cringed with embarrassment for him. It must be difficult having a mother who overindulged in drink, even though everyone in town knew of Mrs. Brenin's little problem

Noah strode across the room and approached his mother, took the drink from her hand and set it on a table. "Never fear, Mother, I am here." He took her hand and kissed it before placing it upon his arm for support.

Marianne smiled at the man's kindness toward his mother as Lizzie led her to stand beside her own mother on the opposite end of the mantel. She drew a deep breath to quell her trembling nerves. After her mother greeted her guests, making special mention of those with prominent positions in the city, and thanking everyone for attending, she deferred to Mr. Brenin for the formal announcement.

The formal announcement of Marianne's life sentence—for an engagement was as binding as marriage itself.

Her blood rushed so fast past her ears, she heard little of what Noah's father said, save for the moment when he proudly announced her betrothal to his son.

Lizzie giggled and hugged Marianne. The crowd clapped and all eyes darted to her, causing a blush to rise on her face. She tried to smile, but the agony in her throat prevented her lips from moving. Daring a glance at Noah, she wondered why he had not made a move to stand beside her and take her hand. Instead, he stood as cold and emotionless as the marble mantel behind him. As people swarmed forward to congratulate the couple, Noah's mother pushed her son toward Marianne. "For goodness' sakes, Noah. She doesn't bite." Her shrill laughter blared over the crowd's murmuring. Noah tugged on his cravat as he inched closer to Marianne as if he, indeed, thought she might chomp on his arm.

Fighting back her anger, Marianne accepted the congratulations and well wishes from the guests with as much grace and enthusiasm as she could muster, though both virtues dwindled with Noah's continual disregard. She hoped he would at least pretend he was not marrying her for her dowry alone. Yet, as the crowd moved past, their happy looks transformed into looks of pity, and Marianne fought back the tears filling her eyes.

Soon the throng moved back to their former conversations and Noah faced her, his blue eyes searching hers uncomfortably. He took her hand and raised it to his lips.

Marianne swallowed. "At last you greet me, Mr. Brenin."

"I hope you can forgive me. I often have trouble tearing my thoughts away from business." He flashed a smile, the brevity of which left her wishing for more. "I meant no disrespect." His eyes took her in again. "You look lovely this afternoon, Miss Denton."

A wave of heat flushed through Marianne at his unexpected compliment. "You are too kind." She smiled and he released her hand.

He glanced over his shoulder toward the door. "But I fear I must beg your forgiveness once again, Miss Denton, for I must leave straight away."

Leave? Marianne shook her head. "Whatever do you mean, Mr. Brenin? You only just arrived."

"Yes, I know, but I must set sail immediately or I stand to lose a great deal of money." The look in his eyes did not affirm the veracity of his statement. Rather, he shifted uncomfortably and avoided her gaze.

The lemonade soured in Marianne's stomach. She leaned toward him. "Regardless, you cannot leave our engagement party," she whispered through clenched teeth.

Her mother eased beside her, perhaps sensing her rising anger.

Noah bowed politely in her direction "Thank you, Mrs. Denton, for such a lovely afternoon."

Marianne's mother eyed him curiously, but she accepted his appreciation with a smile. "You are most welcome, Mr. Brenin. There is more to come."

"Unfortunately, I will not be able to partake of your extended kindness. I am to set sail within the hour." With a nod, he turned and sauntered across the room to join his friend. The two of them exited the parlor. Seconds later, the front door closed with a definitive thud. Once again, everyone looked at Marianne, including Cassandra and Rose, who quickly dashed to her side. Whispers slithered about the room like gossiping snakes and for the second time that night, Marianne wished she could disappear.

"He did not just leave." She heard the spite in her own voice. Not in front of everyone. Not when the party had only begun. Now it would be plain to all that he cared nothing for her or for their marriage.

"I believe he did," Cassandra said.

"Oh dear." Her mother coughed and her face blanched as if she were about to faint. Grabbing her, Marianne led her to a nearby chair. "Rose, get my mother some lemonade, if you please."

Rose skittered away and returned with a glass, which Marianne held to her mother's lips. She took a few sips and then leaned back. "Thank you, dearest. I will be all right."

Marianne set the glass on a table and studied her face as the color returned. Perhaps her mother would recover for now, but blast that scoundrel Noah for upsetting her so.

"I'm so sorry, Marianne," Rose said.

Marianne hung her head, battling a plethora of emotions: embarrassment, shame, sorrow, and finally anger. Clenching her fists, she squared her shoulders. "He's not going to get away with this. Not this time."

❖ CHAPTER 3 ❖

Mr. Brenin, come back here this instant!" Incensed at the man's loathsome behavior, Marianne rushed out the front door after him. Clutching her skirts, she leapt down the stairs and dashed out into the street. "Mr. Brenin!"

Noah halted, shifted his shoulders, and turned to face her. "My apologies, Miss Denton, but I have a ship full of cargo I must get to England as soon as possible."

"You will do no such thing!" Marianne tripped over a stone and stumbled forward. She caught her balance before making a fool of herself and tumbling to the ground. Noah's friend, Mr. Heaton, chuckled as Noah faced forward and continued on his way.

"Go home, Miss Denton." He flung a hand over his shoulder.

"Marianne!" Lizzie's sweet voice filled the air.

"Dearest, come back." Her mother's plea wrapped around her like an invisible rope, halting her, tugging her home to safety and love.

But one slice of her fury severed it in an instant.

"Never fear, Mother, Lizzie, I will return shortly," she shouted as she stomped forward after the two men. Her rage tore away any pride left within her and tossed it to the cobblestones beneath her feet. She knew her behavior only made her shame all the more evident, more humiliating, but she couldn't help her actions. How dare Noah embarrass her in front of everyone, the councilmen, and the mayor? How dare he shame her in such a horrid way? Why, she would be the laughingstock of the whole city. She'd be unable to show her face in any social circle.

One quick glance behind revealed her worst fear. A mob of guests crowded the porch of her home. Some laughed while others looked at her with pity. The latter included her mother, standing alongside her two friends Cassandra and Rose.

But Marianne could not stop. "Mr. Brenin, if you please." She darted before a phaeton. The driver jerked the horse's reins and the animal neighed in protest.

"Watch where you're going!" the coachman shouted. Marianne waved an apology and forged ahead.

"Mr. Brenin!"

Halting, Noah swung about, a look of annoyance twisting his handsome features. Beside him, Mr. Heaton seemed to be having difficulty holding back his laughter. A gust of hot wind tugged at Marianne's curls. Perspiration dotted her neck.

Noah's blue eyes sharpened. "Miss Denton, it is unseemly and most unsafe for you to be chasing me through the city streets."

"Mr. Brenin, it is most rude and incorrigible for you to abandon me at our engagement party."

Noah released a sigh and gazed down the avenue toward the docks, then back at her as if she were an annoying rodent. "I have not abandoned you, miss. I simply have more important—" He halted and flattened his lips. "I have crucial business to attend to. Surely you don't wish to have a sluggard for a husband."

She didn't wish to have a husband at all, if truth be told. Marianne drew a deep breath and composed herself. "What I wish for, sir, is a husband who treats me with respect and doesn't make me an object of mockery before the entire town."

A flicker of sympathy crossed his face before it hardened back to stone. "When I am your husband, you have my word I will never do so."

"How am I to believe you when you so freely disregard me now?"

He smiled, that arrogant half smile that set her blood boiling. "Me? I believe you are the one acting beneath your station, chasing me down the street like a needy little wife."

Marianne contained herself with difficulty. "I am neither needy nor your wife. Can you not spare my dignity with a few hours of your time, sir?"

"Your dignity?" He laughed, his blue eyes sparkling. Removing his hat, he palmed the sweat from his brow. "Is that what this is about? Your dignity? You always did care for the opinions of others."

"Why, you insufferable clod," Marianne spat.

Mr. Heaton chuckled, but was instantly silenced with one look from Noah. The first mate turned toward Marianne, "If I may, Miss Denton, I—"

"You may not, Mr. Heaton." She gave him a scorching look. "Not unless you can convince your captain to return to our engagement party." Marianne eyed Noah's first mate, the man whose daring ways were the talk of the town amongst the ladies. A perfect specimen of manhood save for the tiny scar that sliced through his right earlobe. The twinkle in his eye as he perused her told her he was also a man who had no difficulty drawing female attention.

Yet she felt naught but annoyance at him.

Mr. Heaton shrugged and instead tipped his hat at a lady who passed on his left.

Noah shifted his leather boots impatiently over the cobblestone. "Now if you please, Miss Denton, we must be on our way. I suggest you return home posthaste as the night falls and the crowds appear quite agitated."

"I will do no such thing unless you return with me. How can I face my guests when my own fiancé can't stand the sight of me?"

His eyebrows shot up and he gazed at her curiously, but then he placed his hat atop his head and straightened his coat. "It is not the sight of you that disturbs me, miss, but your attempt to rule over my affairs. Now run along, Miss Denton." He flapped one hand toward her as if to brush her away. "We can discuss this when I return."

Marianne's eyes burned with tears at the man's cruelty, but she willed them away. She would not give him the satisfaction.

Obviously taking her silence as compliance, he swung around and marched down the street, Mr. Heaton by his side. Together, they disappeared into a mob of citizens who were shouting and cursing as one man at the center held up a pamphlet.

"Federalist garbage!" one man yelled.

"I'll not have this treason printed in my town!"

Clutching her skirts, Marianne circled the mob, thankful when they ignored her. Standing on her tiptoes, she peered down Conway Street, searching for Noah's hat. Since he stood a head taller than most men and wore that pompous purple plume, she should have no trouble spotting him. She knew following a man through the streets would not only besmirch her reputation but put her in harm's way, especially as the sun slipped below the buildings and the shadows crept out from hiding, but she could not let him win again. Not this time. This time he would learn that he could not treat her like a child to be bullied whenever he pleased.

Memories assaulted her of the time when she was five years old and Noah had dropped a frog in her bonnet, only to laugh hysterically when she placed it atop her head and screamed. Or the time he had stolen a pie from Marianne's cook, Maggie, and showered crumbs in Marianne's hair and on her dress to incriminate her for the infraction. She had spent two days alone in her chamber and received no pie for a month as punishment. Memory after memory assailed her, fueling her resolve to forge ahead and bring him back. If she had to marry this unscrupulous rogue, then she had better assert herself from the start. He could set sail as often as he liked, he could do whatever he wanted as long as he cared for her mother and sister, and treated Marianne with respect. Was that too much to ask?

Above the bobbing heads, the imperious flutter of his purple plume marked his location. She dashed between two carriages and followed him as he turned down Light Street. A breeze coming off the harbor whirled around her, bringing with it the smell of the sea, of fish, and crab, and the sting of refuse. Tall ships of all sorts and sizes bobbed in the choppy bay, some docked at the long piers that ran out into the water.

She tripped over a brick, and pain seared up her toe and into her foot. Biting her lip, she continued threading her way through the sailors, merchantmen, footmen, and coaches, as well as ladies and gentleman out for a stroll along the bay.

Noah turned right onto Pratt Street and she followed him.

Workers and slaves hustled over the wharves as they carried last-minute goods to the ships. Baltimore had grown so much since the Revolution that it had become the third largest seaport in America. Though Marianne hated the harbor, she was proud of that fact and proud of her grand city. Ignoring the glances and whistles the sailors cast her way, she dashed through the throng and kept her head down to avoid drawing unnecessary attention.

A pianoforte twanged from one of the taverns lining the street as a cacophony of laughter and song erupted from men taking early to their cups. Marianne shivered, though the night was warm. She hated the inner harbor. Not so much because of the lecherous stares from the seamen or because of the danger, but because of the dark choppy sea that stretched its greedy fingers up the Patapsco River. Didn't the sea claim enough victims upon the open waters? Did it have to invade the land as well?

Continuing onward, she avoided looking at the water licking the pilings of the dock as if smacking its lips in anticipation of a meal. She avoided looking at the ominous spot that loomed up ahead.

The spot where they had found her father facedown in the harbor.

His body bloated and pale from spending days in the water. She swallowed a burst of sorrow and shifted her gaze to the warehouses and taverns tucked across the cobblestone street, all the while silently cursing Noah for forcing her to visit a place she'd successfully avoided for three years.

Noah marched onto one of the piers then dashed across a plank that led to a ship. Mr. Heaton followed, and the air instantly filled with Noah's resounding voice spouting orders to his crew.

Heart stuck in her throat, Marianne inched down the wobbling wharf and halted at the foot of the plank. Her feet went numb. On the ship, Noah and another sailor perused a document. Never once did he look her way. She glanced at the name painted in red letters upon the hull. *Fortune.* Of course. A perfect name for a man who cared for nothing but wealth.

" 'Scuse me, miss." A worker hoisting a crate onto his shoulder drew her attention. She stepped aside to allow him to pass.

Other workers loading goods onto the ship passed her by, the plank buckling beneath their weight like a spring. But would that spring snap? Beneath the flimsy plank, claws of foam-encrusted water leapt up in search of unwary victims.

Noah disappeared down one of the hatches, and Marianne knew she hadn't much time. She held her breath and dashed across the plank. The wood shifted beneath her slippers as if it were water itself, but then she felt the firm railing. She looked around, proud of her accomplishment, but not in time to see there were no steps leading down from the ship's railing.

Waving her arms through the air, she tumbled to the deck in a heap of silk and lace. Her skirt flew up, leaving her petticoats fluttering around her.

Chuckles bombarded her from all around, followed by catcalls and whistles. Her face heated.

"Ye ain't supposed to be here, miss." One of the sailors reached out to help her to her feet.

Rising, she released his hand and pressed down her skirts, ignoring the crude comments flung her way.

"Begging your pardon, sir, but I believe I am. I am the captain's fiancée." She thrust out her chin. "And I must speak to him at once."

The sailor, a young man in a checkered shirt, red scarf, and tan breeches, looked her over as if she couldn't possibly be the captain's fiancée. A thick jagged scar ran down his left cheek and disappeared into the scarf tied around his neck. "I expect he went to his cabin, miss."

Marianne turned her gaze away from his disfigurement. "And where might that be?"

But before he could answer, another man grabbed him by the arm and pointed to something above in the yards. The two men climbed aloft, leaving her alone.

Very well. Though she'd never been on a ship before, it didn't appear to be too big. How hard could it be to find the captain's cabin? Marianne sauntered to the hole into which Noah had disappeared and peeked below where a ladder descended into the gloom. Grabbing the rail, she lifted her skirts and carefully lowered herself down the narrow, steep stairs. The smell of aged wood and tar filled her nose. At the foot, she headed down a long corridor, lit by lanterns hooked along the sides. A row of cannons wrapped in thick ropes and sitting on wood carriages lined both sides of the deck. Surely the captain's cabin would not reside next to such dangerous guns.

"All hands aloft!" Feet pounded above her, echoing like drums.

Men passed by her, looks of surprise on their faces. Some tipped their hats, while others stared at her curiously before they sped on their way. The ship seemed to close in on her. Why was everything so cramped down here? How did these men survive in such tight quarters?

"Sir, if you please." Marianne leapt in the path of a sailor. "Can you direct me to the captain's cabin?"

Halting, he eyed her and adjusted his dirt-encrusted neckerchief.

"Come along, Rupert!" a man yelled from above.

The sailor glanced upward and shifted his feet nervously. "It's aft, ma'am," he said before scurrying away.

Aft. Hmm. Marianne wasn't quite sure what this aft meant. Down perhaps? She found another ladder. Surely the captain's cabin was below, away from the noise and clamor where he would have more space and more quiet. A stench that reminded her of rotten eggs assaulted her as she descended farther into the gloom. Holding a hand to her nose, she reached the bottom and continued down another narrow hallway. At the end, a door stood ajar. No lantern lit this room, but the dim light coming in from the hallway revealed nothing but barrels and crates. She was about to shut the door when a tiny meow sounded from the corner. Peering into the darkness, she scanned the room.

"Meow."

"Heave short the anchor!" A man bellowed from above, and the sound of a chain chimed through the ship.

Marianne crept inside the room. "Poor kitty. Down here in the dark all alone." Releasing the door, she felt her way around barrels and chests toward the last place she'd heard the meow. The ship lurched. The door slammed shut. A darkness blacker than she'd ever witnessed closed in on her.

"Meow."

"I'm coming, little one. I'll get you out of here."

A snap that reminded Marianne of the crack of a huge whip crackled the air. The ship jerked again. She took another step forward, feeling the edge of a wooden cask with her gloves. A splinter pierced the silk and into her skin. She winced.

The ship pitched, and she gripped the crate to keep her balance. The sound of wood scraping against wood filled her ears. She inched her way forward. A creak and another scraping noise.

Thump! Twack! The drums and chests came to life around her.

She bumped against something tall beside her. It moved.

"Meow."

"I am here, little one." Marianne reached in the direction of the feline's plea. Warm fur brushed against her glove.

The ship jerked again.

Thunk! Something heavy struck her from above. She crumpled to the floor. The last thing she remembered was the burning pain in her head and the cat licking her face.

❖ CHAPTER 4 ❖

"Ease off the topsails, Mr. Heaton," Noah commanded from his position on the quarterdeck. He clasped his hands behind his back and glanced over his shoulder at his helmsman. "Three points to larboard, Mr. Pike."

"Three points to larboard, Captain," Pike answered.

From his position beside Noah, Mr. Heaton shouted orders that sent sailors leaping into the shrouds and scrambling up the ratlines to adjust canvas.

Closing his eyes, Noah allowed the stiff breeze to blast over him and rake through his hair. He shook his head, hoping to rid himself of the memories of home and the agonizing look on Miss Denton's face. He hadn't meant to cause her shame. Confound it all, he should never have agreed to the match. But what else could he do when the Brenin merchant business had suffered so much this past year?

A situation his father blamed entirely on Noah.

Noah clamped his jaw tight. Would anything ever be enough to make up for what had happened eleven years ago? He had done his best: set records in making the fastest crossing to England, made

31

arduous trips during hurricane season to the Caribbean, and worked tirelessly for months on end. And if not for the American embargo five years ago and the British laws prohibiting Americans from trading with France, he would have doubled their income and not been forced to sell one of their two ships to keep the business afloat.

Then his father would not have insisted Noah accept the engagement to Miss Denton. And Noah would not have been forced to behave the cur yesterday. Now he could not rid himself of the vision of Miss Denton's sorrowful brown eyes. Surely her pain sprouted from pride and not from any affection she harbored for him.

Noah gazed across the sea that spread like a dark blue fan to the horizon. The rising sun flung golden jewels upon the waters and capped the waves in foamy white. He stretched back his shoulders. Upon the sea, he was captain of his ship, master of his destiny. Not like back at home where he was simply William Brenin's incompetent son.

"It is good to be back out to sea, eh, Luke?" Noah asked his first mate.

"Indeed." Luke nodded and gripped the railing. "You there, Mr. Simon, haul taut, hoist away topgallants and jib!" he yelled to one of the sailors below on the main deck then released a sigh. "But our liberty at port was rather short this time."

Noah cocked a brow. "Didn't get your fill of drink and women?"

"Is that possible?" Luke grinned as he scratched the stubble on his jaw.

Noah chuckled.

"We could have at least stayed at your engagement party a bit longer," Luke added. "I barely had two sips of wine."

"You know we had no time to spare."

"Persistent girl. I admire her for that." Luke shoved a strand of black hair behind his ear.

"You refer to Miss Denton, of course." The ship rose over a wave, and Noah braced his boots on the deck, annoyed that his friend had brought the woman back into his thoughts. "I daresay she's acquired a bit of spunk in her womanhood."

"She's definitely not a little girl anymore." Luke's eyes carried the salacious twinkle always present whenever he spoke about the fairer sex.

Noah grunted. "I regret running out on her, but it could not be helped."

Luke tipped his hat down against the bright rays of the sun. "From the look on her face, I imagine you won't have too much trouble persuading her to call off your engagement."

"Which is precisely why our need to set sail worked in my favor. Who could forgive such insolent behavior? Why, I imagine at this moment she's already discussing with her mother and my parents the best way to annul the arrangement."

Pain drummed a steady beat in Marianne's head. She willed it away and tried to slip back into the peaceful repose from which she came. But the agony would not abate. In fact, it worsened. A moan escaped her lips. She lifted her hand and dabbed her head. Her fingers touched something moist and sticky that stirred the pain anew.

A deep purring tickled her ears. She opened her eyes to nothing but thick darkness. Confusion scrambled her thoughts. Where was she? Then the creak of wood and oscillating of the floor sent a shock through her. She jolted upright.

Noah's ship.

Her breath caught in her throat. Something furry leapt into her lap, and she screamed. When she tried to push it off, the creature began purring again. Taking a deep breath, Marianne picked it up and drew it to her chest. "Oh, little one. What happened? How long have we been down here?"

The cat's only reply was further purring as it nestled in her arms. Marianne clung to it, fighting the ache in her head and the rising panic that she was out to sea. Fear scrambled through her like a wicked imp, pinching every nerve. *Lord, I know I haven't spoken to You in a while, but please don't let me be out to sea. Please have mercy.*

No answer came save the creaking and groaning of the wooden planks and the faint rustle of water against the hull—all of which made her plea dissipate into the stagnant, moldy air. She struggled to rise, still holding the cat. With one hand she felt her way through the maze of barrels toward the thin strip of light marking the bottom of the doorway. Opening the wooden slab, she made her way down the same hallway she had traversed earlier. Her head grew light, and she gripped the wall to steady herself.

Shouting and laughter sounded from above. She took the first ladder toward the clamor and the ever-brightening sunlight filtering downward. Squinting, she climbed the final stairs and emerged to a burst of wind and a spray of salty water. Above her, white sails snapped in the breeze. Sailors sat upon the yards, adjusting them with ropes. Other men stomped across the deck. Those who saw her stopped to stare. She gazed toward the horizon and trembled. All around the ship spanned an enormous gaping mouth full of salivating azure water.

The sailors, whose normally boisterous voices could always be heard across the deck, grew unusually silent. Ignoring the unease that slithered down his spine, Noah lowered the spyglass and gazed amidships. His heart seized.

A woman in a cream-colored gown with pink trim stood in the center of the deck. He blinked and rubbed his eyes. Had his guilt over the ignoble way he had treated Miss Denton conjured up visions of the woman to taunt him?

"Captain." Luke's voice jarred him, and he opened his eyes to a look of grand amusement on his first mate's face. "I believe you have a guest."

Noah glanced toward the main deck again, praying his eyes had betrayed him. But no, there, in the middle, stood Miss Denton, frozen as if she were a statue.

Anger simmered in his belly as he stormed toward the quarterdeck ladder and leapt down onto the deck. "Miss Denton, what on earth are you...?"

She faced him, a white cat in her arms, terror screaming from her eyes. A red streak crept down her forehead, seeping from a dark, matted blotch in her hair. She said not a word but looked at him as if he were a ghost. She stumbled, and he dashed to her and grabbed her shoulders. "Miss Denton?"

She looked up at him with wide brown eyes. "I am at sea."

"Yes. I find that fact as astounding as you."

"But I cannot be at sea."

Upon closer inspection, the spot of matted hair was a bloody wound. Noah scanned the deck and found his boatswain. "Matthew, call your wife to your quarters, if you please, and have her bring her medical satchel."

"Aye, sir." Matthew disappeared down a hatch.

Marianne lifted a hand to her head. The cat leapt from her embrace. "Forgive me, Mr. Brenin, but I do not feel very well." She fell against him, and he swept her up into his arms.

The sailors began to crowd around. "Who is she, Captain?" Mr. Weller, Noah's gunner asked.

"Put me down, this instant," Miss Denton murmured.

"How did she get on board?" another man asked.

"I have no idea." Noah glanced up at his first mate. A smirk played upon his lips. "Mr. Heaton, you have the helm."

"Yes, Captain."

Leaving his curious crew behind, Noah carefully navigated the ladder and headed down the companionway toward Matthew's quarters. He entered the cabin and laid Miss Denton on the new coverlet that Agnes had just spread on the bed. Matthew stood near the bulkhead, kneading his hat in his hand.

Miss Denton opened her eyes and moaned.

"Oh my, poor dear." Agnes darted to her side. "Who is she?"

"My fiancée." Noah took a step back. "She appears to have hit her head."

"Don't you worry, sir, I'll attend to 'er right away." Agnes's cheeks reddened as she handed a pewter basin to her husband. "Fetch me some water, Mr. Hobbs."

The short, bald man donned his hat and eyed his captain.

Noah nodded his agreement, and the boatswain scurried out the door faster than his stocky frame would seem to allow.

"Noah." Miss Denton tried to lift herself from the bed but fell back onto the coverlet. "I must return home at once."

"I'm afraid that will be impossible."

"I assure you, it is quite possible." Miss Denton's breathing grew ragged. "Help me up, please." She latched onto Agnes's arm and pulled herself to a sitting position.

Noah huffed his annoyance. "You will lie back down this instant, Miss Denton, and allow Mrs. Hobbs to dress your wound. It is a long voyage and I'll not have you growing ill on my ship."

"Voyage?" Her brow wrinkled as if she could not fathom the meaning of the word. Her chest heaved. "I cannot possibly—"

"Inform me if she does not cooperate, Mrs. Hobbs," Noah interrupted, "and I'll have her strapped to the bed." He used his stern captain's voice in an effort to prevent any further defiance.

Agnes swung a look of reprimand his way, and Miss Denton's face pinched. "You wouldn't dare!"

Noah clenched his jaw. "It would be my pleasure." Then turning, he stomped from the room and closed the door.

The rotund woman with the cheery face of an angel dabbed a wet cloth on Marianne's head. Wincing, Marianne gasped at the sting.

"My apologies, dear." The woman smiled. "But ye've got quite a gash on your head and I need t' clean it."

Marianne pushed the woman's hand away and struggled to rise. The white cat, perched at the foot of the bed, opened her sleepy eyes at the interruption. "Oh, there you are, little one. This is all your fault, you know."

"Seafoam?" The woman chuckled and her chubby cheeks jiggled. "That cat always be gettin' in some kind o' trouble."

Lifting a hand, Marianne rubbed her forehead. "I thank you for your kindness, Mrs. . . ."

"Hobbs, but ye can call me Agnes." The woman dipped the cloth into a basin filled with water and wrung it out. "Whatever happened to ye, miss?"

Sinking back onto the lumpy mattress, Marianne closed her eyes against the throbbing as Agnes rubbed the cloth over her wound. "I was searching for No—the captain. I suppose I got lost. I heard a cat meowing and went into a room to investigate. The rest is a bit of a blur."

"Seafoam." Agnes wagged a finger at the cat. "See the trouble you cause." Agnes's laughter bubbled through the room, causing Marianne's nerves to unwind. But only for an instant. For the rush of water against the hull reminded her of where she was.

She gazed curiously at the cheery lady before her. Why would any woman sail the seas of her own volition? "I don't mean to intrude, but whatever are you doing aboard this ship?"

"Me husband is the ship's boatswain. And not wantin' t' be without him, I signed on as cook." She wrung out the bloody cloth in the basin and set it aside. "But I also do laundry and any doctorin' that needs attendin' to." She opened a black satchel and pulled out a bundle of white cloth. "Me, a surgeon." She chuckled. "The Lord has a sense o' humor, I'd say."

The ship careened to the right, and Agnes gripped the bed frame. Marianne guessed her to be around her mother's age, but any further resemblance stopped there. Where Marianne's mother was petite, frail, and peaked, this woman's pink skin, rotund figure, and sparkling green eyes radiated health.

The snap of sails thundered above, followed by the shouts of the crew. Agnes unrolled the white strip of cloth, sliced a portion off with a knife, and gently wrapped it around Marianne's head.

"Being out at sea doesn't frighten you?" Marianne asked as Agnes tied the bandage and sat back to examine her work.

Her face scrunched. "Afraid? Nay. I love the sea. Was born on a ship in the Caribbean." She stuffed her wiry red hair streaked with gray back underneath her mobcap and took Marianne's hand in hers. "Now don't be afraid. Cap'n Brenin be a good cap'n. But you best be stayin' put for a while. You don't want t' find yourself strapped t' the bed." She grinned, revealing two missing teeth on her bottom row.

"Surely he wasn't serious."

Agnes's brow lifted along with her shoulders. "One thing I know 'bout the cap'n. He's not a man given t' jokin'." She coiled the remaining bandage back into a ball and stuffed it in her satchel. "Truth be told, I don't know what's got into 'im. He's usually a perfect gentleman. I ain't never seen him behave so unmannerly towards a lady."

"I have." Marianne pushed aside the resurging memories of his cruelty as a child. "Perhaps he wears a mask of civility for the benefit of his friends."

"Naw. Mr. Hobbs and I have sailed wit' him for five years. He be a good man, you'll see. An' he'll make a fine husband." Her cheeks reddened.

Marianne had her doubts about that as well, but she thought better than to voice them. Obviously Noah had fooled this woman into believing he was something he was not.

Agnes patted Marianne's hand. "Now get some rest. I'll check on you later." Then standing, she ambled from the room.

Rest? Marianne closed her eyes, trying to drown out the rustle of the sea against the hull and the sound of the wind thrumming in the sails. How could she rest when all that stood between her and a watery grave were a few planks of wood?

Seafoam rose, stretched her legs, and sauntered to lie beside Marianne. Turning on her side, Marianne caressed the cat's soft fur. "I thought cats were afraid of water."

Purring rose to Marianne's ears as Seafoam nestled against her.

"Well, if you can be brave, little one, then so can I." Marianne winced at the throbbing in her head even as her eyelids grew heavy.

The room began to spin, and she slowly drifted into a chaotic slumber filled with nightmares.

Marianne and her mother and sister were without a boat in the middle of the ocean, thrashing their arms through the foamy waves to keep afloat. A small vessel approached. Marianne's father and Noah sat within it, rowing toward some unknown destination. Pleading desperately for help, Marianne called out to them as they passed. But neither man looked her way. She continued to scream and splash to get their attention. But both men kept their faces forward and their hands to the oars. Soon, they slipped away and faded into the horizon, leaving Marianne and her family to drown.

Noah picked up the lantern and set it beside the chart spread across his desk. Using his divider, protractor, gunner's scale, and Mr. Grainger's best weather prediction, Noah had plotted their fastest route to South Hampton. With clear skies and God's good favor, they'd make port in four weeks. After they reached South Hampton and off-loaded their cargo, Noah had arranged to transport silks and fine china to Nevis in the Caribbean, where he expected the wealthy colonists would pay handsomely for the extravagances lacking in the new world. Then at Nevis, he would fill his hold with coffee and sugar to sell in Baltimore. All in all, he hoped to make a year's wages with this one voyage.

Perhaps then his father would see him as a more-than-qualified merchantman. Perhaps then, that gleam of approval Noah longed to see would appear in his father's eyes. Dare he even hope for an added spark of forgiveness? Reaching into his waistcoat pocket, Noah withdrew a handkerchief—his brother's handkerchief. He unfolded it and laid it across the palm of his hand giving it the reverence of a holy object. To him, it was holy. He traced the deep maroon stains that marred its center and then fingered the lace at the edges. His eyes grew moist. "I'm sorry, Jacob." He stared at it for a moment then gently folded it into a tiny square and slipped it back inside his waistcoat.

Clearing his throat, he forced back all emotion then laid down the scale and walked to a cabinet built into the bulkhead. Opening the door, he grabbed a bottle of port and poured himself a glass, then wove around his desk and gazed out the stern window. A half moon lingered over the horizon. The ebony sea seemed to be reaching up toward it, trying to grab hold of some of its crystalline light for itself.

Noah released a sigh. Everything was going well, everything save one tiny detail.

Rap rap rap.

"Enter." Noah expected Luke with the watch report, but instead of the thud of heavy boots, the swish of silk sounded. He spun around.

"Thank you, Mr. Boone." Miss Denton nodded toward the purser as the sailor's eyes met Noah's uncomfortably before he scrambled down the corridor.

"Such a narrow hallway." She gestured behind her. "How do you endure such cramped quarters?"

"The hallway is called a companionway, Miss Denton."

She nodded and swept the cabin with her gaze. "So this is where your chamber is located." She approached Noah's desk, leaving the door ajar.

"My *cabin*, yes."

"Ah yes, I knew that." A dark red stain marred the white bandage swaddling her head, marking the position of her wound. Brown curls dangled on top of the cloth and crawled from beneath it as if they refused to be restrained. The ship bucked. Her eyes widened as she flung out her arms to keep her balance. Curves rounded the folds of her silk gown that glistened in the candlelight.

Shaking off a sudden wave of heat, Noah averted his gaze. "I believe I told you to rest." He circled his desk, fighting back his annoyance at her presence, and poured himself a glass of port.

"I did." She glanced across his cabin again, only this time her eyes seemed to soak in every detail before they returned to him. "All day, as a matter of fact, Mr. Brenin."

"I am called *Captain* aboard my ship, Miss Denton."

"Very well, I will call you whatever you want as long as you return me to Baltimore as soon as possible." The lift of her chin and smug look on her face brought him back fifteen years to a time when she was naught but a spoiled girl flaunting her wealth before a poor merchant's son.

"You are in no position to order me about any longer, Miss Denton. . .or should I say *princess?*" Noah grinned and sipped his port. The sweet wine slid down his throat, warming him.

Her eyes narrowed for an instant, but then she waved her hand through the air. "You may call me princess if you wish, *waif.*"

The word struck him with the same shameful twinge it had when he was a boy.

Her golden-brown eyes snapped his way. "You did naught but tease me as a child."

"And you did naught but belittle me." Noah leaned back on the top of his desk and crossed his boots at the angle.

She bit her lip and began twisting a ring on her right hand.

The look of fear on her face softened the bitter memories of their youth, and Noah released a sigh. "Perhaps we should set aside our childish ways."

"Would that you had decided to do so before you abandoned me in Baltimore." Her sharp tone stabbed him.

"I had no choice. Business before pleasure, you know."

"Pleasure, humph." Marianne leveled a stern gaze upon him. "You looked as if you'd prefer the town stockade to attending your own engagement party."

Noah finished his port and set the glass down. How could he deny it?

A shadow passed over her face, and she looked away. Noah groaned inwardly. He did not wish to hurt her. In fact, it took all his strength to stop from explaining his boorish behavior. Yet perhaps his reasons would hurt her even more. No, the idea to break off the engagement must be hers and hers alone—to spare her reputation, and perhaps her heart.

But what to do with her now? The thought of being forced to

endure her company for months made his stomach curdle. Yet perhaps he could use this time to his advantage. Noah ran a hand over the back of his neck and watched her as she struggled to maintain eye contact with him, despite the trembling in her bottom lip. Yes, he would have plenty of time to convince her that he was the obnoxious cad she believed him to be and that life with him would be unbearable.

"Your silence confirms my suspicions." She pressed a hand over her throat and sank into one of his high-backed chairs. "Let us be honest with each other, Noah." She sighed. "You have no intention of marrying me, do you?"

Marianne awaited his answer, but instead he smiled. "You always were rather forthright, Miss Denton."

"While you were never so." She glanced across the cabin again, a much larger room than she would have expected. Yet everything within it—from the three high-backed Chippendale chairs circling a mahogany desk, to the oversized chest with a heavy iron lock, to the fitted racks that held volumes of books and brass trinkets, and finally to the two swords, a pistol, an hourglass, a map, and various instruments that lined his desk—everything was masculine, and well ordered, just like its master.

Her stomach knotted. He had not answered her question. Yet, how could she force this man to marry her when the very thought of it made her own skin crawl?

"I have every intention of following through with my obligation, miss." He folded his arms across his chest and shifted his blue eyes to the massive trunk perched by an archway that led to his sleeping chamber. A breeze blew in from the open door, feathering the hair that touched his collar. The muscles in his jaw twitched, but he would not look at her.

He was lying. She knew it. "Is that what I am, an obligation? How romantic."

He chuckled. "If you want romance, I suggest you search for it somewhere else—in one of those tawdry novels coming out of London, perhaps?" He quirked a dark eyebrow so at odds with his light brown hair. Then grew serious. "While we are being honest, Miss Denton, you know as well as I that it is your dowry that has drawn us together."

Of course she knew that. Then why did his admission cause her heart to ache? Perhaps because it crushed her childhood dreams of someday finding love and romance in the arms of an admirable man. A man nothing like the one standing before her. But then again, why would she expect anything extraordinary to happen to someone ordinary like her? She folded her hands in her lap. "Have no care, Captain. I do not flatter myself to think otherwise. But your desperation must be exceedingly great to force your agreement to such an undesirable match."

Noah adjusted the cuffs of his white shirt then cocked his head toward her. "What has me quite vexed, Miss Denton, is what benefit this match is for you. It is obvious you loathe me."

"Loathe is a strong word." She batted the air, trying to avoid the question. The smell of wine and leather and aged wood filled her nose. She couldn't very well tell Noah that she and her mother were nearly destitute, that without this marriage, they could not touch the inheritance her father left her and purchase the much-needed medicines to keep her mother alive. She wasn't lying to him. He would receive the seven thousand dollars of her dowry the moment they married. But what he didn't know was that he would receive nothing else, no jewelry, or silverware, satin sheets, china, Persian rugs, or any of the luxuries her mother had been forced to sell this past year. Instead he would acquire only Marianne, her sister, and a sick mother-in-law. So, Marianne simply responded, "Our fathers wished it."

He eyed her curiously. "Your father would not wish you unhappy, miss. I assure you I will not make you a good husband."

Marianne gripped the arm of the chair. Her throat went dry. "Why are you trying to dissuade me when you have admitted that you need my money?"

He shrugged and stared out the open door down the corridor. "I see how my presence upsets you. It would no doubt be pure torture for you should we marry."

"What upsets me is your behavior."

"Unfortunately the two cannot be separated."

"That is not true. People can change if they want to. God can change people."

"What has He to do with it?"

Marianne flinched. "God has everything to do with everything."

"If that is so, then He has much to answer for." He frowned and turned to stare out the stern windows.

"You should not say such things, Noah." Marianne's heart saddened. His family had faced tragedy, as had hers. But she had not forsaken God. Or had she? Certainly her trust in Him had waned.

She struggled to her feet. "Enough of this. I cannot sail to England with you. My mother is ill and needs my help."

He faced her. "She has servants who will attend to her, I am sure."

In truth, no. "Only I can see to her properly. And my little sister will be lost without me. I simply cannot be gone for months."

"Then you shouldn't have snuck aboard my ship."

She stomped her foot, the hard wood sending a dull ache through her silk slippers. "Then you shouldn't have run away from me."

He rubbed the back of his neck, and the features of his face grew tight. She wondered if he still had the same nasty temper he had as a boy. "Confound it all, I stand to make a great deal of money on this voyage, Miss Denton. Perhaps even more than your dowry is worth."

More than her dowry? Then he wouldn't need her. Fear clogged in Marianne's throat. She couldn't allow that to happen.

"But time is of the essence," he continued, "And I cannot waste two days returning you home. I'm afraid you are here for the duration of the voyage. There is nothing I can do about it."

The ship pitched, and Marianne shifted her feet to catch her balance. A salt-laden breeze swirled about the room. The candle flickered, and a chill slid down her back. The mad dash of water against the hull mocked her as fear for her mother battled for preeminence against fear of the sea.

"You don't understand. I cannot be aboard this ship." Tears burned behind her eyes, but she would not disclose her fears and provide him with more ammunition with which to badger her.

"But the fact is you are, miss. By your own accord, I might add. And as such, you will be my guest until we return home. Though nothing like the elegance you are accustomed to, I assure you the ship will be quite comfortable."

Marianne felt the blood drain from her face as dizziness threatened to spin her vision. She grabbed the chair for support and closed her eyes.

Noah's boots thumped across the planks. He took both her hands in his. "You have not yet recovered from your wound, Miss Denton. I'll show you to your cabin."

The gentle way he caressed her fingers sent unwanted warmth through her. She opened her eyes.

"What have we here?" He flipped over her hands. Red, crusty calluses stared up at them both. Marianne snatched her hands from his.

"It is nothing. It must have happened when the crate struck me." She took a step back.

He narrowed his blue eyes upon her.

"Very well, Noah." She conceded to allay his suspicion. "Perhaps I do need some rest. You may show me to my room."

He stiffened at her condescending tone, but it couldn't be helped. It was the only way for her to recover from what he had seen on her hands. If he knew she worked as a common servant in her own house, he would no doubt call the wedding off.

Grabbing a lantern from his desk, he gestured toward the door and gave a mock bow. "This way, miss."

Lifting her nose in the air, Marianne followed him down the narrow hallway, lit by intermittent lanterns to another door not far from the captain's. He opened it to a space no bigger than a closet. A box-framed bed attached to the wall filled most of the room, save for a tiny shelf for belongings. A foul, moldy smell swamped over her.

But Marianne didn't care. She'd grown accustomed to sleeping in a chair by her mother's bedside, so truth be told, the stuffed tick on the bed appeared more than inviting.

After placing the lantern on the shelf, Noah leaned on the door-frame and watched her as she eased past him, brushing his arm. "Thank you, Noah."

His eyes widened and he studied her as if she'd said the sea was made of blue pudding.

She pressed down the folds of her gown and shook her head. "What I meant to say was, I suppose it will have to do."

"Yes, it will. Sleep well, Miss Denton." He gave her a sly wink before shutting the door. His boot steps pounded his exit down the hallway.

Marianne sank onto the knotty mattress. She didn't intend to sleep. She had planning to do. Noah must not have any reason to break off their engagement. Her mother's life depended on it. Therefore, she must discover a way to do one of two things: Either make Noah fall madly in love with her or stop him from making his fortune by sabotaging his ship. The former made her sick to her stomach.

The latter brought a smile to her lips.

❖ CHAPTER 5 ❖

Inhaling a deep breath, Marianne trudged up the ladder that led to the main deck. The sound of her stomach gurgling rose even above the crash of waves against the hull. She had hoped to remain below today where she could more easily forget she was in the middle of the ocean. Besides, she had to plan the best way to sabotage the ship, and she wanted to investigate the lower decks. But the biscuit and jam she'd eaten for breakfast were not cooperating. In fact, they rebelled quite vehemently. She poked her head above deck, and a gust of wind tore at the hair she'd managed to pin up in a loose bun despite the bandage wrapped around her head.

Pressing down her skirts to keep them from flying up, Marianne took the final step above. Fear threatened to send her below. She tried to calm her rapid breathing, afraid the heaving of her chest might tear the gown Agnes had lent her—a garment that had obviously belonged to a much thinner woman than Marianne.

Face forward, she inched her trembling feet to the mainmast, grabbed the rough wood, and squeezed her eyes shut, trying to quell the ferocious beating of her heart. Sounds of footsteps, shouts, the gurgle of water, and creak of wood assailed her ears. Hot rays from a sun sitting high in the blue sky scorched her tender skin.

Lord, I need Your help. I need Your strength. Please grant me Your peace and help me find a way to get back home to my mother. The ship canted, and she planted her feet slightly apart to brace herself, realizing how unfamiliar prayer had become to her. *Please watch over her and Lizzie in my absence. And please help me find a way to ensure Noah marries me.* The remains of her biscuit rose in her throat. She swallowed them down. *Or if there's another way to save my mother and Lizzie without marrying that beef-witted clod. . .* She hesitated beneath a spark of guilt. *Forgive me, Lord.* The ship pitched and a salty spray showered over her. *One more thing, Lord. If You don't mind, please keep this ship afloat. Amen.*

She should have felt better—more at peace—like she used to feel after praying, but instead all she felt was the ever-present anxiety that had plagued her since her father died and dragged the entire family fortune with him into the depths of Baltimore harbor. The notes of Papa's funeral dirge had scarce faded when creditors descended on their home like a pack of wolves to collect on his gambling debts. Though he had not been the most affectionate or attentive parent, Marianne had always believed he would care for his family. When he died, she lost more than a father, and more than their fortune, Marianne had lost her trust.

Her trust in man and her trust in God.

"Miss?" A gruff voice startled her, and she snapped her eyes open to see a tall man peering down at her. The same man who had helped her to her feet when she'd first come aboard—or rather fell aboard. Beneath his floppy hat, thick black hair whipped over his shoulders in the wind. "The captain inquires as to your health." Her gaze shot unbidden to a patch of rippled skin that scarred the left side of his face. He seemed to notice the direction of her eyes and frowned. Shoving aside her ill ease at the deformity, Marianne smiled instead and met his eyes directly.

"Oh he does, does he, Mr. . . ."

"Mr. Weller, miss." Intelligent brown eyes examined her from within a face that, despite the scar, appeared young. He nodded at the death grip she had on the mast. "And he insists you go below if you're not feeling well."

Releasing the mast, Marianne cocked her head. "Insists, you say?" She glanced up at the quarterdeck where Noah stood by the wheel glaring down at her, his purple plume bending to the breeze. She could not make out his eyes in the shadow of his hat.

Ever present, his salacious accomplice, Mr. Heaton, stood by his side.

Retrieving a handkerchief from her sleeve, she dabbed the perspiration on her neck and faced Mr. Weller. "And what is your position aboard the ship, sir?"

He stared agape at her as if no one had ever asked the question. "I am the ship's gunner and supercargo, miss."

"What does a supercargo do?" She could well assume what function a gunner served.

"I handle the transfer of all monies, miss, along with carrying out all selling and buying at each port of call."

Marianne smiled. This man could be very useful to her. "Indeed. Do you know much of the workings of the ship?"

"Aye, miss. I suppose." He tugged upon his red scarf, his brows scrunching together beneath the brim of his hat.

Tucking that information away for a more propitious time, Marianne sighed. "Very well, Mr. Weller, would you do me the honor of escorting me up to see the captain? I should like to speak with him, and I am unaccustomed to the shifting deck."

A slow smile lifted his lips. "Why, yes, miss." He extended his arm, but suddenly snapped it back and shoved his hand into his pocket. But not before she saw that only two fingers remained upon it.

He gestured with his other hand toward the ladder and started in that direction. Marianne had no idea what had happened to this man, but she did know how it felt to be less than perfect, to be flawed. Weaving her arm through his, she pulled his hand from his pocket and gave him her best smile.

He eyed her curiously, then led her to the stairs and up onto the quarterdeck just as "A sail, a sail!" bellowed down from the crosstrees.

"Where away?" Noah yelled, trying to ignore Miss Denton, who took a spot beside him.

"Off our larboard quarter."

Cursing under his breath, Noah raised his spyglass and focused on the horizon. Most likely another merchant ship. Nothing to get overwrought about. Certainly less remarkable than the scene he'd just witnessed amidships. Miss Marianne Denton, highbrow extraordinaire, treating scared and deformed Mr. Weller with not only kindness but also compassion. Even from his position above her, Noah had seen the slight cringe on her expression the moment she caught sight of his face. He'd waited for the expected turn of her nose and polite excuse to leave. Shock gripped him at what he beheld instead.

Now, she stood beside him, one hand lifted to cover her eyes as she peered in the direction of his scope, the other hand clutching the railing in such a tight grip, her fingers reddened. The scent of fresh soap wafted over him—no doubt given her by Agnes. The clean lavender smell—a rare one among sailors—tickled his nose and aroused his guilt. Miss Denton should not be at sea. Born to opulence and ease, she was like a duchess among degenerates aboard this ship of rough, crude sailors.

He adjusted the scope until three sails, glutted with wind, came into view. His chest tightened. Not a merchant ship. He handed the glass to Luke.

"What do you make of her?" he asked.

His first mate studied the ship for several seconds before giving Noah a look of concern. "A British warship."

"Yes." Noah took the glass and nodded. "A frigate was my guess."

"She appears to be gaining, sir." Luke scowled.

Miss Denton faced him, her chest heaving and her brown eyes wide. "Will they attack us, Mr. Brenin?"

Noah flexed the muscles in his jaw. "Captain."

She huffed. "Will they attack us, Captain?"

Noah angled his lips and shrugged. "Why would they?"

"They may try an' impress us." Mr. Pike offered from his position at the wheel behind them.

"Balderdash, Mr. Pike. We have no one on board who deserted the British navy." Yet even as he uttered the confident declaration, his glance took in Mr. Weller, who stood at the foot of the quarterdeck ladder. Though the man hadn't directly deserted the Royal Navy, he had allowed them to presume him dead when the brig sloop he served aboard went down in a squall four years ago.

Mr. Weller's gaze met his, and Noah saw raw fear leap in his eyes at the sight of one of His Majesty's ships heading straight toward them.

"Never fear, Mr. Weller," Noah said. "It will not come to that. However, go below and ready the guns in the off chance we need them." Which they wouldn't, of course. Not only because it would be suicide to go up against a British frigate with Noah's small armament, but because all Noah's dealings with the British had proved them an honorable people. Despite the stories he heard on the docks, Noah did not believe the British would steal Americans to serve on their ships. Regardless, he wanted to give his gunner something to do that would help ease his fears.

"Aye, aye, Captain." Weller nodded and jumped down the ladder.

The ship swooped over a roller, flinging creamy spray across the bow. Miss Denton's knuckles whitened on the railing. She seemed to be having trouble breathing.

Fear. He recognized it well. Mind-numbing, debilitating fear. But of what? The frigate? Him? Or was it an act?

Regardless, he had no time for her theatrics. "Make all sail, Mr. Heaton. That should give them the message that we haven't time to stop and chat."

"Haul taut, sheet home, hoist away topgallants and jib!" Luke directed the crew, and men grabbed onto thick lines while others leapt into the shrouds and scrambled above.

Noah watched them clamber with the confidence of monkeys up into the yards. His palms began to sweat, though his feet remained firmly planted on deck. Yes, he knew about fear. He knew about fear very well.

Shaking it off, he raised his spyglass again, trying to determine the frigate's intentions while keeping his mind off Miss Denton beside him and the way her curves filled out her gown. She'd always been a bit plump, while he decidedly preferred ladies of a more slender figure. Why then, did he find his gaze drawn toward her?

"I hear they take no care for a sailor's nationality or whether they ever served in the British navy," she announced with conviction.

"Pure rubbish, Miss Denton." With glass still pressed to his eye, he kept his gaze locked on the frigate. Sailors scampered across her deck and yards, hauling all sails to the wind. Giving chase. Alarm rose within him.

"Have you taken sides with our enemies, Captain?" Accusation stung in her voice.

Sails thundered above him in an ominous boom.

He faced her, making no attempt to hide his frustration. "I take no side, Miss Denton."

Her nose pinked and her eyes narrowed. "It is common knowledge that the British stop and board our ships and impress our sailors without cause. I would think you, of all people, would be angry at such an affront."

Ignoring her, he cuffed a hand over the back of his neck. "Let fall sheet home, hoist away royals and flying jib!" he bellowed across the deck, sending more men to their tasks. Why didn't the blasted woman go below? "They have not attacked me. Consequently, I have no fight with them."

The ship creaked and groaned as it picked up speed. Miss Denton's face whitened. She clung to the railing as if it were her only salvation. When the ship settled again, she righted herself, keeping both hands on the rail. "So it is all about you, then, Mr. Brenin—I mean, Captain?

You care not a whit for your country."

Luke gazed at them both, a look of pure enjoyment on his face.

Leveling the scope on the British frigate, Noah welcomed the reprieve from staring into those brown eyes as sharp as spears.

"We have the wind off our quarter, Captain," Luke said. "They are losing ground."

Noah snapped the scope shut and angled a weary glance at Miss Denton. "My country, miss, has done naught but impede my merchant business with their blasted embargoes." He studied the slight tilt of her nose. What would she know of sacrifice and hardship surrounded by luxury in her home? When she had never lifted a finger to work for any of her money.

"You speak as a Federalist and a traitor, sir." She pursed her lips and glanced at the British ship. "If they mean us no harm, then why do they chase us?"

"I have no idea, nor do I intend to find out." Noah's blood boiled at her accusation. "And I am no traitor. I love my country as much as the next man."

The sharp censure in her eyes made him reconsider his words. Did he love his country? Truth be told, he'd been so busy making money, he'd never taken the time to ponder what America stood for nor how she differed from other nations.

Miss Denton clenched her fists as if she intended to punch him. She shifted her gaze to Luke. "What is your opinion, Mr. Heaton? Do you love your country or are you more consumed with how she can help you make money?"

"Nations come and go, Miss Denton." Luke shrugged. "One must look out for oneself in this world."

The ship rose over a wave. The blue water surged onto the main deck before finding its escape through the scuppers back to sea. Miss Denton's chest heaved. From anger or fear, Noah couldn't tell. Still she managed to mumble. "I'm surrounded by Judases."

"That depends on your perspective." Luke gave her a patronizing smile before he glanced off the stern. "They've given up, Captain."

"Very well. Strike the topsails, Mr. Heaton." Noah doffed his hat and ran a hand through his hair. He faced Miss Denton, attempting to curtail his anger, but then he realized his plan was to do the opposite—to prove himself to be a beast.

"Since you know nothing of the merchant business," he began. "Nor of sailing, nor of the British Navy, nor even of work itself, might I suggest you keep your opinions to yourself and keep your person off my quarterdeck."

Her expression fell, and her bottom lip protruded ever so slightly. Though they had the intended effect, Noah immediately regretted his words. But he could see no other way to save them both from this unwanted marriage.

"You have not changed at all, Noah Brenin." The flicker of pain in her brown eyes disappeared, leaving them as hard and cold as polished agates. Swerving around, she moved away from him, gripping the railing all the way to the ladder then with careful movements she descended to the main deck.

"And I thought I was the scoundrel aboard this ship." Luke shook his head, uncharacteristic censure filling his eyes.

Noah's shoulders slumped beneath a press of guilt. "Surely that will convince her of my unworthiness as a husband."

"It convinced me."

"The man is a jingle-brained, bedeviled rogue," Marianne grumbled as she made her way to the captain's chamber. . .cabin, whatever it was called, later that evening for supper. *Why, Lord, do You force me to marry such a man?* Any other man would be better than this one.

Pressing a hand over her stomach, she halted and leaned on the wall. The ship canted to the left, and she stumbled to the other side of the corridor. Swaying lanterns flung eerie shadows over the wooden planks that encased her like a coffin. Indeed, she felt as though she had died and gone to hell—a watery grave ruled by the evil King Noah, a man who was not only malicious but a traitor as well. How could she marry someone who did not share her love of country?

She forced herself to continue. Though she would rather turn down Noah's invitation to dine with him and his officers—knowing it only provided him further opportunity to play his cruel games. She also knew she could not gain any useful information about sabotaging the ship by sitting in her cabin. Which was why she intended to arrive several minutes before the scheduled time for supper. Perhaps she could discover something in the room to aid her cause, and if she got caught snooping around she had an excuse for being there.

Gathering her breath, she peered around the open doorframe. In the midst of the cabin, an oblong table was set with pewter plates and mugs. Candles set in brass holders cast an icy glow over the silverware neatly placed beside each plate. A bowl of fruit and decanters of liquid stood at attention in the center of the table. Beyond it, through the stern windows, the setting sun trailed a red and orange ribbon across the horizon, even as tiny stars poked through the darkening sky above.

She took a step inside and her eyes landed on Noah's desk, pushed off to the side. She headed in that direction when an "Um hum" sounded from the corner. Her heart seized and she spun around to see Mr. Hobbs rising from a chair, a mug in hand.

"Mr. Hobbs, I beg your pardon. I didn't see you there."

"Quite alright, miss." He dragged the hat from his head. "I didn't mean t' startle you."

Oh drat, how could she snoop around with him here? "I must have the time wrong. Am I early for dinner?"

"Aye, just a bit."

"Where is No—the captain?" Marianne glanced out the door, uncomfortable at the thought of being alone with this man.

"He went above for a bit, but he'll be back soon." He waved his hat at her and smiled as if sensing her ill ease. "Don't let me cause you any discomfort, miss."

Marianne studied him. With arms and legs that seemed too muscular for his short body and his bald head gleaming in the candlelight, he appeared like an enormous bulldog. And just as ferocious until she looked in his gray eyes and found only kindness.

"Your wife has been most gracious to me, Mr. Hobbs."

"Aye, she's a good woman."

Marianne could not imagine the pairing. Where Agnes was jolly and friendly, Mr. Hobbs was serious and reserved. Where Agnes was rotund and soft, Mr. Hobbs appeared stiff and hard.

An uncomfortable silence ensued, and Marianne turned to go. "I'll return in a few minutes."

"Nay, miss, if you don't mind. I'm glad we got this chance to talk."

Marianne cocked her head. "What do you wish to speak to me about, Mr. Hobbs?"

"I overheard the captain speakin' t' you earlier. Up on deck."

She lowered her chin beneath a twinge as Noah's callous words shot like arrows through her mind.

"It is not like him, you see. I don't want you thinkin' ill of him. He's like a son t' me."

"Though I appreciate your concern I grow weary of everyone making excuses for his ill behavior."

Mr. Hobbs's lips grew taut. "I don't blame you for thinkin' such. Just don't give up on him yet."

"I have no intention of giving up on him, Mr. Hobbs." Though not for the reasons he thought. Not because somewhere deep beneath Noah's hard crust of cruelty, a speck of kindness survived, but instead because her mother's life depended on it.

Marianne glanced at the captain's desk again. "I wonder, Mr. Hobbs if you would oblige me."

"I'd be happy to, miss."

"Since I am to be imprisoned on this ship for months, I've taken an interest in sailing and navigation. Could you point out the captain's instruments and their function to me?"

"Of course." Mr. Hobbs threw back his shoulders and met her at the captain's desk. "What would ye like to know?"

Marianne pointed in turn at each instrument and asked its function and name, which Mr. Hobbs was more than eager to explain.

"So what would happen if the captain's charts were to be lost?"

"He'd have t' use the stars to guide him, I suppose."

"What about this one." Marianne picked up the odd-looking brass triangle with the curved bottom. "The sextant, was it? What exactly is it used for again?"

"Where's the rum?" Mr. Heaton's deep timbre filled the room, and Marianne glanced toward the door, quickly setting the sextant back upon the desk. The first mate's dark hair, tied behind him in a queue, matched the black breeches he'd donned. A white shirt, encased in a black waistcoat with gold embroidery completed his ensemble. "Forgive me, Miss Denton. I did not realize you had arrived already." He gave her a roguish grin that he no doubt expected would send her heart fluttering. She squelched any such reaction. She knew his type. He was handsome and he knew it. And he used it to his advantage. Marianne had resigned herself long ago that she would never know how it felt to stir a man's passions by the mere sight of her. And for the most part, she was happy for it.

For the most part.

Noah marched into the room like a captain in command, and her heart quirked a traitorous flutter in her chest. *What is wrong with me?* He tossed his bicorn onto a hook on the wall and eyed his guests. One brow lifted when his eyes landed on her. "Miss Denton, you came?"

"I was invited, was I not?"

"I didn't expect the pleasure of your company."

"I did not wish to deny you of it." She hid her annoyance beneath a sarcastic smirk.

Mr. Heaton grabbed a decanter from the table and poured himself a glass of whatever vile liquor it held.

Noah approached her, pointing at his desk. "What, pray tell, do you find so fascinating among my things?"

"Miss Denton wanted to—" Hobbs began.

"Mr. Hobbs was instructing me on the fine points of navigation, if you must know." Marianne interrupted before the man gave her away.

Noah folded his arms across his brown waistcoat. "I had no idea you had such interests."

"Nor the mind to grasp them?"

He smiled.

Luke dropped into a chair, a grin on his lips.

Mr. Hobbs shifted his stance and gazed between them. "Truth be told, Miss Denton has a keen mind an' a quick understandin'."

Marianne smiled at the elderly man. "Why, you are too kind, Mr. Hobbs."

"Hmm." Noah scratched the stubble on his jaw.

A sailor entered with a tray balanced on his shoulder. Another man followed him, and they both began placing platters of food on the table: biscuits, cheese, a steaming bowl of some sort of soup, and a block of salted meat.

The spicy scent of stew wafted over Marianne. Her mouth watered and her stomach clenched at the same time. Whether it was seasickness or the constant terror of being upon the ocean, Marianne found her appetite had shriveled.

She thanked Mr. Hobbs and moved away from the desk, deciding it would be best to make her exit now before she had to endure any more of Noah's scorching wit.

The ship tilted and one of the sailors stumbled. A glass decanter flew from his tray and crashed to the floor, bursting into a hundred crystalline shards.

"My apologies, Cap'n." The sailor growled as he knelt to pick up the mess.

"No need, Mr. Rupert," Noah said. "Just attend to the mess, if you please."

A red slice appeared on one of Rupert's fingers, and Marianne withdrew her handkerchief from her sleeve and knelt beside him. Taking his hand in hers, she wrapped the bloody appendage. "Be careful, Mr. Rupert." She smiled and his hazel eyes lifted to hers, shock skimming across them. "Let me help you." She began picking up pieces of glass when a hand touched her arm.

"No need, Miss Denton. He can manage."

She looked up to see Noah's brow furrowed as tight as a wound rope.

"Of course." She rose and felt warmth flush through her. What was she thinking? A lady of fortune did not assist servants. Her gaze scanned Mr. Heaton, Mr. Hobbs, the other sailor, and Noah all staring her way.

"If you'll excuse me, gentlemen, my head suddenly aches. I believe I'll forfeit my dinner tonight."

The curious look remained on Noah's face. "Allow me to escort you to your cabin."

She waved a hand through the air. "I know the way. Enjoy your dinner, gentlemen." And with that, she swept out the door.

Making her way down the hallway, she chided herself for her mistake. Noah must never know how destitute she and her mother were. If he did, it would only fuel his desire to call off the engagement. And that must never happen. Not as long as Marianne had anything to say about it.

She stepped inside her cabin and shoved the door closed then leaned against the hard wood. Her plan was set in place. Now all she had to do was wait for the captain to leave his cabin.

❖ CHAPTER 6 ❖

A rap sounded on her cabin door, and Marianne stopped the pacing she'd taken up for the past several hours as she waited for the sounds of laughter to dissipate from the captain's cabin—which they had done an hour ago. Still she could not get up the courage to do what she had to do. Not until she could be sure Noah was either gone from his cabin or fast asleep.

She opened the door to Agnes carrying a tray laden with cheese, biscuits, a mug, and a basin of water along with her medical satchel.

"Thank you, Agnes. You are too kind." Marianne stepped aside, allowing the elderly woman to enter and set the tray upon the shelf. The sharp smell of cheese drifted on a salty breeze that followed the woman inside, sweeping away the stagnant air that filled the tiny cabin.

"I heard you did not partake of the captain's meal, miss." Agnes's breath came out heavy and fast. "So here's some food fer you an' some water t' clean up wit'."

Shutting the door, Marianne's concern rose at the pale sheen covering Agnes's normally rosy face. "Please sit, Agnes. You look tired."

"I thank you, miss." Agnes moaned as she lowered herself onto the mattress.

"You don't have to serve me, Agnes. I am sure your duties occupy much of your time."

Agnes plucked a handkerchief from her belt to dab her forehead and neck. "Oh, I don't mind. It is nice havin' another woman aboard. Besides, the cap'n ordered me to attend to your every need."

Marianne flinched. "I doubt that."

One gray eyebrow rose nearly to the lace fringing Agnes's mobcap. "For bein' his fiancée, you don't know him very well."

"On the contrary, I grew up with him." Marianne reached for a slice of cheese from the tray and took a bite.

"Pish." Agnes batted the air. "All little boys can be rascals from time t' time."

The cheese soured in Marianne's mouth even as her stomach reached up hungrily to grab it. "He was extraordinarily devilish." She sat beside Agnes. The woman smelled of wood smoke, fish, and spices—not unpleasant odors. In fact, they comforted Marianne.

Agnes chuckled, causing the skin around her neck to jiggle. "It has been my observation that most young boys only tease girls they fancy."

"Don't be ridiculous." Marianne snorted. "I assure you, nothing but disdain spurred him on."

Agnes brushed a lock of Marianne's hair from her face. "Poor dear, you seem so out o' sorts aboard this ship."

Marianne's throat burned at the woman's kindness. She hadn't realized how much she needed a friend, someone whom she could confide in, someone who cared. "I worry about my mother. She is very ill."

Agnes patted her hand. "I am sorry t' hear of it, miss. It is so hard to be away from those we love, especially when they are not well." She clucked her tongue. "How unfortunate you wandered aboard when you did."

"Indeed." Marianne twisted the ring on her finger as a hundred scenes crept out from her childhood memories—scenes of Noah's cruel antics and how he always got the best of her. "Do you have family in America?" she finally asked Agnes.

Agnes's eyes drooped in sorrow. "We did. Mr. Hobbs and I. We had two sons. Both died of the grippe before they reached manhood."

The ship creaked and groaned as it rose over a swell. Marianne's heart shriveled. She couldn't imagine such a horrific loss. "I am so sorry, Agnes."

Agnes cleared her throat, and the momentary moisture disappeared from her eyes. "It was a long time ago. I suppose that's why me and Mr. Hobbs have latched onto Noah. He's like another son to us."

Marianne wondered how such a self-centered boor could make anyone a good son, yet the woman seemed sincere in her approbations. Perhaps the bond between them afforded Agnes some sway over the thickheaded rapscallion—a sway Marianne could use to her advantage. "Would you speak to the captain for me?" she ventured. "Beg him to turn the ship around?"

"Oh no, no, no, dear." Agnes gave an incredulous laugh. "When Noah sets his mind t' make port and sell his goods, there ain't nothing can stand in his way."

Marianne shook her head, her hopes crushed once again. "With men, it seems everything revolves around wealth." Just as it had with her father.

Agnes jerked her head back. "Money? No." Her eyebrows drew together. "That's not the way of it with Noah. It's his father who drives him so hard." She leaned toward Marianne. "If you ask me, I'd say Noah don't care much for the money itself."

"Then why did he leave our engagement party in order to set sail as if the delay would cost him more than he could bear?"

"Did he, now?" Agnes huffed and put an arm around Marianne, drawing her close. "Shame on him. Not like him at all."

Marianne grew weary of everyone's approval of the man. Even though she'd seen little of him these past eleven years, she'd observed nothing about his recent behavior to indicate he'd changed from the churlish imp he had been as a young boy.

"I'm sorry he pained you, miss. Noah lives under a heavy burden these days. Lord knows, I've been praying for him t' let it go."

Marianne bit back a snide remark. What burden could the man possibly have that compared to hers? He worried about pleasing his father, about making money, while she worried about saving her mother's life.

Agnes studied Marianne's expression, obviously mistaking it for one of curiosity. "As his wife, you'll find out soon enough."

The thought brought Marianne no comfort, neither the marrying, nor the discovering of Noah's burden. For now all she needed him to do was turn the ship around and return to Baltimore.

Beads of perspiration lined Agnes's forehead, and she dabbed them away. "He's a good man. I'm sure you'll be very happy."

Marianne swallowed. "I do not seek happiness. Why should anyone expect happiness in this life? Doesn't God's Word portend of trials and troubles and tribulation?" The cheese turned to stone in her stomach, and she pressed a hand over it. In these past years, Marianne had come to believe those verses more than the ones promising joy and peace and abundance.

"Whatever do you mean?" Agnes gave Marianne a motherly look of concern. "Life has its struggles, t' be sure, but there are also many fine moments as well—right fine moments."

"Perhaps, but if I do not look for them, then I shall not be disappointed." Marianne stood, pressing down the folds of her gown. "I am not the sort of person who is destined for greatness. I am an ordinary girl who will live an ordinary life."

"Such a glum outlook, my dear." Agnes took Marianne's hands in hers. "And you are far from ordinary."

Marianne warmed at the affection brimming from her friend's eyes. But then Agnes's face blanched, and she pressed a hand upon her rounded belly.

Marianne grabbed her arm. "Are you ill?"

"Just out o' sorts a bit." Agnes batted the air. "I'll be all right. Now"—she turned and grabbed her satchel—"let me redress your wound and then I'll let you retire."

"Thank you, Agnes, but I haven't been sleeping very well since I boarded."

"The captain neither." Agnes grabbed the bowl of water and plucked a fresh bandage from her bag. "I saw him on deck just a bit ago, staring off into the dark sky as he often does during the night."

Excitement tingled Marianne's veins, and she hardly noticed as Agnes redressed her wound. Hopefully Noah's nighttime stroll would give her plenty of time to slip into his cabin and steal his navigational instruments.

"Thank you, Agnes," Marianne gave her a peck on the cheek as Agnes opened the door to leave.

"I'll leave you to your rest, dear. God bless you."

Marianne watched until the woman faded into the shadows, thinking of what she was about to do. God had not blessed her in many years, and He certainly would not bestow any blessing on her current task. But something had to be done to convince Noah to head the ship back to Baltimore. She was on her own.

Easing into the hallway, she inched her way to the captain's cabin. With a click that seemed to echo like a gong through the corridor, she opened the door and slipped inside. Moonlight poured in through the stern windows in a waterfall of silver that dusted across Noah's desk. The spicy scents of a supper long since consumed swirled around her.

After listening for any sounds coming from the sleeping chamber or the hallway, Marianne made her way to the desk and scanned its contents. Spotting the sextant, protractor, and gunner's scale, she quickly grabbed them and turned to leave. But her eyes latched onto a bottle of ink, and a devilishly naughty idea made her lips curve upward. Setting the instruments back down, she picked up the ink bottle and uncorked it. She studied the map for the best location then slowly turned the bottle over. Thick, black liquid oozed from the lid and spread on the area beside the coast of England into a burgeoning puddle of pitch that covered the sea like lava from a volcano. She smiled and set the bottle on its side, hoping to make it appear as though it tipped over on its own.

Placing her hands on her hips, she studied her artwork with satisfaction.

"Now to find a place to hide you," she whispered to the implements as she picked them back up.

Thud. Thud. Thud. Boot steps echoed in the hallway

Muffled voices and laughter jarred her nerves and strung them tight.

Marianne froze. Her heart thundered in her chest. The mad dash of the sea against the hull seemed to be laughing at her.

Thump. Thump. Thump.

"I daresay, you'll be the death of me, Luke." The captain's voice grew louder.

Marianne's eyes darted around the room. Nowhere to hide. Beneath the desk? No. She whirled around. The sleeping cabin.

Dashing across the room, she dove into the tiny room no bigger than a wardrobe and stubbed her toe on the bed frame. She bit her lip against the groan rising in her throat. The cabin door creaked open and in stomped Noah, and from the sound of the other voice, Mr. Heaton. Lantern light peeked around the corner of the chamber door as if trying to expose her. She folded into the deepest shadows and leaned against the wall. Her chest heaved. Her blood pounded like drums in her ears.

"Confound it all! What's this?" Noah yelled.

Boot steps thundered.

"My chart is ruined!" A foul word spewed from his mouth, stinging Marianne's ears.

"What a mess," Mr. Heaton exclaimed. The rustling of paper filled the room. "How will you chart our course?"

Noah snorted. "I have another one."

Marianne's heart sank. Perspiration trickled down her back.

Drawers opened and scuffling sounded, as no doubt the men sopped up the spilt ink.

"Have a drink with me, Noah. You look as though you could use one." Mr. Heaton said.

The sound of a chair scraping over the wooden planks met Marianne's ears. "Very well. A small glass, if you please."

Chink. Glass rang on glass.

"To a safe voyage," Luke said.

"A safe voyage," Noah replied.

Marianne's heart refused to stop thumping against her ribs. *Oh Lord, please get me out of this.* Silence ensued. After several long minutes, curiosity overcame her fear. Keeping to the shadows, she inched beside the bed and crept into the far corner, which gave her a narrow view of the other room. Noah sat on a chair, his legs stretched out before him. Seafoam sprawled in his lap. He ran his fingers through her fur with one hand while he sipped his drink with the other.

"I believe this long voyage will be far more interesting with Miss Denton aboard." Mr. Heaton leaned back against the top of Noah's desk, drink in hand.

Marianne flung a hand to her mouth. Her mind whirled at the man's remark. Interesting? She had always thought herself rather dull.

Noah eyed his friend. "She has a bit of pluck, doesn't she?"

The cat nestled against his chin. Noah smiled and scratched her head. Marianne shook her head at the tender way he caressed the animal—so at odds with his ruthless character.

Mr. Heaton rubbed the stubble on his jaw. "Very entertaining, indeed. I look forward to your banter with her."

"My torment of her is not for your entertainment. And it pains me to treat her so."

Noah's expression remained stoic. Not a trace of humor could be found either in his voice or on his face. Marianne could make no sense of his statement. If it pained him to insult her, why did he continue?

Mr. Heaton laughed. "And the easy way in which she went to the aid of Rupert. I thought you said she was a highbrow used to a life of ease, surrounded by servants."

Noah shrugged. "It must be a ploy of some kind."

A ploy, indeed. Marianne gritted her teeth.

"Come now, Noah. I know you all too well. The woman enchants you."

"You're drunk."

"She's not at all like Miss Priscilla."

Marianne's ears perked.

"No. She is not." Noah set the cat down, and the feline swept her almond shaped eyes toward Marianne where they remained for several seconds. *The blasted cat knows where I am.* Marianne stiffened, barely allowing a breath to escape her lips. She gave the cat a pleading look that she hoped conveyed in cat language what her heart screamed. *Please, from one woman to another, do not betray me.* Finally, Seafoam lost interest and leapt upon Noah's desk.

"The two women are quite the opposites." Noah stared into space.

"Will you call on her in South Hampton?"

But he's engaged to me! Anger stole Marianne's fear. What a swaggering, lecherous cur!

"Though I would love to, no. It would not be right. I am engaged, after all."

"But if you have your wish, that may not last long."

"Perhaps, but while I am bound thus, I will honor my commitment."

Honor his commitment? Admiration sparked within Marianne. It felt oddly out of place in regard to Noah. Yet the fact that he would even so much as entertain interest in another woman while he was engaged to her doused it immediately.

Noah slapped the remainder of the drink to the back of his throat. "Leave me to my rest, Luke."

Mr. Heaton finished his drink and set his glass down. "Very well." He headed for the door.

Noah stopped him. "Before you retire, check on the watch and ensure the next one will be awakened on time. I will not tolerate further laggardness on this ship."

"Aye, aye, Cap." Luke grinned as he stepped backward through the door and closed it.

Panic turned Marianne's legs to wobbly ropes. This was it. He wasn't leaving his cabin. What would he do to her when he caught her? Remembering the instruments in her hands, she quickly stuffed them beneath his mattress and backed up as far as she could against the wall, awaiting her fate.

Noah shrugged off his coat then began unbuttoning his waistcoat. He tore it off, tossing it to the chair then tugged the cravat from his throat.

Oh no, Lord. Please don't allow him to disrobe. Marianne squeezed her eyes shut, but they refused to close completely, leaving a small slit beneath her lashes. Should she alert him to her presence? No. Perhaps he would still decide to leave for some reason.

Lord, make him remember some command to issue or some ship detail to attend to.

He slipped the shirt over his head then sat down to remove his boots. The sculpted muscles in his chest and arms glistened in the lantern light. Marianne could not tear her eyes from him. She'd never seen a man's chest before, and it both fascinated her and caused an odd feeling in her belly.

He stood and began fumbling with the buttons of his breeches. The ship canted, and Marianne darted into the other corner where she could not see him. Perhaps he would fall into his bed and take no note of her.

"Meow." Something warm and furry rubbed against her leg.

Opening her eyes, she saw Seafoam's white shadow lingering by her feet. Silently, she gestured for the stupid cat to go away, but it continued circling the hem of her skirt. "Meow."

Footsteps stomped. Marianne held her breath.

A half circle of light advanced upon her shoes, then crept up her legs.

"What have we here?"

❖ CHAPTER 7 ❖

A pair of wide brown eyes, streaked with terror, stared up at Noah. He shook his head. The woman amazed him. The last place he would have expected to find Miss Denton was hiding in his sleeping cabin. And for the life of him, he could find no reason for it, save one, which would be an impossibility.

"Pardon me, Noah. I seem to have gotten lost." The fear fled her eyes, replaced by her usual lofty manner as she attempted to brush past him.

"A condition you seem to be making a habit of aboard my ship." He moved to block her. A chuckled erupted from his throat.

She planted her hands on her waist. "I fail to see what is so amusing."

Seafoam jumped onto Noah's bed and plopped down, eyeing them both.

Noah set the lantern down and leaned on the doorframe. A grin overtook his lips as he realized he could have some fun with this awkward situation. "On the contrary, finding you so close to my bed in the middle of the night is quite amusing, or should I say, rather pleasing." He winked.

Her chest heaved. Her gaze flitted about the tiny room, avoiding him entirely. A red hue crept up her neck onto her face like a rising tide.

She lifted a hand as if she were going to push him, but when her eyes met his bare chest, she seemed to think better of it. "If you please, Noah, I need some air."

He stepped aside before she swooned. Then grabbing the lantern, he followed her out into his cabin and placed it atop his desk. He faced her, searching his memory of his conversation with Mr. Heaton for anything the lady should not have overheard.

"Good night, Noah." She kept her head lowered and headed for the door, but he darted in front of her.

"Not just yet, Miss Denton."

She backed away. "I am tired and wish to retire now." The scent of her lavender soap swirled around him

"Then why are you in my cabin?" Noah lowered his head to peer into her face, but she kept her gaze upon the deck.

"If you insist on keeping me here, would you at least do me the honor of donning your shirt?"

He chuckled. That she was an innocent did not surprise him. That his unclad chest affected her, he found oddly pleasing.

"Are you quite sure, Miss Denton?" He quirked a brow.

She raised her chin, her face twisting in disdain as another flood of crimson blossomed over it. "How dare you?"

"Perhaps you cannot wait for our wedding night?"

Her brown eyes simmered. "Why you insufferable cad." She raised her hand to slap him.

He caught it and lifted it to his lips for a kiss, eyeing her with delight.

She studied him then released a sigh. "You tease me, sir." Snatching her hand from his, she stepped back. "But what would I expect from you?"

Moving to the chair he grabbed his shirt and slipped it over his head. His glance fanned over his desk where his chart had been and he spun around. "You. You ruined my chart."

She averted her gaze and began twisting her ring. "Why would I do that?"

Brown curls swayed in disarray around a fresh bandage devoid of blood. Her lips pressed in their usual petulant manner, and her petite nose pinked as it always did when she was distraught.

"To force me to return to Baltimore, perhaps?" He took a step toward her. She retreated.

Then squaring her shoulders, she placed her hands atop her rounded hips. "Who is Priscilla?"

Noah couldn't help but grin. So she *had* heard their conversation. Shame settled over him, but he shrugged it off. He had done nothing wrong. "A friend."

"How dare you toss your affections to another when you are engaged to me."

"I can assure you, miss. I never toss my affections anywhere."

Marianne studied him. A word of truth at last, for she doubted the man cared for anyone but himself. Then why was she behaving the jealous shrew? His thick chest peeked out from within his open shirt. The sight of it befuddled her mind. How could she think clearly with his firm muscles staring her in the face?

Yet something else caused unease to clamp over her nerves. Why wasn't Noah furious with her for ruining his map? Instead of chastising her and tossing her from his cabin, he seemed to find the incident amusing.

Which only further infuriated her.

He sat back against his desk and released a ragged sigh, then rubbed the back of his neck as if he had the weight of the world sitting upon it. Agnes's words regarding his burden resurfaced in Marianne's thoughts, and she wondered for a moment what was troubling him.

She should leave. She knew she should leave. Especially now that he no longer blocked her way, but perhaps she could garner some useful information.

"Why do you work so hard for your father?"

His eyes widened. Finally he said, "Unlike you, I wasn't born to privilege. I must work to survive."

"I cannot help the situation of my birth." She huffed. "But you can cease holding it against me."

He tilted his head and examined her as if he could not fathom what she said. "Fair enough," he conceded with a semblance of a grin.

Marianne glanced at the closed door and realized how improper it was for her to be alone with him in his cabin. Yet aside from her reputation—which she doubted anyone on board would care to sully with gossip—the only thing in danger was her pride from his continual insults.

The ship rose over a wave, and she raised a hand to the wall to keep from stumbling. "I don't know how you tolerate this constant teetering. If not for these walls, we would all be thrashed to and fro with each wave."

"Bulkheads."

"Oh, who cares?" She huffed. Releasing the wall, she balanced her way to one of the chairs closest to the door and sat down. "I've seen little of you for eleven years. Your father would visit quite often before my father died, but you were never with him."

"I was at sea."

Marianne nodded, remembering the event that had sent him there. "I was sorry to hear about your brother."

He snapped his gaze away and stood, turning his back to her. "It was a long time ago."

"Unlike you, he was always kind to me."

Noah's back stiffened, and he crossed his arms over his chest. "Yes, Jacob was kind to everyone. Generous, wise, and. . ." He faced her and shrugged. "Well, everything I am not."

Though she could not argue with his statement, Marianne's heart sank at the look of agony on his face. Word around town was that Jacob had died in an accident aboard a ship. Though she longed to know the details of his death, the anger and despair etched on Noah's countenance silenced her.

Her own sorrow at her father's death remained an open wound on her heart. Perhaps they could find some common ground on that alone. "I understand your pain."

His tight expression softened, but the hard look in his eyes remained. "I am sorry for your loss, as well, Miss Denton, but I doubt you understand what I have suffered."

Marianne tugged on a lock of hair, her ire surging with the rise of the ship over another swell. "I understand the loss of someone you love, Noah. Will you credit that to my account or do you hold a monopoly on grief?"

He snorted. "You may suffer as you wish, miss."

"How kind of you," she retorted then chided herself. There was no sense in lowering her behavior to his reprehensible level. Besides, it was obvious he still felt the sting of his brother's death. Until that dreadful day, the Brenin twins had been inseparable. "My mother tells me God brought her the comfort she needed when my father passed. Perhaps you should pray?"

"You may also do the praying, as you wish."

"You don't believe in God?"

"I believe He exists. I simply don't think about Him often. Nor do I think He considers me." The muscles in Noah's neck tightened. "I have discovered it best to keep myself out of the focus of the Almighty's scope, lest I displease Him in some way and suffer the consequences."

Sorrow burned in Marianne's throat. Such a low opinion of God. "Surely you don't believe that. God will bring you comfort, Noah. And hope for the future." She twisted the ring on her finger. Did she believe that? Yes. God had indeed comforted her and her mother. She had felt His presence during their grief. She knew He was real. But in truth, her hope was not in this world. In this life, she had lost all trust that God would work things out for good as He said in His Word. Even so, it broke her heart to see Noah so far from the only One who could help him.

"He can lead you and guide you," she went on. "Grant you wisdom and show you His plan for your life."

"There is no plan, Miss Denton. The sooner you strike that thought from your mind, the sooner you will start to live your own life." He gripped the edge of his desk until his knuckles grew white. "No, a man makes his own plan, his own destiny. As I am making mine."

"And doing so well at it." Marianne straightened her back. "Pray tell, once you have my fortune, will you continue to exhaust yourself year after year, piling up wealth to supply your endless pride?"

"You find me greedy?" He chuckled, his blue eyes sparkling as if he found delight in her insult. But hadn't he always responded to her attempts to inflict pain on him with the same insolent laughter? As if she were of so little importance that she could not possibly affect him at all.

"You don't know me, Miss Denton."

"Then why marry a woman you don't love? To do so only to please your father seems unlike someone who is so"—she paused, searching for the right word, and upon finding none chose the first one that had come to mind—"self-centered."

The lantern flickered, casting golden flecks on the tips of his hair. He scratched his chin, this time not laughing at her barb. "There is much you don't know."

"Pray tell, enlighten me, since I am to be your prisoner for months."

"Prisoner? I am crushed." He laid a hand on his heart even as one side of his lips curved in a mocking grin. "I prefer to call you an unwilling passenger."

"You may prefer all you wish, Captain, but that does not make you correct."

"Your wit has improved with age."

"Yours has not." Marianne remembered Noah and Luke's conversation about her pluck. "But I am happy to entertain you."

"It was Luke who remarked so. Me? I fail to find pleasure in your company, princess." He lowered his gaze but not before she saw a flicker of regret in his eyes. Nevertheless, his words cut deep—deeper

74

than she would have expected. Why was she subjecting herself to his cruelty?

She rose to find her legs unsteady. "It was you who insisted I stay in your cabin."

"To discover the depth of your traitorous activities." His grin had returned, but it lacked its usual luster.

"Since that has been established, I shall relieve you of my company." Marianne swung around.

"Established, you say?" He chuckled. "The only things we have established are that my chart is ruined and that you seem to enjoy lurking about a man's chamber in the middle of the night."

She swerved about. "How dare you! What are you implying?"

One dark eyebrow rose and he gave an innocent shrug. "Nothing. But if you didn't come here to ruin my chart, what am I to think?"

"You insufferable rogue." Marianne narrowed her eyes, then swung about.

"Good night, Miss Denton."

"Good night, Mr. Brenin." She opened the door.

His blaring voice halted her. "And rest assured, I fully intend to keep my cabin locked in the future."

Noah spread his new chart atop his desk. Morning sunlight sprinkled glistening particles of dust across it as he pinned the corners down with the instruments he'd found stuffed beneath his mattress. He chuckled. He had to give the woman credit. She didn't give up and accept her fate as most women would. Persistent and stubborn. Just like when she was a little girl.

Straightening his stance, he threw his arms over his head and stretched. Exhaustion tugged on his eyes. After Miss Denton had left, he'd barely slept an hour. And that hour had been fraught with nightmares—visions of raging seas and black angry skies, of yards high above the deck flung effortlessly to and fro by the screaming wind, of blood on the planks below.

His brother's blood.

He patted the handkerchief in his pocket and shook his head, trying to dislodge the tormenting memories. But the pain in his heart felt as raw as it had the day of the tragedy. The day Noah lost his will to live.

Why, when Noah spent so much of his energy keeping his past buried had Miss Denton so carelessly brought it to mind? Yet he also could not shake the pained look in her eyes at his cruel remarks. But he had no choice. Blast it all. He'd truly enjoyed their conversation. The sympathy beaming from those brown eyes had caught him off guard. She *did* understand his pain—perhaps not the depth of it—but her concern had broken down some invisible wall between them. Then all her talk of God, not preachy, but out of true concern for him. He had felt his defenses weaken. And he couldn't allow that to happen. She must be the one to break off their engagement. It was the only way for her to save face and for Noah to appease his father. Then with the added wealth this trip would bring, everyone would be happy. Perhaps he could even consider a courtship with Miss Priscilla in South Hampton.

He pictured the lady in his mind. With curves in all the right places and hair of golden silk, she was the picture of feminine beauty and charm. The daughter of a wealthy solicitor, she carried none of the pretensions and snobbery one would expect of someone of her class. Although Noah had no formal understanding with Miss Priscilla and he'd only spent a few short days with her, he sensed she was as enthralled with him as he was with her. Her father did, however, require that any suitors must be worth at least one thousand pound a year before he would agree to a courtship.

A sum Noah could make no boast of. Not yet.

He rubbed the back of his neck. Then there was his own father—who would disapprove of Miss Priscilla based solely on the fact that Noah chose her. Another disappointment credited to his ledger. A debt that if Noah could not settle soon, would prohibit him from ever being able to make his own decisions. Which was why he desperately needed this voyage to be successful.

Rap rap rap.

"Enter," Noah said. Matthew ambled in, a tray in hand. The sting of rum-laced tea and stale biscuits greeted Noah's nose as the older man set down his load.

"Apologies sent from my missus, Cap'n, but she's a bit indisposed. 'Fraid ye're going t' have t' do with this simple fare this morning."

"Indisposed?" Noah's alarm rose. He circled the desk. Usually a vision of robust health, Agnes rarely took ill.

"A slight fever, is all." Matthew yanked his hat from his bald head. "Miss Denton attends to 'er."

"Miss Denton?" Noah assumed she'd still be tucked in her bed at this early hour.

Grabbing his waistcoat from the back of the chair, Noah thrust his arms through the sleeves, then lifted the mug and took a sip of tea. The taste soured in his mouth. He liked his tea with sugar, but that was a luxury they could ill afford.

Matthew shifted his bare feet over the floor and stared at Noah.

"Thank you, Matthew. Is there something else?"

" 'Bout Miss Denton." Matthew's eyes crinkled at the corners. "If I may speak wit' ye."

Noah puffed out a sigh. Miss Denton again. He had hoped to occupy his mind elsewhere today.

"I 'eard her cryin' last night in her cabin." Accusation fired from his voice.

The sails thundered above as they shifted in the wind, the sound pounding Noah's guilt deep into his heart. He hadn't meant to make her cry. Leaning back on his desk, he sipped his tea, suddenly wishing he could drown himself in it.

"The missus was speakin' t' me 'bout her. Poor girl's mother is ill, an' she's needed at home."

"I realize that, Matthew." Shrugging off his remorse, Noah tightened his lips. "But I have a schedule to keep and cannot alter it for the actions of one foolish girl. I'll take her home in three months.

Her mother will not suffer overmuch during that time. In fact, she appeared quite well the day of the engagement party." Noah set down his mug and began strapping on his belt. "Besides, I fear Miss Denton will use any excuse she can to get me to return her home."

"Even so, Cap'n. Her poor mother will be worried sick over what happened t' her."

"Considering that Miss Denton darted down the street after me, I'm sure she will solve the puzzle soon enough." Noah had no time for such nonsense. Blast the woman for weaving her way into Hobbs's sentiments.

Matthew tossed his hat down and eyed Noah with more authority than his position allowed. "What's this all about, Noah? It is not like you t' be so cruel and selfish."

Noah studied the man who had been more of a father to him than his own. "Trust me, Matthew, I am not proud of my behavior. But it serves a higher purpose."

"If yer talkin' about God, I doubt He has much t' do wit' it."

God again. "No. I'm referring to a plan which will free both Miss Denton and me from a marriage neither of us desires."

"So." Matthew folded his beefy arms across his belly. "You're being cruel to her for her own good, eh?"

"Precisely." Noah buttoned his waistcoat and snapped the hair from his face. It was true after all. Along with aiding his plan to break free from his father's control.

A ray of sunlight stroked Matthew's bald head, making him look almost angelic, despite his formidable frame. His dark eyes narrowed into pinpoints of judgment. "I've known you for many years, Noah. And you're a good man deep down in there." He pointed at Noah's chest. " 'Bout time you figure that out for yourself and did the right thing."

Still steaming over Matthew's rebuke, Noah strode toward the man's cabin where Agnes rested. He shouldn't allow his boatswain such liberties with his opinion. Noah was captain after all. But the old man had been there countless times when Noah needed fatherly advice. How could he turn him away simply because his advice was not what Noah wished to hear?

He knocked on the door. A female voice bade him enter, and he opened it to see Agnes lying in bed, her glazed eyes peering at him from within a puffy face, flush with fever. At her feet, Seafoam lay curled in a ball. Beside her, Miss Denton sat dabbing a cloth over her forehead. Marianne's eyes swept over him before she quickly returned to her ministrations. No greeting? He could hardly blame her after his behavior the night before.

"Noah." Agnes smiled. "What brings you here?"

"To inquire after your health, of course." Noah took a step inside and was assailed with the stale smell of infirmity. "I heard you were not feeling well."

Miss Denton wrung the cloth out in a basin of water.

"Oh, I suppose I'll live." Agnes tried to laugh, but it came out as a cough. She tugged at the lace of her nightdress that appeared to have a stranglehold on her neck. "Just a wee bit hot and me stomach's twistin' and turnin'."

"Is there something I can get you?" Noah wove around the bed and drew a chair on the other side from where Miss Denton sat. Seafoam pried open her sleepy eyes to look his way.

"No thank you, my boy. Marianne has been an angel, takin' care o' me all through the night."

Through the night? Noah gazed at Miss Denton as she laid a cloth over Agnes's forehead.

"I apologize, Noah, for not makin' yer breakfast," Agnes said.

Noah took her hand. "Madam, you think that concerns me? The crew will make do. All that matters is that you get well." Her hand felt warm, but not too warm. He brushed the back of his fingers across her cheek. Hot, but he'd felt worse. His alarm dissipated.

Only then did Miss Denton look at him with the most peculiar stare before she quickly averted her eyes.

The ship pitched and her eyes widened a moment. A sail snapped above.

Rising, Seafoam stretched and made her way to Noah, jumping into his lap. The old cat had been a gift from their father to both Noah and Jacob on their first crossing to England nearly fourteen years ago. A kitten at the time, she had grown up on this ship, knew every crevice and cranny, and had feasted on her fair share of rats. Noah scratched beneath her chin, and Seafoam stretched her neck upward and purred in response. This old cat and the handkerchief in his pocket were the last things Noah had that had belonged to Jacob.

Agnes squeezed his hand, jarring him from his thoughts. "Order Marianne to her cabin to get some rest, Noah. She's been here all night."

"Order her?" Noah chuckled. "I don't believe anyone can order Miss Denton to do anything she doesn't want to do."

Marianne's lips lifted at one corner, and she favored him with a sly glance before facing Agnes. "I am well, Agnes. When you rest, I will rest right here beside you, in case you should need anything."

"You are too good to me, dear." An exchange of affection passed between Agnes and Miss Denton that caused Noah to shift in his seat. For a woman accustomed to ordering servants about to please her every whim, Miss Denton's care for this dear sweet woman was quite baffling.

And Noah didn't like it one bit.

Emerging from the companionway, Marianne slid her shoes tentatively onto the upper deck. She'd been avoiding coming above, loathe to face the endless sea. But after spending two nights and three days in the stagnant, sickly air of Agnes's cabin, she risked confronting her fears in order to get a breath of fresh air. Thankfully, Agnes's fever had abated, and she slept soundly now. She'd be back to her old self soon.

Noah truly cared for Agnes. Marianne had seen it in his eyes as he held her hand. She had heard it in the soft tone with which he addressed her. And Seafoam. Marianne had never seen a man so affectionate with a cat. And a cat so attached to her master. She began to think there was more to this man than she first assumed. Yet that did not change the fact that he did not wish to marry her. Nor that he planned to do so out of obligation to his father. At least she hoped that was still his plan. That he harbored feelings for another woman didn't bode well on that front.

Fatigue hung on her shoulders and weighted down her eyelids.

Squinting against the afternoon sun that sat a handbreadth above the horizon, Marianne made her way to the round object they used to heave the anchor, bracing herself against the surge and roll of the ship as she went. Somehow the vessel's constant sway seemed less dangerous below where if the ship canted and she tumbled out of control, the walls could break her fall. But here above deck, what would stop her from toppling overboard? She gripped the wooden heaving tool and drew in a deep breath of the stiff breeze that swept past her, bringing with it a hint of salt and fish.

Sailors scampered by, tipping their hats in her direction as they passed. Shielding her eyes, she glanced above where men lumbered over the yards with as much ease as if they strolled along Market Street. Another blast of wind rushed over her, cooling the perspiration on her neck. Forcing down her fear, she dared a glance at the vast waters that held the tiny ship captive. Azure blue waves spread to a glowing horizon, each swell capped with golden crystals of sunlight. The ship bucked and a salty spray showered over her. She jerked back, brushing the drops from her arms.

"Miss Denton," a deep voice startled her, and she turned to see Mr. Weller standing beside her. "Good afternoon t' ye."

"Thank you, sir."

"We haven't seen much of you above deck these past few days." He adjusted the red scarf that seemed to be permanently attached to his neck.

"I've been attending Mrs. Hobbs."

"Aye, we ain't got a decent meal in quite some time. I hope she gets well soon." He frowned. "Not that I only care about me food. She's a kindly lady, too."

"Never fear, she's recovering."

He gazed toward the horizon. "The sea is beautiful in the afternoon. If you come t' the foredeck it feels like yer a bird, flyin' across the water." He gestured for her to follow him.

"Oh no, I couldn't, Mr. Weller." She swallowed. "I'm perfectly saf—I mean content here."

He cocked his head and a slow smile spread on his lips. "Yer afraid of water?"

She gave him a sheepish grin, wondering if she should confide in him. Despite his scarred face, nothing but sincerity shone from his brown eyes. And he had always been kind to her. She leaned toward him. "Dreadfully."

The ship bucked and he placed a hand atop hers, "Nothin' to be feared about, miss. This ship is the sturdiest craft as ever I sailed."

"But ships like these do sink, do they not?"

"Aye, from time t' time." He doffed his hat and scratched his thick head of charcoal black hair.

A wonderful idea planted itself in her mind. This man must know a great deal about ships—especially this particular one. "I'll make a bargain with you, Mr. Weller. I'll brave the foredeck if you'll explain just how sound this ship really is."

He extended his arm. "Ye've got a bargain, miss."

Noah sprang onto the deck to the sound of feminine laughter. His eyes soon discovered the source. At the bow of the ship stood Miss Denton and Mr. Weller, of all people. Her, gripping the railing. Him, steadying her with a hand on her back. They held their heads together as if they were old friends.

An uncomfortable feeling skittered across Noah's back. What would Miss Denton and Mr. Weller find in common to discuss so intimately? Why, Mr. Weller rarely spoke to anyone since Noah rescued him from St. Kitts and gave him a job aboard the *Fortune.*

Forcing down his annoyance, Noah took the ladder to his position on the quarterdeck. After greeting Mr. Pike, who was positioned at the helm, he stood at the stanchions with hands clasped behind his back. He attempted to divert his gaze to the sea, but his traitorous eyes made their way back to Miss Denton and Mr. Weller. Where most women would cringe at the man's deformities, she treated him as if he were the Earl of Buckley dropping over for tea.

Wasn't it enough he'd been forced to witness her kindness toward Agnes? Now this? Why, sooner or later he might have to admit he admired the lady. And that would not aid his plans in the least. Not in the least.

Marianne smiled at her new friend. No longer noticing the rippled skin on the left side of his face or his missing fingers. "So there's nothing that can penetrate the ship's hull save a massive rock or a cannon shot?"

"That be correct, miss. Unless"—he winked—"you were to take an ax to it, I suppose."

Which she would never do. The last thing she wanted was to cause the ship to sink. "And what of these ropes?" Releasing her death grip on the railing, Marianne clung to one of the massive lines that stretched taut up to a sail above. But she already knew the answer. Nearly as thick as her wrist and covered with tar, it would take hours to slice through with a knife.

Mr. Weller grinned. A single gold tooth twinkled in the setting sun. "Nay, these lines are fast and hard. Nothin' can break them 'sides a heavy ax or grape shot. Besides, ye'd have to sever more than one o' them to do any damage."

The ship pitched and with it, Marianne's heart. She clutched the railing with both hands again and tried not to look down at the foamy water sliced by the bow of the ship. Without access to the captain's cabin, she must find another way to disable the vessel.

She gazed upward. "And the sails?"

"Sturdy as steel cloth. Nothing but fire or the blast from a ship's gun could penetrate them."

Marianne bit her lip. Neither would suffice without endangering the crew, and she couldn't do that.

"You are a kind lady, miss." Mr. Weller smiled and ran a thumb down the scar on his face. "Most women avoid speakin' t' me." He shrugged and stared at the churning water at the bow. "I suppose my appearance scares 'em."

Marianne's heart shrank. Though she had no disfigurement, how often had she been slighted in favor of more beautiful ladies? She raised a haughty chin. "Then, I daresay, they are missing out on know-ing a very knowledgeable, courteous, and chivalrous gentleman."

"Gentleman?" He guffawed. "Ain't never been considered to be such."

She smiled at his easy manner then grew serious. "May I be so bold as to ask what happened to you?"

He tugged his scarf up as if suddenly self-conscious of his scar. A sail above them thundered in an ominous snap. "I was a gunner's mate onboard the British warship, the *Hibernia*, of one hundred and ten guns"—he took a deep breath—"an' durin' a battle wit' a French frig-ate, our gun exploded. I lost three o' me fingers and a scrap of hot lead struck me face."

Marianne's stomach grew queasy. "How horrible."

"Three other sailors lost their lives, includin' a young powder boy who was no more 'an thirteen."

"Thirteen." Marianne's head began to spin. She could not imagine the horrors of enduring a battle at sea, let alone such a tragedy. The glaze of painful memories clouded Mr. Weller's eyes, and she longed to take his pain away, to say how sorry she was, but words failed her.

"Aye. They say the gun deck is the most dangerous place to be durin' battle."

The ship rose then plunged over a swell. Seawater misted over her. Normally, she would find it refreshing from the heat, but to her, it seemed like spit from the mouth of a monster.

Mr. Weller's hand pressed against her back to steady her. Though she rarely allowed any man such liberties, she appreciated his strong support and felt no threat from his touch.

"So you see, there's naught to be 'fraid of. Unless we end up in a battle with a warship." He chuckled. "Unlikely since we are simple merchantmen."

"Then why does the captain arm the ship?" Marianne gestured behind her toward the three cannons that lined the top deck on each side and the two that perched off the stern.

"Just for defense, miss, I assure ye."

Marianne released a ragged sigh. It sounded as if the only way to prevent Noah from reaching England would be an enemy attack. And even if she could arrange that, it wouldn't bode well for any of them. Her hope dwindling, she gazed out at sea, squinting at the setting sun. Perspiration slid down her back. Out there, beyond the sun, was her precious country, her precious city, her precious home. And every swell they traversed meant they were that much farther away. *Mother, I'm trying to come home.* Fear tightened her chest. Would Lizzie be able to care for Mama without Marianne? Who would do the cooking, the mending? Who would administer Mama's medicines? She faced Mr. Weller and offered a conciliatory half smile.

"Indeed, Mr. Weller, it does sound as though the ship is indestructible."

"Aye, as I've told you. Unless we come under attack or a squall disables the rudder, ain't nothing will stop us from reaching our destination."

"The rudder? How would I. . .I mean how could that happen?"

He leaned on the railing. The sails above cast half of his face in shadows while the sun cast a golden glint on the other half. His brown eyes so full of life found hers. With a strong jaw and cheekbones, he could be considered a handsome man, if one could ignore his scars. Which she found increasingly easy to do. And he was young. She guessed he couldn't be older than thirty years.

MaryLu Tyndall

"A shot to the rudder would do it." He smiled. "Or running aground during a storm, or by the strain o' a storm on the wheel. Or I suppose someone could chop through the tiller ropes, but I don't see why anyone aboard would do that."

"Why not?" Marianne dared not hope.

"That would leave us unable to steer, save by the sails, and that would be difficult." He glanced above. "O' course that can be repaired right quick."

She bit her lip. "Then it seems as though we are destined for England."

"The captain's a driven man when he's got a cargo full of goods. No, I expect the only thing that would turn 'im around is if he lost his cargo somehow and had nothin' to sell."

Lost his cargo.

Marianne's heart leapt. She smiled. Of course. Why hadn't she thought of that? What reason would Noah have to continue to England if he had no goods to sell?

If his precious cargo met with some unforeseen disaster?

❖ CHAPTER 8 ❖

Marianne ran the back of her sleeve over her moist forehead and stared at the soup bubbling atop the iron stove. She wanted to assist Agnes—still taken to her bed—by preparing the evening meal. But in light of the strange odor wafting up from the gurgling slop in the copper kettle, she was beginning to regret that decision. It wasn't as if she hadn't cooked before. After her mother dismissed most of the servants, Marianne had taken up the duty of preparing the meals. But she'd done so in a well-equipped kitchen, not in a dark, cramped ship's galley with only a smidgen of spices and foods to use in the preparation of her meal.

Ignoring the sweat streaming down her back, she grabbed a cloth and opened the oven door where several whole chickens roasted on spits over the fire. Hot air blasted over her, carrying with it a juicy, spicy fragrance that made her mouth water. At least the chicken would taste good. She silently thanked God that she hadn't been forced to slaughter the poor birds herself. Mr. Weller had gladly assigned that duty to one of the sailors.

Closing the oven door, Marianne took a step back, if only to remove herself from the heat for a second, and bumped into the preparation table. How did Agnes, a much larger woman than Marianne, work in such tight quarters?

She sensed, rather than heard someone watching her and looked up. Mr. Heaton leaned against the doorframe, arms folded over his chest. He smiled. "Smells delicious."

"Thank you, Mr. Heaton." Marianne returned his smile, ignoring the slight quiver of unease at his presence. "I am hoping the taste will agree with the smell." She studied the tall, muscular man. His hair, as dark as a starless night, was so at odds with his clear blue eyes. Eyes that took her in as if she were some strange apparition.

"Can I help you?" she asked. The soothing smell of baked dough swirled about her nose, and she jumped. "Oh no, my biscuits!" Using the cloth still in her hand, she removed the oven tray and turning, dumped the browned biscuits into a large basket. At least she hadn't managed to burn this set. She dropped the tray to the table and began plopping dough onto it for the next batch.

"Is there something you want, Mr. Heaton? I am quite busy at the moment." Though he had given her no cause for alarm and had always been cordial, his reputation among the ladies in Baltimore as a libertine and a rogue made her stomach clench in his presence—especially since she found herself alone with him.

"Just surprised to find you here, miss." His deep voice held no malice. "Noah led me to believe you hadn't done a day's work in your life."

Marianne sighed. That had been true of her once—a lifetime ago, before her father died. "Noah knows very little about me."

He stepped forward and reached to pluck one of the biscuits from the basket. Without thinking, Marianne slapped his wrist, her anger overcoming her reason, for she didn't know whether Mr. Heaton was a man one could slap—even playfully—without repercussions. To add to her discomfiture, the distinct smell of rum filled the air between them. She knew the smell. Knew it quite well, along with the memories it invoked of her father.

Relief came, however, when Mr. Heaton chuckled, his mirth reaching his blue eyes with a twinkle. "Noah knows little about you? I would say that to be true of you, as well, regarding him."

"I've known Noah since I was five and he was six. Can you attest to the same?"

"No, but these past five years I've lived in these quarters with him for months at a time. Can you attest to the same?"

Marianne could see why women's hearts fluttered at his rakish grin that was both sensuous and charming.

"I cannot imagine how you have suffered his company that long." She snorted.

He chuckled and rubbed the scar on his right ear. "Or he mine."

She cocked her head. Though appearing the rake in every way, she sensed something deeper within him—a kindness, a genuineness—that set her at ease. "Do you enjoy life at sea, Mr. Heaton?"

"I do. There's freedom here on these waves, miss. And adventure. You never know what will happen. Take you, for instance. Who would have guessed you'd be sailing with us on the crossing."

"Yes, I quite agree with you on that." Marianne plucked a ladle from its hook and stirred the fish soup. "So you crave freedom and adventure. What else stirs your soul, Mr. Heaton?"

"Wealth." His answer came too quickly. Too resolutely.

Marianne huffed her disappointment. "Indeed? What of charity, kindness, loyalty, honor? Have they no place in your life?"

He shrugged. "They do not fill empty bellies."

"And your belly is all that concerns you?" She looked his way, wondering if her blunt comment would prick his ire. But he only returned a grin.

"At the moment, yes." He eyed the biscuits. "I am quite hungry."

"Then you have come to the right place." Marianne plucked one and handed it to him.

He took it and lifted his brows. "Thank you, miss. I won't tell a soul."

"Do you have family in Baltimore, Mr. Heaton?" she asked.

He swallowed the bite of biscuit in his mouth. The usual cocky expression faded from his face. "My parents are dead."

"I'm sorry." Marianne stepped toward him, the soup dripping from the ladle onto the floor. She knew well the pain of losing a parent.

He lifted his gaze, shifting his eyes between hers—eyes filled with pain and the slight glaze of alcohol, eyes that instantly hardened. "No need. It was a long time ago."

"But that kind of pain can last for years."

He jerked his hair behind him then lowered his chin.

Grabbing a cloth, Marianne knelt to clean up the spilled soup, chiding herself for prying into this man's personal life.

"How is your wound?" he asked.

Rising, Marianne felt the bandage wrapped around her head. Aside from an occasional itch, she'd all but forgotten it was there. "It gives me no pain."

He chuckled. "I heard it was Seafoam who lured you into your trap below."

"My father always told me my love for animals would cause trouble for me." She smiled then sorrow gripped her at the memory.

She cleared her throat and began spooning biscuit dough onto another tray.

"That cat is a smart one," he said. "I'll warrant she knew exactly what she was doing."

Marianne's hand halted in midair. "What the devil do you mean, sir? I am now a prisoner aboard this ship. How could that be a smart thing to cause?"

Her outburst bore no effect on his insolent grin. "You are good for him."

Lifting the tray, she opened the oven and shoved it inside, slamming the door with a *clank*. "For whom?"

He gave her a devilish smile.

"Noah?" She swung back to the stove to examine the soup. "Absurd. He hates me and I him."

"I doubt that."

"Oh, really? What of Priscilla?"

His eyebrows shot up. "That vain peacock? She's nothing but an empty box wrapped in ribbons and lace."

"So she is beautiful?" Marianne stirred the soup a little too vigorously. Why did she care?

"Very. But she is a bore, if you ask me."

Marianne didn't want to ask him. Didn't want to hear any more about the silly woman.

"Supper will be ready in a few minutes, Mr. Heaton."

"I'll call Mr. Hobbs to gather the messmen, miss." He plopped the rest of the biscuit into his mouth, gave her a wink, and left.

"Dinner is served."

Noah glanced up from his desk to see Luke entering the room with Matthew scrambling in behind him, carrying a tray of steaming food.

"Have you heard of knocking?"

"Not when we bring such delicious fare." Luke kicked the door shut as Matthew set the tray on top of Noah's charts. The savory scent of chicken and the aroma of fresh biscuits filled Noah's nose and he licked his lips. "I thought your wife was still indisposed."

"Aye, that she is." Matthew and Luke exchanged an odd glance.

"Then am I to assume that she prepared this food from her bed?" Noah stood, irritation grinding his nerves at whatever secret the two men shared.

Luke lifted his brows, a mischievous look on his face. "Miss Denton cooked the meal tonight."

Noah allowed the words to needle through his mind, seeking a thread of reason. He dropped his gaze to the plateful of glazed brown chicken and two biscuits. Beside it, a spicy fish scent spiraled upward from a bowl of steaming soup. His mouth watered.

"Quite tasty if you ask me." Matthew licked his lips.

"Miss Denton made this?" Noah eyed them both curiously.

Luke crossed his arms over his chest. "I saw her myself."

Tearing a piece of chicken from the bone, Noah tossed it in his mouth. Tender, moist, and somewhat flavorful. "Astonishing."

"Though not as good as your wife's cooking, Matthew, this is certainly satisfying, especially since I thought I would go hungry tonight." Noah bit into a biscuit, surprised when he found a buttery soft texture within the hard crust.

Seafoam nudged his arm and meowed.

"Even the cat knows good cookin' when she sees it." Matthew laughed.

Noah picked up Seafoam, scratched her head, then set her down on the deck. "Go below and find a rat to gnaw on. This meal is mine."

"Not bad for a woman who never did an ounce of work her entire life." Luke's voice rang with sarcasm.

A vision of blistered hands invaded Noah's thoughts. Who was Miss Denton? Certainly not the spoiled little chit who would go crying to her mama whenever a speck of dirt appeared on her dress. Certainly not the princess who would call a servant over to pick up a handkerchief she had dropped. And then snub her nose at Noah when the maid instantly complied. Either this Miss Denton was not Miss Denton at all, but an imposter, or she deserved a chorus of cheers for such a convincing performance.

Marianne shot up in bed, her heart pounding. Had she overslept? So exhausted after cooking for hours, she'd fallen onto her mattress in the hopes of getting a few hours' sleep before putting her plan into motion. Dashing to the porthole, she searched for any hint of dawn, but the night still hung its dark curtain over the sea. A myriad of stars winked at her as if prodding her onward. She must make her way down to the hold to discover a way to ruin Noah's cargo. Even as the thought sparked her to action, guilt rapped on the door of her conscience. But she would not answer. She couldn't. Her mother's life depended on it. Besides, when she and Noah married, Noah would have all the wealth he needed, and he wouldn't need to work so hard. She was actually doing him a favor.

Striking flint to steel, she lit the lantern on the table, then tucked a knife she'd taken from the kitchen into the pocket of her gown.

She swung the door open, cringed at the loud squeak echoing off the bulkheads, then tiptoed out into the hallway, or companionway, whatever it was called. She listened for any sounds from sailors who might still be about, but nothing but the bone-chilling creaks and groans of the ship and the rush of water against its hull met her ears. From what she had observed, most of the men slept through the night in a section beneath the forecastle by the bow, while the other half kept watch on the top deck, the two groups switching every four hours. Noah's officers slept in separate cabins.

Which meant Marianne could slip into the hold undetected.

Lifting the lantern, she made her way down the steep ladder, and thought to say a prayer for her success, but then decided against it. Though God rarely answered her prayers, she was sure this was a petition He would not only refuse to answer but would frown upon.

The narrow steps creaked and bowed with each footfall. Moisture formed on her neck and arms. At the bottom of the ladder, Marianne scanned the dark hallway to her left and recognized the door of the cursed room that had entrapped her aboard this ship in the first place. The stench of mold, stale water, and something akin to rotten eggs assailed her, and she flung a hand to her nose. Nausea waged a battle in her stomach.

When it passed, she lifted the lantern and scanned the area to her right. Another set of stairs descended to an open lower level stacked to the ceiling with crates, barrels, and huge sacks.

Gathering her courage, she inched down the final ladder. The *pitter-pat* of tiny feet filled the hold, sounding like raindrops on a roof. *Drat.* Marianne froze. Rats. *Oh Lord, maybe I will pray after all. If You are so inclined, Lord, please keep the filthy beasts away from me.* At the bottom, she took a step over the pebbles scattered across the hold floor. The light from her lantern arched before her like a golden shield.

Long, furry tails disappeared in the dark gaps between the crates.

She trembled. Resisting the urge to turn around and run to the safety of her cabin, she swallowed her fears and continued onward. She had no choice. *For you, Mama. If you could see me now, you'd be so proud of me.* Unlike Papa who rarely had a kind word for her unless he was well into his cups.

Perspiration slid down her back and dotted her forehead. The sea pounded against the sides of the ship as if it knew what she was about and wanted to stop her. Could it break through the wooden hull and grab her? Mr. Weller had said no.

Several barrels of water and rum sat within easy reach of the bottom of the ladder. But she was not interested in those. Placing one foot in front of the other, she inched her way down an incline to a lower section. Once there, she began examining the crates one by one. As far as she could tell, most were filled with iron tools and fabric. She moved to another section of barrels. Water and rum for the journey no doubt. But it was the sacks that interested her the most. Flour from the mills at Jones's falls in Baltimore and rice from Charleston.

Even if she managed to open the crates, she could not damage iron and besides, the only way to be rid of it would be to haul it up on deck and toss it to the sea—unlikely given her lack of strength and the fact that her deed would not go unnoticed.

But the flour and rice. She smiled. And rum and water. A terrible combination.

From the corner of her eye she glimpsed something too large to be a rat moving. Marianne gasped, and grabbing the lantern tighter, swung in that direction. What other repulsive creatures lived down here? A loud squeak shot through the dank air. Oh my, maybe it was a very large rodent. She gulped.

Then out from the shadows strolled Seafoam, a squirming rat in her mouth. Marianne backed away in horror even as her heart settled to a normal beat. The cat pranced up to her and dropped the rat proudly at her feet. Trouble was, it wasn't dead. Hobbling across the pebbles, the poor beast tried to make its escape. Seafoam leapt in the air and pounced upon it, this time killing it.

Nausea resurging, Marianne pressed a hand to her stomach as Seafoam deposited the lifeless rodent at Marianne's feet, then glanced up at her as if seeking approval.

Despite her queasiness, Marianne couldn't help but smile at the cat's kindness. "For me?" She set the lantern atop a barrel and stooped to pet the cat. Seafoam purred affectionately and circled her, rubbing against her legs.

"You are a brave hunter, little one. But you may have your prey. I've already eaten." Marianne scooped the cat up in her arms and snuggled against her, cheek to cheek. Noah's scent filled her nostrils, sending an odd warmth through her. She remembered the gentle way he had nestled the cat against his chest—in such contrast with his harsh, all-business demeanor.

"I have work to do, little one." She set the cat atop one of the crates, and Seafoam plopped down and began licking her paws and rubbing them on her face.

Marianne pulled the knife from her pocket. "Now, I know you and the captain are good friends, but you must promise me you'll keep silent about this, agreed?"

Seafoam stopped her grooming and yawned before continuing.

"I shall take that as a yes." Then, knife in hand, Marianne swung about and began slashing through the sacks of rice.

❖ CHAPTER 9 ❖

Noah shut his cabin door and trudged down the companionway in as foul a mood on the start of this new day as he'd been for the past three. He ran a hand through his hair and plopped his hat atop his head. Although he'd intentionally avoided Miss Denton during that time, he'd heard enough about her from everyone around him.

"Miss Denton is so kind." "Miss Denton is so generous with her time and strength." "Miss Denton is so witty, smart, capable, honest." Could he not escape the woman? Had she cast a spell on everyone around her? Everyone save him. For he knew the real Marianne Denton. Pompous, spoiled, and self-serving. At least that was the way he remembered her. And the reason he had teased her so as a child.

Weaving around a corner, he nodded at a passing sailor and scaled the ladder to the upper deck in two leaps, ascending to where he hoped to continue evading the woman. For she rarely came on deck. Why she confined herself to the heat and stale air below, he could not fathom. No doubt it was part of her plan, along with her drastic change in character, to invoke his sympathies so he would take her home.

But Noah was no fool.

Sunlight struck him along with a cool ocean breeze, feathering the hair against the collar of his shirt. Agnes's bubbling laughter bounced over him, drawing his gaze to a group of sailors clustered around the mainmast. In their midst, sitting atop a chair, sat Miss Denton with a rope tying her and the chair to the mast. Agnes perched upon a barrel beside her, a huge smile on her chubby face. Noah halted and tried to rub the strange apparition from his eyes.

The sailors chuckled at something Miss Denton said, and she graced them with a smile before returning her attention to a book laid open on her lap.

" 'And the king spake and said to Daniel, O Daniel, servant of the living God, is thy God, whom thou servest continually, able to deliver thee from the lions?' " she quoted.

She reads the Bible to my men. Frustration boiled within Noah. He glanced at Luke who was leaning on the port railing, Matthew beside him, both their gazes riveted upon her.

Noah marched over to them. "What is going on here?"

"I believe your fiancée is reading from the Holy Book." Luke made no attempt to hide his smirk.

"She is not my. . ." Noah flatted his lips. "I can see that. But why?"

"It's the Sabbath," Matthew said as if that should clear any confusion. He shifted his bulky frame. "She marched up here and announced that she'd be performin' Sunday service for those men who'd be interested." He shook his head and chuckled. "An' bless me sailor's soul if most o' 'em didn't come a runnin'."

Noah gritted his teeth. "Why on earth is she strapped to the mast?"

Matthew raised an eyebrow that was nearly as bald as his head. "Because the poor girl is afraid of the water. You sure don't know much about your own fiancée."

"Confound it all!" Noah ran a hand over the back of his neck as frustration tightened his muscles. "Afraid of the water. Is that what she told you?"

"She didn't have to. It's obvious." Luke shrugged.

"She's merely attempting to get our sympathy."

Matthew's head jerked back as if Noah had struck him. "Are you sayin' she's pretendin'? Now why would she be doin' that?"

"To convince me to return her to Baltimore, of course. She's not the sweet innocent she pretends to be. Beneath that benevolent facade rages a pompous shrew." Noah's harsh tone faded, unable to carry the weight of words he wasn't sure he still believed. "And blast it all, Luke, why are you listening? You don't even believe in God."

"She has a unique way of telling the story of Daniel in the lion's den. Very amusing."

"And that, gentlemen"—her cheerful voice brought Noah's eyes back to her—"is why we must always have faith, even in the midst of hopeless times."

"Amen." Agnes clapped her hands together, her full cheeks rosy once again.

"Me wife surely finds pleasure in 'er company." Matthew spit to the side.

"She's no doubt starved for female companionship." Noah growled. "Enough of this." He stormed amidships.

Miss Denton gently closed the Bible and lifted her gaze to his. Brown eyes, glistening like cinnamon in the sunlight, scoured over him.

"Service is over. Get back to work!" he barked. The men scattered across the deck like rats in daylight.

"Never mind him, dear." Agnes leaned over and untied the rope around Miss Denton's waist then helped her to stand.

Noah rolled his eyes. "Matthew, get that chair stowed below where it belongs."

"Aye, Cap'n." His boatswain ran to the mainmast and hoisted the chair in his arms.

Agnes ambled past Noah, adjusted her apron, and pursed her lips. She didn't have to say anything. Her motherly look of reprimand did its work on Noah's conscience.

"Sail on the horizon. Off the starboard quarter!" Mr. Grainger shouted from above.

Thankful for the interruption, Noah plucked his glass from his belt, moved toward the railing, and lifted it to his eye.

"What has put you in such a foul mood today, Captain?" Miss Denton's voice was soft and assured.

Ignoring her, he gripped the glass tighter and focused on the horizon where the slight shape of a white sail reflected the morning sun. Too far to determine whether she be friend or foe.

He lowered his glass. "It won't work, Miss Denton."

She screened her eyes from the sunlight and gazed up at him with more innocence than seemed possible to feign. "What won't work?"

"Your trying to charm my crew to garner their sympathy."

Her forehead crinkled. "I am doing no such thing. It is Sunday by my best calculation, and the crew deserves a chance to worship." A pink hue colored her nose. "I'm surprised at you for not initiating a proper service while out at sea."

"The sails are gone now, Cap'n," Mr. Grainger reported.

Noah slapped his spyglass shut and faced her. "For one thing, I doubt God notices when people worship Him, and for another thing, Miss Denton, this is a merchant ship, not a chapel, and these men wouldn't be caught dead in church when they are in port." She gazed across the water as if pondering his words, her face pinching. Yet she remained silent. No snide comments, no sharp rebukes, no haughty insults.

Where was the spoiled little goose he'd known as a child? The one he found such pleasure in taunting. He had thought being mean to her would be easy, that he could pick up right where he'd left off eleven years ago. How was he to know the goose had transformed into an angel during those long years, making it all the more harder to follow through with his plan?

Yet he must not falter. For her own good.

"You think my men enjoyed your sermon, Miss Denton? They only attended because it took them away from their duties."

She swept her eyes to his, a moist sheen covering them. Noah hated himself for causing it.

"I'll leave you to your commanding, Captain." Then avoiding his gaze, she teetered over the wobbling deck and disappeared below.

Heavy fog wrapped around the ship. Marianne leaned over the railing and peered through the mist. Below, the sea chopped against the hull so close she could almost reach out and touch it. Claws of foam reached toward her. One touched her hand and she leapt back. Her breath clumped in her throat. Dashing over the deck, she screamed for help, for anyone. But the only answer came in the creaks and groans of the ship—chiding her, berating her.

She was all alone.

She darted to the railing again. Gurgling sounded. She glanced down. Massive bubbles surfaced from below. The sea had risen and was now within her reach. They were sinking! Laughter rode upon the mist and taunted her ears. She peered into the fog. A small boat formed out of the eerie haze

"Hello there!" she yelled. "Help me, I'm sinking."

All eyes in the boat shot to her. Her father, her mother, Lizzie, Noah, Luke, Agnes, and Matthew Hobbs. They smiled and waved at her as if nothing were amiss.

"Help me!" Marianne shouted. "Over here!"

They no longer seemed to hear her or even see her.

A figure appeared near the bow of the small craft—glowing in white light, shining and brilliant. He held up a lantern and faced forward as the boat drifted farther away.

And disappeared into the fog.

Marianne jerked up in bed. Her breath leapt into her throat. She laid a hand on her heart to quell its violent thumping. Tossing her coverlet aside, she swung her feet onto the floor and dropped her head into her hands. *Oh Lord. What does this mean? Will everyone I love abandon me? Even You? Can I trust no one? Why has all this happened to me? Father's death, Mother's illness, our poverty, my forced engagement, and now me upon this ship. Why have You abandoned me?*

"I will never leave you."

Marianne brushed the tears from her face. A spark of hope lit in her heart. Had she heard from God or merely imagined His voice? She looked up. Thunder rumbled in the distance. A mist as thick as the one in her dream slithered into her cabin. She stood, hugging herself against the chill. The rush of water against the hull sounded like a thousand voices taunting her, belittling her. *Trust? You can't trust Him.*

She twirled the ring on her finger. The ring her father had given her. The only thing of value he had ever given her. Before he left her and her mother all alone in this world. Marianne should have sold it when she'd had the chance. The money from the sale would provide a few months of food and medicines. Why hadn't she sold it? The silver felt cold and hard against her fingertips, and she released the band.

You couldn't trust your own father. How can you trust God?

Groping for the tiny table at the foot of her bed, she felt for her flint and steel and with trembling hand, struck it to light her lantern. The glow spread over her cabin, chasing the darkness back into the corners.

"I am the light of the world: he that followeth me shall not walk in darkness, but shall have the light of life." The scripture from John flooded her mind. But her doubts resurrected to do battle with the holy words. Marianne's heart thrashed wildly. She didn't know why. Something evil, something dark seemed to hover in the room ready to pounce upon her. She donned her dress and shoes, swung open her door, and headed up on deck. Better to face her known fear than to suffer below with her demons.

A cool night breeze fingered the tendrils of her loose hair as she emerged on deck and made her way to the capstan, which she had learned was the name of the drum-shaped heaving tool she liked to cling to. Light from a full moon cast a milky haze over the ship, making it look dreamlike as it floated on the ebony sea.

A watchman up on the quarterdeck tipped his hat in her direction. After settling against the sturdy wooden frame, she dared a glance across the sea. The moon hung over the horizon like a giant pearl, its milky wands setting the waves sparkling in silver light.

"It shall be established for ever as the moon, and as a faithful witness in heaven."

Another scripture from the Psalms floated through Marianne's mind. The moon was God's faithful witness. Was He trying to tell her that He still loved her and was with her? A lump burned in her throat, and she swiped a tear from her cheek.

"Trust Me."

Releasing the capstan, Marianne took a step toward the railing. She grew weary of all the struggles in her life, weary of feeling so incredibly alone, but most of all she was weary of always being afraid. She slid her other shoe across the wooden planks. The ship rose over a swell, and she threw her arms out on either side to steady herself. Another step. *Lord, can I trust You?*

As if in answer to her question, the ship plunged, and she nearly stumbled. Her heart thumped against her ribs. A spray of saltwater stung her face.

No. I can't. She slowly retreated.

Right into a firm hand on her back.

She whirled around to find Noah behind her. She wobbled.

"Steady now." He gripped her shoulders.

Shrugging off his hands, she backed away from him, only to realize she was but inches from the railing. She dashed toward the capstan and gripped its familiar firm wood. Even in the moonlight, she could see the look of confusion on his face.

He proffered his elbow. "Milady, may I escort you to the railing? I believe that's where you were heading before I interrupted?"

Marianne hesitated. Why was he being kind? She could not trust him. Squaring her shoulders, she lifted her chin. "I can make it on my own, thank you, Noah."

"Captain."

Did the man's arrogance never end? "Captain Noah."

"Just Captain will do." He grinned.

Releasing the wood, Marianne started out again for the railing. "What brings you up here in the middle of the night?"

He chuckled. "I could ask you the same. But it's not the middle of the night. Dawn will be upon us in minutes."

Marianne inched her shoes over the planks, forcing down her fear, determined to prove to this man that she was no coward. "Do the floors on this ship ever stop wobbling?"

Noah grinned. "Decks. The floors on a ship are called decks, Miss Denton."

She grimaced. "What does it matter? You know what I mean."

"If you are to spend months aboard, you should know the terminology so you aren't mistaken for a landlubber."

"But I am a landlubber." She huffed. "A landlubber who has no intention of becoming a seaman—or seawoman."

Noah walked beside her all the way to the railing as if he cared whether she fell. Marianne gripped the railing, the perspiration from her hands sliding over the wood. Taking a spot beside her, he inhaled a deep breath as he gazed upon the obsidian sea. He shook his hair behind him. Moonlight washed over him, setting his sun-bronzed skin aglow and dabbing silver atop the light stubble on his jaw. He planted his feet part and clutched the railing, the muscles in his arms flexing beneath his shirt. He seemed to have the weight of the world upon him, and Marianne tore her gaze away before any further sympathetic sentiments took root.

Facing her, he studied her intently.

Marianne stared at the railing, the moon, the fading stars, anywhere but at the liquid black death upon which they floated or the liquid blue death in the eyes of a man who hated her. "Can I help you with something, Captain?"

"It's true then."

"What?"

"You *are* afraid of the sea." He glanced at the tight grip her trembling hands had on the railing.

She hated that it was so obvious. She hated showing this man any weakness. "You need not concern yourself with me, Captain."

"As captain, I must concern myself with everyone on board." His brows lifted. "What has me quite baffled, miss, is in light of this fear, why you would steal the very instruments which will aid us to shore. What were you planning on doing with them? Tossing them overboard?"

A wave of shame heated Marianne's face. She took a deep breath and tried to ignore the sea rushing past them not twenty feet below. "If you must know, yes, that was exactly my plan."

He chuckled. Which further angered her. "I assure you, miss, I've been at sea long enough to know how to navigate without them. Difficult as it would be, it would only delay our reaching the safety of land." He leaned toward her until she could feel his warm breath on her neck. "I would abandon your efforts to turn this ship around, Miss Denton. Mark my words, we will make it to England as well as our other ports of call."

Marianne gave a smug huff. England perhaps, but once he discovered she had ruined his precious cargo, he'd have no choice but to return home to Baltimore. "We shall see, Captain Noah."

"Yet your perseverance and ingenuity are commendable."

"A compliment?" Marianne faced him. "Have a care, Captain, or a crack may form in your heart of stone."

Noah's smile was rewarded by the curve of Marianne's lips. Surprisingly, it warmed him from head to toe. Her brown eyes shimmered in the silver light of the moon now dipping beneath the sea. Why hadn't he ever noticed how beautiful her eyes were? She had removed her bandage, allowing her hair to flow like liquid cinnamon down her back.

Resisting the urge to run his fingers through it, he folded his arms across his chest.

The woman was an enigma. How terrifying the past days must have been for her in light of her fear of the sea. Yet here she was up on deck. Her bravery, her kindness to those she should consider beneath her, her willingness to cook and care for the sick, hammered away at the imperious image he had formed of her as a child. Was she playing him for a fool? Nothing but sincerity burned in her gaze. He wanted to hate her for it. But at the moment, he could find no trace of that emotion in his heart. Quite the opposite, in fact.

She broke the invisible thread between their gazes and glanced away. "What brings you on deck so early?"

"This is my favorite time of day." Even as he said it, a soft glow spread across the eastern horizon, chasing away the dark night. "See there." He pointed. "Dawn arrives. A new day. Fresh beginnings."

Marianne twisted the ring on her finger and eyed him curiously. The light brushed golden highlights over her hair and face, and Noah swallowed down a lump of admiration. Confound it all, what was wrong with him?

The ship bucked, and Noah placed a hand on her back to steady her. Salty mist showered over them and her chest began to heave. "Never fear, Miss Denton, you are quite safe aboard this ship."

She shot him a look of disbelief. "Are you so determined to make your fortune that you cannot spare a few days to return a frightened woman—your fiancée—to her home?"

The muscles in Noah's jaw tightened. "You do not know my father."

"What has he to do with it?"

"This is his ship, his cargo. He and Mother depend on me for their survival."

"A heavy burden to bear alone." Her voice sank with genuine concern.

How quickly she transformed from a woman demanding her way to one who cared for his concerns. He looked away from the sympathy pooling in her eyes and thought of his demanding father, hoping to resurge the anger and guilt that kept him strong. "I must apologize for my mother's behavior at the engagement party. She has taken to an excess in drink as of late." He lowered his chin. "It is an illness with her." Confound it all, why was he telling her this?

She laid a hand upon his, jarring him. "No need to apologize, Noah. Many people who have suffered tragedy find succor in spirits.

It is understandable." She offered him a timid smile. "I am sorry."

Noah felt her sorrow—genuine sorrow that began to melt a part of his heart he wasn't ready to let soften. "I do not want your pity," he said in a harsher tone than he intended. He snatched his hand from beneath hers.

She clutched the railing again and flattened her lips in disappointment just as Noah's mother always did when he'd done something wrong. As he always did.

Unlike his father, Noah's mother never chastised him openly. She didn't have to. Noah's failings and weaknesses lurked about their home, hanging from the dark corners of the ceiling like heckling specters. Which was why he preferred to be at sea. He patted the pocket inside his waistcoat. "My mother drinks because I failed her. I failed her and my father. But I will fail them no longer."

Her brows drew together. "Certainly your father understands there are things that affect your fortune that are beyond your control."

"The only thing he understands is success."

A breeze lifted the soft curls of her hair and brought with it the fresh smell of dawn seasoned with a hint of salt. Why was she not angry at him for snapping at her? Why did he battle the strong desire to apologize for all the pain he had caused her?

"Anyone can see you are a more than competent captain."

He cocked a brow. "A compliment? Have a care, Miss Denton. A crack may form in your heart of stone."

They both laughed.

The sun fanned its rays over the sea, brushing golden light over her face.

Unable to resist any further, he took a strand of her hair between his fingers and relished in the silky feel of it. Her sweet feminine scent drifted over him.

Her eyes widened, searching his.

"A sail. A sail!"

Noah slowly tore his gaze from her brown eyes, and for the first time, he felt the pain of their loss. He shifted his attention to the horizon.

"Where away, Mr. Grainger?"

"She's to leeward, sir, about four leagues," the lookout shouted.

Marianne remained frozen beside the railing while Noah marched away, spyglass raised to his eye. Stunned not by the sighting of another ship, but by the tender look on Noah's face as he fingered her hair. What had just happened? She had no idea, but she hadn't time to consider it as the ship exploded in a flurry of activity at the appearance of their new guest. After ordering one of his men below to wake the crew, Noah took a stance on the quarterdeck to study the intruder. Within minutes, sleepy-eyed sailors sprouted from the hatches like gophers from their holes. Luke gave her a wink as he passed and took his place beside his captain.

"Hoist all sail, up topgallants, and courses!" Noah ordered. "Mr. Pike, veer to starboard!"

Mr. Heaton repeated the orders, addressing certain sailors to specific tasks.

Marianne's blood pounded in her ears. Men jumped into the shrouds and scrambled aloft until she could barely see them. They ambled across yards to loosen the sails, dropping them to catch the wind.

"She's British," a man above yelled. "A warship. A frigate."

Following the line of Noah's scope, Marianne spotted the object of excitement. A red-hulled ship, sporting three masts and crowded with sails, stood out stark against the rising sun. White foam leapt upon her bow as she split the dark waters and bore down upon them.

With her heart in her throat, Marianne made her way up onto the quarterdeck and clung to the mast behind the helm. At least from there she could hear what was happening.

Noah slammed the glass shut and slapped it against his palm. Then turning, he spotted one of his sailors. "Run up our colors, Mr. Lothar."

Within minutes the American flag sprung high into the wind on the gaff of their foremast.

"What do they want do you suppose?" Mr. Heaton asked.

"I don't intend to find out." Noah narrowed his eyes upon their pursuer, his face a mask of confidence and command. No hint of fear glinted from behind his sharp blue eyes as he directed his men to their tasks—men who were quick to obey, their expressions displaying trust in their captain. Mr. Weller leapt upon the quarterdeck and stood beside Noah.

"They have the weather advantage," he said.

"I can see that." Noah scratched his chin. "But we are much lighter and swifter. We can outrun them."

"Should I ready the guns, Cap'n?" Mr. Weller clawed nervously at his scarf with his two remaining fingers. "Just in case."

Guns. Marianne swallowed. Surely they wouldn't engage in battle with a British warship?

Noah gave him a curious look. "No need. We will not allow them to get close enough." He looked aloft and then off their bow and the confidence slipped from his face. "Mr. Pike, I told you to bring her to starboard."

The helmsman hefted the massive wheel and grunted. "Cap'n, she ain't respondin'."

Noah marched to his side, gripped two of the spokes and assisted him.

"They're gaining, Cap'n," Mr. Heaton shot over his shoulder.

"The sails are stuffed wit' wind." Mr. Weller scratched his head. "Why haven't we picked up speed?"

Noah released the wheel and rubbed the back of his neck.

The helmsman gazed up at his captain. "It feels like we're draggin' an anchor."

Marianne's heart lurched. She threw a hand to her mouth. "Oh drat."

All eyes shot toward her.

Noah marched toward her. "What have you done, Miss Denton?"

❖ CHAPTER 10 ❖

Marianne watched as Noah emerged from the companionway, his face twisting with rage. His eyes latched upon her like arrows about to fly from their quiver as he made quick work of the ladder to the quarterdeck. His officers followed timidly behind him, their faces reflecting fear. Fear, she assumed, for what he might do to her.

He stormed toward her. Marianne cringed, not daring to release the mast.

"Do you know what you have done?"

"Ruined your rice and flour?" she answered sheepishly.

A cannon blast cracked the peaceful sky with a thunderous *Boom!*

Marianne jumped and stared in that direction, but Noah's eyes never left her.

A splash sounded where the ball dropped into the sea.

"A warning shot, Captain," Mr. Heaton shouted from his spot by the quarterdeck railing. "I believe they want us to heave to."

"Confound it all! More than ruined my cargo, Miss Denton." Noah seemed to be having difficulty speaking. "You have filled my hold with bloated rice and sticky paste and caused the ship to move as if she were a pregnant whale."

"I'm sorry, Noah, I could think of no other way to—" She halted, fear strangling her voice at the crazed look in his eyes.

He backed away and clawed a hand through his hair. "Now we are caught like a fish in a net."

She glanced from him to the frigate and back again. "I thought you said we had nothing to fear from the British." She forced a ring of hopefulness into her voice.

He pointed a sharp finger her way, his face purpling. "Whatever happens is on your head, miss. Mark my words." Then turning, he stormed toward the railing.

Within minutes, the British ship came alongside and kept pace with them. Men scrambled in formation across her deck, some in blue uniforms, others in red—all of them armed. Entangled within the lines above, men in redcoats pointed muskets their way. The charred mouths of fourteen cannons gaped at her from their ports on the main deck.

What had she done, indeed.

Noah eyed the British Naval Ensign flapping at the peak of the frigate's mizzenmast as a man dressed in what looked like a captain's uniform stepped onto the bulwark and held a speaking trumpet to his mouth.

"This is His Britannic Majesty's frigate *Undefeatable*. What ship are you and where are you bound?"

Noah cupped hands around his mouth. "We are an American ship out of Baltimore, the *Fortune,* with a cargo for South Hampton, Noah Brenin commanding." Noah took a deep breath to quell his rising fear. He had traded with the British for years—had friends on English shores. Surely when they discovered the *Fortune*'s nationality and their peaceful business, they would leave them be.

The British captain raised the speaking trumpet again. "Heave to at once, Captain, and prepare to receive a boarding party."

Noah shook his head. Surely they would see reason. He raised his hands to his mouth. "We harbor no deserters, sir, and cannot be delayed." He studied the frigate as he awaited a response. Sleek, tight lines and sturdy sails made her swift upon the seas. The barrels of a hundred muskets gaped at him from the tops. Not to mention the fourteen charred muzzles winking at him from her deck. A tremble went through him.

The captain turned to speak to someone beside him. Soon the air resounded with the thunderous fury of a cannon blast. Gray smoke blew back across the British ship, obscuring part of their forecastle. Once again, the ball heaved harmlessly into the sea just astern of the Noah's ship.

"They be within our range, Cap'n." Mr. Weller's horror-filled eyes bulged as he transfixed them on the British warship. "Let's give 'em a bit o' American 'ospitality, eh?"

Noah shook his head, "We cannot fight a British frigate and hope to win. We would all be killed." Confound the blasted woman! He expelled a deep breath and closed his eyes for a moment then opened them to see the terror etching upon his gunner's face. "Mr. Weller, I will do my best to protect you."

Mr. Weller returned a knowing nod, but the fear never left his eyes.

"Go fetch my pistols and sword, if you please. No, belay that." Noah spotted Mr. Boone on the weather deck and gave him that same order then turned back to Mr. Weller. "Get below and tell the men to arm themselves. Then stay out of sight."

With a salute that gave Mr. Weller's naval experience away, he dashed across the deck. Noah returned his gaze to the frigate. A blast of wind punched him with the sting of gunpowder. He rubbed the sweat from the back of his neck. For the first time in his merchant career, he was trapped—caught in the sights of fourteen guns, eighteen-pounders, from the looks of them. A broadside of which would sink him in minutes. He had no choice but to surrender and hope the captain was a reasonable fellow. Why wouldn't he be? Despite the stories of illegal impressments that had made their way to Baltimore, most British naval officers were men of honor.

If Noah were a praying man, he would have lifted a petition to the Almighty, but he'd given up on God caring about him a long time ago. Noah was on his own now as he had been for years. Straightening his shoulders, he gathered his resolve to preserve his ship and the lives of those upon it.

He eyed his first mate. "Mr. Heaton, heave to."

Luke gave him a wary look and laid a hand on Noah's shoulder in passing as he barked the orders that would lower sails and halt the ship.

No sooner had the ship eased to a slow drift, than a cutter aboard the frigate was swung from its chocks and lowered into the water on their leeward side. From what Noah could make out, a lieutenant, a midshipman, ten marines, and five sailors clambered into the boat and heaved off from the hull.

Mr. Boone returned from below and handed Noah his weapons. After strapping on his sword, Noah turned toward the mast where he'd last seen Miss Denton, expecting to find she had gone below. But there she stood, leaning against the massive wooden pole, terror and remorse burning in her gaze.

"I'm sorry, Noah," she said.

He marched toward her. "No time for apologies, miss. You need to get below."

She shook her head. "I caused this, and I will accept the consequences of my action."

Grabbing her arms, he peeled her from the mast and led her to the ladder. "Do as I say for once, Miss Denton." She ceased struggling and lowered her chin.

Noah halted. "Muster the men amidships, Mr. Heaton," he ordered Luke, who was strapping on his own weapons. His first mate's eyes met his. No fear, only anger seared in his dark gaze, making Noah glad for the first time that he'd chosen such a courageous man for first mate. For never had he needed the man's bravado and stalwart spirit more than he did now.

He urged Marianne down the ladder onto the main deck. She trembled, and his anger diminished. Despite her guilt in causing their present predicament, she must be more terrified than he. "Get below, Miss Denton, and you will be safe." Yet he heard the uncertainty in his voice. "Hide in—"

He was interrupted by a bellow from below. "Drop the manropes!"

He turned to Marianne. "Do as I say." Then he nodded for his men to oblige. Fear rose to join his anger for the lady. He had no idea what type of man this captain was, but he had heard stories of innocent women being captured from merchant ships as well as men.

Seven sailors, followed by ten marines clambered over the bulwarks and landed with resounding authority on the deck of the *Fortune*. A man dressed in white breeches and a blue coat that sported three gold buttons on the cuffs sauntered toward Noah. "Good morning, Captain. I am Lieutenant James Garrick, first lieutenant of His Majesty's ship, *Undefeatable*. This is Mr. Jones, our senior midshipman." He gestured toward a boy no more than twenty, standing beside him as he shifted slitted eyes over Noah's crew.

Noah lengthened his stance, trying to use his height to intimidate the shorter man. "Why has your captain stopped my ship, Lieutenant Garrick? We are but simple merchants. Our countries are not at war."

"War?" The man snickered "We need no war to reclaim what is ours." He glanced over the crew and waved a hand to his men. "Search below and be quick about it." He smiled. "You've got deserters from His Majesty's service in your crew, and by God, I'll have them."

Marianne backed against the break of the foredeck. She hoped to hide behind the swarm of Noah's sailors crowding the deck. She could not go below. Not when this invasion was all her fault. What if Noah or one of his men were to get hurt—or worse, killed? How could she live with herself? If there was any way to prevent bloodshed, she must stay above to offer her hand—or her reason. *Oh Lord, forgive me for*

putting everyone on this ship in danger. Why have You allowed the British to capture us? Her thoughts sped to Agnes, and she prayed the woman would remain out of sight. And Mr. Weller as well. Poor Mr. Weller.

Noah stepped forward, the purple plume of his hat waving in the breeze. His blue eyes turned to ice as he glared at the lieutenant. "I am Captain Noah Brenin, and I do not welcome your visit, sir. In fact, I protest this pretence as piracy. I can assure you my crew are all Americans and you, sir, are wasting your time."

Mr. Heaton and Mr. Hobbs took positions on either side of Noah, sentinels guarding their captain.

"Indeed." The lieutenant fingered sideburns that extended down to his pointy chin. "If that is so, we shall be gone before you know it. Now assemble your men in the waist, if you please."

Noah gripped the hilt of his sword. "You have no right, sir."

Marianne held her breath. The wind stopped as if pausing to view the unjust spectacle below. Perspiration slid down her back. Along with her admiration of Noah's courage, rose fear for his safety. *Please, Lord. Do not let them fight.*

"Ah, but we do, Captain." The lieutenant held out his hand. "I'll take that sword and your pistols, too."

Noah scowled and crossed his arms over his chest.

"And your officers as well." The man's glance took in Mr. Heaton and Mr. Hobbs. "And anyone else who has the stupidity to believe they can best His Majesty's Navy," he shouted to the crew.

Mr. Heaton's eyes narrowed. He fisted his hands, and for a moment, Marianne thought he would lunge at the man.

Noah raised his hand, holding him at bay. "If this is a friendly visit, Lieutenant, what need do you have of our weapons?"

"Ah, defiance, but what would I expect from you rebel Americans?" Lieutenant Garrick aimed his pointy finger toward his ship where the muzzles of fourteen cannons, primed and ready to fire, gaped at them from the frigate's deck. "Any resistance will be met with force, Captain."

Even from where she stood, Marianne could see the muscles in

Noah's jaw tense. "Would your captain kill his own men to prove a point?" he asked.

"If he had to." Lieutenant Garrick shrugged. "But I assure you. . ." He thumbed toward the line of marines standing in formation behind him. "I would have no trouble quelling any dissension and escaping this"—with lifted nose, his glance took in the deck—"rotted bucket you call a ship before we sink her to the depths." Again, he held out his hand and Noah, his eyes simmering, drew his sword and handed it hilt-end to the infuriating man, nodding for Mr. Heaton and Mr. Hobbs to do the same.

Noah stepped to the center of the deck. "Line up, men!"

Marianne's heart sank. Was there nothing to be done?

The sailors shuffled into tattered lines around the mainmast. Their eyes skittered about as their fearful mumblings drifted to Marianne on the wind.

The royal marines, resplendent in their red jackets and white pants marched forward to face the sailors, their black boots thumping over the deck. The bayonets at the tip of their muskets reflected the sun's rays in blinding brilliance. Lieutenant Garrick, a tall, angular man with a pointy nose to match his chin, took up a pace before the men. He called for any who were British subjects to step forward. When none did, he began addressing each man.

Marianne watched in horror as the British scoundrel questioned the crew regarding their nationality and date of birth. All the while Noah's face grew a deeper shade of purple. "I assure you, lieutenant, these men are no more British than you are an American."

Ignoring him, the lieutenant turned as the soldiers he had sent below leapt onto the deck, dragging Agnes and Mr. Weller with them. Agnes tore from the British sailor's grasp and slapped him on the arm. "How dare you, you beast!"

The man raised his hand to strike her. Marianne screamed. Mr. Hobbs flew at him, his face mottled with rage. He crashed into the sailor and toppled him to the ground. Noah marched toward the brawl. The British sailors laughed as the two men tumbled over the deck.

Agnes threw her hands to her mouth. Marianne dashed to her side and clung to her arm. The older woman trembled as her husband punched the British sailor across the jaw. The man fell to the deck. "You'll not be touchin' me wife, mister." Mr. Hobbs wiped the blood from his cut lip and stood.

The marines turned in unison to aim their muskets directly at him. Noah halted.

Marianne's throat went dry. Surely they wouldn't shoot him. The grin that had taken residence on Lieutenant Garrick's lips during the altercation faded, and he snapped his fingers. "Assist Mr. Cohosh to his feet, and"—he pointed toward Mr. Hobbs—"string that defiant traitor up on the yardarm."

Noah froze. A blast of hot wind struck him. His blood pooled in his fists. No. He would not allow his friend, the man who had been more a father to him than his own, die such a cruel death.

Agnes let out an ear-piercing wail. Marianne clung to her, but she seemed to be having difficulty keeping the woman from falling. Her pleading eyes met his.

Two of the marines grabbed Matthew's arms.

"I protest, sir!" Noah pushed his way over to the lieutenant. "This man was only defending his wife."

"Protest all you like, Captain. This man has struck a sailor in His Majesty's Navy, and he must pay the price."

"This man is not a British citizen, nor in your navy, and therefore does not fall under your twisted justice."

Lieutenant Garrick's eyes flashed. "Nevertheless, it can serve as a warning to you all."

Marianne stormed toward the pompous man. "Lieutenant. You will do no such thing!" she said with an authority that belied her gender.

With raised brow, the lieutenant swerved to face her. Noah tensed. What was the foolish woman doing drawing attention to herself?

She put her hands on her hips and gave the lieutenant one of her

I-know-far-better-than-you looks that always made Noah's blood boil.

"And what have we here?" The man's eyes swept over her. "Ship's cook? Seamstress?"

Noah gestured from behind the British officer for her to stop and say no more.

She glanced at him but continued nonetheless. "I am Miss Marianne Denton, the captain's fiancée."

Noah blew out a sigh and shook his head.

"Ah, even better." The lieutenant grinned, glancing at Noah.

"Please, sir, do not harm this man. I beg you." The limp sails flapped thunderously above them, adding impetus to Marianne's demand.

"And what will you offer me in exchange?"

She narrowed her eyes. "I have nothing to offer you, sir."

Noah stepped forward before Miss Denton dug her own grave and all of theirs as well with her unstoppable mouth. "Ignore the woman, lieutenant. She's mad with fever." He gave her a stern look and pushed her behind him, but not before he saw the fury in her eyes.

"I am not—"

"Now, I insist you leave my ship at once." Noah interrupted her. "You have found no British deserters."

"But I have not finished." Lieutenant Garrick said in an incredulous tone, peering around him at Miss Denton. "Besides, I need to inquire after *your* citizenship, Captain, and your first mate."

"We were both born in Baltimore. I in 1786 and he in 1784."

The lieutenant stared at him for a moment, shifting his eyes onto Luke. Then he shrugged. "I don't believe you. In fact, from today forward you and your first mate can consider yourselves British seamen."

Panic squeezed the blood from Noah's heart. "This is outrageous, sir! We are Americans."

"Americans." The word spit like venom from Lieutenant Garrick's lips. "Nothing but rebellious British colonials." He flung his hand through the air.

Luke charged toward the arrogant man, fists curled and ready to strike. The marines snapped their muskets in his direction. Noah leapt in front of him and forced him back.

The lieutenant laughed. "You will soon learn proper discipline under the strict rule of Captain Milford."

He turned toward Miss Denton. "And I believe I'll take you up on your offer, miss. In exchange for this man's life, you will come with me." He gestured toward Matthew who stood beside his wife, his arm draped over her trembling shoulders.

Miss Denton's eyes grew wide, and she swallowed.

"Leave her be!" Noah barreled toward the man, his only thought to save Marianne, but the point of a bayonet pierced the skin on his chest, halting him. A red spot blossomed on his white shirt, and he took a step back.

Lieutenant Garrick gave him a look of disgust. "No, I will not leave her be. The captain is in need of a new steward. The last one fell overboard during a storm. Quite tragic."

Miss Denton's face paled as white as the sails.

"Yes, I believe she'll do quite nicely." Garrick shifted his gaze to Noah. "That is unless you prefer me to hang this man of yours?" He wrinkled his nose in disdain at Matthew.

Behind the lieutenant, Miss Denton shook her head furiously at Noah. He blinked. She willingly exchanged her life for Matthew's—a man she barely knew?

The lieutenant scanned the crew one more time. The creaking of the ship and flap of canvas filled the silence as each man held their breath and avoided his gaze.

His eyes latched upon Mr. Weller. "You look familiar to me."

"I don't know you, sir." Weller's face remained a stone, save for the sweat glinting on his scarred cheek.

Noah's stomach knotted.

The lieutenant eyed Mr. Weller up and down, his gaze landing on his missing fingers and the scar on his face. "A gunner, perhaps?"

"I never been in your navy." Mr. Weller spat to the side.

"Your accent betrays you, sir." Lieutenant Garrick gestured for his men to grab Mr. Weller as well.

Shock replaced the fear on Weller's face as two marines clutched his arms and dragged him to the railing. Yet he didn't struggle. Instead, his expression turned numb as his lifeless eyes raked over Noah in passing.

A marine grabbed Marianne's arm. He dragged her to the bulwarks. She winced and began to tremble as they approached the railing, but the soldier took no note. Every fiber within Noah itched to charge the man as Luke had done, to fight this incredible injustice, but he knew it would only cause bloodshed.

There was nothing he could do.

"Oh my poor dear," Agnes wailed after Marianne.

Sweat slid into Noah's eyes, stinging them. He glanced one more time over his shoulder at the remainder of his crew, their eyes reflecting both their relief at not being chosen and their fear for him. Matthew took a step forward, Agnes leaning in his arms. At least they had been spared. Matthew nodded his way. A look of understanding passed between them, and Noah knew the man would care for his ship and if possible, find a way to rescue them.

It was the only hope Noah could cling to as he swung over the bulwarks and dropped into the boat that would take him, his men, and Miss Denton to a fate worse than death.

❖ CHAPTER 11 ❖

Sandwiched between two officers—Lieutenant Garrick walking before her and another man behind—Marianne descended a set of wooden steps beneath the quarterdeck and proceeded down a gloomy passageway aboard the *Undefeatable*. Familiar smells burned her nose— moist wood, tar, and the sweat of men, of hundreds of men from what she'd seen above deck.

Each step sent her heart crashing against her chest. A thousand horrifying visions of her future flashed like morbid captions across her mind. Unlike Noah, she did not entertain the notion that any honor existed among these British officers. She had heard the stories of their atrocities inflicted upon American sailors—and she believed them. A shudder overtook her. She stumbled, and the man behind her nudged her forward.

She thought of Noah and Mr. Heaton. What horrors were they presently facing? And Mr. Weller. Poor Mr. Weller. But she hadn't time to contemplate their fate, as hers was about to be revealed. At the end of the passageway, a man dressed in a red coat, white breeches, with musket in hand, guarded a door she assumed to be the captain's.

Lieutenant Garrick knocked. A gruff "Enter" followed, and Garrick swept open the door, ducked beneath the frame, and ushered Marianne inside. A massive oak desk faced her and behind it, tearing spectacles from his rugged face, rose a man whose height caused him to lean slightly forward lest he bump his head on the ceiling—or deckhead, whatever they called it. Thick black hair, veined with gray, sprang from the confines of a ribbon at the back of his neck as if unwilling to be restrained. He shifted his broad shoulders beneath his dark blue coat, causing the golden threads of his epaulettes to quiver.

Lieutenant Garrick doffed his hat. "We found three deserters aboard the ship, Captain Milford."

The other officer took a position just inside the door.

Marianne swallowed, searching the captain's eyes for any trace of kindness or decency, but all she found was an intelligence that astounded her and a cruel indifference that frightened her to the core.

He tugged on the sleeves of his coat, the three golden buttons at the cuffs glimmering in the sun's rays that streamed in through the stern windows.

Sensing a hesitancy in the man, Marianne stepped forward. "If I may, sir. They were not deserters, you see—"

"You may not, miss!" the captain barked, forcing the remainder of Marianne's words into a clump in the back of her throat.

"Very good, Mr. Garrick." He shifted gray eyes onto his first lieutenant. "See that they are settled and given their assignments." He rounded the desk, keeping his eyes on Marianne. "And who might this be?"

Lieutenant Garrick lifted his chin. "I thought she would do nicely as your new steward, Captain."

"Indeed?" The captain appraised her as one might a piece of fine furniture or a prize horse. Marianne shifted beneath his impertinent perusal and dared a glance at Lieutenant Garrick behind her.

Gone was the smug facade he'd worn on board the *Fortune*. Instead the man kept his eyes leveled forward and his back straight. "Since we lost Jason in the storm," he added with a tremble in his voice.

The officer's stance of temerity before his captain caused a new gush of fear to rise within Marianne. What sort of man *was* this Captain Milford?

"I'm aware of that, Mr. Garrick. Do you take me for a fool?" The captain snapped, spit flying from his mouth. Then as quickly as his fury had risen, his features softened, and he grabbed a lock of Marianne's hair and rubbed it in between his fingers. He lifted it to his nose. "Has she any training?"

Marianne stiffened. "I would appreciate you not speaking about me as though I were too ignorant to understand you, sir."

The captain's gray eyes chilled, and for a moment she thought he would strike her. But then he broke into a chuckle. Lieutenant Garrick smiled.

The captain speared him with a sharp gaze "That will be all, Mr. Garrick. Attend to the new recruits."

With a salute, Garrick turned and left.

"No, you remain, Mr. Reed." Captain Milford's words halted the other officer.

Marianne's breath grew rapid. Determined not to show her fear, she met the captain's gaze without wavering. Interest flickered in his eyes as he circled her, one hand behind his back. Arrows of sunlight beamed through the stern windows and angled across a cabin much larger than Noah's aboard the *Fortune*. The bright rays skimmed over the desk, the chairs, and a bookcase holding numerous tomes, decanters, and glasses. Two unlit lanterns swung from hooks on the deckhead. A sleeping chamber took up the far left corner. Conspicuously absent, however, were the cannons. Marianne had always heard British captains kept cannons in their cabins, ready for use. Also odd was the row of potted plants that lined the stern window casing.

Captain Milford completed his assessment and stood before her, his gray eyes sharp. "So, miss. Have you?"

"I beg your pardon." Marianne shifted her shoes over the edge of the painted canvas at the room's center.

He gave an exasperated sigh. "Any training as a steward?"

Encouraged by the spark of kindness drifting over his expression, Marianne turned pleading eyes his way. "Captain, I beg you. My name is Marianne Denton, and I am a citizen of Baltimore, Maryland. I am no one's steward, sir. In fact, I wasn't even supposed to be on that merchant ship."

The gold fringe on his epaulettes shook as the wrinkles at the corners of his eyes folded in laughter. "Allow me to enlighten your understanding, Miss Denton. You are no longer a citizen of Baltimore. You are my steward. You will prepare and lay out my clothing, bring me my meals, scrub this cabin, and help keep my affairs in order." His tone rang through the cabin like a death knell. "Is that clear?"

Marianne closed her eyes. *This cannot be happening.* "Captain, if I may indulge your patience. My mother is very ill. I must get back to her as soon as possible."

"Enough!" He thrust his face toward her. "My mother died while I was at sea. You will soon learn that we all must make sacrifices."

His hot breath, tainted with alcohol, fanned over her skin. Turning, he stormed toward his desk and poured a glass of amber liquid from a glass carafe. He sipped it and took up a pace before the stern windows.

"Many sailors have woeful tales, miss. If I allowed everyone off this ship who had some tragedy ashore, I'd be sailing it myself."

He fingered the leaf of one of the plants. "Isn't that so, my lovely?"

Marianne flinched. Was the captain toying with her? "But I am not a sailor. I am an innocent lady."

He tossed the remainder of his drink to the back of his throat then slammed the glass to his desk. Turning, he brushed invisible dust from his dark blue sleeves. "Do I look presentable, Mr. Reed?"

"As always, Captain." The man's guttural voice drifted from behind her.

"Very well. Very well, indeed." He glanced across the cabin as if trying to remember something, his eyes growing dull and lifeless.

The ship moaned over a swell, and Marianne steadied her shoes against the rising deck.

"Captain?" The officer behind her said. "Your orders?"

He shook his head. "Ah yes. Prepare the ship to get underway, Mr. Reed."

"And the lady?"

"Show her to the steward's quarters."

Marianne took a step forward. "But, Captain, you cannot hold an innocent civilian."

He eyed her and the former sharpness in his gaze returned. "I assure you I can, miss. I can do whatever I wish. I am master of this ship. I can either treat you as my steward or as a prisoner and lock you below. Which would you prefer?"

Marianne pursed her lips and tried to quell both her anger and her fear. She must choose the option that afforded her the most freedom—freedom to help Noah and his crew, and freedom to escape.

Noah lined up with his men on the deck of the *Undefeatable*, awaiting their inspection, and gazed at the *Fortune*—his ship, his father's last ship—as it sailed away over the choppy azure waves. He supposed he should be happy the two nations were not at war for if they were, the British would most certainly have taken his ship and cargo as prize. Though his body had accepted his fate, his mind was cast adrift in a sea of impossibilities, unable to anchor into anything solid, anything real. On his right stood Luke, his hands crimped into permanent fists. On his left, Weller shifted from foot to foot, muttering to himself.

Across the deck, sailors busied themselves with various tasks: scrubbing the deck, tying knots, coiling rope, shining brass, hoisting lines, and unfurling sail as the ship prepared to get underway. Not a square foot of space could be found unoccupied. And weaving among the organized chaos, marched masters' mates, shouting orders as they snapped their stiff rattans against their palm to ward off any dissension.

Lieutenant Garrick popped up from beneath the quarterdeck where he had disappeared moments before with Marianne. *Oh God, please keep her safe.* Noah surprised himself with the first prayer he had uttered in eleven years.

The lieutenant took up a pace before them, placing one hand behind his back. "You three men will be assessed as to your skills and assigned to different watches and positions." He halted and scoured them with a haughty gaze. "A word to the wise. This is a British navy vessel, a disciplined fighting machine, not the unorganized piece of flotsam from which you came."

Noah grimaced, and Luke leveled such a burning gaze upon the man, Noah feared it would sear him clean through.

Garrick didn't seem to notice, so obsessed was he with his commanding performance. "Captain Milford suffers no fools on board, nor does he brook any nonsense. The sooner you accept that, the better things will go for you."

Mr. Weller mumbled something.

Luke gave a defiant grunt, bringing the lieutenant's gaze down on him along with his pointy finger. "I perceive we shall have trouble with you." He cocked his head. "Nothing that a few licks from the cat won't change." He chuckled.

Noah tired of the man's supercilious display.

He nudged Luke with his elbow and shook his head, hoping his volatile first mate would heed the warning. He had heard of men being lashed with the cat-o'-nine who had barely survived. The cruel punishment was inflicted aboard His Majesty's ships for the slightest infractions and was the reason so many of their crew deserted.

Which was what Noah intended to do. And exactly the reason that he and his men had to submit to this man's pompous authority—for the time being.

The sails snapped above. The ship lurched, and Noah ran the sleeve of his shirt across his sweaty brow.

"He won't give you any trouble, Lieutenant. Just show us where to go." Perhaps then he could speak to the captain. Surely a man in command of such an exquisite warship would have the decency and honor to see how great an injustice had been enacted upon them. Any reasonable man could come to no other conclusion save that Noah and his friends were but neutral American merchantmen and not British navy deserters.

Garrick's spiteful gaze shifted to him. "Mr. Simons," he yelled over his shoulder. "Take these men below. Instruct the surgeon to look them over from stem to stern and have them make their mark on the ship's articles. Issue them their slops, mess gear, and hammock, and see to their assignments."

"Yes, sir." A short, squat man with a considerably large bald head approached and led Noah and his crew below deck.

A deep gloom enveloped Noah as he descended the ladder— a darkness and heat that was oppressive, stifling. Perhaps it was the number of sailors crammed into this tiny space. Men seemed to fill every crack and crevice, each one of them busy attending to some task. Down one more deck and they met the surgeon—a pale, thin man with bloodstains on his shirt and sweat layered on his brow. After gazing into their open mouths and squeezing a few muscles, he pronounced them all fit for duty.

Next, Mr. Simons escorted them to the purser's cabin. A thick man with leathery skin leaned on the counter and pointed toward a parchment containing various marks and signatures. "Make yer mark here, if you please."

Noah fingered the quill pen. "And if I don't?"

Mr. Simons laughed, and he and the purser exchanged a glance. "You don't want to be findin' that out, now. The cap'n deals harshly wit' mutineers."

"How can we be mutineers if we aren't in your stinking navy?" Luke grumbled.

Mr. Weller nudged Noah. "We better do it, Cap'n." His voice emerged as a childish whimper.

"Very well." Noah signed the paper and handed it to Luke. "It won't matter anyway."

"Welcome t' His Majesty's Navy." The purser chortled after they had all signed, "Here's yer slops and gear." He tossed each of them a bundle that upon further inspection contained tin cups, plates, a hammock, and clothing that smelled as if it hadn't been washed since the last owner had worn it. After changing and storing their gear in the berth, Noah and his men followed Mr. Simons back up on deck.

As Noah emerged above, he blinked and squinted like some nocturnal animal trapped in the sunlight. "Mr. Simons, can you tell me what became of the lady who was brought on board with us?"

"Don't know nothin' about that. I imagine she's wit' the cap'n."

Noah's throat closed. Surely the captain would do her no harm. Would he?

Mr. Simons drifted past them and pointed at Luke. "You are assigned to larboard watch." He thumbed over his shoulder to a man dressed in trousers too small for his tall frame. "Kane'll show you the ropes."

"I've been sailing ships all my life." Luke huffed his disdain. "I doubt Mr. Kane can show me anything."

"What he'll be showin' you is how to do what you're told an' keep your mouth shut." Mr. Simons's heightened voice held a warning as his baleful eyes narrowed upon Luke. With a shake of his head he continued, "And you." He stopped before Mr. Weller. "Gunner's mate. Since I see you already had a run in wit' a canon," the purser added with a laugh.

The scars on Mr. Weller's face seemed to scream in defiance, yet he simply nodded as a glaze of placid acceptance covered his dark eyes.

"Get below and report to Mr. Ganes."

Mr. Weller slogged off. Noah's gut tensed in defiance.

"And you." Mr. Simons squinted up at Noah. "Weren't you the cap'n aboard that ship?"

"I was."

"Well, now you're a topmastman."

Noah's heart stopped. He glanced up at the towering masts that stretched into the blue sky. "Do you have any other positions?"

Mr. Simons eyed him curiously. "No, but if you're afraid of heights, I guarantee you'll overcome that right quick." Again he laughed, and

Noah had the impression he spent his day laughing at his own jokes.

"Report to Blackthorn there. He'll get you situated."

Noah glanced over at the large, crusty looking fellow standing by the shrouds then back above. Men walked across the yards and foot-ropes as if they were wide city streets.

A vision of his brother, laughing and scrambling up the ratlines and around the lubbers' hole at the mast top, filled Noah's mind.

Gripping the lines, Jacob had glanced down at Noah, a wide grin on his tanned face. "Watch how easy it is, you jellyfish!" he shouted.

Right before...

Noah's life had changed forever.

He froze. His body felt as heavy as an anchor. He could never go up there. If he did, he was sure he would die.

❖ CHAPTER 12 ❖

Marianne followed the officer called Reed, a tall, polished man with neatly trimmed coal black hair, out of the captain's cabin and down two doors to a room even smaller than the one she'd been given aboard the *Fortune*.

"The steward's quarters, miss. At the captain's orders, a fresh gown left by one of the sailor's wives has been laid out for you on the bed. I suggest you put it on." His deep voice held the monotonous tone of someone either terribly bored or in complete control of any errant emotions.

She swung to face him. "Mr. Reed, I beg you. Surely you can see I do not belong here." She searched his eyes for a speck of compassion. "I am but an innocent lady, born and raised in Baltimore."

A hint of disdain crossed his gaze. "That you were born in Baltimore, I will not question. That any of you seditious Americans are innocent, I refuse to believe." He lifted a haughty brow and looked above her as if the sight repulsed him.

"We won our freedom from Britain honorably and fairly. Or do you insist that all peoples bow before your great nation?"

"Not all. Only those who owe us the very debt of their existence." The *whomp* of sails thundered above and the ship canted. Marianne gripped the doorframe for support, and Reed gave her a look of annoyance. "Though it appears you are no stranger to servitude, I doubt you are accustomed to the quality of service the captain requires."

"How dare you? You do not know me, sir."

"Guard your tongue, miss. I am an officer and will be addressed with respect." He waved a hand through the air. "I'll send Daniel to instruct you in your duties." And with that, he nudged her inside and closed the door.

Marianne slumped onto the thin, knotty mattress and hung her head. A beam of sunlight struck the ruby in her ring and set it aglow. She twisted it and thought of the day her father had given it to her for her twentieth birthday. He had looked so dapper in his maroon coat and brown trousers with the tips of his styled hair grazing his silk cravat. It was the only time Marianne felt as though he approved of her, if only a little. She could still picture her mother sitting in the chair by the hearth, holding Lizzie against her breast—just a year old at that time. A warm glow, akin to the one within her ruby, swept over Marianne at the memories. They had been a happy family once.

Falling to her knees, she dropped her head onto the mattress. *Why, God, why? I don't understand. What purpose could it have served to take Papa from us?* Tears blurred her vision. *And now this? Captured and enslaved on a British warship. Help me understand.*

The deck tilted, and Marianne's knees shifted over the floorboards. A splinter pierced her gown and into her leg. A pinprick of pain shot up her thigh. Yet no answer came from God. The booming crack of sails above and the crush of water pounding on the hull were answer enough. God had a plan, of that she was sure. However, it was surely a plan that did not consider her or her family's happiness.

"Oh Lord, please take care of Noah and his men. It's my fault they are here," she sobbed. The rough burlap scratched her face, and she lifted her head into her hands. Tears slid down her cheeks and dropped onto the coverlet, forming darkened blotches. "And if You can spare a moment, please look after Mama. I miss her so much. Please do not let her die." The tears flowed freely now, and her body convulsed beneath a flood of them until she had none left.

"Miss! Miss!" A child's voice drifted over Marianne. "Miss!" Someone tugged on her arm. "Miss, wake up!" Marianne searched through the fog in her head, trying to remember where she was.

The British ship!

She snapped her eyes open to a face so sweet and innocent, she thought she might have died and gone to heaven. If not for the ache in her head and the cramps in her legs—and the teetering of the ship beneath her as it sailed through the deadly sea.

"Who are you?" Marianne struggled to sit, then rubbed her eyes.

"I'm Daniel, miss." He glanced out the half-opened door. "Sorry t' disturb you, but the captain will be wantin' his cabin attended to before his noonday meal." With brown hair the color of cocoa and eyes as bright as lanterns in a dark sanctuary, the boy's presence seemed to scatter the forebodings of doom that had consumed her cabin.

"What time is it? How long have I been asleep?" Marianne pushed the hair from her face.

" 'Bout an hour, miss." Daniel smiled, revealing a perfect set of white teeth. "I came by 'efore but figured you needed the rest due to being impressed an' all." He said the words as if this sort of thing happened all the time. Well, perhaps on this ship, it did.

He clipped his thumbs into the waist of his oversized blue breeches. "We best be hurryin', miss."

"Very well." Marianne struggled to stand, then leaned her hand against the wall to steady herself as the ship rolled. She pressed down the folds of the maroon gown she'd donned. A scandalous color, to be sure. But she didn't wish to vex the captain by not accepting his gift. "I suppose you're here to instruct me in my duties."

"Aye." The boy beamed and flung dark hair from his face. Clear brown eyes shone with an invitation for friendship.

An invitation that, despite her circumstances, Marianne couldn't help but accept.

For the next two hours, Daniel instructed Marianne in the fine art of being a captain's steward. The list of duties was exhausting. Not only did Captain Milford want his meals brought from the cook on time, his uniforms delivered to the laundry and returned promptly, and his daily attire laid out each morning, but also the floor of his cabin scrubbed, his rug shook out, his desk and shelves dusted, and the silver on his sword hilts, chalices, and trays polished every day.

"What of these plants?" Marianne asked Daniel as she glanced over the assortment lining the stern window frame. From what she knew of horticulture, one was a strawberry bush, one a lime tree, another a patch of onions. The others she could not name.

"Oh no, miss." Daniel's eyes widened. "You must never touch those. Only the captain cares for his plants."

"A curious thing to see on a ship, is it not?"

"Aye miss. But the cap'n is a curious man, if you ask me."

Yes, she had noticed. "How do you know so much about caring for the captain?"

"I used to help the captain's last steward a bit." Daniel's voice sank. "Before he fell overboard." He shrugged. "An' I guess the captain's partial to me."

"I can see why." Marianne pressed a hand over an ache in her back and glanced out the stern windows. The distant horizon rose and slipped beneath the frame as the ship traversed each ocean swell. Though rays of sunlight brightened the entire cabin, making it almost cheery, they also increased the temperature. Withdrawing a handkerchief from her sleeve, Marianne dabbed at the moisture on her neck and thought of how miserable it must be on deck in the direct sun.

"Have you seen my friends?"

Daniel opened a jar of some type of oil and dribbled some onto a soiled cloth. He nodded.

"Are they well?"

"Aye, miss."

"Can you get a message to them for me? To the tall one with the light brown hair."

Daniel's eyes lit up. "Aye, the cap'n?" The smell of lemons and linseed filled the room.

"Yes." Marianne bit her lip. No doubt Noah would still be so furious that he would not wish to hear a peep from her, but she needed to know how he and the others fared. She'd never forgive herself if something happened to them. "Can you tell him I'm sorry and ask him if there's anything I can do?"

Daniel nodded his understanding as he knelt to scrub the floor.

Marianne plopped beside him and grabbed another rag. "How old are you, Daniel?"

"Eleven." His voice rang with pride.

"What are you doing on board this ship?" She poured oil on the rag and mimicked Daniel's method of polishing the deck. "Is your father aboard?"

He halted for a minute, then continued scrubbing. "I was impressed, same as you."

"Impressed? Stolen?" Her fears began to rise for the boy. "You're an American?" Why hadn't she noticed the absence of the distinct British lilt?

He beamed. "Aye, from Savannah."

The poor lad. Marianne laid a hand on his shoulder. "Where are your parents?"

"Back home, I suppose," he said without looking up from his task.

Marianne stood, her indignation rising with her. "How can the Royal Navy steal little boys away from their parents? Have they no shame?"

"I was on a merchant ship, same as you." He shrugged and gave her a peaceful smile, completely at odds with the alarm she felt. "It is the way of the Royal Navy, miss."

"That does not make it right," she huffed. "What do you do here on board?"

Rising to his feet, he lengthened his stance. "I am a powder boy, miss."

Marianne drew a sleeve over her damp forehead, wincing when she touched her wound. "Powder boy? What does a powder boy do? I thought most gentlemen no longer powder their wigs."

"No, miss." He giggled. "I run the powder to the guns when we're in battle."

Gunpowder? She thought of Mr. Weller. "But isn't that dangerous?"

"Aye." His eyes widened once again as if he were about to tell her a grand secret. "Just a fortnight ago, when we was firing upon a French warship, an enemy shot crashed through the gun deck and my friend William had his face blown clear off."

Marianne threw a hand to her mouth, both at the gruesome event and the casual, unfeeling manner in which Daniel relayed it. The things he must have seen. The horror and bloodshed. How unconscionable for so young a boy. Yet he seemed not to bear the fear one might expect. In fact quite the opposite.

"He's in heaven now." Daniel announced with a calm assurance that reinforced her impression. He stood.

"We must get you off this ship at once." Marianne drew him to her breast.

He pushed her back and gazed up into her eyes. "I know, Miss Marianne. That's what you came for."

"Whatever do you mean?" She brushed the hair from his face.

"Why God sent you."

"Sent me? I don't understand." Had the poor child gone mad in his imprisonment?

Yet the clarity in his brown eyes spoke otherwise. "Yes, miss." He smiled. "God told me there'd be a lady and three men coming to rescue me.

"And here you are."

Heart stuck in his throat, Noah eased his bare feet out onto the foretopsail footropes. The yard he gripped shuddered in the wind, and his sweaty fingers slipped over the rough wood.

"New to the top?" the man called Blackthorn said as he made his way out across the yard ahead of Noah.

"You could say that." Noah barely managed to squeak out the words before a blast of wind tore them away. Instead of the light steady breeze, interrupted by occasional gusts below, the wind here in the tops remained constant and strong like the persistent front line of an enemy attack.

An attack in which Noah believed he would be the first casualty.

"I thought you was the cap'n." Blackthorn said.

"I was. . .I am."

Blackthorn chuckled. "Sink me now, ain't never heard of a captain afraid of heights."

Despite Noah's attempts to hide it, the horror strangling his gut had obviously taken residence on his face.

"Ah now, you'll get used to it. Just don't be lookin' down. Keep a firm grip on the jackstays and beckets and make sure you have a good step before you take it. You'll do fine." He slapped Noah on the back, causing him to grip the yard tighter.

"Sorry," Blackthorn muttered.

As Noah and the other four men spread upon the footropes, waiting orders from below, he ignored Blackthorn's advice not to look down. He hoped to catch a glimpse of Miss Denton, if only to see how she fared. Had the captain harmed her? Had he locked her below? Such a brave lady. If she were as frightened of the water as Noah was of heights, she possessed far more courage than he imagined, for he could not stop the trembling that had gripped him since he leapt up into the shrouds.

His eyes latched onto the captain standing by the binnacle, feet spread apart and hands clasped behind his back. Both the commanding tilt of his nose and the three gold buttons on his cuffs gave away his rank. At least he wasn't below with Miss Denton.

"Strike the foresail!" The order bellowed from below, and the men began to loosen the lines keeping the sail furled.

"What is your opinion of the captain?" Noah asked Blackthorn.

The huge man, who looked more like a bear balancing on a high wire than a sailor accustomed to the topmast, leaned casually against the yard as if he were leaning against a railing below.

"Milford?" He angled toward Noah's ear. "Crazy ole rapscallion, if you ask me. Some say he's been at sea so long he's gone mad. He can be as vicious as a rabid wolf one minute and kinder than Saint Joseph the next." He scratched the hair sprouting from within his shirt. "Trouble is, you never know which one you're gonna get."

Noah loosened the first knot and moved to the next one. The edges of the thick sail began to flap in the wind. He swallowed and tried to steady his hands. "Do you think he would harm a woman?"

"Ah, you're thinkin' of your lady friend." Tearing through a stubborn knot, Blackthorn shook his head. "I don't think so. As long as she does what she's told."

Noah grimaced. The woman never did what she was told!

He studied the captain. The man carried himself with a commanding, capable presence, albeit with an overdone pomposity. But surely that went with the position. Noah could not conceive that a British officer and a gentleman would imprison simple merchantmen against their will, let alone an innocent woman. As one commander to another, Noah intended to reason with him the first chance he got. And if that didn't work, there was always the possibility of escape.

Lieutenant Garrick popped on deck from below, the usual scowl twisting his thin lips.

Blackthorn cursed under his breath. "I'd stay away from that one, if I was you."

Noah inched his way across the ratline. His sweaty feet slipped over the swaying rope, and he gripped the yard. Following Blackthorn's gaze, Noah snorted as Garrick leapt upon the quarterdeck and took a stance behind his captain. "I believe I've had my fill of Lieutenant Garrick already."

"Ambitious and cruelhearted." Blackthorn grumbled. "If he had 'is way, half the crew'd be keelhauled."

"Let go clewlines and buntlines!" ordered the man below, and the mastmen began lowering the lines that would free the sail to the wind.

Noah pointed toward another man in a lieutenant's uniform who took his post beside Garrick. "What of him?"

"Reed? He's a good egg, for the most part, I suppose." Blackthorn loosened a line and part of the sail dropped, flapping in the wind. "Just a bit full o' hisself, if you ask me. His father's a member of Parliament, they say—which is why he got this commission." The wind whistled through the gaps of two missing teeth on his bottom row. He snapped his mouth shut. Though towering over Noah's six feet and with the muscle to match his height, Blackthorn's easy manner and kindness made him appear less threatening.

"You're not British," Noah said.

"Me? No. Pure American I am. From Savannah, Georgia."

"Impressed, then?"

"Aye, a year ago. I was a waister on a merchant ship. Captain took me an'"—he hesitated and looked down—"me bosun."

"A year?" Noah stared at him aghast. "You haven't tried to escape?"

Blackthorn's dark eyes seemed to lose their luster. "Aye, we did. Or at least we tried. I was flogged, but the cap'n tossed me bosun to the sharks. God save his soul."

"Let fall! Sheet home!" More orders from below.

But all Noah heard was Blackthorn's words *flogged* and *tossed him to the sharks.* And his terror-stricken heart shrank. "But I hear people desert the navy all the time."

Blackthorn gave him the measured look of a man who had traveled a particular road more than once. "They don't ever let their eyes off us Yankees." He released the sail. The canvas lowered further, slapping furiously at the wind's attempt to conquer it. But it fought a losing battle, for air soon filled every inch of the sail with a thunderous roar, stretching it taut and snapping the lines.

"No, you best accept your fate, Mr. Brenin. There ain't no way off this ship."

❖ CHAPTER 13 ❖

Marianne set the tray of pea soup, roast chicken, and tea down on the captain's desk. "Your dinner, Captain."

He grunted and tossed down the documents he studied then eyed her above the spectacles perched on his nose. "You're late."

"The cook extends his apologies, Captain. He is behind on his duties today due to his gout acting up again."

"Addle-brained sluggard." Captain Milford tore off his spectacles and leaned his nose over the food. "Smells like pig droppings."

"I can take it back if you like."

"No no. I'll eat it." He waved her off. "If I waited for a decent meal around here, I'd starve to death. Dismissed."

Relieved to leave his presence, Marianne swerved about.

"Belay that!"

She froze.

"My cabin deck is dirty."

Marianne slowly turned to face him, forcing down her frustration. "Captain, I spent an hour this morning on my knees scrubbing and polishing each plank. I assure you it is as clean as it can possibly get."

He narrowed his eyes and rose to his most ominous height. His chair scraped over the wooden floor, sending a chill down Marianne's spine. Grabbing a bottle from his shelf, he poured himself a drink and took a sip. "Are you telling me that I don't know my own deck?"

A giggle rose in Marianne's throat at the absurd question. She forced it down, fairly certain this man would not find the same humor in the situation. "I was unaware, Captain, that one could become quite so intimate with one's deck." She'd meant to say the words in a light-hearted tone in hopes of bringing levity to the situation, but her voice carried more sarcasm than witticism.

His face mottled in anger, and he marched toward her. Every muscle in Marianne's body tensed. Why couldn't she keep her snide comments to herself? She felt his gaze boring into the top of her head, yet she kept her eyes leveled upon the gold buttons lining his white lapel. His chest heaved beneath them. Would he strike a woman? Would he lock her in the hold? She had no idea what to expect from this capricious man.

Releasing a brandy-laced breath that sent the hair on her forehead fluttering, he stepped back. Then he swung about and stormed back toward his desk. "And my uniform was not laid out properly this morning, miss. . .miss. . ."

"Denton, Captain." Surely he knew her name after a week.

"Yes, Denton." He plopped back into his chair and gripped his side as if it pained him. "My last steward was much better."

Marianne clenched her hands into fists. Her ring pinched her finger, bringing along with the pain familiar feelings of inadequacy. She'd never worked so hard in her life for so little appreciation—as the muscles in her legs and back could well attest. "I am still learning, Captain." Her voice came out as though it were strained through a sieve.

"Nevertheless," he barked, his gray eyes firing. "I do not tolerate slothfulness on my ship."

Slothfulness? Of all the. . .

"And what is that gash on your head?" He leaned back in his chair and sipped his drink.

Shocked by his sudden interest, Marianne dabbed the tender scar. "A crate fell on me aboard the merchant ship. Knocked me unconscious, which is how I came to be—"

"You should have my surgeon look at it." He interrupted with a wave of what could only be construed as disinterest in her tale.

Marianne shuddered. She had seen the man he called the ship's surgeon. "I would prefer that he didn't."

"Preposterous." He frowned. "You will—"

A knock on the door interrupted them, but before the captain could respond, it opened to reveal the object of their discussion. The pale man with a perpetual gleam of sweat on his brow angled his head around the door, reminding Marianne of a snake spiraling from its hole. "Time for your medicine, Captain."

With barely a glance her way, he slithered past her. In fact, since she'd come aboard, not once had the physician acknowledged her presence during his frequent visits to the captain's cabin.

"Good, good," Captain Milford mumbled. "You are dismissed, Miss Denton."

Marianne turned to leave but not before she saw the surgeon pour something from a flask into the captain's drink. A sharp odor, one she was quite familiar with from her mother's medications, bit her nose. *Laudanum.*

Tucking the information away, she slipped down the companionway, determined to use these precious moments of freedom to go above deck. She'd been stuck below for a week attending the captain's every whim, and she desperately needed to feel the sun on her face. And maybe catch a glimpse of Noah. To see how he fared, and Luke and Mr. Weller as well.

Squinting against the bright sun, she emerged onto the main deck to a gust of chilled wind and the stares of myriad eyes.

"Back to work!" The *crack* of a stiff rope sliced the air, drawing her gaze to one of the petty officers who raised his weapon to strike one of the sailors again. Swallowing her repulsion, she scanned the ship, searching for Noah and his crew, but none of their faces appeared from among the throngs of seaman. Fear crowded her throat. Were they imprisoned below? Above her, at the rail of the foredeck, a line of marines stood at attention, their red and white uniforms crisp and bright, their golden buttons gleaming in the sun.

Threading her way through the bustling crew, Marianne made her way to a spot at the port side railing just beneath the foredeck where no sailor worked. Turning her back to the sea, she swept another gaze across the deck and was rewarded when Luke's coal black hair came into view. It shimmered in the hot sun like a dark sea under a full moon as he—along with a row of men—tugged upon a massive rope.

"Heave!" a sailor shouted.

Moist with sweat, Luke's face reddened. His features twisted with strain as he yanked on the stiff line.

Lieutenant Garrick dropped down from the quarterdeck and headed toward the row of men. "Mr. Kane, what have I told you about being too soft on the crew?" he shouted. "Why, my mother could pull a line harder and faster than these wastrels. This one in particular." He pointed straight at Luke.

Luke, his hands still gripping the line, slowly raised a spite-filled gaze to Lieutenant Garrick. Marianne's breath halted. *Don't say anything, Mr. Heaton. Please don't say anything.* For she had heard how cruel the British could be.

"See the way he looks at me?" Lieutenant Garrick gave an incredulous snort. "An officer in His Majesty's Navy. Strike him, Mr. Kane. Strike him every time he dares look you in the eye." An insidious smile crept over Garrick's lips like an infectious disease.

Luke faced forward again. The muscles in his jaws bulged, but much to Marianne's relief, he said nothing.

Mr. Kane shook his head. "Aye, aye, sir." And proceeded to lash Mr. Heaton across the back with his braided rope. Luke did not flinch, did not move. Not even a wince crossed his stern features.

With a satisfied grin, Lieutenant Garrick sauntered away, head held high.

Marianne swung about and clung to the railing. Better to face the sea than watch that horrible man strut about like a despotic peacock. The sun cast a blanket of azure jewels over the water. Marianne's palms slid over the railing. Her knees wobbled as her fear hit her full force. How could something so beautiful be so deadly?

Her head grew light as a bell rang twice from the forecastle, announcing the passing of time on the watch. One o'clock from what she had learned.

"Aloft there, trim the foretopsail!" a sailor shouted.

Shielding her eyes, Marianne glanced upward. Men lined the yards of the foremast at least eighty feet above her. And right in the middle of them stood Noah, his bare feet balanced precariously over a thin rope. His stained blue jacket and brown trousers flapped in the wind as he clung to the yard in front of him. A large man standing next to him leaned over and said something. Noah's gaze shot to Marianne. Her heart flipped in her chest. Though she could not make out his expression, she sensed no anger emanating from him. In fact, just the opposite. An unexpected bond kept their eyes locked onto one another like an invisible rope, a rope Marianne did not want to sever for the odd comfort it brought her. Odd, indeed. Coming from a man who had more reason to dislike her than ever before, and she, him, for his unwillingness to bring her home and marry her.

The ship plunged over a swell, but despite her fear, she kept her gaze upon him. The smells of salt and fish and wood filled the air and twirled beneath her nose. The dash of the sea against the hull accompanied by creaks of tackle and wood chimed in her ears. Yet, she could not tear her gaze from him. He looked well, unharmed. And she wanted more than anything to talk to him.

"Ease away tack and bowline!" a man shouted from below. And the lock between them broke as Noah swerved his attention to his task, inching over the footrope. Inching slowly over the footrope. Very slowly. While almost hugging the yard. Was he frightened? *Lord, please protect him up there.*

"Quite dangerous in the tops, you know." A familiar voice etched down her spine, and Marianne lowered her gaze to the superior smirk upon Lieutenant Garrick's face.

"Noah is a capable seaman." She replied, taking a step away from him. He followed her as if they danced a cotillion at a soiree.

"You do say?" He glanced up again, his black cocked hat angling toward the sails. "He doesn't seem too steady on his feet, if you ask me."

"I don't believe I did ask you, Lieutenant." She gave him a sweet smile, instantly regretting her unrestrained tongue.

He dropped his gaze, sharp with malice, and eyed her from head to toe.

Marianne shuddered.

"Heave to!" One of the master's mates bellowed. The sharp crack of a rope sounded, and Marianne looked up to see the man whom Garrick had spoken to earlier following out the lieutenant's orders across Luke's back. Mr. Heaton's muscles seemed to vibrate beneath the strike. She cringed.

"Life can be quite difficult aboard a British frigate, Miss Denton," Lieutenant Garrick said, his eyes narrowing into slits.

A gust of hot wind blasted over Marianne. The loose strands of her hair flung wildly about her. She brushed them from her face and stared out to sea, hoping her silence would prompt the annoying cur to leave.

"Especially for a woman."

Perspiration dotted her neck.

He lifted a finger to touch a lock of her hair.

Raising her jaw, she stepped out of his reach. "What would you know of being a woman, Lieutenant?"

"Oh, I know much about what women need." The salacious look in his eyes made her skin crawl. "Sleeping on a lumpy mattress, no proper toilette, clean gowns, or decent food." He clucked his tongue. "Not befitting such a lady."

"Pray don't trouble yourself over it, Lieutenant. I shall survive." *And much more happily if you scurry away to the hole from which you came.*

He leaned toward her, his offensive breath infecting her skin. "Yet you can do so much more than that, miss."

Bile rose in her throat. "And how would I do that?"

He lifted one shoulder and scratched the thick whiskers that angled over his jaw down to his pointy chin. "Kindness, Miss Denton. Kindness to a lonely man like myself."

His words drifted unashamed through her mind, shocking her sense of morality. Did he mean what she thought he meant? Unaccustomed to such vile advances, or any advances at all for that matter, she nearly lifted her hand to slap him, but thought better of it. Instead, she directed her stern eyes upon his. "My Christian kindness I offer to everyone, Lieutenant Garrick. Any further affections will never be yours." *There went her mouth again.*

His gaze snapped to the sea, his jaw twitching in irritation. "I perceive you are unaware to whom you speak, Miss Denton. Perhaps I should enlighten you." He gave her a caustic grin. "My family possesses more land and wealth than you could ever hope to see in your rustic, underdeveloped colonies." He gazed at her expectantly as if waiting for her to swoon with delight.

Marianne fought down her rising nausea. "How lovely for you, sir. But, I fear you waste your time boasting of your fortune to me. Unlike the sophisticated *haut ton* in London, I place more value on honor and dignity than title and money."

"Savage Yankees," he spat, his face reddening. "If we were not on this ship, the strictures of polite society would not allow me to even speak with you, let alone offer you my attentions."

"Then I shall pray we reach port soon so you will be forced to forsake such a silly notion."

"Lieutenant Garrick!" Captain Milford's booming voice stiffened Garrick immediately. "Report aft!"

Garrick frowned. His eyes narrowed and beads of sweat marched down his pointy nose. "We shall see, Miss Denton. A few weeks on board a British frigate might persuade you otherwise. But, mark my words, I am not a patient man." He gripped her chin between his thumb and forefinger until pain shot into her face. Then releasing her with a thrust that sent her face snapping to the side, he marched away.

Another blast of wind tore over her. A sail above cracked in a deafening boom that seemed to seal her fate.

Marianne threw a hand to her throat, trying to check the mad rush of blood. *Lecherous swine.* She stilled her rapid breathing and gripped the railing.

Oh Lord, a mad captain, a ship full of enemies, a lecherous lieutenant. . . And no one to protect me.

Noah slid his aching bones onto a bench and leaned on the mess table. Dangling from two ropes attached to the deckhead, the oak slab swayed beneath his elbows. But he didn't care. Anything was better than swaying to the hard, fast wind up in the yards. Though he had tried to hide it, his legs still wobbled like pudding long after descending the ratlines and jumping to the main deck where he had resisted the urge to bow down and kiss the firm planks beneath his feet.

Luke eased beside him while Mr. Weller took the opposite bench. From amongst a crowd of howling, jabbering men, Blackthorn emerged and slapped a platter filled with salted pork, mashed peas, hard tack, and a bowl of steaming slop into the center of the table before he took a seat beside Luke. Noah sniffed, hoping a whiff of the food would prod an appetite that seemed to have blown away with the wind, but all he smelled was the foul body odor of hundreds of men.

Dinner was the best part of the day, according to the crew, most of whom swarmed the large space below deck that also served as their berth. Now, with hammocks removed and tables lowered from the bulkheads, hundreds of sailors crammed into the room, gathered with their messmates, and stuffed food into their mouths while they shared their day's adventures, told jokes, and relayed embellished tales of the sea.

Noah wanted no part of it. Nor did he ever want to go aloft again. A week in the tops and his fear had not subsided one bit. He glanced at his first mate and gathered, from the strained look on his face, that he fared no better.

"How goes it?" he asked Luke as he reached up and grabbed the mess pouches from hooks on the bulkhead and flung them on the table. The men opened them and pulled out their utensils.

Grabbing a hardtack from a pile, Luke took a bite and winced—Noah guessed—at the hard-as-stone shell around the biscuit. Luke tossed it down. "Great, if you call spending the day in the blaring sun heaving lines pleasurable."

"Try spending the day spit polishing the guns." Weller moaned.

"You're going t' have to toughen up, lads," Blackthorn said. "This is your life now. The sooner you accept it, the better." He dipped a ladle into a kettle of foul-smelling stew and slopped some into Noah's bowl.

The putrid smell of some type of fish rose with the steam and stung Noah's nose. Perhaps it would suffice to soften his hardtack. Yet when Noah dipped his biscuit into the steaming concoction, it remained as hard as a brick. His stomach pained, and setting the biscuit aside, he tipped the bowl and drained it as quickly as he could. At least it was warm.

Along with the shouts and laughter assailing him from all directions, Noah sensed the piercing gazes of several pairs of eyes. He looked up to see men from the surrounding tables periodically staring at Noah and his friends as they made comments to their companions. Not pleasant comments, he surmised, from the disdain knotting their features.

"Ignore them." Weller grabbed his share of salted pork and plopped it onto his plate. "Some don't take kindly to us bein' Americans."

Luke gave a sordid chuckle. "And here I thought we were British deserters." He downed his stew as Noah had done and wiped his mouth on his sleeve.

"They know exactly who we are." Blackthorn poured liquid from a decanter into tin cups. "An' most o' them lost family in the Revolution." He set a cup before each of them. "One cup o' beer for each of you."

The ship canted to port, sending the lantern above their table swaying like a drunk man. Waves of golden light pulsated over the dreary scene.

Mr. Weller cast a glance around him and mumbled under his breath.

Noah eyed his gunner with concern. "I'll get you out of here, Weller, I promise." Though at the moment, he had no idea how he would accomplish such a feat.

"I place no blame on you, Cap'n." Weller tugged at his scarf. "I knew the risks when I signed on wit' yer crew." He gulped his drink then wiped his mouth on his stained sleeve. "Best not to make promises ye cannot keep."

Noah's stomach shriveled. Is that what he was doing? Promising something beyond his reach, beyond his ability? The permanent etch of disappointment lining his father's face rose to crowd out Weller's visage.

"Why can't you be like your brother? Why must you fail at everything?"

Noah swallowed and stared into his cup, longing to see his brother in the liquid reflection, rather than his own face staring back at him. What would Jacob do? No doubt something heroic.

Blackthorn scanned the raucous crowd of sailors as if searching for someone. "Like I said, square up, lads, and get used to it. I'm afraid you're here to stay."

Grabbing his cup, Luke downed the beer in two gulps then slammed it down with a thump. "Square up, you say? Any more squaring up and my back will turn to leather."

Noah ground his teeth together. He'd thought he'd seen the petty officer whipping Luke repeatedly. He glanced behind Luke at the red stripes lining his shirt. "What did you do to deserve that?"

"Nothing." Luke stretched his back and winced. "That weasel Garrick ordered me to be lashed every time I looked the master's mate in the eye."

"So don't look him in the eye," Noah said.

A mischievous grin toyed with Luke's lips. "It cannot be helped, I'm afraid."

Noah shook his head and chuckled. "Your insolence will be the death of you yet."

Blackthorn squeezed his cup between his bearlike hands. "Sink me, you'd be smart to stay away from Garrick. Don't look at 'im. Don't speak to 'im. Just do your duty." He lowered his chin. "He'll beat a man senseless for the smallest infraction."

Two tables down from them, the men's voices rose in ribald laughter as if they'd heard his declaration. A look of pained understanding passed between Weller and Blackthorn.

Noah leaned forward and studied the beefy man. "You?"

Blackthorn shifted his dark eyes toward Noah—eyes filled with restrained defiance. He nodded. "These Brits are a cruel breed."

"I'll drink to that." Weller lifted his cup.

Noah remembered seeing Garrick speaking to Marianne earlier that day on deck. The drink soured in his throat. "Lieutenant Garrick, would he hurt a woman?"

Blackthorn gave a cynical snort. "I'd tell your lady to steer clear o' 'im as well."

"Confound it all, we must get out of here." Noah swore under his breath.

A midshipman passed the table, offering them a callous glance. They all grew silent.

"I was like you when I first came here," Blackthorn whispered after the man was out of earshot. "Rebellious, bold, determined to escape." He craned his neck forward and eyed them each in turn. "You best get that thought out of your mind straightaway. They'll either beat the life out o' you so you don't want t' live no more, or they'll kill you." He thrust his spoon at them. "An' that Garrick had it out for me from the beginnin'."

Noah took a bite of pork as he pondered Blackthorn's statement. His jaw ached from trying to chew the tough meat. No doubt the man had suffered much during the year since he'd been impressed. But despite his declaration, Noah had no intention of being a guest on this ship that long.

"Do your best to avoid Lieutenant Garrick's bad side, Luke." If only he could give Miss Denton the same warning. Noah gulped down his beer. The pungent liquid dropped into his belly like a rogue wave.

"We'll be off the ship soon enough," he added, hoping to offer the encouragement his men needed to go on, even if he didn't believe it himself.

Blackthorn groaned and shifted wide eyes over the room. "Don't be talkin' like that. We could all be flogged for desertion even at the mention of it."

"Blasted Yankees!" A curse shot their way from the agitated crowd.

Noah eyed Mr. Weller. With his eyes downcast, he had taken up the habit once again of mumbling to himself—the same trait he'd had when Noah found him at Kingston after he'd escaped His Majesty's Navy the first time. Guilt churned in Noah's gut.

Luke downed his stew and tossed the bowl onto the table, adding, "What did you do before your career in His Majesty's Navy, Blackthorn?"

"Me?" Blackthorn chuckled, revealing his two missing teeth. "As I told yer cap'n here, I was taken from a merchantman out of Savannah." He released a heavy sigh. "Where I left a pretty wife, heavy with child." Again, he surveyed the crowd around them as if looking for someone.

"Indeed?" Luke seemed as surprised as Noah had at the revelation.

"Aye, a good Christian woman—a true saint she be—who redeemed me from"—he cleared his throat—"me prior life."

Luke's eyes lit up. "Ah, a sordid past? I'm intrigued."

"Nothin' I'm proud of, t'be sure." Blackthorn scooped some mashed peas into his mouth. "Some o' the things I did haunt me worst nightmares. But then again, if I'd stayed in that"—he scratched his thick chest hair—"profession, I wouldn't be in me present situation. An' I wouldn't have met me dear, sweet Harriet, either."

The ship tilted. Bowls and cups slid over the sticky table, but no one seemed to care. Noah rubbed the sweat from the back of his neck. Shouts and curses speared toward them from a group of sailors in the distance where a heated argument began.

A young lad wove through the crowd and headed for their table. Blackthorn's eyes latched upon the boy like a lifeline in a storm. His shoulders lowered. "Daniel, where you been?" He mussed the boy's brown hair and urged him to sit opposite him, beside Weller.

"I'm well." The boy's smile took in everyone at the table.

"You weren't at mess for near seven days." A twang of worry spiked Blackthorn's voice.

"I've been taking my supper with Miss Marianne." He gazed proudly up at the burly man.

"Miss Denton?" Noah's heart leapt. He'd been desperate for information regarding her wellbeing but had found no one who could tell him anything.

"Aye." Daniel nodded and grabbed a biscuit. "Helping her learn how to be the cap'n's steward."

A steward? Noah couldn't help but grin. She must be having as tough a time adjusting to servitude as he was to the tops. "How does she fare?"

Daniel bit into the biscuit, crumbs flying from his mouth. "She's well. I like her. She's nice." He said the words with such innocent conviction, it startled Noah.

Nice? Not exactly the way he would describe Miss Denton. Nevertheless, his body tensed as he forced the next question from his lips. "Has the captain. . . Has she been harmed?"

"No, sir. He works her mighty hard, but no harm will come to her." Noah released a breath.

"The cap'n ain't like that," Blackthorn added. "He's no abuser of women."

Despite Lieutenant Garrick's behavior, perhaps Noah's belief in the honor of British officers stood true. The realization only reinforced his desire to seek an audience with the man. Surely the captain would see reason to release them once the situation of their impressments was explained to him in detail. But every time the captain had been on deck, Noah had been in the tops, and when he wasn't in the tops, he was forbidden to wander the ship. The only time he was free to slip away was in the middle watch of the night between the hours of midnight and four in the morning, and he dared not disturb the captain's sleep.

Blackthorn scooped some pork and mashed peas onto a plate and shoved it in front of Daniel. The boy grabbed a chunk of meat and took a bite. He shifted in his seat and his gaze suddenly flew toward Noah. "Oh," he said as if just remembering. "I have a message for you from Miss Marianne."

Noah flinched.

"She says she's sorry. And she wants to know if there's anything she can do to help."

Sorry. Was she truly sorry for all the pain she had caused them or was she simply sorry that she endured that pain along with them? Renewed anger coursed through Noah's veins, but he forced it back. Anger over the past would not serve them now. He must focus on the future. Perhaps Miss Denton could help them. She not only had the captain's ear, but she would be privy to his private conversations.

"Tell her to keep her ears open. Will you do that?" he whispered across the table.

"Yes, sir." Daniel's eyes sparkled in the lantern light. "You can trust me."

"Good boy. Report back to me what she tells you. And keep it to yourself."

Weller mumbled as Daniel shifted the mashed peas around his plate.

Blackthorn groaned. "I don't want you puttin' the boy in danger."

"I'm only asking him to tell me what he hears." Noah cupped the back of his own neck. "There's no harm in that."

A fiddle chirped in the distance, the twang keeping cadence with the creak and groan of the ship. Men began to clap and sing to the music.

"I'll be okay, P—Mr. Blackthorn," Daniel said. "These men have come here to help us."

Noah blinked. "What do you mean?"

Daniel straightened in his seat. "God told me in a dream that a lady and three men would come and rescue us from this ship."

Luke chuckled and stared into his empty cup as if in doing so, he could conjure up more beer.

Blackthorn reached across the table and mussed the boy's hair again. "What's got into your fanciful head now, boy?"

Daniel giggled but then shrugged. "I'm just telling you what God told me." He took a sip of his drink. "And then you came." He glanced at Noah with a confidence that inferred he would accept no other explanation for their capture.

"Well, I can assure you being impressed into the navy was not my idea." Noah offered.

"No sir. It was God's."

Noah eyed the boy. If what the boy said was so, then he had even more things to be angry with God about.

"If there is a God, He has abandoned us." Weller muttered loud enough for all to hear. "For I know fer a fact, the Almighty would ne'er set foot on a British warship."

"There is no God, Mr. Weller." Luke's bitter tone startled Noah. "There cannot be. Not in a world as unjust as this one."

Yet his first mate's declaration sparked a memory in Noah's mind. He paused to study his first mate. "I thought your parents were missionaries."

"My parents are dead." Luke scowled and rubbed the scar on his ear.

Blackthorn shook his head. "Sink me, you'd all believe in God if you met me wife. The sweetest spirit I ever came across."

Noah's thoughts took an odd drift to Marianne. "I assure you gentlemen," he plopped a piece of pork into his mouth and instantly regretted it as the unsavory clump hardened in his throat. He forced it down. "There is indeed a God. But I have found Him to be a harsh taskmaster. One who does what He pleases and yet who is impossible to please Himself."

"Sounds like your father." Luke snorted.

Noah slouched back into his seat, allowing the perverse connection to settle into his reason. He opened his mouth to respond when the air filled with blasphemies.

"Blasted Yankees!" a man yelled.

"Ill-bred rebels!" another brayed. Noah looked up to see a mob forming around them. "My pa died in your revolution." A particularly hairy man with pockmarks on his face leaned his hand on the edge of the table.

Luke slowly rose. "And how is that our fault, you callow fool?"

The man spit into Luke's bowl.

Noah stood and held an arm out, restraining his first mate from charging the man.

"That one is uglier than a pig struck with a hot iron." Another man beside the first pointed at Weller. "Don't ye Yankees know how to handle your guns?"

The mob laughed.

Confound it all, now Noah was getting angry. "He lost his fingers on one of your British ships. Therefore, it is your master gunner's incompetence which should be called into question."

The pockmarks on the man's face seemed to deepen. He grabbed the platter of their remaining pork and tossed it against the bulkhead. The chunks of meat fell to the floor with heavy thumps. "You'll see," the man said in a loud voice. "We'll beat you ignorant dawcocks an' send you runnin' to hide behind yer mama's skirts." He clipped his thumbs inside his belt. "Then maybe I'll be the new major o' one of the barbaric outposts ye call a town." He glanced over his friends and they all joined him in laughter. "An' yer mama can clean me shirts."

Luke grabbed the man by the collar and tossed him backward through the mob. He stumbled and crashed into a mess table. Shouts and jeers erupted from the men, none too pleased when their meager stew spilled over the table from the overturned pot. They shoved the man back toward Luke.

The pock-faced man collected himself. Without hesitation, he slammed his fist across Luke's jaw.

Shouts assailed them from neighboring tables as men rose from their meals to witness the brawl. Wide-eyed, Weller struggled to his feet.

Blackthorn grabbed Luke by the arm. "Let it be." His voice held more than a warning. It held terror.

"Please, sir." Daniel headed toward Luke, but Blackthorn pushed the lad behind him.

Noah barreled forward. He must stop this madness before the officers took note.

Luke's dark eyes narrowed into seething points. Jerking from Blackthorn's grip, he raised his fist. Noah shoved himself between Luke and his assailant and grabbed Luke's hand in midair.

"Let me at him, Cap'n." Luke struggled.

Noah shook his head and forced down Luke's arm with difficulty.

"I told ye all Yankees are milksops," the other man chortled and his friends joined in.

"What have we here?" The stout voice of a marine sergeant scattered most of the rats back to their tables. The officer's boots thumped authority over the deck.

"Nothin', sir." Blackthorn stepped forward. "Just a disagreement."

"And as usual, I find you in the middle of it." The man gave a disgruntled moan. "Anxious to meet the cat again, Mr. Blackthorn?"

Blackthorn's jaw stiffened. "No, sir."

"That American insulted our navy, sir." The pock-faced man pointed at Luke. His voice transformed from one of spite to one of humble subservience.

The marine stopped and eyed Luke. "He did, did he?"

"An' we couldn't let it go without speaking up for King George's navy."

In lieu of a hat, he placed his hand over his heart. "Long live the king."

"To the king!" A muffled toast echoed halfheartedly through the room.

Noah clenched his fists. Surely this officer would see reason. "Sir, if you please, this man approached our table and insulted us without provocation."

"I care not what was said." The marine sergeant adjusted his cuffs. "All that concerns me is who struck the first blow?"

"He fisted me first, sir." The pock-faced man gestured again toward Luke. The rest agreed.

"I protest." Noah thrust his face toward the man.

"Regardless." A malicious grin writhed upon the marine's lips. "Perhaps we need to teach you barbaric Americans who is truly in command. "Come with me." He pointed toward Noah and Luke. "The captain will decide your just punishment."

❖ CHAPTER 14 ❖

Marianne pushed the rag over the brass candlestick for the thousandth time. Her fingers ached. Her back ached. And the sharp scent of polish stung her nose. Her only consolation lay in the fact that everyone aboard this ship shared her suffering from overwork. Most of the sailors were young boys far from home or older men torn from their families by impressment gangs back in England. Too illiterate to read the posts sent from loved ones, they carried the missives in their pockets if only to make them feel close to those they left behind.

She stopped to steal a glance out the cabin windows, before which the captain stood, tending his plants. Outside, the lantern perched upon the stern showered a haze of golden light over the captain, highlighting the gray in his hair and making him look almost peaceful—almost.

As if to contradict her thought, he cursed and mumbled something she couldn't make out as he moved from plant to plant with his watering jug.

Then suddenly he swung around. His eyes glazed with the mad look she'd grown accustomed to these past few days. "Odds fish, aren't you done yet?"

Marianne examined the shimmering brass. She thought she'd been done hours ago, but the man saw flaws no human being could ever see. She held the two holders up to him with a questioning look on her face, hoping her annoyance didn't show on her features.

He set down his jug and grabbed the half-full glass of brandy he'd been nursing all night. "I suppose they will do." His voice sounded heavy with defeat and something else. . .a hopelessness that seemed to thicken the air around him.

Rising, Marianne set the brass holders atop his desk and tucked the cloth in the pocket of her skirt. "Captain, if I may ask a favor?"

He grunted.

Marianne had come to interpret that as permission to continue, so she took a step forward. "If you would indulge me, Captain, and if your men would approve, I could read their missives from home to them. I mean, for those who are not schooled in their letters." Though she normally would resist doing anything to help the British, she could not fault these young impressed sailors for being aboard this warship. It was bad enough they'd been forced into naval service, but to not be able to read comforting words from home, or to have to wait for an officer's good humor to read them. . . Tragic. If she must remain imprisoned aboard this ship, perhaps she could at least bring some joy to others in the same position.

Captain Milford sipped his brandy and stared at her as if she'd asked permission to sprout wings. "The midshipmen often read their letters to them. But if you wish. It matters not to me."

"Thank you, Captain." She turned to go.

"Stay. Sit down for a moment." He cocked his head toward a chair, and Marianne groaned inwardly. *Drat.* It had been a long day. Her muscles screamed for rest.

Slipping onto a chair cushion, she stretched her aching back and waited. Only seven days of endless serving and cleaning had passed, yet it seemed like a thousand. And all she saw before her was a multitude of similar days strung together in a muddled line of misery that screamed into eternity. Though she had long ago decided against trying to understand God's purposes—especially when one tragedy after another had struck her family—she found a need growing within her to know the reason for this current madness. She refused to believe the explanation Daniel had given that her that she had been sent to rescue him. Just the fanciful notions of a young boy.

Drink in hand, Captain Milford dropped into a chair in front of his desk. He released a long sigh and stared at the canvas rug beneath his boots. During their forced time together the past few days, Marianne had caught him staring at her more than once, not in a licentious manner, but more as if he wished to converse with her.

As if he were lonely.

"You remind me a bit of my Elizabeth." An awkward smile rose on his lips.

"Indeed?" Marianne wondered if he was paying her a compliment or an insult. Though from the wistful expression on his face she guessed it was the former.

"She was a woman I knew once. Many years ago." He stared off into space as if he were traveling back in time. "Smart, courageous, kind." His eyes snapped to her. "Though you're no beauty like she was."

Marianne lowered her chin. Had he said smart, courageous, and kind? Yet all she heard were the words "no beauty." Why did the flood of pain caused by such insults always drown out the compliments to her character?

"Blast it all, I've hurt your feelings," he growled in a tone that carried no apology. "Women are far too sensitive."

Marianne twisted the ring on her finger until the ruby glowed in the lantern light. "What happened to her?" she managed.

He gulped the last of his drink and slammed the glass down on his desk. Marianne flinched. Rising, he waved a hand through the air then gripped his side. "It matters not."

"I'll warrant you have a family of your own back in England, Captain." She realized her error too late as every line on his face tightened and his eyes flitted about the room as if in search of something.

Finally they settled on her in a cold, hard stare. "And why would you think that?"

Marianne had no response save the nervous gurgling of her stomach.

He stormed toward her. "The Royal Navy is my family, Miss Denton. Been my family all my life. Was my father's family and his father's family before him."

Marianne stared down at his boots and concentrated on the exquisite shine, compliments of her hard work that morning. She didn't want to look up at the intimidating man towering above her. She didn't want to look into those volatile eyes, serene one minute and explosive the next. "I'm sorry."

"Why are you sorry?" he bellowed. Thick hands grabbed her shoulders and yanked her to her feet.

She stared straight into twitching, gray eyes. The scent of brandy stung her nose. Gathering her bravado, she tugged from his grasp and took a step back. "It seems a rather lonely existence, Captain." She kept her voice steady, despite her quivering belly. "And I would appreciate you keeping your hands to yourself. No gentleman would employ such crude manners."

If he intended to strike her or lock her in irons, she preferred that he simply proceed without delay. For every time she was in the captain's presence, she felt as though she were walking one of those thin ropes in the top yards, waiting to be shoved off to the deck below.

A tiny vein pulsed in his neck just above his black neckerchief. The hungry sea dashed against the hull and tipped the ship slightly to larboard. Marianne braced her feet against the deck and her soul against another onslaught of this man's deranged outbursts.

Instead, he broke into a chuckle and swung about.

"The navy's been good to me," he continued the conversation as if nothing had happened. Perhaps to him, it hadn't. "Why, I've seen exotic places most people never see. I've fought in glorious battles that have changed the course of history." He rounded his desk and caressed one of the leaves of his plants. His rock-hard expression softened.

"Tender precious things, aren't they? Grew them from seeds. Just one little seed"—he gestured the size with his thumb and forefinger—"and you can grow a tree that will feed a family."

Marianne released a sigh at the change in his demeanor. He seemed to respect those who took a stand against him, or at the very least, her courage had caused him to shift back to the calm, reasonable captain, not Captain Maniacal, who so often appeared out of nowhere.

"Perhaps you should have been a farmer," she said.

Captain Maniacal returned. His face reddened. "Begone, Miss Denton. I tire of your company."

Before she made it to the door, a knock sounded. The captain growled a curse that made her ears burn, then he shouted for the intruder to enter. A man dressed in a marine sergeant's uniform gave her a cursory glance as he passed. Her heart leapt in her throat as Luke followed on his heels. His brows lifted at the sight of her, and he winked in passing. But it was Noah's blue eyes that latched upon hers that sent her blood racing. She took a step back and leaned on a nearby chair for support. Instead of anger, she saw relief on his face as he perused her. A faint smile lifted his lips.

Behind him, another marine nudged him forward. Lieutenant Reed brought up the rear.

Noah looked well. They both looked well. She silently thanked God.

"What is this about?" Captain Milford grumbled. "Can't a man enjoy his evening without interruptions!"

"Sorry to disturb you, Captain." Lieutenant Reed stepped forward and saluted. "But it appears these Americans have been stirring up trouble with the crew. As well as disrespecting the Royal Navy."

It took all of Noah's strength to stare straight ahead and not turn for another look at Miss Denton. Although she appeared well, and young Daniel had said as much, Noah longed to hear it from her own lips.

"Causing trouble, you say?" The captain's sharp tone brought Noah's focus back on him. A much larger man in person than he appeared from the tops, the captain took a step away from the windows, wobbled, then crossed his arms over his chest.

When the marine had first announced they were to see the captain, Noah's hopes had lifted. At last he would have an audience with the only man who could set them free. Surely, once he explained the altercation during dinner as well as the circumstances of their impressments, this officer, this man of honor, would see reason. But now as Noah stood before the man, the haughty lift of the captain's shoulders and the scowl on his face did not bode well for that notion.

"Well, speak up. What happened?" the captain said.

"Captain, nothing but a—" Noah began.

"Not you, deserter!" Captain Milford barked and spittle landed on his desk.

"Captain," the sergeant said. His voice quavered. "This man started a fight with another crewman and insulted His Majesty's Navy."

Luke skewered him with a glare. "That's a lie and you know it."

"We are not deserters, Captain," Noah said.

"Silence!" the captain shouted. He plopped into his chair as if it took too much strength to keep his bulky frame standing. Black hair, streaked with gray, sprang like the edges of an old broom about his shoulders. He gripped his side then turned to the Lieutenant. "What say you, Lieutenant Reed?"

"I was not present during the altercation, Captain. I have only the marine sergeant's testimony."

"Hmm." Captain Milford's tired, gray eyes focused on Luke. "A fight you say? What was the cause?"

"An insult to the navy, sir," the marine stated.

"Did you hear this insult?"

"No, sir."

Luke grimaced. "I made no such slur, Captain."

The captain rose and adjusted his coat. His angular jaw flexed and gray eyes, alight with cruelty, shifted over the men. Fatigue drew the lines of his tanned face downward.

"Who struck who first?" he demanded.

The sergeant coughed. "I believe it was this man who threw the first blow, sir." He gestured toward Luke.

"Your crewman insulted our country, Captain," Noah said, not wanting the lie to go unchallenged. "And my man here merely gave him a little shove."

"Your country," the captain mumbled. "You have no country but England." He snorted and narrowed his eyes at Noah, then shifted them to Luke. He released a sigh, heavy with boredom, and rubbed the bridge of his nose. "Well, I shall take my marine's word over that of these two deserters."

Noah shook his head as his hope for justice faded completely before this blustering man.

"You both are in violation of Article 22 of the Articles of War which prohibits all fighting, quarreling, and reproachful speech aboard a Royal Navy ship. Since this is your first offense, I'll spare you the cat." The captain waved a hand toward Luke. "Lock him in irons below. No food or drink for two days. Perhaps that shall suffice as a lesson to you, sir, that I do not tolerate brawls on my ship."

Marianne gasped and all eyes shot to her.

"With all due respect, Captain—" Noah stepped forward.

"This is madness," Luke interrupted. "I did nothing wrong."

"Hold your tongues or I'll have you both flogged!" The captain's left eyelid began to twitch. "You are British sailors now, not crude, undisciplined Americans."

"We are *not* British sailors," Luke spit out through clenched teeth.

"Make that three days," the captain said. "Shall we go for four?"

Noah elbowed his friend and shook his head. Luke scowled but remained silent.

"Captain, please!" Marianne's sweet voice flowed over Noah from behind like a refreshing wave. He glanced over his shoulder at her. She stepped forward, her anxious gaze shifted from him to the captain. "Have mercy, I beg you."

The captain cleared his throat and for a moment—a precious, hopeful moment—the harsh glare in his eyes lessened. "I told you to leave, Miss Denton." His steely voice softened as he addressed her. She remained firmly in place. Noah blinked. How had the woman worked her charm on such an ill-tempered beast?

The captain snapped his gaze back to Luke. "Take him," he ordered the marine, who promptly tugged Luke by the elbow and led him toward the door. Noah tried to give his friend a reassuring look before he left, but Luke's gaze remained on the deck.

The marine sergeant smiled, while his companion Lieutenant Reed stared ahead, his lips set in a stiff line.

Captain Milford turned flashing eyes toward Noah. "And this one? What did he do?"

"He, too, was in the midst of the altercation, sir." The marine announced proudly.

"You're the captain of that merchantman we boarded, aren't you?" Captain Milford studied Noah as one would an insignificant organism beneath a microscope.

"Yes, I am, sir." Noah searched the captain's eyes for the honor, the integrity, he had hoped existed in the commander of a British warship. But instead, he found nothing but an apathetic cruelty that set the hairs on his arms standing straight.

"Ah, but you are no longer a captain of anything." Milford circled his desk and planted his thick boots in front of Noah.

"Captain, my men and I are not deserters." Despite the man's obvious derision toward them, Noah had to convince him of their innocence. He leveled a stern gaze upon Milford, captain to captain. "We are American citizens stolen from my ship without cause. Your man Garrick did not even examine our papers."

A slow smile lifted one corner of the captain's mouth. "Tsk tsk. I have no time for woeful tales." He exchanged a glance of amused annoyance with the marine.

"I have friends in South Hampton, Captain," Noah went on, "who can vouch for my character and integrity."

"To the devil with your character and integrity, sir! You and your men are sailors in His Majesty's Navy. You will forget your past. Forget your ship. Forget your country." Milford thrust his rigid face toward Noah. The odor of brandy and sweat filled the air between them. "I run a tough ship, and I'll not stand for insubordination, sir. Do I make myself clear?"

Noah stiffened. The captain swung about and grabbed a glass from his desk, giving Noah a chance to steal a glance at Miss Denton who was behind Lieutenant Reed. Desperation poured from her brown eyes. Desperation for him or for herself, he couldn't tell. Regardless of her culpability in their dire situation, a warship was no place for a lady.

He faced forward. Knowing he might not have another opportunity to speak to the captain in person, he must try to win Miss Denton's freedom. He must risk the captain's temper once again. "Permission to have a word with you, Captain."

Giving a disinterested huff, Captain Milford poured himself a drink and waved him on.

"It's about Miss Denton."

The topic brought the captain's cold gaze back to Noah.

"She's an innocent, captain. She's not a seafaring woman, sir, and found herself on my ship quite by accident."

He glanced at Marianne. Shock filled her misty eyes.

The captain sipped his drink. "Nevertheless, she is here now."

"I appeal to your honor, sir." Noah took a bold step toward him. Surely an officer in the Royal Navy would do no harm to an innocent woman. "She is a civilian. A proper lady with fortune and status in Baltimore. By the laws of civilized warfare, please return her to her home."

"You appeal to my honor, do you?" Captain Milford chuckled. "I have been in enough wars to know, sir, that there is nothing honorable about the men who fight them. You ignorant, savage Americans"—he pointed at Noah with his glass—"ever a source of amusement." He glanced at Reed but the man remained a statue.

The marine sergeant chuckled.

Anger flared in Noah's belly. "Yet I do believe it was we ignorant, savage Americans who defeated Britain's best army and navy and sent you scurrying back to England." He knew he sailed on dangerous seas, but Noah could not allow the insult to his country, to his countrymen, go unchallenged.

The captain's face turned a dark shade of purple. "The presumption, the audacity, sir! I should have you flogged!" He set down his goblet and moved toward Noah.

Marianne gasped.

"Mark my words, young captain"—Milford crammed a finger toward Noah's face—"should our nations meet at war again, we shall squash your American spirit as well as your pathetic military forces and reclaim the land that belongs to us!"

Noah didn't flinch, didn't blink, didn't allow the fury boiling within him to rise to the surface. He had once thought that a country so steeped in traditions of honor and glory, so rich in the history of fighting for their own freedom, would never consider stealing the freedom of others. Now he knew differently. Now he knew better.

Captain Milford's dark brows arched. "For your insolence, sir, you will scrub the weather deck day and night for as long as your slick-tongued friend is locked below."

Noah's breath clogged in his throat.

"And if you are caught sleeping while on the job," the captain leaned toward him, a greasy smile on his lips. "The penalty is death."

After a sleepless night that left her eyelids as heavy as anchors and her head throbbing, Marianne attended her duties with the mind-numbing routine of a longtime servant. She fetched and served the captain his breakfast and then helped him on with his uniform, brushing off specks of invisible dust. Afterward, she ushered him on deck, promising to have his cabin sparkling by the time he returned.

She'd learned to ignore his insulting quips and constant grumbling and placate him with feigned agreements hidden behind an occasional smile. He was British, after all, and who could argue with a man who believed he came from a master race destined to rule the world. Mad or not, when he straightened to his full commanding height and raised his voice to its most vociferous capacity, her insides melted in fear. But she'd learned that not soon after such an incident, his shoulders would sink and his voice lower and he would speak to her as if he hadn't just called her every abominable name he possessed in his vast vocabulary.

Leaning on her knees, Marianne scrubbed the wooden planks of the captain's floor and thought of her mother and Lizzie. Without Marianne's marriage or a certificate proving her death, her mother would never be able to touch Marianne's inheritance. Another year and her beloved family would run out of money to live on. And then what would they do? Marianne's chest grew heavy. If she had not taken matters into her own hands aboard Noah's ship, and ended up a prisoner on a British frigate, Noah would have returned her home after his voyage. Now, because of her lack of faith, none of them would ever see home again.

Lord, I'm sorry I didn't trust You. Yet with the utterance of the words came the realization that she still didn't trust God—that she no longer truly knew how to trust anyone. *Please, God, if You're listening, please help my family.* But her prayer seemed to dissipate into the humid air of the cabin.

The scent of linseed oil and lemons burned her nose. Pain shot into her legs and angled over her back. She grew accustomed to the constant aches, welcomed them, in fact, as punishment for bringing such tragedy upon herself, her family, and her friends. Friends? Could she call Noah, Luke, and Mr. Weller friends? Would they consider her as such? And why, lately, did her thoughts center on the one man who had caused her the most grief—Noah Brenin?

She cringed at the thought that he'd been up all night scrubbing the deck above. And poor Luke, locked in irons below. She must do something to lessen their strict punishments. Yet her attempt to bring up the subject with the captain that morning had resulted in yet another outburst of his fury.

Noah had risked punishment on her behalf. She could not shake the thought, nor could she imagine why he would do such a thing, when she was the one who had put them all in this horrible situation. The door squeaked open and in walked Daniel, wearing his usual bright smile, torn shirt, and breeches. His hands were tucked behind his back as if he were hiding something from her. His eyes sparked with excitement. "Hello, Miss Marianne!"

Sitting back on her haunches, she returned his smile. "Hello, Daniel."

"I brought you something." He swept out his hands and handed her a book.

On closer inspection—a Bible.

Marianne set down the cloth and allowed him to place the holy book on her open palms. She gazed down at it with an affection that surprised her. As a child, she had enjoyed hearing her mother read aloud the wonderful stories it contained. As she grew, she immersed herself in its loving words whenever she needed wisdom or comfort. But, much to her shame, Marianne had not read from the precious book in quite a while—not since her father died. "Is this yours?"

"Yes, miss. But God told me you needed it more than me right now."

"Oh, indeed?" Marianne laughed. "But I really can't accept this."

"You must. Not forever." He shrugged. "Just until you help rescue me."

"Oh, Daniel." Marianne set the book atop one of the padded chairs and began scrubbing again. "I am not so sure you have heard from God. How am I going to help you escape when I can't even help myself or Mr. Heaton and Mr. Brenin?"

Yanking a cloth from a pile, he dabbed some oil on it and began scrubbing beside her. "It don't matter, miss. God'll help you."

"God help me?" Marianne concentrated her scouring over a particularly stubborn patch of dried dirt. "He has better things to do." Much better things or He wouldn't have allowed her father to die, wouldn't have allowed her mother to become ill and wouldn't have allowed their family fortune to blow away in the wind.

Or Marianne to get stuck aboard Noah's ship.

Or her to become a slave to a mad captain.

Halting, she sat back and gazed at the rays of morning sunlight reflecting off Daniel's dark hair and surrounding him with light as if he were precious to God.

While she remained in the shadows.

"I fear you have the wrong lady, Daniel, I'm just a plain, ordinary woman. I am nobody special. And I won't do anything important." She sighed. "I'm terrified of water. I can't take care of my mother and sister properly, and I can't even keep a man's interest long enough so he'll marry me."

Daniel snapped the hair from his face and gazed at her forlornly. "Beggin' your pardon, miss, but there ain't nobody ordinary in God's Kingdom."

Marianne held up the Bible. "I'm not like the people in here: Moses, Abraham, Elijah, Paul, all great men that God used."

"And Daniel." He stopped scrubbing and smiled. "He was a prophet."

"Yes, he was." She wiped a smudge of dirt from his face with her thumb and remembered her Bible lesson to the men on board Noah's ship. Daniel in the lion's den. *And that is why we must always have faith, even in the midst of hopeless times.* She could still hear her voice so full of feigned conviction—a masquerade of the strong woman she longed to be.

"And I am God's prophet, too. He told me so." Daniel's brown eyes sparkled.

Marianne moved to another spot and continued her scrubbing. The boy's childish innocence warmed her heart. Let him have his dreams, his illusions, his hopes. They were probably the only things keeping him alive on this horrid ship.

"What of Esther?" he asked.

Marianne searched her mind for the story her mother had read to her long ago. Ah yes, the queen. "She was beautiful." Not like Marianne.

"Rahab?"

The old stories flooded her mind like rays of sunshine on a cloudy day. Rahab was the harlot who hid the spies of Israel so they could defeat Jericho. Definitely not like Marianne. "She was brave."

"I know what story is like yours." Daniel's eyes widened with delight. "How about Gideon? His clan was the weakest in the tribe of Manasseh, and he was the least in his father's house. Yet God used him to defeat the Midianites with only three hundred men."

Shaking her head, Marianne grabbed the bottle of oil and shifted to a fresh spot on the deck. "I know you mean well, Daniel. And I'm sure God has great plans for you. But my life has been fraught with tragedy. I can never seem to rise above the struggles, to conquer them like others stronger than I." She continued her scrubbing. "I fear God will do what He wills in this world and in my life, and I will always be what I am—a plain, ordinary girl."

She circled the rag over the wooden planks. Round and round like the monotonous circles of her life until her wrists ached and perspiration beaded on her neck. Tears burned behind her eyes. She could not fathom where they came from or why they appeared. Something about Daniel's words, his enthusiasm, his faith, tugged upon a yearning in her heart—a longing, beneath her bitterness, to be something more.

He touched her hand, stopping her. "You don't think God loves you, do you?"

Halting, Marianne drew a deep breath and looked away. She'd never truly considered the question.

Daniel shook his head. Strands of hair hung down his cheek. "Even your name means that God loves you. Marianne, taken from Mary, the mother of our Lord. She was an ordinary girl from an ordinary family. And look how important she was in God's plan."

She gazed at him, astounded by his wisdom. But she could not allow these fanciful notions to take root. For if she did, if she started to believe God truly loved her, if she believed she was special and that He had a plan for her life, then the next disappointment, the next tragedy would rob her of her will to go on.

And then she would end up facedown in the Patapsco River like her father.

"Of course, I know God loves everyone." She shrugged, hoping to shrug away her tears as well, along with the hope that had ignited them.

"You know it up here." Daniel pointed to his head. "But not in here." His hand flew to his heart.

Pouring more oil on her cloth, she leaned over and buffed the wood into a shine. "I believe I'm going to heaven, but I expect nothing else from this life."

"You'll see that you're wrong." Daniel smiled. "When God tells me something it always comes true. He told me a beautiful woman and three men would come on the ship and save me and my da—save me."

Beautiful woman? Marianne chuckled. Now she was certain she was not the woman in Daniel's prophecy. Looking into his hope-filled—no, faith-filled—eyes, she wished with all her heart that she could make his vision come true. But she couldn't. All she could hope to do was to try to alleviate some of Noah and Luke's discomfort during their punishments. A glorious thought occurred to her which might be the solution she sought, but she couldn't do it alone.

She brushed the hair from his face. "Daniel, do you know where Lieutenant Reed is?"

He gave her a perplexed look and glanced out the window. "He may be in the wardroom, miss. He likes to have a cup o' tea about now. What do you want him for?"

Though Lieutenant Reed's stiff, portentous exterior would normally dissuade her from seeking him out, the expression on his face last night and the way he shifted his feet uncomfortably when the captain had unleashed his temper led her to believe there may exist a smidgeon of compassion behind his stuffy facade.

"I want to ask his help to lighten the captain's sentences upon Mr. Brenin and Mr. Heaton."

Daniel's exuberance of only a moment ago faded beneath an anxious look. "I doubt he'll help you, miss. 'Sides, when the captain issues a punishment, it stands. I ain't never seen"—his eyes snapped to hers—"Oh, I forgot to give you Mr. Noah's message."

"Message?" She ignored the tiny leap of her heart. "When did he give it to you?"

"At supper last night before those sailors stirred up trouble. He asked how you were. Seemed real concerned as to your welfare."

The statement uttered in such innocent sincerity sent warmth down to her toes. She shook it off, had to shake it off, but it stubbornly remained in light of Noah's brave appeal to the captain.

Daniel laid his cloth aside and stood. "He wants you to keep your ears open for anything you hear about where the ship is heading or any plans the captain has."

"He wants me to spy?" she whispered, excitement tingling over her skin.

"Aye, miss." He glanced out the door. "An' I can deliver messages back and forth between you."

Marianne's mind whirled with the possibilities.

The ship bucked, nearly spilling her bottle of oil. She grabbed it and steadied her stomach against a wave of nausea.

"I 'ave to be goin' now," Daniel said.

Marianne struggled to her feet. "Thank you for your help, Daniel. And for the Bible."

"My pleasure, miss." Then, after a friendly wave, he disappeared out the door.

Tossing the cloth aside in favor of a more important task, Marianne left the captain's cabin and descended one level for the officer's wardroom. Air, heavy with the smell of tar and damp wood, filled her nose—a not altogether unpleasant scent. Or perhaps she was just growing accustomed to it. Making her way down the companionway, she kept both hands raised, ready to brace herself against the bulkhead should the ship try to knock her from her feet. She couldn't help but smile at her growing knowledge of the names assigned to parts of the ship—names she had not known a month ago.

Rap rap rap. She tapped on the open door of the wardroom and put on her best smile for Lieutenant Reed as he glanced up from a steaming cup of tea. His brow furrowed. "Are you lost, Miss Denton?"

"No, sir. May I have a word with you, please?"

He scanned the room, no doubt checking to see if they were alone. Small cabins that were enclosed by little more than stretched canvas on wooden frames, lined either side of the oblong table at which he sat. Officers' cabins, Marianne surmised. A cupboard at one end held plates, cups, and cutlery as well as a variety of swords, muskets, pistols, and axes.

"Make it quick, miss. You should not be down here." Lieutenant Reed stood, scraping his chair over the deck. He adjusted his black coat, the three gold buttons on each of his cuffs and one button on each collar glimmering in the light of a lantern that swayed overhead.

She clasped her hands together and took a timid step within. "It is about Mr. Heaton and Mr. Brenin."

She detected a flinch on his otherwise staunch demeanor. "And?"

"You know as well as I they do not deserve their punishment."

"It does not matter what I know or don't know." He snorted and plucked his cocked hat from the table. "All that matters on this ship is what the captain says."

Marianne twisted the ring on her finger. "Even if it is unjust and ruthless?"

"You would do well to curb your tongue, miss. The captain is not above issuing the same punishments for a quarrelsome woman."

She studied the stiff man for a moment, gauging him. She knew Noah had risked punishment for her. Could she do less for him? Something deep within Mr. Reed's hazel eyes told her he agreed with her, despite the indifferent shield he attempted to hide behind.

"You know as well as I that the captain is not himself," she whispered.

A flicker of understanding darted across his eyes before they glanced away. "I know no such thing, miss." He tugged on his neckerchief. "I could report you for such subversive words."

"Then do so, Lieutenant." Marianne no longer cared. If she were to suffer for trying to correct a terrible injustice, then so be it.

Lieutenant Reed shifted his stance. "Order must be maintained on board, miss, or we would be unable to defend our country. There must be a commander aboard this ship just as there must be a king over a country or chaos would ensue."

"Order, yes, but cruelty, no." Marianne gripped the back of one of the chairs. "And permit me to correct you, sir, but chaos ensues when leaders wield their power without impunity. As is happening on this ship."

Lieutenant Reed studied her and for a moment she thought she'd won him to her side. But then he lengthened his stance and settled his bicorn atop his head. "I can do nothing for you."

"Will you at least allow me to bring some food and water to Mr. Heaton?"

Hazel eyes sparked at her from beneath the pointed edge of his hat. "What you do in the middle of the night is of no concern to me." One cultured brow rose slightly before he marched out of the room.

❖ CHAPTER 15 ❖

Noah stretched his stiff shoulders and legs, trying to loosen the tight knots that held his muscles captive. Taking his place in a line of sailors on the main deck, he waited to receive a cup of grog. He'd been scouring the deck for forty-three hours. His head pounded, and his eyelids felt like iron pilings. One glance at his hands told him they were white, wrinkly, and raw from the incessant scrubbing. A flurry of hot wind swirled around him, tugging at his hair and cooling the sweat on his brow and neck. He drew in a deep breath, relishing the smell of the sea. Just another twenty-nine hours. He could do it. . . He had to do it.

As he slogged forward in line, Noah felt Miss Denton's presence on deck. He had no idea how, but when he glanced over his shoulder, there she was. She seemed to be looking for someone. Their eyes met and for a moment he thought he saw concern flicker within them. For him?

A midshipman, Blake, if Noah remembered, ordered the boatswain to blow his pipe. "For all you men who cannot read, Miss Denton has offered to read your letters from home without cost before you go

174

below for your evening mess."

Read letters? Noah nearly gasped. Why would she do that? She hated the British. A sailor rolled a barrel over for her, and she perched upon it and adjusted her skirts. The setting sun set her hair aflame like glistening cinnamon and cast an ethereal glow over her radiant skin. She smiled at the men forming a circle around her.

Grabbing his ladle of grog, Noah downed it and returned to the foredeck where he'd left off scouring the oak planks. At least they allowed him food and drink. He couldn't say the same for Luke. He cringed at what the man must be enduring chained below in the dark, dank hold.

Picking up the holystone, Noah continued his work while keeping an eye on Miss Denton. Truth be told, he found it difficult to keep his eyes off her. One by one, the men approached her. With a smile, she took each man aside and read the contents of his missive in private. Visibly moved, some of the sailors clutched their letters to their chests as they ambled away while others broke into tears upon hearing what their loved ones had to say. What astounded Noah the most was the kind gestures and gentle way she addressed each man—each British man.

His thoughts drifted to Miss Priscilla. Memories of their brief time together focused more clearly in his mind. Her dismissive, commanding attitude toward the servants in her home, the way she jutted out her chin and looked the other way when they passed the impoverished in the city streets.

Truth be told, in light of Miss Denton, Priscilla's beauty began to fade.

Noah's gaze latched upon Lieutenant Garrick, who stood at the helm of the quarterdeck, his beady eyes riveted upon Miss Denton. What Noah saw in those eyes made his stomach curdle—a look he'd seen in many men's eyes when they sought only one thing from a woman.

A surge of protectiveness rose within Noah that surprised him. But how could he protect her from a man who wielded nearly as much power as the captain himself?

Soon, the group of sailors surrounding Miss Denton dissipated, and a bell rang from the forecastle. Noah counted the chimes as they echoed over the deck. Eight bells. Which meant it was four in the afternoon, the end of one watch and the start of another.

But that made no difference to Noah. He must stay at his task.

Miss Denton rose and started across the deck. She gazed up at Noah ever so briefly—too briefly—when Mr. Weller approached her, holding out a missive he must have had on him when he'd been impressed. Noah frowned. Why hadn't he trusted Noah to read it aboard the *Fortune*?

One of the sailors bumped into Mr. Weller in passing. The same pock-faced man who'd caused trouble with them below. Weller stumbled from the impact, but kept his ground. "Monsters are hatched not birthed. You ain't got no family." He chortled and gazed around him, eliciting the chuckles of other sailors.

Weller glared at the man and curled his fists. The scars running down his face and neck reddened. *Do not strike him, my friend.* Noah silently pleaded. *Or you'll end up like me, or worse.* Leaping to his feet, Noah scurried down the foredeck ladder, shoving men aside in order to save his friend from doing something that would warrant a lashing.

Miss Denton's voice shot across the deck, halting him. "You will take that back this instant, Mr. . . . Mr. . . . "

The sailor froze, studied her for a moment, and dragged off his hat. "Wilcox, miss."

"Do you judge a man by his scars, Mr. Wilcox? Or do you judge a man by his character?" She pointed at Weller. "These scars are evidence of Mr. Weller's great bravery during battle. Have you any to compare?"

The man's spiteful eyes narrowed as Noah made his way toward Miss Denton. Yet despite the fury storming on the man's face and his defiant stance, Miss Denton held her ground. She placed her hands atop her hips. "Apologize at once."

The man hesitated, spit to the side, then spun on his heels and marched away.

Releasing a sigh, Noah approached her. Admiration welled within him, along with the realization that the woman he'd known as a child no longer existed. He wanted to tell her that she should curb that reckless tongue of hers on board this ship. He wanted to tell her that she was the bravest woman he'd ever met.

But the loud shout of a petty officer behind him halted him. "Get back to work, Brenin! Or the cap'n will hear of this!"

Miss Denton gathered her skirts and their eyes met. She smiled at him before she descended the companionway ladder, and Noah's heart soared in the brightness of that smile.

Marianne crept forward, peering through the gloom of the sailor's berth below deck. Her toe struck something sharp, and she bit her lip to keep from crying out. Daniel turned and laid a finger over his mouth then proceeded around a corner and into a large area filled with hammocks that swayed back and forth with each movement of the ship. At well past midnight, Marianne hoped most of the crew would be asleep. Her fears were allayed when nothing but snoring, occasional grunts, and the creaking of the ship combined into a discordant chant. Gesturing for her to wait, Daniel disappeared among the oscillating gray masses. The lantern the young boy held cast eerie shadows over the scene as he wove between the sleeping mounds, making them look like giant cocoons—cocoons out of which woman-eating insects could burst forth at any minute. A chill overcame Marianne at the thought, and she hugged herself. Her nose curled at the stench of sweat and filth that hung in the room like a cloud.

Moments later, Daniel returned and beckoned her onward. On the other side of the room, seated on the hard floor, his legs in irons hooked to the deck, sat Mr. Heaton, his head reclining on his knees. Beyond him, a marine, musket gripped in his hand, slouched against the bulkhead fast asleep.

Kneeling beside Luke, Marianne touched his arm, and he jerked his head up, tugging on his chains. The clanking dissipated amidst the snores and creaks.

He gaped at her, rubbed his eyes, and then blinked. "Miss Denton, what are you doing here?" he whispered.

"Shhh." She glanced at the marine. "I brought you some grog and a biscuit."

He looked over his shoulder, alarm tightening his features. Stubble peppered his jaw, and his black hair hung limp over his shoulders. Even in the dim lantern light, Marianne could make out a purple bruise circling his swollen eye.

"Do you know what they'll do to you if you're caught?" he whispered, then glanced at Daniel keeping watch not three feet away. "And you, too."

"It will be all right." The assurance in the boy's voice gave Marianne an odd sense of comfort.

"Be gone with you, Miss Denton." Luke dropped his head back onto his knees.

Ignoring him, she nudged his chin up and lifted the cup to his lips. "Drink this and be quiet, Mr. Heaton."

She tipped the mug, and he gulped the liquid, releasing a sigh when he had drained the last drop.

"I never thought stale water and rum would taste so good."

"Here." She handed him two biscuits. "Don't leave any crumbs." She smiled.

A snort sounded from one from the hammocks. Another man cried out in his sleep. The guard shifted his weight and scratched his nose.

Marianne froze, her eyes shifting from Mr. Heaton to Daniel.

Taking the biscuit, he gestured for her to leave. She started to get up.

He grabbed her arm. "Thank you," he mouthed.

Her heart pounding, Marianne dashed between the hammocks and followed Daniel up one deck. She held the bundle containing another two biscuits close to her chest.

"Thank you, Daniel." She leaned and kissed him on top of his head. "Now get some sleep."

"Where are you going, miss?" He looked at her with concern.

"I'm going to check on Mr. Brenin."

Noah lifted the collar of his coat to shield his neck from the evening wind that despite the summer month carried the bite of the cold north Atlantic. Though he could tell from the stars and sun that they sailed a southwest course, he had no idea where they were heading or what his plan should be once they got to their destination. Struggling to his feet, he stretched his cramped legs and blew into his hands to try to spark some life back into his stiff fingers.

He scanned the deck. Save for the helmsman, and two lookouts, the rest of the crew was no doubt fast asleep below. Even the poor marine assigned to guard him seemed deep in slumber as he slouched against a railing on the foredeck. Good. That would give Noah a chance to take a respite from his hard labor.

Off their starboard port, a half moon winked at him as waves frolicked in its glistening light as if they hadn't a care in the world. He envied them. He hung his head, fighting back a wave of exhaustion. Sorrow and shame followed close on its wake. He had lost his cargo, lost his father's last ship, and lost all means of providing for his family. Regardless that the fault lay elsewhere, his father would consider it Noah's responsibility and hence, Noah's failure. And a failure he was.

Even if he managed to escape, without his father's merchant business he would be nothing but an impoverished sailor. No doubt Miss Priscilla would refuse to even see him. Yet it was not her pretty face he found drifting unbidden into his mind of late. It was the face of another woman, not nearly as striking, but a face that shone with its own unique brilliance. Noah stared at the holystones by his feet—the ones he'd been using to scour the deck for the past fifty-two hours. Confound it all, he should be angry at Miss Denton, not dreaming of her like a love-sick schoolboy.

An invisible weight tugged upon his eyelids as he plodded across the deck trying to get the blood pumping in his legs again. How long could a man live without sleep? Another twenty hours to go. He could make it. He had to make it. To fall asleep meant certain death.

Noah spun on his heels and headed in the other direction. A lady dressed in a fiery maroon gown glided over the deck. Her brown hair shimmered. He rubbed his eyes. No doubt the lack of sleep caused him to hallucinate. But then he smelled her sweet scent—Marianne—and he opened his eyes to her creamy face awash in moonlight. "Are you real?" he asked.

"Quite, Mr. Brenin. And I bear gifts." She held out a biscuit to him. Her sweet smile nearly stole his breath away.

Despite her kind intentions, Noah's fear for her safety rose at her foolishness. "You shouldn't be here," he said, ignoring the offer of food despite his growling stomach.

"I shouldn't be many places these days. However, it is on my account you are scrubbing these decks all day and night with no rest in sight." She avoided his gaze. "Thank you, Mr. Brenin, for trying to help me. Though I can't imagine why you did after I put you on this ship in the first place."

After a quick glance across the deck, Noah took her arm and led her to a more secluded spot behind the ship's boats. He ran a hand through his hair. "Despite what you may think, I am still a gentleman, and this is no place for a lady." Is that why he had risked punishment to save her? To appease his gentlemanly duty?

A breeze stirred the tendrils of her hair circling her face. She brushed them back and studied him. "Why aren't you angry with me? I've ruined your life. I've caused you and your friends great harm and loss."

"Who says I'm *not* angry at you?" He folded his arms over his chest.

She studied him. "Your eyes."

"Humph. Then I shall have to speak to them about keeping quiet from now on." He couldn't help but smile.

Her nose pinked and she lowered her gaze. "You mock me, sir."

He shook his head and laid a finger beneath her chin, raising her eyes—sparkling brown eyes so full of sincerity and kindness—to his. "I was angry at you, Miss Denton. But what purpose does it serve? You were only trying to get home to your mother." He sighed. "Perhaps I should have returned you to Baltimore at your request. I was so obsessed with getting my goods to England." He rubbed the back of his neck and gazed out to sea. "Now I have no goods and no ship."

"Thanks to me." Her voice sank.

"Egad, but ruining my cargo." He chuckled. "Quite imaginative. I suppose it is fair recompense for all the pranks I pulled on you as a child."

"It was a means to an end." She gave him a sad smile. "I take no pride in the action." She held out the biscuit to him again. He took it this time, allowing his fingers to linger over hers. Why, he didn't know. But her touch had a curious effect upon him, sending tendrils of warmth up his arm. "They are permitting me to eat."

"I know." Her eyes misted with tears. "I thought it would help you stay awake. I brought another one." She held out her bundle, but he pushed it back, shoving the biscuit into his pocket. He had more important matters on his mind than food. "How are you?"

The ship rose over a swell. She stumbled and Noah grabbed her waist to steady her, drawing her near. Her alluring scent filled his nostrils and his body quickened. Confusion hammered through his mind. He wasn't supposed to desire this woman, this woman who had snubbed her nose at him as a child, this woman who was both plain and plump. He was supposed to be convincing her to break off their engagement. Though he wondered if that truly mattered anymore.

He glanced down at her. Her brown eyes shimmered with surprise, and something else. . .ardor? Her skin glowed in the moonlight, her lips parted slightly. And in that moment, he saw nothing plain about her. Even the feel of her rounded curves beneath his hands sent heat into his belly. He released her and backed away.

She averted her gaze.

"How is your head?" He gestured toward the spot where her wound had been, now barely discernable beneath her hair.

She dabbed her fingers over it. "It heals nicely." She gave him a curious glance from the corner of her eye. "If not for this wound, none of us would be on this vile ship."

"Indeed. And you would still be with your mother."

"And you would have made your fortune and be attending soirees with Priscilla and have no need of. . ." She lifted a hand to her nose.

"Have no need of what?"

She waved a hand at him and turned her eyes to the sea.

Noah shifted his bare feet over the deck. Guilt assailed him and he didn't know why. He had done nothing wrong. Was she concerned for her mother? "Is your mother ill as you said?"

She shot fiery eyes his way. "How dare you? I wouldn't lie about such a thing."

He shrugged. "I thought you were exaggerating so I would return you home."

She looked back out to sea.

"I'm truly sorry that you are separated from her." He wanted to erase the pain from her face and see the sparkle return to her eyes.

"She'll die if she doesn't get her medicines. And without me to care for her. . ." She inhaled a sob and lowered her gaze. "I tried to explain to the captain that I can't be here. . ." She rubbed her hands together in frustration, and Noah noticed that they seemed raw, rough.

He took one and flipped it over, examining it in the light of the mainmast lantern. Red blotches marred skin that was streaked with cuts and scrapes. "He works you to death."

"He is particular about the way things are done."

Noah shook his head. In all that she had endured, she never once complained. Without thinking, he placed a light kiss upon the blisters on each hand. She gasped, yet she made no move to take them from his grip. He ran his thumb over her skin. "Does he hurt you?"

She shifted bewildered eyes between his, then shook her head. "The captain is a lonely, bitter man. Truth be told, I think being at sea so long has befuddled his mind."

"He certainly wasn't open to reason the other night." Noah continued caressing her fingers, relishing in the feel of her skin. She gazed across the deck, anguish flickering in her eyes.

Concern for her, for her safety, for her family, flooded Noah like never before. "I will get you off this ship, Miss Denton."

"How?"

"I don't know. But I will find a way." He leaned closer to her. "I promise we will not be here forever."

The wind whipped the curls around her face into wisps of glittering cinnamon.

"Do not promise me anything, Noah. Promises are too easily broken." Sorrow glazed her eyes.

And Noah wanted more than anything to prove her wrong. His thoughts shifted to Lieutenant Garrick and the way he had hovered over Marianne on deck, the way he had looked at her. Noah's muscles tensed. "What does this man Garrick have to say to you?"

Her hands trembled. She pulled them from his grasp and hugged herself. "He is a cad, of course, but he is harmless." Her voice lacked conviction.

"I am not so sure." Noah caught her eyes with his. "Stay away from him."

"I assure you, Mr. Brenin, that is my intention."

The deck tilted again. Marianne reached for his hand. The melodious purl of the sea played against the hull, and Noah had the strangest urge to dance with her across the deck.

"Unless, of course, you plan on charming him as you have the captain?" His tone taunted her. But he meant his words. She possessed a unique charm he could no longer deny.

"Charm?" She huffed. "Surely you jest. I have not charmed a soul in my life."

"I am not so sure." Noah fingered a silky strand of her hair. What was wrong with him? Surely exhaustion had taken over his reason.

She stepped away. Her chest heaved. Then she glanced up into the tops. "They work you hard as well."

Stunned by the concern in her voice, he nodded. "Ah yes, the top yards."

"Is it safe?"

"Safe?" His laugh came out bitter. "It's not safe anywhere on the ship."

She lowered her gaze. Her delicate brows furrowed. "You are frightened of the height?"

Though the man in him wanted to deny any fear, something about her made him willingly admit it. "How can you tell?"

"I am not unfamiliar with fear." She gazed across the molten dark waters and took a deep breath.

"You seem to handle your fears much better than I."

"Don't let me fool you, Mr. Brenin."

"I wouldn't think of it." He smiled.

He glanced aloft, then back down at her eyes—penetrating eyes full of compassion. And something within them bade him to bare his soul. "My brother fell from the t'gallant yard."

Her mouth opened.

"He was teaching me to sail."

She laid a hand on his arm. "Oh, Noah."

He jerked from her, chiding himself for saying anything, for invoking a sympathy he did not want. "It doesn't matter."

Marianne swallowed the lump in her throat even as her eyes burned with tears. "Of course it matters. It wasn't your fault, Noah."

He turned away. "How do you know?"

News of young Jacob's death had spread quickly through Baltimore, but no word followed as to the cause. An accident was all they'd heard. Afterward, Noah never accompanied his father when the man came to visit Marianne's family.

"I know you, Noah."

"Do you?" Agony burned in his eyes. He ground his teeth together. "I caused him to fall." He tore his gaze from her. "I challenged him to race up through the ratlines and around the lubber's hole while I timed him."

Marianne stepped toward him, but he raised a hand to stop her.

The ship bucked, blasting them with salty spray.

"It was my idea." His voice cracked. "He was teasing me because of my fear. It made me angry, so I challenged him to best a time only a seasoned topman could match." He hung his head.

A gust of wind whipped over them. Noah's Adam's apple leapt as he swallowed. "I held his bloody head in my hands and watched him die."

Marianne's vision blurred. The horror of it. The agony. She could not comprehend. Her throat burned as she tried to gather her thoughts, but they refused to settle on anything rational, on anything comforting. She laid a hand on his arm. This time, he did not resist.

"You meant him no harm, Noah. It was an accident." Yet her words seemed to fall empty upon the angry waves thrashing against the hull.

"Tell that to my father." Noah frowned. "Jacob the good son, the smart son, the brave son." He shifted moist eyes her way. "He wished it had been me who'd died."

Marianne shook her head, wanting to comfort him, but not finding the words.

"And I've spent a lifetime trying to make it up to him." He gripped the railing and stared out to sea. "But nothing I do will ever be enough."

The weight of his guilt pressed down on Marianne. How could anyone live with this kind of pain, this burden? No wonder Noah was driven to succeed. It wasn't for the money, for the prestige, it was in payment for the death of his brother.

And his father had encouraged it, fostered it. It was, no doubt, why Noah had agreed to marry her—a woman he didn't love.

"I miss him." He rubbed his eyes again then straightened his shoulders. "Forgive me, Miss Denton. It seems exhaustion has loosened my tongue."

"There is no need for apologies." Marianne longed to comfort him but, as in most things, she felt woefully inadequate to the task. She took his hand in hers and squeezed it. "No one can bear the weight of this, Noah. You must let it go." A tear slid down her cheek.

He stared at her curiously. Lifting his hand, he wiped her tear with his thumb then caressed her cheek. His touch sent a wave of heat across her skin that made her thoughts swirl and her body reel.

It meant nothing, she reminded herself. He was beyond exhaustion. He was angry and despondent. Surely any woman with a listening ear and a caring heart would suffice to appease his loneliness. Marianne knew she should leave. She needed to leave, but the look in his eyes held her captive—a look that slowly wandered down to her mouth and hovered over her lips as if only there could he find the sustenance he needed. Marianne's breath halted in her throat.

Then he lowered his lips to hers.

A quiver spread down Marianne's back. Warmth flooded her belly. Noah's lips caressed hers, playing, stroking, hovering. His hot breath feathered over her cheek. She drew it in, filling her lungs with his scent. He caressed her cheek, her neck, and ran his fingers through her loose curls.

Laughter shot through the night air, startling her and jerking Noah back.

"That ought to keep the blasted Yankee awake." One of the watchman chortled to another man who'd just leapt on deck.

Heat flamed up Marianne's neck. She attempted to regain her breath.

Noah's jaw tightened. "My apologies, Miss Denton." Then avoiding her gaze, he marched away.

Marianne laid a hand on her stomach and stared out to sea. Not exactly the reaction she expected from the first man she allowed to kiss her.

❖ CHAPTER 16 ❖

Marianne fell onto her bed and sobbed. Her first kiss. She should be elated, filled with joy. For she had never thought any man would find her alluring enough to kiss unless it was forced upon him by marriage. Why then did she cry? Sitting up, she wiped the tears from her cheeks and tried to regain her senses, traitorous senses that had danced in a delightful flurry when Noah's lips touched hers. Not simply touched, but caressed as if he truly cherished her.

But that couldn't be. Especially not Noah Brenin.

Noah had not slept in nearly three nights, she reminded herself. The moonlight, the late hour, the slap of the sea against the hull, and Marianne lending a caring ear to his woeful tale, all combined to create an atmosphere, a desire that was, if not imaginary, surely ephemeral. In his weary delirium, Noah had simply given in to the manly desires Marianne's mother had warned her about.

Then why did she care?

This infuriating, reckless boy who had done nothing but make her life miserable as a child, who had shunned her and teased her until she cried herself to sleep at night. This oaf who had abandoned her at their engagement party.

Then why did she wish for something more?

Why did he consume her thoughts day and night? And why did the touch of his lips on hers send a warm flutter through her body?

A kiss. She'd been kissed at last. Marianne smiled and brushed her fingers over her lips. She had no idea it could be so pleasurable.

But in that pleasure she also sensed a power that could rip her heart in two.

Following a line of crewmen, Noah lifted his heavy legs and climbed through the hatch onto the main deck. He rubbed his eyes against the glare of the rising sun that promised a warm day ahead. When the watchman had relieved him of his punishment at four in the morning, he could hardly believe it, for he had begun to think his penalty was more eternal than hell itself. Stumbling below like a drunken man, he had crawled into his hammock. Two hours of sleep. Two hours of precious slumber was all he'd been granted in the wee hours of the morning. But it was the sweetest sleep he'd ever had. In fact, he hadn't even heard the boatswain's cries "All hands ahoy. Up all hammocks ahoy," nor the scrambling of his mates unhooking their bedding around him. Not until Weller and Luke—who had been released at the same time as Noah had—dumped him from his hammock and he fell to the hard deck below did he snap from his deep slumber.

Noah's thoughts sped to the kiss he had shared with Marianne last night. No, it was not last night, but the night before. After she had fled the deck, the rest of that night and all the next day and night had blurred past him in turbulent shades of gray and white and black like a fast-moving storm. Visions of her maroon gown, brown hair, and full lips mingled with holystones and oak planks into a disjointed mirage that had him wondering if he had only dreamed of the kiss.

But no. He could still feel the tingle on his mouth. What madness had possessed him to taste her sweet lips? What madness had possessed her to accept his advance? Whatever the disease, he hoped there was no cure. She had responded with more passion than he would have guessed existed within her. For years, he thought her nothing more than a pretentious prig. When in reality. . . His body warmed at the remembrance. Was it possible she cared for him? Or did she kiss him out of pity or to make amends for what she had done? Since he had not seen her in over a day, he had no way of knowing.

"To your stations!" a boatswain brayed, and the crew scrambled to take their assigned watches across the deck where they would assist with the sailing of the ship or perform necessary maintenance. Normally the crew swept and holystoned the deck each morning, but due to the gleaming shine glaring from the wooden planks—thanks to Noah—he had saved them at least that chore.

One would think they'd thank Noah instead of shower him with grimy looks of contempt.

Flinging himself into the ratlines, Noah followed Blackthorn to the tops, trying to shake the cobwebs from his weary brain even as his old fear rose like bile in his throat. If he could not keep his concentration, he might end up a pile of broken bones and blood splattered on his clean deck—a tragedy after all his scouring.

"Good to 'ave you back," Blackthorn said as they positioned themselves on the footrope.

A gust of salty wind clawed at Noah's grip on the yard. "I'd like to say the same, my friend, but I'd rather be on the deck than up here where only birds and clouds have God's good grace to be." Noah tried to blink away the heaviness weighing down his eyelids.

Blackthorn smiled. The wind whistled through the gaps left by the two missing teeth on his bottom row. "Sink me, I'll look out after you."

Noah nodded his appreciation.

The ship pitched over a wave, and Noah gripped the yard. His feet swayed on the footrope. Every rise and fall and roll of the ship seemed magnified in the tops. His legs quivered, and Blackthorn clutched his arm. Though the morning was young, sweat slid down Noah's back, and he wondered how he would survive the day.

The sharp crack of a rattan split the air, drawing his gaze below to where Luke and his watch mates battled a tangled rope. His first mate winced beneath the strike even as the petty officer glanced at Lieutenant Garrick at the helm. For approval? For direction? Or to plead with the lieutenant for mercy? Noah couldn't tell. Regardless, Garrick nodded at the petty officer then chuckled at his fellow lieutenants lined up at the quarterdeck stanchions like cannons in a battlement. None joined him in his mirth.

Luke swept his gaze up to Noah. Even from the tops, Noah could see the bruises covering his face. Released from his irons around the same time Noah had been sent below, they'd barely managed to grunt at each other before they took to their hammocks.

The ship plunged down the trough of another swell, and Noah hugged the yard and curled his bare toes over the rope. After his heart settled to a normal beat, he turned to Blackthorn. "What has Luke done to incur such wrath from Lieutenant Garrick?"

"Sink me, who knows with that blackguard?" His friend spit to the side. "He hates everyone, 'specially Yankees. Before they assigned me t' the tops, he used to have me whipped too."

"Reef the topsail!" the order came from below. Men on deck began hauling the tackles. Noah bent over the yard to pull in the reef lines, but he had difficulty keeping his mind on his task. If he didn't get Miss Denton and his men off this ship soon, he doubted any of them would survive.

At six bells before noon, or eleven o'clock, the bosun's shrill pipe halted the men in their work. "All hands on deck!"

Thankful for the temporary reprieve from the harrowing heights, Noah followed his crew down the ratlines to the deck below. Still slower than a fish through molasses, he always landed last on the planks. But he would wager that he was the most grateful for the solid feel of wood beneath his feet.

Captain Milford emerged onto the deck in a burst of pomposity.

His crisp, white breeches, stockings, and waistcoat gleamed beneath a dark coat that was lined with buttons shimmering in the bright sun. Black hair, streaked with gray, was pulled taut behind him. Traces of strength remained in the muscles that now seemed to sag with weakness. Climbing the quarterdeck ladder, he took his spot at the railing before the helm and looked down on his crew.

The bosun piped the men to attention and called them to muster in the waist. The marines, fully decked in their red coats and white pants with bayonets gleaming formed a line before the men. The petty officers fell into jagged rows behind them, while the midshipmen and officers assembled in crisp ranks on the quarterdeck, immediately aft of the mainmast.

Captain Milford stepped forward.

Wiping the sweat from his brow with his sleeve, Noah lingered near the back of the mob, anxious for possible news of the ship's destination. But instead of good news, the captain bellowed, "You shall witness a hearing and subsequent punishment of a fellow crewman. Remain orderly and in your ranks."

Noah bristled beneath the excitement in the captain's voice.

"Master of Arms, bring forth the prisoner," the captain shouted and Noah's throat went dry, hoping it wasn't one of his own men. Relief allayed his fears when the master dragged forward a middle-aged, beefy sailor whose neck seemed to disappear beneath his head. He halted before the railing, his face lowered and the irons around his hands clanking.

Noah's heart went out to him. Luke and Weller pressed in on either side of Noah and gave him a look of trepidation.

"Let us proceed. Read the charges," the captain shouted.

As the master at arms read from a list of offenses, a flash of red caught Noah's eyes. Miss Denton stood by the larboard railing at the break of the quarterdeck, trapped by the conflux of crewmen. Terror screamed from her expression, and Noah wondered if it was the close proximity of the sea or the proceedings that frightened her.

". . .and threatening a shipmate with a knife," the master at arms concluded.

The captain eyed the man with disdain. "What do you say for yourself, Mr. Bowen?"

Mr. Bowen shook his bucket-shaped head and dared to glance at his captain. "No, sir. I only found the knife on deck an' picked it up."

Blackthorn edged beside Noah. "This won't be pretty."

"Sentence has not yet been pronounced," Noah reminded him.

"It will be. And soon. I ne'er seen the captain turn down an opportunity to flog one of 'is men." Blackthorn shifted the muscles across his back. "I got the scars t' prove it."

Noah eyed his back as if he could see beneath his shirt. "For what?"

"Insubordination t' an officer. At least that's what they said."

The captain grumbled and turned to Lieutenant Reed. "Lieutenant Reed, did this man attack his shipmate with a knife or not?"

The lieutenant's jaw twitched. "I cannot say, Captain. I was not present."

The captain turned to his right. "And you, Lieutenant Garrick."

The man licked his lips. "Yes, Captain. I saw it plain as day."

Captain Milford scanned the crew. "Will anyone speak up for this man?"

Though mumbles coursed through the crowd like distant thunder, every sailor kept his gaze lowered and his mouth shut.

"I will not tolerate brawls aboard my ship, Mr. Bowen. Save your fighting for the French, should any of the cowards show their faces out at sea." He withdrew his hat, spurring the same action from his officers and crew. Then in a blaring voice devoid of all sentiment, he read the Articles of War appropriate to the offense. At their conclusion, he turned to the boatswain. "One dozen lashes should do it, Mr. Simons."

The prisoner visibly jerked as if he'd already been lashed. His whole body began to tremble—a tremble that Noah felt down to his own bones.

Three men lifted the main hatch and attached it to the gangway with its bottom fast to the deck. Two marines led Mr. Bowen to the grating, stripped him of his shirt, and tied his hands to the top of the iron frame. Silence consumed the ship. Only the angry thrash of water and the groans of shifting wood screamed their protest of the proceedings.

The sun, high in the sky, lanced the crew with burning rays. Yet no one moved. Sweat slid into Noah's eyes and he blinked. He glanced at Miss Denton. Her hand covered her mouth. Her eyes were wide with horror. *Go below, you foolish woman. No need to see this.* As if she read his thoughts, she turned and shoved her way through the crowd then disappeared below.

Noah wished he could escape as easily. Though he understood the need for discipline aboard ship, he had no stomach for cruel torture.

The captain snapped his hat atop his head. "Do your duty, Mr. Simons."

The bosun's mate took the cat out of a red sack and stepped forward, pushing the crew back to make room for his swing.

He raised his arm and flung the cat across the man's back. A howl that reminded Noah of the cry of a wolf shrieked from the poor soul. Jagged ribbons of red appeared on his back.

Beside Noah, Luke fisted his hands and crossed them over his chest, his face mottled in anger.

Noah surveyed the crew. Weller was nowhere to be seen. Good.

"Is there nothing we can do?" he asked Blackthorn.

Blackthorn shook his head. "It's the way of the navy. If you step in, your fate will be the same."

The cat whistled through the air and landed with a snap upon the man's back once again. The crew remained silent, almost as if they saw their own future flashing before their eyes.

Another strike tore at the man's flesh. The sails thundered above them.

Noah turned around. Fury tore through him. He'd never valued his own country and the justice and freedom for which she stood more than he did at this moment. Why had he so flippantly allied himself with a people who restricted others' freedom, who stole innocent men from their ships and enacted such cruelty without censure?

Mr. Bowen's howls of pain speared the air, sealing the conviction forming within Noah. He would find a way off this ship. He would be free again and when he was, he would spend the rest of his life defending his country against the sharp whip of tyranny.

Marianne fluffed the captain's mattress to remove the lumps and smooth the feathers—just as he liked it—while in truth, she'd rather fill it with large, jagged rocks. She couldn't help but wonder how the man who had been flogged fared. No doubt he would not be lying in his hammock tonight—at least not on his back. Though thankful she'd escaped witnessing the event, she had not been able to escape the man's heart-piercing howls. Howls that infiltrated every wooden plank and beam until the very ship seemed to scream in defiance. Dropping to her knees, she had prayed for him, for that was all she knew to do. It seemed so inadequate.

She stood and placed a hand on her aching back and peeked at the captain sitting at his desk mumbling to himself. It had been a long day. She prayed he would dismiss her shortly and take to his bed. Especially since she doubted she could curtail her anger toward him given his actions today.

A knock sounded on the door. Her hopes dashed when at the captain's bidding, three officers entered, Lieutenant Garrick and Lieutenant Reed among them. They stood at attention before Captain Milford's desk and removed their hats.

"You summoned us, sir."

Leaning on the doorframe of the sleeping cabin, Marianne glanced at the captain. After his evening meal and usual three glasses of brandy, plus the laudanum the surgeon had just poured down his throat, it was a wonder he could sit up. Yet he rose from his chair as alert as if he'd just arisen from a sound night's sleep.

He straightened his white waistcoat. "We shall be arriving in Antigua in seven days, gentlemen, where I expect to receive my orders. At that time. . ."

He continued on with further instructions regarding watches and shore leave, which Marianne shrugged off in light of the first piece of information. Excitement set her head spinning. They would make port soon. Surely that fact would aid Noah in formulating his escape plans.

Turning around, Marianne busied herself laying out the captain's nightshirt and cap while she listened for any further news that might be of use. But there was nothing of note save that very few of the men would be allowed a brief time ashore.

"Now go on. I need my sleep." The captain dismissed them with a wave of his hand. Lieutenant Garrick's brows lifted when he saw her. He gave her a wink that slithered down her spine before he followed his friends out the door.

Marianne approached the captain. "I've laid out your nightshirt, Captain, and fluffed your mattress. Is there anything else I can do for you?" Anger stung her tone, but he gave no indication that he took note of it.

Instead, he sank into his chair, his face twisted with thought. Then he raised hard eyes upon her. "Anything else?" He cursed. "Odds fish, can you tell me why my men rebel against me?" He slammed his fists on his desk. Marianne jumped.

"I don't know what you mean, Captain."

"That blasted Bowen." He reached for his glass, then leaned back and sipped his brandy.

All through the afternoon and evening, he'd been muttering about the flogging earlier that day. Why? Guilt? Marianne doubted it. His anger suggested another conclusion. Perhaps he feared the disrespect of his men. Perhaps he feared losing control of his ship.

Gathering her courage, she took a step forward. "I do not believe he meant to defy you, Captain."

"Defy!" He jumped up and began pacing before the stern windows, rubbing the glass of brandy between his hands. "Mutinous dogs. How dare they conspire against me?"

Marianne tensed. "Sir, I am unaware of any conspiracy."

Before she even finished the words, he circled the desk. His gray eyes flashing, he stormed toward her. The smell of brandy and the fish he'd had for dinner filled her nose. He eyed her up and down. "You are probably a part of it."

The ship canted. Stumbling, Marianne grabbed onto the edge of his desk. The lantern flickered, casting eerie shadows over his face. She swallowed and determined not to flinch, not to show him that her stomach had just dropped to the floor. "You know that's not true, Captain."

His expression loosened like the unwinding of a tight rope. He released a sigh. "You think me harsh, don't you?"

Yes, I think you are a mad, cruel man. She bit her lip to hold back the truth lest she find herself at the end of a cat-o'-nine tails. But it snuck out anyway. "Yes," she said, then braced herself.

The captain let out a loud chuckle. He lifted his glass in her direction, the alcohol sloshing over the sides. "I like you, Miss Denton. Honesty. Quite refreshing."

"If honesty is what you want, Captain, I have plenty of it." She dared to take the opportunity to acquaint him with her opinion of the injustices she'd witnessed.

He walked to the stern window and stared out into the black void of night. A spray of twinkling stars beckoned her from the darkness.

At his silence, she continued, "Mr. Bowen did not receive a fair trial today, and you know it. You never gave him a chance to defend himself. And his punishment was far too cruel."

He swung around. A spray of brandy slid over the lip of his glass. His face scrunched. "What do you know of keeping discipline on a ship this size?"

Marianne stared wide-eyed at him, hoping he wouldn't charge toward her again.

Facing the stern, he snapped the brandy into his mouth. He attempted to set his glass down, but he missed his desk, and it crashed to the floor in a dozen glittering shards. As if unaware of the mess, he turned to examine his plants, brushing his fingers over their leaves.

A lump formed in Marianne's throat. The captain was a harsh man to be sure. But at times like these when he was in one of his dark pensive moods and well into his cups, he seemed more like a little boy than a man. A broken, lonely little boy. Grabbing one of her dusting cloths, she knelt by the desk and began to carefully pick up the shattered pieces.

"You are a good woman, Miss Denton. Not much of a steward, if I do say so." He chuckled. "But kind, quick-witted, completely agreeable. Your tranquil mannerisms and feminine gestures soothe an old man's soul."

Marianne halted, stunned by his compliments. She was surprised that they affected her so, for she gulped them in like a starving woman long deprived of food. Unbidden tears burned in her eyes. Blinking them back, she continued picking up the glass pieces, afraid to look up into his face. Afraid to discover he only taunted her.

"You are generous and wise and honest," he continued. "Qualities difficult to find among ladies these days."

A tear slid down Marianne's cheek and landed on a glass shard. She picked it up. The sharp edge caught her finger and sliced her skin. Pain shot into her hand. She dabbed the blood with the cloth and picked up the few remaining pieces. In all his years, her father had never once spoken a word of praise to Marianne. He had not been a cruel father—had never raised his voice at her, had never impugned her character. He had simply not been the type of man who freely offered his approval. So she found it ironic that this man who could be so cruel could also speak so highly of her.

Bundling the cloth around the glass, Marianne wiped her face and stood. She had never known her father's opinion of her. She had never known whether he was proud of her. And not until this moment did she realize how desperate she was to hear any approbation at all. She set the cloth down on the desk and raised her gaze to the captain.

He smiled and shifted his eyes away uncomfortably, but she sensed no insincerity in his expression.

He leaned on the window ledge and gripped his side. "I don't feel too well."

Marianne darted to him just in time to catch him before he fell. His weight nearly pushed her to the floor, but slowly she managed to lead him to his sleeping chamber.

"Perhaps some sleep will make you feel better, Captain." She eased him onto his mattress.

"Yes, yes. Quite right. I need to sleep." He plopped his head down on his pillow and lifted a hand to rub his temples.

With difficulty, Marianne managed to swing his massive legs onto the mattress, and then she stared down at the man who, with his eyes closed, looked more like a gentle old grandfather than the captain of a British warship.

Memories assailed her of another time, long ago, and another man. A man very dear to her. As she gazed upon the captain, he slowly transformed into that man—her father, Mr. Henry Denton, home late from a night of drinking and gambling.

Shaking the bad memories away, she removed the captain's boots one by one, unaware of the tears sliding down her cheeks until one plopped onto her neck. How many nights had she done this same thing for her father? How many nights had Marianne cared for him when her mother had been unwilling? How many nights had Marianne gone out with one of the footmen to drag her father from a tavern and bring him home?

Too many.

Until that last night when he didn't come home at all.

The captain mumbled and patted her hand. "That's a good girl. A good girl."

Grabbing the wool blanket, Marianne laid it atop him and tucked it beneath his chin. She batted the moisture from her face. Would she ever stop missing her father? Would she ever forgive him for leaving her?

Resisting the urge to plant a kiss upon the captain's forehead as she'd done with her father, she turned to leave.

"I should have been a farmer, you know," he stuttered, his eyes still closed.

Marianne took his hand. Rough, sea-hardened skin scratched her fingers. His eyelids fluttered and he moaned. A farmer? Yes, she could see him as a farmer. Yet instead of fertile ground to till and tender plants to tend, he plowed His Majesty's ship through tumultuous seas and raised rebellious boys to be officers. No wonder the man was miserable and half-crazed. He had missed his destiny.

"You still can be a farmer, Captain. You still can." But her words fell on deaf ears as the captain started to snore. She released his hand and blew out the lanterns in his cabin, then left him to his sleep.

Pushing her sorrow away, she made her way down the passageway. She must find Daniel and give him the news about Antigua.

She didn't have far to go as she nearly bumped into the young boy when he came barreling down the ladder from the quarterdeck. She ushered him into her room. "I have news to give Noah," she whispered as she lit a lantern and sat upon her bed.

He plopped beside her. "Aye, that's why I was headin' t' see you."

"How did you know?" She eyed him quizzically. He grinned. "Oh, never mind." She leaned close to him. He smelled of brass polish and gunpowder. "Tell Noah that the captain expects to make port in Antigua in seven days, will you do that?"

His white teeth gleamed in the lantern light. "Yes, Miss Marianne, I will. That's good news." He grabbed her hand. "Maybe that is where we are supposed to escape."

"Perhaps. I don't know. I don't see how we can with all these sailors and marines guarding us."

"That's okay, miss. God knows, and He can do anything."

Marianne sighed and brushed Daniel's hair from his face. She wished more than anything that she possessed his faith. "We shall see."

"You don't trust God, do you, Miss Marianne? You don't trust in His love." He leaned his head on her shoulder. "Oh, Miss Marianne, you must. You simply must."

"I'm trying, Daniel." She swung her arm around him and drew him near. "It's just so hard when nothing but bad things happen to me."

"How do you know they're bad?" He pushed away from her.

"What do you mean?"

He shrugged. "You can't know what God's purpose is for the things that have happened until you see the end. It's like the end of a good story, miss. Everything looks real bad until you get to the last chapter."

Marianne couldn't help but laugh at his enthusiasm, but inside, the wisdom of his statement jarred her to her core.

"I best be gettin' back. That Garrick's been keepin' a strict eye on me." With a grin, he slipped out the door, leaving her alone with only the slosh of the sea against the hull for company.

With a huff, she lay back on the bed and tried to calm her nerves. But Daniel's words kept ringing through the dank air of the cabin, refusing to be drowned out by the sounds of the ship.

"How do you know?"

❖ CHAPTER 17 ❖

Noah leaned his aching back against the hull and propped his elbow on the mess table. With a bit of pork stew and weevil-infested tack in his belly, and the anticipation of a good night's sleep, he wouldn't have expected the angst tightening his nerves. Perhaps it was the vision embedded in his mind of Mr. Bowen's torn flesh and with it, Noah's increased urgency to escape this British prison.

"How do you fare, Luke?" he asked his first mate who'd been too busy shoveling food into his mouth to talk.

Luke released a heavy sigh and stretched his shoulders. "Better than Mr. Bowen."

"I'll say." Weller grunted from his seat beside Luke.

Next to Noah, Blackthorn stared blankly at the bottom of his mug.

Noah pointed toward Luke's empty dish. "Apparently this slop transforms into a king's fare when you haven't eaten for three days." He shoved his own half-eaten meal away. His nose wrinkled as the bitter smell rose to join the stench of hundreds of unwashed men.

"Miss Denton brought me some biscuits." Luke smiled, then winced and dabbed at the purple bruise marring his left cheek.

Noah's brows shot up. "She did?"

"Yes, her and that lad, Daniel."

Blackthorn raised his gaze from his cup.

"Down in the berth, with all those men?" Noah asked. The woman was a source of constant surprise.

"Yes. In the middle of the night. The marine who guarded me was asleep." Luke sipped his beer.

Weller grunted and scratched his head, jarring a few strands of his stiff black hair.

Noah gazed over the mess room, trying to make sense of Luke's words. Sailors hovered over tables, their faces twisted in the dim, flickering lantern light. Shouts, insults, jeers, and chortles shot through the room like grapeshot.

Daniel emerged from the fiendish throng like an angel escaping hell. Blackthorn's stiff features relaxed at the sight of him. "Where have you been, boy? Had me worried about you again."

"Sorry." The boy gave Blackthorn a sheepish grin. "I had to wait for Miss Marianne to leave the captain's cabin."

"How is she?" The enthusiasm in Noah's voice drew the men's gazes his way.

"She's well. She has a message for you." Daniel slid in between Blackthorn and Noah. He grabbed a biscuit from Noah's plate.

"Well, spill it, boy." Blackthorn elbowed the lad. "We are all friends here."

Daniel's eyes lit up. "Antigua. We're to anchor in Antigua in seven days."

The news sang in Noah's ears like a sweet melody. Hope rose within him. He tousled the boy's hair. "Good job, lad."

Blackthorn's coal black eyes skewered Noah. "You ain't thinkin' what I think you're thinkin'."

"Pa, they're here to rescue us," Daniel said.

Noah flinched. "Pa?"

Luke's eyes widened, and Weller lifted his gaze.

Blackthorn huffed and stared back into his mug.

"Sorry, Pa." Daniel lowered his chin.

"Our secret is out, I suppose." Blackthorn growled.

Noah glanced between Blackthorn and Daniel and wondered why he hadn't seen the resemblance before. Same dark hair, same piercing, brown eyes. "Why hide your relationship?"

"So the captain nor Garrick don't use the boy against me." Blackthorn scratched the hair springing from the top of his shirt. The lantern flame set his eyes aglow with fury. . .or was it fear?

Noah's jaw tensed. Would anyone be so cruel as to use a man's son against him? Yet after what he'd witnessed today, he wondered if any honor and kindness existed among these British officers. "Rest assured, we won't tell anyone," Noah said. "Right, men?"

"Aye," Weller muttered.

"Of course." Luke nodded.

Daniel leaned in and shifted eyes alight with glee over the men. The lantern above them squeaked as it swayed in its hook. "You should know my father used to be a pirate."

"Indeed?" Luke's brows lifted and again he winced as if the action pained him. From the look of the swollen puffy skin around his eye, Noah could see why.

"Sink me, ain't nothin' to be proud of, son." Blackthorn leaned back, scanned the table, then shook his head when he noticed all eyes were riveted on him. "Only for a year. Sailed wit' a vile man by the name o' Graves. A fittin' name, to be sure, for he put many people in theirs." He let out a sigh. "Some o' the worst years of me life."

"Unimaginable, man." Luke's tone was incredulous. "Surely you enjoyed the freedom, the adventure?"

Blackthorn blew out a sigh. "At first, mebbe, but it is a lifestyle without honor, and without honor, what does a man possess of any value?"

Luke grunted. "So you quit?"

"Nay, I wasn't strong enough for that." Blackthorn fingered his stubbled chin. "I met Daniel's mother and she reformed me, so t' speak." He smiled. "I was settin' me life straight, tryin' to obey God's commands and make an honest livin'." The lines on his face fell. "But then our merchant ship got captured."

Daniel looked up at his father with such affection it caused a lump to form in Noah's throat and made him wonder what it would be like to have a son of his own someday. Would his son look at him with similar admiration or would he look at Noah with the same disgust with which Noah looked upon his father?

"It ain't your fault, Pa." Daniel glanced at Noah. "Pa thinks this is punishment for his time as a pirate."

"I killed men." Blackthorn hung his head.

A vision of Jacob lying on the deck, blood pooling beneath his head, filled Noah's thoughts. So had he. If there was one thing he understood, it was the weight of such guilt.

"God forgives you, Pa. He told me."

The words pierced Noah's heart as if the boy had directed them at him instead of Blackthorn. Did God forgive Noah as well? And if He did, would that make the guilt go away?

Blackthorn patted the lad's head. "My son fancies himself a prophet."

Weller gave a cynical laugh, then stared at the boy. "Perhaps you can tell us if we'll ever get off this ship."

Daniel sat tall. "I can, mister. And we will. In Antigua."

"Isn't that one of Nelson's dockyards? The main British port in the Caribbean?" Luke frowned.

"Aye." Weller's brown eyes seemed to darken, even as his golden tooth gleamed in the lantern light. "The place is brimming with naval officers and marines. Ain't no way we can escape there. We'd be picked up for sure. Then hung for desertion."

The ship tilted, creaking and groaning. The lantern above them swayed, shifting its light back and forth over the group as if searching for one worthy of its brightness. The bulk of its glow settled on Daniel.

"Not for sure, mister." Daniel's eyes sparkled with youthful exuberance.

Blackthorn sipped his drink. "Though I ain't too sure I believe it anymore, I'd listen to me son, if I were you. He's rarely wrong. In fact, he's a miracle hisself."

"How so?" Noah asked.

Blackthorn rubbed a finger over the gaping holes where two teeth had once stood. "My wife could bear no children, being past the age. We resigned ourselves to being childless. So, I went off to sea. She took a position as governess in the mayor's home. But she never stopped praying for a baby. Then a little more than eight months after I left Daniel came along. The physician called it a miracle." Blackthorn put his arm around the boy and seemed to have difficulty containing his emotions. "He's been the light o' our lives e'er since. Though I'm sure your ma is right furious at me for takin' ye to sea." He swallowed and glanced away. "She must be overwrought with worry o'er what happened to us."

"A miracle child, eh?" Noah elbowed Daniel and the boy grinned.

"My son inherited his strong faith from his ma," Blackthorn gazed with pride upon the lad. "Me? Me feet stand on more solid ground."

The boy's features crumbled. "But God told me Miss Denton and these men would come to free us." He looked up at Noah. "It's what you're supposed to do."

Whether God sent him here or not, Noah knew all too well what he had to do. He had to find a way to get Marianne and his crew off this ship. "It may be our only chance." Noah eyed each man in turn. "What have we got to lose?"

"Our lives," Weller grumbled.

"You call this life?" He paused, looking at each man in turn. "I'd rather be dead." Noah leaned toward Daniel. "Tell Miss Denton that we shall make our escape in Antigua."

Marianne stepped onto the weather deck. The evening breeze, stiff with the scent of brine, swirled around her, cooling her perspiration. Pressing a hand against her back, she tried to stop the ache that had taken residence after yet another day of scrubbing and polishing and buffing and listening to the mindless chatter of the captain. Thankfully he made no mention of her tucking him into bed the night before or of his disclosure of his preference to be a farmer. She hoped he had forgotten, but after his foul mood and gruff mannerism all day, she doubted it, for he exhibited all the signs of a man with wounded pride.

Despite the captain's belligerent behavior, Marianne found her spirits lifted after Daniel gave her Noah's message. Did he have a plan? Could they really escape? She dared not allow her hopes to rise for she didn't think she could survive another disappointment. However, if she did hope just a little, if she did believe they might get off this ship, that meant she would have to put her trust in Noah. She cringed at the thought of trusting anyone again.

The ship rose over a swell, and she balanced her sore feet over the planks, amazed at how accustomed she had become to the sudden roll of the deck. Now, if she could overcome her fear of the fathomless expanse of blue surrounding them, she might enjoy these trips above. Inching her way to the break of the quarterdeck, she gripped the wooden railing and drew a deep breath of the moist air. The sun waved a farewell ribbon resplendent with peach, saffron, and maroon across the horizon.

She surveyed the ship. A few watchmen sauntered about, paying her no mind. Apparently, she had become as normal a feature aboard this ship as any of the sailors. Whether that was a good thing or not, she couldn't say. The clamor of voices, *clank* of plates, and *twang* of a fiddle wafted up from below where most of the crew partook of their dinner, or mess as they called it—an appropriate description based on what she'd seen. The captain and his officers ate much better. And thankfully so did she.

Her thoughts drifted to Noah, and she wondered how he fared. She knew the British sailors treated the Americans poorly, and it saddened her to think he was suffering. Odd, when not two weeks ago, she had wanted to strangle him. What had changed? What had transformed the repugnant brat into a chivalrous gentleman?

She ran the tips of her fingers over her lips and thought of their kiss.

Her belly warmed at the memory.

Truth be told, she wished she could stop thinking about the kiss or about Noah at all. But she could not. And that frightened her more than anything—even more than being trapped aboard this ship. Day and night she wondered about him. How was he faring in the tops? Did they beat him? Did he sleep well? And whenever she came on deck, she searched him out, desperate for a glimpse of him. What was wrong with her? She was behaving like a silly schoolgirl.

She loved him.

The realization stormed through her like a mighty gale. And like a gale, it threatened to tear her to shreds. For Noah had made his desires quite plain. He did not wish to marry her. He had a sweetheart in South Hampton. Marianne was no fool. She knew all too well that any union between her and Noah would only be motivated by his need of her wealth.

But she couldn't allow him to be so miserably matched just to appease his father's guilt-induced mandate.

She loved him too much.

No, if they ever got off this ship and back to Baltimore, she would grant Noah his wish and break off their engagement. She had done him enough damage, caused him enough pain. That way he could silence his father's demands and marry Priscilla—beautiful, cultured Priscilla. Her insides crumpled at the thought.

She would find another way to provide for her mother and sister and purchase the medicine her mother needed. *Oh Lord, please heal my mother. Please take care of her and Lizzie in my absence.* Her heart ached to know how they fared.

"Don't cry, Miss Denton." The slippery voice sent a chill over her. She knew who it was before she turned around.

"Lieutenant Garrick." Marianne batted the moisture from her face. "You frightened me."

The grin on his thin lips turned her stomach sour. "What has you so distraught, my dear?" He slithered beside her at the railing, effectively backing her against the head of the quarterdeck.

Her nerves tightened. She faced the sea. The last traces of the sun slipped below the horizon. "I am concerned for my mother and sister back in Baltimore."

"Ah yes, apart from loved ones. It is the price we pay to serve in His Majesty's Navy." He brushed his coat, drawing attention to the gold stripe and three buttons lining his cuff.

Marianne twisted her ring. Was he trying to impress her? She dared to stare into his narrowed dark eyes. "I am not in His Majesty's Navy." Her sharp tone sent one of his eyebrows into an imperious arch.

"I believe you are mistaken, Miss Denton, for last I heard you are aboard the HMS *Undefeatable* serving as Captain's steward."

"Not by choice."

"Don't be so naive." He ran a thumb down the whiskers outlining his pointed chin. "Most of these men are not here by choice."

"Perhaps if they were, you wouldn't have to strip the flesh off their backs to force their loyalty." She regretted her brazen statement as soon as it left her lips.

A look akin to a demon's scowl came over Lieutenant Garrick's face. Darkness seeped from his eyes.

Marianne's blood turned cold. She glanced across the deck, now murky in the falling shadows. No one was in sight.

He flashed a superior grin. "How could a woman understand the ways of the greatest navy in the world?"

Marianne thought to tell him she hoped never to understand but decided for once to keep her mouth shut.

"It is a lonely career, Miss Denton. Like you, I miss the companionship of family and friends from home." He leaned toward her, his eyes absorbing her from head to toe. The stench of alcohol hung upon his foul breath. "The companionship of a woman."

She backed against the quarterdeck. Her heart thrashed against her chest. The ship plunged down a wave, sending a spray of saltwater over them. Marianne quivered.

"Ah, you shiver, Miss Denton. No need to be afraid. I will protect you." He caressed her cheek.

She jerked away. "And who will protect me from you?"

He grinned. "No one, I suppose. Which is why you should simply give me what I want. It will go much better for you."

Marianne's feet went numb. She dug her nails into the wood behind her. *Lord. Please. Help me.* If she screamed would anyone come to her aid? Would anyone stand up for her against Lieutenant Garrick?

Raising his arm, he pressed his hand against the quarterdeck, blocking her exit. "Ah, I assure you, no one will cross me, Miss Denton. I am second in command and have the captain's favor, and everyone on board this ship knows it."

Her chest heaved for air. She lifted her shoulders. "Then what is it you want, Lieutenant Garrick?"

"I thought you'd never ask." In an instant, he closed the distance between them and crushed his body against hers.

Marianne struggled. She tried to pound her fists against his chest. She tried to kick him. But the weight of his body pinned her to the quarterdeck. His mouth clawed hers. Spit and salt stung her lips. She squeezed her eyes shut and willed herself to wake up. *Just a nightmare. Only a nightmare.* She tried to scream, but only a pathetic squeal groaned from her throat.

Then a deep growl of fury filled the air.

Marianne felt the weight of Lieutenant Garrick's body lift from hers. She struggled for a breath. *Thump!* The sound of something heavy hitting the wooden planks caused her to open her eyes. The lieutenant lay on the deck, one arm hung over the railing, his chest heaving. His sordid features twisted in a mixture of shock and rage.

Before him stood Noah, muscles flexing, fists clenched. His hair hanging around his firm jaw. He turned to her. "Are you all right?"

She nodded, stunned as much by his concern, the fear for her that she saw in those blue eyes as by what he had just done.

"Do you know who I am?" the lieutenant roared. "I'll have you court-martialed and hung for that, Yankee!" He struggled to his feet and straightened his jacket.

The men on watch approached from all sides. Lieutenant Reed's tall, dark form lurked at a distance. Blackthorn headed toward them from across the deck.

Garrick turned and addressed his audience. "You saw it. He struck me!"

"I only pushed you aside to keep you from accosting this woman." Noah ran a hand through his hair. "Or is ravishing women an acceptable pastime allowed officers according to your precious Articles of War?"

Garrick laughed and stormed toward him. "You will die for this, Yankee dog. I hope the trollop is worth your life."

Noah lifted his fist to strike the man.

"No, Noah!" Marianne screamed and grabbed his arm, but he tore it from her grasp.

Blackthorn darted to Noah's side and shoved him back, staying his hand.

Noah struggled against the massive man, but Blackthorn held him in place. "Garrick will have you hanged."

Garrick chuckled. "How noble, Mr. Blackthorn. But I fear your efforts are in vain." He grabbed his hat from the deck and plopped it atop his head. "The man already hit me, and he will pay the penalty. And in case you aren't familiar with our *precious* Articles of War, the penalty for striking an officer is death."

❖ CHAPTER 18 ❖

Noah raised his hands to scratch his face. The iron manacles clanked in protest as they bit into his wrists. Whips of sun lashed the back of his neck as streams of perspiration slid beneath his shirt. Though exhaustion attempted to drag his chin down, he refused to lower his head in defeat. The shrill of the boson's pipe pierced the air. His stomach soured.

Footsteps thundered over the deck as the crew mustered amidships for the trial.

His trial.

The captain glared down at him from the quarterdeck. The supercilious smirk on his face suggested a perverted glee at the punishment of others. To Noah's left, Luke, Weller, and Blackthorn huddled together, lines of fear etched their faces. He hoped the young lad Daniel had gone below out of sight of such horror. He hoped the same for Marianne.

But a flash of maroon linen caught the corner of his eye, dashing his hopes. She stood at the top of the quarterdeck ladder, anguish burning on her features. Confound the woman! He didn't want her to witness his shame, to see him like this, beaten and chained. Nor did he wish to witness the pity, the sympathy now spilling from her lustrous brown eyes.

When he'd seen Garrick's body crushed against hers—heard his lecherous grunts and lewd comments—all reason, all fear had abandoned Noah. The only thing that mattered was protecting her. He was not sorry. He would do it again. He would take whatever punishment their twisted sense of justice meted out to him.

Even death.

Except that would leave Marianne alone with no one to rescue her the next time. Noah grimaced until the muscles in his jaw ached. The hot wind pounded on him, yanking his tangled hair. Above him, the masts creaked under the strain of canvas glutted with the breath of the sea.

Noah barely heard the captain call the inquiry to order or the master at arms read the charge. *Assaulting an officer.* Hushed murmurs of fear rose from the crew. They no doubt knew the fate that awaited him.

"Silence!" the captain shouted. "This is but an inquiry into the charges, Mr. Brenin. If I deem you guilty, you will await a court-martial when we reach port. Now, what do you have to say in your behalf?"

Noah squinted up at him, the captain's silhouette a dark shifting blotch against the brightness of the noon sun. "I did not strike Lieutenant Garrick, Captain. I merely protected the honor of a lady."

Garrick laughed. "I see no lady aboard."

The crew chuckled, drawing a fierce "Order!" from the captain who pounded his fist upon the railing.

"Lieutenant Garrick, what is your side of it?"

The slimy toad, who stood beside Milford, turned to his captain. "I was conversing with Miss Denton, your steward."

"I know she's my steward, blast you!" The captain fumed, sending the lieutenant back a step.

Garrick adjusted his coat and continued, "As I said, I was conversing with Miss Denton when Mr. Brenin charged me and knocked me to the deck. There was no cause for it that I could see other than his vicious Yankee temper."

The captain eyed Garrick with suspicion. No doubt, the man's arrogant belligerence had not missed the captain's notice. "No other cause, you say?"

Garrick shifted his boots over the deck and took a pompous stance. "Isn't it obvious, Captain? He's jealous."

Lieutenant Reed, standing to the captain's left, snorted.

Noah snapped the hair from his face. "Not jealous, sir, but concerned for the lady."

Murmurs sped through the crowd, silenced by one look from Captain Milford.

"Hmm." The captain eyed Noah. "Regardless of the cause, you know, sir, I could have you court-martialed and hanged for striking an officer."

"Lieutenant Garrick is lying." Marianne's bold declaration drew all eyes to her.

❖

Yet she could not allow such atrocious lies to go unchallenged. Nor could she allow Noah to die for her without at least trying to save him.

His blue eyes met hers. The fear and admiration within them gave her the courage to continue.

The captain's jaw stiffened, and his dark brows drew together as if he couldn't believe she had the audacity to speak in front of the entire crew. She knew that look. He was about to unleash his mad fury on her and order her below. She took a step toward him. "I beg you, Captain, hear me out. Lieutenant Garrick assaulted me, and this man came to my rescue. He did not strike the lieutenant but merely pulled him from me." She gazed at Noah and smiled. "To save me, Captain."

Noah's brow furrowed.

"That is pure rubbish, Captain. I—" Garrick began, but with a lift of the captain's hand, he was silenced.

Marianne prayed that reason reigned in the captain's mind this day instead of laudanum-induced hysteria.

Captain Milford scanned the assembled crew. "Were there any other witnesses?"

Midshipman Jones took an unsteady step forward. He dragged his hat from his head, revealing the smooth face of a young man no older than eighteen. "When I came upon them, Captain." His voice quavered. "I saw Lieutenant Garrick on the deck and this man"—he pointed toward Noah—"hovering over the lieutenant, his fists clenched as if he'd struck him."

Garrick smiled.

"Thank you, Mr. Jones." The captain nodded his approval. "Anyone else?"

One crewman separated from the crowd. "That's what I saw, Cap'n, except this one, Blackthorn, was holding Mr. Brenin back from striking the lieutenant again."

The ship pitched over a wave, and Marianne gripped the railing at the head of the ladder. Her chest tightened, but not due to fear of the sea this time. This time, all her fears focused on the future of one man.

One very special man.

The wind whipped the flaps of Captain Milford's coat. "Very well. That will suffice." He faced Marianne with a true look of regret. "The word of three men against yours, Miss Denton. It is admirable that you speak up for your fiancé, but I'm afraid your testimony is of no account."

Marianne's head grew light. She pressed a hand over her chest to steady her heart. What could she say? What could she do to stop this madness? It was bad enough she'd gotten Noah impressed, but she could never live with herself if she got him killed. "They are lying, Captain, I beg you!" Her voice trembled.

Her gaze locked upon Lieutenant Reed, his eyes downcast, red hands clasped tight behind his back. The muscles in his jaw bunched and relaxed as though engaged in battle. He had been there last night. *Why didn't he say something?*

"Lieutenant Reed?" she shouted. He turned guilt-ridden eyes to hers.

"That is enough, Miss Denton!" The captain faced the crew. "Mr. Brenin, you will be confined below until we make port where a proper court-martial can be held." He gave Noah a shrug that fell short of a sympathetic gesture. "Based, however, on this evidence, it's a surety they will condemn you to death."

Death.

Noah allowed the finality of the word to sink into his gut. If it was his time, he expected it to take an uncomfortable residence there, but instead it shot off the deck and bounced over the bulwarks in rebellion until a gnawing ache formed in his belly.

Marianne gasped. He glanced at her. Terror screamed from her face and something else. Pity? Sorrow? He couldn't tell from where he stood. Sweat streamed into his eyes and he shook it away.

Lieutenant Reed turned to his captain. "Captain, if I may speak. I saw the entire altercation, sir."

The captain's features stiffened. "Odds fish, man, why didn't you say something before now?" he barked.

"I had hoped not to speak on behalf of the Americans." Reed nodded toward Marianne. "However, conscience dictates that the truth be known. It is as Miss Denton describes. Lieutenant Garrick attacked her, and Mr. Brenin came to her rescue. As far as I saw, he did not strike the lieutenant."

Noah's breath returned to him. He saw Marianne grab hold of the railing as if she might swoon.

Lieutenant Garrick's face puffed out like a sail at full wind. "What the devil are you saying, sir? The verdict has already been issued."

The captain studied Lieutenant Reed. His gray eyes flashed. "And what of Mr. Blackthorn restraining him?"

"That is true." Reed said. "The lieutenant called Miss Denton a foul name, and it appeared as though Mr. Brenin intended to strike him."

The ship swooped over a wave as if elevated by the truth. Noah steadied his bare feet on the hot deck, too afraid to hope for a different outcome—any outcome beside the one that placed him in a grave.

"This is madness." Garrick gave a nervous chortle.

"Silence!" Captain Milford faced Noah. "Mr. Brenin. What say you? Was that your intent?"

Noah raised his shackled hands to wipe the sweat from his brow. *Clank.* The iron had grown warm in the hot sun and burned his skin. Would the punishment be the same if his intent had been to strike an officer? Would he lose his grip on life once again? Yet he could not lie. "That was my intention, Captain."

The captain adjusted his coat and stared out to sea, weighing Noah's fate on the scales of his madness. The azure water crashed against the hull as if cheering him on.

"Very well." He faced Lieutenant Garrick. "You will restrain your lecherous passions aboard my ship, sir, or, regardless of your connections, it will be you at court-martial next time. I will not tolerate such dishonorable conduct under my command."

The lieutenant's face flushed, and his eyes narrowed.

The captain looked down on Noah. "And you, Mr. Brenin. Strike or attempt to strike an officer again, and you'll wish for death." He waved a hand through the air. "Two dozen lashes."

Though preferable to swinging from a rope, the words lanced across Noah's heart as if he'd already suffered the wrenching blows. Vivid images flashed across his mind—images of what one dozen strikes had done to the last man to suffer such a verdict.

Marianne cried out, and he wondered in his clouded mind whether she shrieked out of horror for his punishment or whether she truly cared for him.

The crew doffed their hats as Captain Milford opened the Articles of War and read the rules regarding Noah's infraction. But he heard none of it.

His mind was numb. Muted sounds of the crew tossing curses his way, of the hatch grating being lashed to the deck, the snap of sails, the thunder of the men's footsteps as they assembled to witness his shame—everything blurred before him. His feet dragged over the deck as they led him to the grating. Splinters pierced his skin. The bosun tore off Noah's shirt. The searing sun struck his bare skin as they removed his irons and bound his hands above his head.

Noah's last thought was of Marianne. He hoped she'd gone below. He hoped the captain would not punish her for speaking out on his behalf.

The pounding of drums sounded.

He closed his eyes.

He heard the cat-o'-nine being pulled from the bosun's mate's bag.

Crack.

Raw pain seared across his back, simmering deep into his flesh.

Snap.

A thousand hot knives sliced through his skin.

Thwack.

He dug his forehead into the iron grating and ground his teeth together.

Blood dripped on the deck by his feet.

Crack.

Sharp bits of the metal cut into his face. His head grew light.

And darkness welcomed him.

Holding a lantern out before her and clutching a bundle to her chest, Marianne crept down the dark passageway. The sway of the ship knocked her against the bulkhead, but she quickly righted herself and continued. Tying the bundle to her belt, she gripped the railing and descended the narrow steps of one of the ship's ladders. Long since faded, the laughter and shouting of the crew had been replaced with snores, grunts, and the ever-present creak of the ship—a sound Marianne had come to believe was nothing but an ominous warning that the hull was about to break apart.

Ignoring that terrifying thought, she descended another level. Rats scattered before her sphere of light, the pitter-patter of their feet echoing through the ship. Swallowing, she shoved aside her fear of the crew, the rats, the sea, knowing she must attend to Noah. She halted at the bottom of the ladder and lifted her lantern. Darkness filled every crack and crevice. Remembering the directions Daniel had given her, she turned left.

Hopefully toward the sick bay where Noah lay recovering.

Apparently his wounds had been so devastating, the surgeon decided to keep him overnight instead of allowing him to return to his hammock.

Rounding a corner, she entered an open space. Wooden bed frames, holding stuffed mattresses, hung from the deckhead and swayed with each movement of the ship. Glass covered cabinets containing bottles of all shapes and sizes stood against the far bulkhead. Medical instruments, including what looked to be a saw and a hatchet, hung from hooks on the opposite wall.

Gathering her courage, she stepped forward. The light from her lantern landed on a man's bare back, ripped and torn like a hunk of meat at the butcher's shop. Noah. She gasped. Her stomach lurched.

She dashed to the wooden table.

His eyes popped open, and he whispered, "Hello, Miss Denton. I hope you'll forgive me for not getting up."

Half-laughing, half-crying, she pulled up a chair beside him and sat down. Setting the lantern atop another table, she took his hand in hers. The metallic smell of blood filled her nose.

His brows lifted then lowered when he saw her tears. "Not to worry, Marianne. The surgeon says I'll be good as new in a few days." Half his face was flattened against the table, making his words slur.

"Noah, I'm so sorry." Marianne could not hold back the tears. "What can I do to help you?" She gripped his arm and shook it in her fury.

He winced. "You can stop doing that for one thing."

"Forgive me." She released his hand. "I've made a mess of things."

"It wasn't your fault that bedeviled rake attacked you."

"No, but it is my fault we are all on this ship in the first place." *And you stood up for me—protected me. Why?* She longed to ask him, but the look in his blue eyes captivated her. Myriad emotions crossed over them: frustration, pain, and one that sent her heart fluttering—regard.

"Why are you here?" he asked.

"Oh." Marianne untied the bundle and opened it on her lap. "I have brought bandages and aloe for your wounds."

"Aloe?" He rose on his forearms, his face contorted in agony.

"It's from the captain's plants. I stole a leaf. It's for healing of the skin." She tried not to stare at the firm muscles rounding in his arms.

"Stole? Confound it, woman. He's not a man to trifle with."

"I can handle him."

Noah released a heavy sigh. The harshness in his gaze faded. "You came down here to attend to my wounds?"

Marianne smiled. "As I have said. Now lie back down and be still."

"Yes, ma'am." He chuckled then winced as he lowered himself to the wooden table.

Marianne spread the milky gel over a strip of cloth and gently laid it across his back. She pressed lightly.

He groaned.

"My apologies." Marianne studied his wounds, searching for the best place to apply the aloe next. The cat had done its work. Streaks of red, torn flesh crisscrossed Noah's back as if he'd encountered a very angry bear with very large claws. She pressed a hand to her stomach at the sight as bile rose in her throat.

"How does it look?"

"Not bad."

"Liar."

She chuckled.

"Did you watch?" he asked.

"No." Marianne shook her head. As soon as the flogging had begun, she'd slipped below. "I am a coward." She spread aloe on another strip of cloth and laid it on his back.

"You are anything but a coward." He winced. "I am glad you didn't witness it."

She finished laying aloe-covered cloths over the worst areas then plopped to the chair. Tears spilled from her eyes.

He reached out a finger and lifted her chin. "Don't cry, Marianne. It will be all right."

He used her Christian name. Twice now. The sound of it on his lips sang like a sweet melody in her ears. "You risked your life to protect me."

She swallowed. "Why?"

"I couldn't stand by and watch you get ravished, could I?"

Was there no other reason? "Other men would have."

She brushed a strand of hair from his face. But not him. Not Noah. He'd proven himself to be an honorable man of integrity and courage, even, dare she say, kindness. Not at all like the little boy she remembered.

The ship swayed, groaning and creaking. Lantern light flickered across his prominent chin, strong jaw, and blue eyes—sharp despite the pain he must be feeling.

"Oh, Noah, we are all trapped in this living hell. I fear for you and Mr. Heaton and Mr. Weller and young Daniel."

He wiped a tear from her cheek and allowed his thumb to linger there. "Never fear. We shall escape."

"But how?" She leaned in to his hand and found comfort in its warmth and strength. Memories of their kiss sent her pulse racing. Would she ever feel his lips on hers again? What was she doing? She jerked away from his touch. Fanciful, romantic hopes were not for women like her.

"When we make anchor at Antigua," he answered. "I will figure something out."

She couldn't imagine what plan would succeed with so many officers always watching them, but she smiled nonetheless. Hope would make Noah recover sooner. Hope was what had kept her mother from giving up and dying.

"Don't worry, princess." He reached up and caressed her cheek. "I will get you off this ship."

Princess. Yet the gentle tone in which he offered this spurious title in no way resembled the sarcasm of his youth. Marianne's thoughts jumbled as he brushed the back of his hand over her skin. His masculine scent filled the air between them. And all she wanted was for that moment to never end. For if and when they escaped, she would lose him. Lose him to his merchant business, lose him to Priscilla.

She looked down under his intense perusal. Bloodstains spread across the deck, reminding her that life didn't always end up well. Perhaps she should tell Noah the truth about her fortune. Perhaps she should get it over with before she'd lost so much of her heart, she would never reclaim it. "I must confess something."

"Yes?" He ran a thumb over her chin.

"My mother and I have not been completely forthright regarding our engagement."

Noah could not imagine to what Marianne was referring, nor did he care at the moment. All that concerned him was the look of complete admiration and care beaming from those rich brown eyes.

When had the shrew transformed into an angel? Despite the pain lancing across his back, his heart filled with an affection for her he hadn't thought possible. He could not seem to stop caressing her cheek. So soft. So moist with tears—tears for him.

"My inheritance." She began twisting the ring around her finger.

"It doesn't matter now." Noah surprised himself at the veracity of his statement. For he truly didn't care about the money anymore. Nor about his father's merchant business. All that mattered was this precious creature before him and that he must do everything in his power to protect her.

"I suppose you're right, but I need to tell you anyway." She lifted her lashes. "There is nothing but the seven thousand dollars of my inheritance left." She spat out the words so quickly, their meaning left him stunned.

He stopped caressing her cheek. "But my father informed me the Denton fortune is worth thirty thousand."

Her gaze followed his retreating hand. "It was. Before my father gambled it all away."

Gambled? Noah shifted his back. Pain stretched across his skin like a tight, fiery rope. He remembered spotting Mr. Denton at the card tables now and then, but no more than most men in the city.

"Playing cards and some poor investments," she added.

"He lost everything?" Instead of anger, sympathy rose in Noah's chest.

She nodded and stared at the empty bundle in her lap. "Everything but my inheritance which was locked in a trust until I married."

"The house?"

"Mortgaged."

"The furniture? Silverware? Family heirlooms?"

"All sold."

"And the engagement party?"

"A pretense. A sham. Paid for by weeks of not eating."

Noah eased up on his forearms and stared at the bloodstained wood beneath him. "That's why your hands are blistered. Because you worked."

"When we dismissed our servants, we had no choice." She shifted hopeful eyes to his. "I'm sorry, Noah."

Noah's mind reeled. "So that's why you were eager to announce our engagement."

Marianne swallowed. "It's not what you think. You see, my mother is very ill. We can't afford her medicine without my dowry."

Realization dawned on him. They had used him. Like a pawn in some sordid scheme. Once Marianne married him, releasing her inheritance, she intended to use the money on her mother's medications. Not to support the Brenin merchant business. And who would fault her? Certainly not even Noah's father would choose business over someone's life.

Anger tightened the muscles in Noah's back. They cried out in pain. He had been used, the thought repeated. But how could he fault her when his family had done the same thing? They intended to use the Denton fortune to further their own aspirations. But at least they made no pretense about their motives.

"So you conspired to trap me, eh?" A sudden pain shot from his back into his head, and he gritted his teeth.

Her chest rose and fell rapidly. "I did no such thing. Our fathers wanted us married. My mother and I merely agreed to it."

"Under false pretenses," he growled. "At least I was honest in my reasons for marrying you." Then a second thought struck him—she never truly wished to marry him. Even though her behavior on board the *Fortune* spoke otherwise. Even though the ardor he'd seen in her eyes recently and the way she had kissed him screamed otherwise. She needed him only for his signature on a marriage license and his "I do" at a ceremony. A heavy weight sank to the bottom of his stomach. Noah had been used all his life.

And he was tired of it.

"So now you know." She gathered her things and rose, her chin lifting in that petulant tilt he remembered as a child. "And you have my word that if we ever get off this ship, my first order of business will be to break off our engagement."

Noah cringed. Sorrow weighed upon him, forcing his forehead to the table. Wasn't that what he had wanted? Wasn't that what he had tried to prod her into doing on board his ship? Then why didn't her agreement seem like a victory? "Most kind of you." He kept his tone dull, too angry and too proud to let his feelings show.

She turned her back to him and he saw that the hand by her side trembled. When she swung back around, tears pooled in her eyes. "Why did you kiss me the other night?" Despite her obvious effort to appear indifferent, the sorrow in her voice cut into Noah's heart.

He longed to jump from the table and take her in his arms. He longed to tell her that he'd kissed her because he thought she was kind, generous, and beautiful—because he thought he loved her. But she had lied to him. Used him. Like everyone else. "Why did you kiss me back?" he replied without emotion.

Her nose pinked and she drew a trembling breath. "You have your wish, Mr. Brenin. You are free of me. If we ever get off this ship, marry Priscilla, marry whomever you want, but you will never marry me."

❖ CHAPTER 19 ❖

Noah eased over the yard, his sweaty hands clinging to the backstay.

The foreman brayed from below, and Noah and his fellow topmen began hauling in the lower topgallant sail. Beside him, Blackthorn grunted with the exertion as he took up the slack for Noah. Five days had passed, and Noah's back still flamed as though a dozen branding irons lay across his tender skin. Yet the captain had ordered him back to work. Every move of his arms, every shift of his weight, sent searing agony across his torso.

A heavy gust of wind struck him, and he tightened his grip. Though the breeze cooled the sweat on his hands and neck and eased the fire on his back, in his weakened condition, it threatened to shove him to the deck below.

Blackthorn's worried eyes assessed Noah as the crew folded the heavy sailcloth and began tying it. Noah attempted a grin to reassure the man that he was well.

Well—as long as he didn't look down to the deck ninety feet below him. Well—as long as nothing so much as a feather brushed across his back.

He'd not seen Marianne since she'd stomped out on him in sick bay. Why she was angry, he had no idea. She had deceived him, snuck aboard his ship, caused them to be impressed into the navy, and created the circumstances that resulted in his flogging. Yet she dared to raise that smug nose of hers and be cross with him. Him? He would never figure women out. Especially not this particular one. Her moods were as fickle as the captain's.

Just minutes before her anger, nothing but admiration—dare he hope—affection shone in her gaze. But it had all disappeared just as quickly as she had, leaving him alone in the darkness. Though he'd been angry at first at her deception, the more he'd considered it, the more he understood that it blossomed from a love for her mother. She'd had no choice but to agree to the engagement and keep her true inheritance a secret. Her mother's life depended on it. And how could he fault her for such undaunted affection? It was admirable, in fact.

Like most things about Marianne.

Besides, he had behaved the unconscionable cad to her not only in their youth, but on board his ship. Surely he could forgive her, given the circumstances. What bothered him the most was that he wished she'd had an entirely different reason for agreeing to marry him in the first place.

The wind gusted against him as he tied the final knot, tying sailcloth tight to the yard. The spicy scent of rain bit his nose.

The ship plunged down a rising swell. Bubbling foam swept over the bow. Noah's breath halted as he clung to the yard. He hoped he wouldn't be called upon to strike the upper yards and set the storm sails in these rough seas.

"A storm approaches." Blackthorn pointed to the dark clouds swirling over the eastern horizon.

A storm approached indeed. For tomorrow they arrived at Antigua. And Noah had made up his mind. One way or another, regardless of the danger, regardless of the threat of death, tomorrow they would escape.

Marianne dipped her cloth into the black grease and rubbed it over the captain's boots, buffing as hard as she could in an attempt to achieve the impossible shine he demanded. Normally her hands ached, but if she imagined the boot to be Noah's face, they seemed to soar effortlessly over the leather. Oh, how she wished she could scrub that insolent scowl from his lips as easily.

Lips that had sent a warm quiver through her belly with a simple touch.

How dare he judge her for betraying him when his reasons for marrying her were as self-serving as hers?

She had thought... No. If she dared to admit it, she had hoped that after all they'd been through, her inheritance wouldn't matter to him.

"You are a fool, Marianne, the biggest fool of all." She blew a section of hair from her forehead. "A fool for ever thinking that a handsome, honorable man like Noah Brenin would ever love you." The look she'd mistaken for affection in his gaze had been merely gratitude for her ministrations. For how quickly it had transformed into one of fury when he'd discovered her deception.

Yet wasn't that what she had wanted? Wasn't that why she had told him? To invoke his anger at her duplicity so he would stop looking at her like he had been the past few days. Like he cared for her. Like he wanted her.

Like no one had ever looked at her before.

A look she would never see again.

Emptiness invaded her heart at the realization.

The captain marched in, grunted his salutation, and proceeded to the stern windows. Picking up a watering jug, he began tending his plants. From the look of exasperation on his face, Marianne knew better than to engage him in conversation, so she continued her work.

An ear-piercing howl filled the cabin. "What happened to my aloe?"

Marianne's heart clamped. She'd forgotten about the missing leaf, and suddenly wondered why he hadn't noticed until now. He swung around, face fuming, eyes latched upon her.

Midshipman Jones appeared in the doorway.

The captain scowled in his direction. "Burn and blast your bones, what is it now, lad?"

"Lieutenant Garrick's compliments, Captain, but we've spotted a sail."

The captain slammed down his jug, spilling water on the charts laid out across his desk. "Clean this up at once!" he barked at Marianne. Then grabbing his hat, he followed the midshipman aloft.

Thank You, Lord. Marianne breathed a sigh at the temporary reprieve. With any luck, the captain would forget the aloe upon his return. After dabbing up the water, she set the boots aside and went above. They had not spotted a sail since boarding this horrid ship. Were the guests friend or foe? She couldn't keep her hopes from rising.

But as soon as she emerged above, those same hopes fell to the hot deck beneath her shoes. Too small to be a French warship, it was most likely a merchant or a privateer, neither of which would take on a British frigate.

The *Undefeatable* pitched over a rounded swell, then swooped down the other side. Balancing over the teetering deck, Marianne inched toward the capstan, not daring to venture to the railing in such rough seas. Bloated, foamy waves billowed all around the ship. The wind clawed at her hair, loosening it from its pins. The scent of salt and rain swirled about her, and she glanced at the dark horizon. She gripped the wood. Her knuckles whitened. *Lord, please don't send a storm our way.* How many horrid tales had made their way back to Baltimore of ships that had sunk to the depths during a squall where not a soul on board was ever seen again?

Unable to stop herself from seeking a glimpse of Noah, she glanced aloft and found him clinging to the third yard above her on the mainmast. Her pulse quickened at the sight of him. With his broad shoulders stretched back and his bare feet gripping the swaying ratline, he seemed more comfortable in the heights than he had been at first. Blackthorn said something to him, and Noah's hearty laughter spilled down upon her like a warm spring shower. She shook off the sensation, not wanting to relish in the new and frightening feelings the man invoked in her.

Especially when nothing would ever come of them.

The crack of a rattan split the air, drawing Marianne's gaze to the petty officer hovering over Luke. Mr. Heaton released the rope and rose to his full height, leveling dark, snapping eyes toward the officer and then at Lieutenant Garrick who stood behind him.

"Again! For your insolence, sir," Garrick commanded, and the petty officer struck Luke once more. Grimacing, Luke bent to pick up the rope and took up his spot in line. His black hair hanging in his face did not hide his fury, and Marianne wondered how much a proud man like Luke could take before he retaliated.

A satisfied smirk on his face, Garrick surveyed the deck, his eyes halting when he saw her. A superior grin crept over his lips. His eyes grew cold, and he started toward her, but Marianne nodded toward the captain at the helm.

Following the direction of her glance, Garrick gave her one last look of scorn, then spun about.

Though she knew her reprieve was temporary, Marianne breathed a sigh of relief. The determined look in Lieutenant Garrick's slitlike eyes told her that he would not be easily swayed from his objective. And for some reason—perhaps because she was the only woman aboard—his objective was her. She must be careful not to be found alone again anywhere on the ship. Perhaps she could appeal to the captain. He displayed some admiration toward Marianne—at least when he had his wits about him. Not to mention she had a feeling that he had lessened Noah's sentence on her behalf. Perhaps if she expressed her terror of Garrick to the captain, he would keep the licentious lieutenant at bay.

Thunder pounded its agreement in the distance as the ship crested a wave and salty spray misted over her.

"Blast her! She's taunting us." The captain's bellow could be heard above the rising howl of the wind. He snapped his scope shut and set his jaw in a firm line. Off their larboard quarter, the unknown ship's sails appeared, then quickly disappeared behind the foamy peak of a surging wave, only to reappear as the vessel crested the roller. Marianne wondered why they weren't chasing the small craft as they'd done with Noah's.

Her answer came quickly from Lieutenant Reed's lips. "She's aweather of us, sir. With the oncoming storm, we'll never catch her."

"I am aware of that, Mr. Reed," the captain spat.

Daniel appeared at Marianne's side, bracing himself so sturdily upon the tilting deck that he had no need to hold on. He smiled up at her, his dark hair tossing to and fro in the wind. "That ship will save you." He nodded toward the ship that dared to tease the HMS *Undefeatable*.

Marianne wrinkled her brow. "I'm sorry, Daniel, but that ship is no match for this one. I fear they are doing nothing but infuriating the captain. Which is never a good thing."

His eyes twinkled as if he knew a grand secret.

Thunder roared again. Thick, black clouds churned in a sooty witches' brew over the horizon, spreading dark fingers up to steal the light of the sun not yet halfway across the sky. A light mist descended upon them. Marianne shivered.

"Take in topgallants and royals!" Lieutenant Reed yelled from his post beside the captain, causing more orders to be shouted across the various stations.

Glancing aloft, Marianne saw Noah inch his way alongside a dozen other men farther up the mainmast. She thought of his brother's tragic death and she shuddered. *Lord, protect him.*

A yellow flash lit up the seas, followed by a jet of gray smoke. The air pounded with the blast of a cannon. Marianne raised a hand to her throat, staring at the audacious vessel who dared fire upon His Majesty's royal frigate. Her hopes for rescue had just begun to rise when the shot fell impotent into the foamy sea several yards away.

A string of vile curses flew from the captain's mouth. He paced the quarterdeck, stopping to stare at the pesky ship though his long glass. Despite the mad rush of wind, she heard bits and pieces of his dialogue. "Show them... How dare they? They don't know who..." He ceased his pacing and took a commanding stance.

"A signal shot." Garrick laughed. "Too far away and too absurd to be a warning."

Captain Milford fumed. "A signal for whom? For what purpose?"

Marianne leaned toward Daniel. "What ship is that?" she asked, but the boy's attention was riveted aloft where excited chatter filtered down from above. She glanced back at the vessel. The gray sails faded against the darkening horizon and soon disappeared.

"That'll teach them!" the captain brayed as if he'd been responsible for the ship's retreat.

"It's a good ship, Miss Marianne." Daniel's voice rose above the wind, and he took her hand in his. "A good ship."

Marianne chuckled. "You are a curious lad, Daniel."

"Is that a good thing?" The mist pooling on his long lashes sparkled.

Giving his hand a squeeze, Marianne smiled. "A most excellent thing."

The mist transformed into raindrops that tapped over the deck and sounded like applause. Applause for what, Marianne didn't know. Perhaps for the ship that had dared to fire upon them, or perhaps for this young boy beside her who seemed more angel than human. As if to confirm her thoughts, Daniel held out a hand to catch the drops of rain, then he closed his eyes and lifted his peace-filled face to the wind, treasuring the moment. Innocent trust and glee in the midst of such chaos. She envied him.

Further commands to lower sail echoed across the ship. Shielding her eyes from the rain, Marianne looked aloft to see Noah descending. Her heart skipped as the details of his face came into view.

The captain grumbled, handed command of the ship to Lieutenant Reed, and dropped below deck. Marianne should follow him and tend to her duties below or risk his wrath, but the identity of their curious visitor kept her feet in place. Perhaps Noah could offer more information than Daniel's "good ship."

The rain fell harder, and Marianne drew Daniel close, dipping her head against the drops and the buffeting wind. The deck tilted, and she tightened her grip on the capstan. Her legs trembled.

Noah landed on the deck with a thud. He winced and stretched his shoulders beneath his wet shirt. The fabric clung to his corded muscles as red bands appeared across his back. Swinging about, his gaze landed on her and remained. He ran a hand through his wet hair and attempted a smile. Despite the rain, heat rose up her neck at the intense look in his eyes. Not the anger she expected. Quite the opposite, in fact.

Luke joined him, drawing Marianne's attention. She inched her way closer to them, keeping Daniel by her side.

Noah gave his first mate a look as if they shared a grand secret. "Did you see what I saw?" he said to Luke.

Luke smiled and lifted his brows. "I did, indeed."

"What did you see?" Marianne edged between them.

"That ship." Noah gestured to the span of agitated, foamy sea where the gray sails of the vessel had last been seen. "I'd know that ship anywhere."

Marianne shook her head.

"It was my ship, the *Fortune*."

❖ CHAPTER 20 ❖

The ship bucked. Marianne's feet lifted off the deck, and she tumbled against the bulkhead of her tiny cabin. Wind howled. Waves battered the hull with the fury of a jealous lover pounding on the door to his beloved's bedchamber. Dropping to her knees, Marianne gripped the bed frame and leaned her head against the mattress to resume her prayers. The sharp smell of aged burlap filled her nose.

Oh Lord, please do not let us perish in this storm.

The ship rose as if the great sea monster, Leviathan, had picked it up. Marianne clutched the wooden frame. The splinters bit into her skin.

Lightning flashed. An eerie shroud of gray passed through her cabin before plunging the room back into darkness.

Terror sent her mind reeling with visions of herself sinking beneath the violent waves. Gurgling, fuming water filled her mouth, her lungs and stole her last breath. She resumed her prayers. She prayed for her mother and sister back home. It may be the last chance she had to lift them up before God. *Oh Lord, take care of them please. Heal my mother and send someone who will provide for them.*

Thunder cracked a deafening boom in response. The ship trembled, mimicking her own body. The deck careened to the left. She propped herself against the bulkhead. Her thoughts went to the *Fortune* they'd spotted earlier. No doubt Matthew, Agnes, and the crew suffered in the midst of the storm as well. *And protect them, too, Father.*

Yet they had come.

The excitement in Noah's voice at the sight of his ship had been unmistakable. But Marianne dared not join in his optimism. A rescue seemed as impossible as this frigate surviving the ferocious gale that pummeled them.

The ship pitched, then dove. Something thumped to the floor. Groping in the dark, Marianne found the Bible Daniel had lent her. Clutching the Holy Book to her chest, she realized she'd not once opened it since he'd given it to her. "Oh Lord, forgive me. If you save us from this storm, I promise I'll read Your Word."

Yet even those words seemed to fall on empty ears as the ship bolted again. Marianne tumbled into the leg of the table attached to the bulkhead. Her arm throbbed.

Struggling to stand, she supported herself against the door and gazed out the heaving porthole. The sea splashed against the glass, only to be torn away by the howling wind. Lightning shot a white devil's fork across the sky. A chorus of thunder gave a demonic chuckle in its wake.

Marianne hugged herself. She squeezed her eyes against the tears threatening to spill down her cheeks. Her hope that God was indeed the personal God Daniel claimed Him to be faltered beneath a plethora of unanswered prayers and the continual storms that assailed her.

Storms that now seemed to culminate in the ferocious gale lashing the ship.

A strip of light seeped beneath her door, drifting over her shoes. *Pound pound pound.* She felt rather than heard someone knocking and moved to answer it. The oak slab began to open, pushing her back.

A burst of light filled the cabin and in walked Noah, lantern in hand.

Without thinking, she fell against him and clung to his shirt. She didn't care that he didn't love her. She didn't care that he didn't want her. She didn't care what propriety dictated. All she cared about was feeling his warm strength surround her. At least she would not die alone.

One thick arm embraced her and drew her close. Marianne buried her face in his shirt drawing a whiff of his scent. He hung the lantern on a hook and wrapped his other arm around her. Muscles as firm as wood encased her in a warm cocoon—a cocoon from which she never wished to break free.

"Never fear, Marianne. It will be all right."

"We shall all die in this storm," she sobbed.

He chuckled, and the rumble in his chest caressed her cheek.

The ship canted. Bracing his boots upon the deck, he gripped her tighter. "No, we will survive, I assure you. This is but a tiny squall."

"A tiny squall?" She lifted her gaze to his. Only a few inches separated them. His blue eyes drifted over her face as if soaking in every detail. They halted at her lips.

Her body warmed, and she pushed off of him. "Forgive me. My fear has relieved me of my senses."

"I made no complaint." A playful glint lit up his eyes.

Her heart leapt. Why wasn't he angry with her? Anger she could deal with. Hatred even. But not the desire, not the ardor she now saw burning in his gaze. The ship bolted, and she thumped against the bulkhead.

He gripped her shoulders. "Why didn't you tie yourself to the bed as you were instructed?" His gaze took in the ropes scattered across the deck.

"And drown in my bed when the ship sinks? I could not bear it."

His chuckle soothed her frayed nerves. He led her to the bed and gently nudged her down on the mattress. She gripped the frame and glanced out the undulating porthole. Surely if he found humor in the situation, the storm could not be as bad as it seemed.

He gathered the wayward ropes. "We will not sink. I've seen far worse than this out at sea."

"Truly?"

He smiled and ran a finger over her cheek. "Truly." Kneeling, he brushed the hair from her face. "Now, may I?" He held up the ropes.

"Tie me up?" She gave him a playful smile. "Wouldn't you enjoy that?"

His deep chuckle filled the cabin as he took her hand in his. "I did tease you quite harshly as a child, didn't I?"

Marianne swallowed, forcing down a lump of traitorous hope at his kindness. "If you call dipping my hair in tar teasing, I suppose. However, I prefer to call it cruelty."

Releasing her hand, he ran his fingers through her loose hair. "And such glorious hair, too."

Her mind whirled. Her breath threatened to burst through her chest. He was toying with her again. That was all. "Mother had to cut so much of it off that I looked like a boy for months."

"I doubt that would be possible."

Her insides dissolved. She must keep her wits about her. She must focus on his bad traits, on his ruthlessness. "And remember when you released a jar full of locusts in my bedchamber?"

He chuckled.

"I see nothing humorous about it." Marianne crossed her arms over her chest and she looked away.

Lightning flashed. The ship swooped over a swell. Noah grabbed her shoulders and drew her near.

Her heart thumped, but not from the storm this time. She lifted her gaze to his. Compassion and strength radiated from his eyes. She pushed back from him. "You've changed."

"Indeed?"

"Pray tell, what transformed the impish waif into a gentleman?" she asked.

His lips curved into a half smile that warmed her from head to toe. "A gentleman, you say?"

She looked away. "Don't let it swell that big head of yours."

With a touch to her chin, he brought her back to face him. "I wouldn't dream of it." He lowered his gaze. The lantern swayed above them, casting shifting shadows across the cabin. "Everything changed after my brother died."

Marianne watched as Noah's shoulders seemed to sink. He shrugged and played with the frayed edges of the ropes still in his hand. "Tragedy has a way of changing one's perspective."

She nodded, her thoughts drifting to how much her life had changed after her father's death.

"As well as reveal one's shortcomings." He sighed. "Then when I was unofficially promoted to captain of my father's ships, I had to grow up in a hurry."

As had Marianne. Forced to carry the burden of care for her ailing mother and younger sister, she found her imperious manner quickly crushed beneath the humbling rock of poverty.

Still kneeling before her, Noah shifted his weight to his other leg, seemingly oblivious to the oscillating deck. "And you, my princess, what transformed you into an angel?" he asked.

Heat burst onto her cheeks. *Angel?* "I was a bit of a highbrow, wasn't I?"

One side of his mouth lifted. "A question I shall refrain from answering."

Thunder bellowed. The sea rumbled against the hull.

"I was, and you know it." Marianne smiled then grew serious. "The same thing that changed you, I suppose. Tragedy." She gazed into his eyes, longing to see what emotions flickered there, but the lantern light swayed back and forth, giving her only glimpses of their deep blue color, taunting her. "I am sorry, Noah, for deceiving you about my inheritance." She swallowed. "There was no excuse for it."

"Yes there was." He took one of her hands again. "You did it for your mother. I understand."

Marianne's vision grew blurry.

He leaned toward her and whispered in her ear. "I'm truly sorry, Marianne, for every cruel joke I played upon you. The antics of a young brat." His hot breath tickled her neck. "Will you forgive me?"

Shock rendered her speechless. She'd never thought she would hear those words from Noah Brenin's lips. No doubt his guilt had gotten the better of him. "I'll consider it." She gave him a playful smile. "But you didn't come here to reminisce about our childhoods, did you?"

"I knew the storm would frighten you."

Sincerity rang in his voice. A lump formed in Marianne's throat, and she looked down.

His finger touched her chin, lifting her gaze to his. "Now will you allow me to tie you to this post so you don't injure yourself?"

She shook her head. That would mean she'd have to rely on him to untie her later on. She would have to trust that he'd remember and that if the ship sank, he'd come for her. "I cannot."

He frowned. "You don't trust me."

"Should I?"

The ship bucked and he balanced his knees on the deck. "Haven't I given you enough reason to?"

Remembering their childhood, she lifted a brow.

"As of late, I mean."

She sobered. "Yes, you have. But trust does not come easy for me, Noah." Thunder roared in the distance. "Everyone in this world has let me down."

Noah frowned and ran a thumb over the lines on her palm. "If you mean your father, I'm sure he never intended to cause you or your mother pain."

Tears burned behind Marianne's eyes. She watched Noah's thick, callused thumb caress her fingers, so small by comparison. His tenderness, his compassion wove its way deep into her soul, coaxing out of hiding a secret she'd never shared with anyone. "There's something you don't know." The words flew off her tongue before she'd had a chance to stop them.

He looked at her.

"My father's death was not an accident." Marianne squeezed her eyes shut. "He killed himself."

Noah's heart shriveled. *Killed himself.* Of all the horrors to endure. . .

"So, you see, he left us of his own free will," Marianne continued.

"Abandoned me, my mother and my sister." Though her voice remained composed, even cool, the moisture filling her eyes betrayed her.

"I'm sorry, Marianne." He didn't know what else to say. He'd suffered much rejection in his life but never something like that. "No doubt the shame of losing the family wealth was too much for him." Something Noah could well understand.

"It was his job to take care of us," she went on. "His responsibility to love us. And he let us all down." A tear slid down her cheek. "He and God."

He brushed the tear away with his thumb, his insides crumbling. "You can't blame God for what your father did."

"No? Then why hasn't He answered any of my prayers since? It's like God and my father both abandoned me at the same time."

Noah lowered his gaze. He understood that sentiment, for he had barely spoken to the Almighty since his brother fell to his death.

The ship rose—the pitch not as fierce this time. He squeezed her hand. Thunder rumbled from a distance. He tossed down the ropes, suddenly angry at her father. Angry at the man's cowardice. Angry that any man could leave his family uncared for—unprotected. Angry at what the man had done to this angel sitting before Noah.

The lantern light shimmered over her brown hair, setting select strands aflame in glistening red. He ran his fingers through it again, delighting in the soft curls swaying like waves over the shabby coverlet.

Her brown questioning eyes the color of rich mahogany searched his, yearning. How could he have ever found her plain? How could he have ever wanted her to break their engagement? A man would have to be a fool to let such a treasure escape his grip.

The ship bucked. He drew her close and held her tight. Her sweet breath feathered his jaw. He rubbed a thumb over her cheek and lowered his lips until they were but an inch from hers. Her feminine scent swirled around him, but she did not move, did not jerk away. He pressed his lips upon hers.

Sweet and soft, they met his kiss, caressing, loving. She clung to him, and his body responded. Heat waved through him as he absorbed himself in the taste of her.

His mind reeled with glorious thoughts. If they got off this ship, if she would still marry him, if she would allow him to, he'd vow to take care of her and protect her for the rest of her life.

Thunder bellowed. He withdrew. His heavy breaths matched hers, filling the air between them. Doubts assailed him. Had he truly won her affection or was her ardor born out of her desperate need for him to unlock her inheritance?

He studied her eyes still glazed with passion. No. That was not the kiss of a woman pretending affection.

"What was that for?" she asked softly.

He cupped her chin. "You enchant me, Miss Denton."

Shock sparked in her eyes.

"In fact you always have." Even when she was young and spoiled and full of herself. Something about her had grabbed hold of him. Which was probably why he'd bullied her so much.

A tear formed at the corner of her eye. "I've never enchanted anyone."

He smiled. "I doubt that."

Her nose pinked as it always did when her emotions ran high. He placed a gentle kiss on it.

Shouts filtered up from below. A gray hue swept the darkness from the porthole.

"I must go." Reluctantly releasing her, he stood and grabbed the latch of the door. "A new day dawns, my love. A grand new day." He winked. "For tonight we will escape."

"But how, Noah?" Fear skittered across her gaze.

"Trust me."

Unable to sleep after Noah left, Marianne bound her hair up in a loose bun, dabbed a moist cloth over her face and neck, and went to the galley to fetch the captain's breakfast of oatmeal and a biscuit. Carrying the tray, she nodded toward the marine who stood guard outside the cabin, then entered when the captain screamed her name.

"Where have you been? I've been awake for hours," he grumbled as he flipped his coat tails and took a seat at his desk.

"My apologies, Captain, but it's not yet eight bells, and I had no way of knowing you had risen." She squelched the frustration in her voice and instead kept her tone lighthearted.

This seemed to appease him as he took to his meal with gusto, all the while muttering about making port in Antigua, about meeting Admiral Pellew, and being entertained on the flagship. Marianne listened intently for any valuable information that she might pass on to Noah as she brushed off his dress uniform and polished his boots before laying them out beside his bed. But the only thing of import she gleaned was the captain's mention of receiving orders for his next mission—a mission he seemed most anxious to embark upon.

After he left, Marianne quickly scrubbed and polished the deck, eager to go above as soon as possible. With her eyelids heavy from lack of sleep and her chest still wound tight from last night's frightening storm, she hoped some fresh air would both revive and calm her. She hoped, too, that it might clear her head, still whirling with what had transpired between her and Noah last night.

As she rose above deck, a flurry of morning activity met her gaze. The majority of the crew were on their hands and knees holystoning the decks. Midshipmen sauntered about issuing orders at the petty officers who were armed with rattan canes with which to strike any laggards. A light breeze, fresh and crisp from the storm, wafted over Marianne, and she inhaled a deep lungful as she carefully made her way to the larboard railing. Above her, Captain Milford and his officers stood upon the quarterdeck, like masters of the sea, ruling the ship and the men upon it with an iron scepter.

Shielding her eyes from the rising sun, Marianne dared a glance aloft, seeking the cause of the ceaseless confusion in her mind and the odd feeling in her belly. But Noah's eyes had already locked on hers. A flicker of a smile lifted his lips.

"Land ho!" a cry came from above and all eyes scoured the horizon. A gray mound broke through the endless sea off their larboard bow.

Despite her doubts that Noah could orchestrate their escape, excitement flared in Marianne's chest at the sight of land. She'd been at sea so long, she was beginning to wonder if the earth hadn't been swallowed up by this vast blue ocean.

As the ship grew abuzz with activity, Marianne clung to the railing and did her best to keep out of the way. She did not want to go below and miss seeing the island grow as they drew near.

The sun rose into a clear cerulean sky that held no trace of last night's storm. She wished the same were true of her own heart, for she could not stop thinking about Noah's tenderness toward her—or his kiss. Heat rose up her neck in a wave. Though Marianne had no experience in the matter, she couldn't believe a man would kiss a woman with such passion unless he harbored some affection for her.

"You enchant me." His words bubbled in her heart like a fresh spring, soothing the parched places and dashing the cobwebs from the corners. She longed to embrace them, believe them, and allow her heart to soar with the hope that he truly loved her.

Yet somewhere deep down, fear arose, fear that it was just a dream, a cruel joke. He had made no declaration of affection, no declaration of intent. Perhaps he had simply been trying to allay her fears of the storm.

"Trust me." His last words to her echoed in her heart. And right now, she wanted to trust him more than ever.

Blinking the fatigue from his eyes, Noah focused on wrapping his toes around the footrope as tightly as he could. He elbowed Blackthorn and nodded toward the island that had just been announced as Antigua. Never had a piece of land looked more beautiful. With its sea of green vegetation swaying in the wind and its sparkling blue harbor, the island appeared more Eden than a British outpost. Each minute brought them closer, and soon Noah made out a thicket of masts bobbing in the harbor.

Blackthorn's tepid grin fell short of the enthusiasm Noah longed to see. In fact, the doubt screaming from the man's expression began to stomp on Noah's excitement. Yet he couldn't blame him. The last time Blackthorn had attempted to escape, he'd lost a friend and gained a flogging. But things would be different this time. Noah had made a promise to a certain special lady, after all.

He glanced down to the object of that promise, still clinging to the larboard railing. He loved her. This woman he'd once thought to be a plain, plump, and pompous woman. But she was none of those things to him anymore. When he weighed her on the scales against Miss Priscilla, Miss Priscilla became the common shrew and Marianne the beautiful lady. How could he have been so wrong?

She gazed up at him and smiled. His body reacted to the remembrance of their kisses.

A gusty breeze tore over him, the sweet smell of earth and life riding atop the scent of the sea. Though Noah had long since stopped believing in miracles—especially when it came to his own life— if Daniel had indeed heard from God, then maybe, just maybe the Almighty would grace them with a miracle now. At least for the sake of the boy and his father.

Noah glanced down at the quarterdeck where the captain stood, flanked by his officers. Two quartermaster's mates gripped the huge wheel as they took direction from the sailing master.

"A leadsman in the chains, if you please," the captain bellowed, and one of the sailors dropped the lead-and-line into the water to determine its depths as they approached the harbor.

"Hand the courses!" a command bellowed from below. "Release topsails!"

More hands clambered above to help Noah and the others carry out the captain's orders. The humid Caribbean air swamped around him. Sweat streamed down his back and stung his wounds. Once the courses were taken in, the frigate slowed, and calls from the forechains indicated they had plenty of depth to maneuver.

Noah dared a glance at the burgeoning harbor—a huge, glittering, turquoise bay separated in half by a hilly spit of land. The ship canted to starboard and headed toward the right fork. He squinted against the glare of sun on wave to see the dichotomy of ornately decorated brick buildings standing beside shabby wooden taverns and primitive thatched huts—all three dotting the harbor and extending into the green hills. The clamor of bells along with the squawk of gulls filled the air. An impressive gathering of ships of the line, ensigns flying high, bowed in the water like courtiers before the king.

"Prepare the anchor!"

Men scrambled to remove the lashings from the anchor catted to the starboard bulwark.

The quartermaster hoisted the ship's flags up on the halyard. They snapped in the warm breeze.

Noah climbed down to the deck as the order to back the foretops was given. Luke and several waisters hoisted on the lines to bring the bare yard around. As they passed what Noah assumed was the flag-ship, captain Milford gave the order to fire a salute and the starboard-forward-most gun roared its booming greeting.

Marianne covered her ears, and Noah gave her a gesture she hoped would allay her fears as one after another of the guns fired until six had spent their powder-only loads. Four thunderous booms cracked the sky in response from the flagship.

When the ship had slowed to but a crawl, Captain Milford gave the order to let go the anchor, and with a mighty splash the iron claw dove into the turquoise bay. The captain disappeared below, then emerged moments later in his full dress uniform. He climbed down into a boat that had been lowered in his absence and hoisted off from the frigate with a boatful of sailors at the oars. Excitement crackled in the air as the crew expressed their hope that they would be chosen to go ashore.

Noah's excitement joined with theirs. The others tasted rum and women.

But he tasted freedom.

❖ CHAPTER 21 ❖

Marianne swept through the captain's cabin, busying herself with dusting and making sure the captain's instruments and trinkets were in a line just as he demanded—even though everything had already been set in place. A quick glance out the stern window at the graying sky tinged with pink told her that it would soon be dark. The captain had been gone for hours and by the sound of the thrumming of feet above and the constant harping of an off-key fiddle, she guessed the crew was as anxious as she was to discover their next mission.

She yawned and opened her eyes wide, lest her lids drop like weights to her cheeks. Though she longed to retire for the night, she must remain awake and alert enough to play the spy when the captain returned. Noah and the others depended on her for any information that would tell them the best time to make their escape.

She had already poured the captain's nightly port and laid out his nightshirt. Glancing over the cabin, she searched for something to occupy her time and keep her awake when thumping sounded in the passageway. The door flew open, crashing against the bulkhead. Captain Milford charged in like a drunken bull, stuttering and staggering, and entangling himself in his dark blue coat as he tried to remove it. Lieutenant Garrick and Reed followed after him on a gust of hot wind tainted with sweat and rum.

Garrick gave her a salacious grin. Ignoring him, Marianne moved to the captain's side and helped him ease out of his boat cloak, then she hung it up in the armoire. The captain plopped into one of his stuffed chairs and released a heavy sigh. His officers stood at attention before him.

"What are you worthless toads still doing here?" he barked. "Go inform the crew that we are at war and will set sail as soon as the provisions are brought on board in the morning. And send up the surgeon."

At war? Marianne flinched. *Leaving in the morning?* Drat. Then they would have to escape tonight.

"Very well, Captain," both men said at once and then exchanged looks of disgust. For each other or for their captain, Marianne didn't presume to know. After saluting, they hurried out and closed the door, leaving Marianne alone with the drunken man.

Gathering her resolve, she knelt before him and tugged on his left boot. Though he was capricious, volatile, even cruel at times—not to mention half-mad—she no longer believed he would hurt her. He gazed at her with lifeless, wavering eyes. "You're a kind woman, Miss Denton. Would that I had a daughter like you."

The compliment settled over Marianne like a wet blanket—cold, uncomfortable, and unfamiliar. How she had longed to hear such approbation from her own father. A sudden need to cry burned in her throat.

"Did you enjoy your trip?" She kept her voice nonchalant and her focus on her task. One boot removed. Now for the other.

"The food was to my liking. The company, however, atrocious." He leaned his head back and closed his eyes.

"But surely your time with the admiral was rewarding?" Marianne grabbed his boots and stuffed them into the armoire.

"That blowhard. He doesn't know a great captain when he sees one.

Why, I fought beside Nelson at Copenhagen. I captured the French frigate *Vainqueur*. Not many men can make such a boast."

"But you mentioned war, Captain. Is it true?" Marianne inched her way back to him, clasping her hands together.

He gave a maniacal chuckle. "Aye. Your puny nation of rebels—if that is indeed from whence you hail—had the audacity to declare war on Britain a month ago. Can you believe it?"

A surge of pride lifted Marianne's shoulders—pride in her country, in her brave men and leaders. "I can. Since I have recently found myself beneath your unjust rule."

He flashed angry eyes her way and started to rise, and for a moment, Marianne feared she had stepped over the line. Then he sank back into the chair. "Never fear, we shall squash your pathetic rebellion within days." He laughed. "And you will once again be a subject of the crown."

"I am subject to no one, sir."

"And yet it would appear otherwise." He peered at her through half-closed eyes. "I need a drink."

"Perhaps you've had enough." Or perhaps she should allow him his liquor. It might loosen his tongue enough to supply her with further information. Or it might knock him unconscious, which would never do.

Wincing, he pressed a hand on his side. "Where is that blasted surgeon?" His head fell against the back of the chair, eyes closed and mouth open.

Marianne darted to his side. She must think of something to keep him talking. "Captain, captain." She shook his arms. "Tell me what happened to your side that it pains you so."

"Battle wound. Struck by a wooden spike this thick." He lifted his head for a moment and held his hands out to demonstrate the size of a skewer that would have killed him had it struck any part of his body.

"Oh my, Captain. How brave you are."

He drifted off again, and Marianne stomped her foot on the deck. She must discover his orders. Leaning forward, she whispered into his ear, "I'm sure the admiral has sent you on another important mission."

"Important. Balderdash!" His eyes popped open and he tried to stand. Marianne backed away and watched as he swayed like a spindly tree in a storm before falling back into the chair. "I'm to assist the HMS *Guerriére* patrolling the northern colonies and intercept and destroy the American ship USS *Constitution*. *Assist!*" he hissed, spittle flying from his mouth. "Me, an honored captain!"

Marianne smiled. Resisting the urge to run and find Daniel, she gazed at the man, reeling with drink and despair, before her. The lines on his face seemed especially long, making him look older than his fifty-three years. An ache formed in her heart for him. His bitterness, discontentment, and loneliness kept him locked in a prison that was far more formidable than the ship was to Marianne.

He lifted his head, mumbled something unintelligible, and then dropped it back again. The surgeon could not be relied on to arrive, and she couldn't very well leave him like this.

"Come now, Captain, let me help you to your bed. A good night's sleep and things will look better in the morning, to be sure." She eased her arm beneath his.

"I don't need your help!" He shot to his feet then tumbled to the left. Marianne reached out to catch him before he fell. His weight landed like a huge sack of grain across her shoulder, shooting pain down her back. She stumbled but managed to stay upright. A flood of alcohol-tainted breath stung her nose.

"Well, I suppose I do need help." He chuckled.

The door creaked open, and the surgeon appeared beside her. "Here, I'll take him, miss. You can go on now," he said, wiping sweaty strands of hair from his forehead.

Releasing the teetering man, Marianne spotted Daniel standing at the door awaiting her message, expectation flashing in his eyes. But as she stared at the surgeon's satchel and thought of the laudanum within it, then glanced over the bottles of rum lining the captain's shelves, a glorious thought occurred to her. A wonderful, mischievous thought.

Balancing the makeshift raft on his back, Noah inched his way up the companionway ladder. He peered above deck and scanned for any watchman looking their way. Nothing but a sliver of a moon smiling at him from the horizon and a gentle breeze laden with the scent of tropical flowers greeted him. He gestured for the others to follow and crept across the deck, keeping to the shadows and clutching his only weapon, a jagged piece of wood, close to his chest. One glance behind him told him that Blackthorn, Daniel, Weller, and Luke followed close upon his heels. Not a sound, not a footstep emanated from the group as they inched toward the quarterdeck. Well past midnight, the crew was fast asleep, all save a few watchmen above.

But he would take care of them.

War. The words Daniel conveyed to him earlier still spun in his mind. So President Madison had declared war. A month ago Noah would have been furious at the news. A month ago his main concern would have been the success of his merchant business. But much had happened since then.

America had every right to defend herself against the bullying tactics of Britain. And, by God, Noah would do all he could to aid his country's efforts to shake off their tentacles of tyranny.

Not the least of which was to escape this ship.

A shape formed out of the darkness. Noah threw his hand up and halted as did those behind him.

The sound of deep snoring filtered over him like a soothing balm. The watchman sat on the deck just beneath the quarterdeck ladder, his chin on his chest, fast asleep. Noah eyed the musket in the man's grip and thought better of trying to pry it from him. Instead, he swept a glance across the foredeck where he expected to find another watchman at his post. Instead a dark mound lay crumpled beside the mast. Noah scratched his head. Though only a few men were assigned night watch when anchored at a British port, he had not expected them both to be asleep—a condition that if discovered would mean their certain death.

Perhaps God *was* on his side, after all.

He inched up the quarterdeck ladder and past the helm where another watchman lay curled in a ball by the wheel. Astounding. Shaking his head, he passed him and made out a shape by the mizzenmast. He hoped it was Marianne. After Daniel had delivered the message that they were to set sail in the morning, Noah had sent the boy back to her with the request that she meet them at the larboard stern at four bells of the middle night watch.

As she came into view, his heart leapt. Milky moonlight trickled over her, transforming her hair into chocolate and her skin into rich cream. Instead of the fear he expected to see on her face, a catlike grin played upon her lips as she held up a dark uncorked bottle.

"What's this?" he whispered as the others crowded around. He set down the tiny raft.

"It *was* laudanum," she replied.

"Was?"

Luke chuckled.

Marianne gestured to two empty bottles perched at the foot of the mizzenmast. "The watchmen were quite eager to have an extra ration of grog." She smiled. "A special concoction of rum and laudanum does wonders for a good night's slumber."

Noah brought her hand to his lips. "Clever, brave girl. But how were you able to steal the captain's rum and the laudanum?"

"The captain sleeps soundly." She shrugged. "And I slipped the laudanum from the surgeon's pouch while he put the captain to bed."

Daniel darted to her side and gave her a hug. "I knew you could do it, Miss Marianne," he whispered.

She returned the lad's embrace.

Weller mumbled something and Blackthorn, with a thick rope looped over his shoulder, took up a position at the helm, scouring the deck with his nervous gaze.

Marianne retrieved the two empty bottles, walked to the railing, and tossed them into the water. Their splashes joined the slap of waves against the hull. Facing them, she drew a breath as if trying to gather courage from the humid air around them. "Where is our boat?"

"There is no boat." She inhaled a tiny breath and Noah stepped toward her. A breeze played with a rebellious curl lingering at her neck. He longed to touch it, if only to soften the words he had just spoken.

Even in the shadows, he could see the whites of her eyes widen. And a tiny wrinkle appear between her brows. "How are we to get to shore?"

Noah took her hand. "We swim."

"But I can't swim." Her hand trembled and she tried to tug it from him, but he fastened his grip and led her back to the mast. Releasing her, he grabbed the tiny raft. "I made this for you. You can float on it. I'll pull you along."

Marianne gazed at the tiny piece of wood—part of a crate, from the looks of it. Every nerve in her body rebelled. "I can't possibly." Terror constricted her throat. She couldn't breathe.

Daniel looked up at her. "It'll be all right, Miss Marianne."

She glanced toward the port town. Nothing but a few blinking lights remained to mark the row of shops, taverns, and warehouses she'd spotted earlier in the day. Miles of water as dark as coal stretched between them and those lights. And in the middle, a maze of British warships barred their passage.

"But how. . .impossible. . .it won't hold me."

Noah shook the crate and then struck it with his hand. "It's sturdy. It will hold you, I promise."

Lowering herself into a small boat would have been difficult enough—something she had spent the day preparing herself to do—but trusting a crate no bigger than a man's chest was beyond the pale. A milky haze eased over the dark waves like an eerie mist. She hugged herself.

"We are all strong swimmers, miss." Luke urged her with his eyes. "We'll help you to shore."

"Aye, miss." Mr. Weller approached, a frown etched across his forehead. "No need to worry. I wouldn't let nothing happen t'you." He fingered the scar on his neck then tugged his scarf up over it.

The sea licked its greedy tongue against the creaking hull of the ship. Marianne's head grew light. Drawing Daniel close, she stepped back into the shadows and leaned against the mizzenmast for support.

Mr. Weller's gaze skittered nervously over the deck. "We must go."

Blackthorn left his post, crept to the railing, and began tying his rope to the gunwale. Weller and Luke joined him.

Noah's eyes reached out to her like a lifeline. "Trust me." He extended his hand.

Marianne swallowed. She wanted to trust him. She wanted to be able to trust someone again. She wanted to get off this ship. But her will was having difficulty forcing her body to comply. She nodded and lifted her hand to take Noah's outstretched one...

...when a sinister voice blared over them, tinged with sarcasm. "What have we here?"

Clutching Daniel, Marianne slipped into the shadows toward the stern.

Noah froze, his shoulders slumped. Beyond him, Lieutenant Garrick stood hands on his hips and a bestial smirk on his thin lips.

Marianne covered her mouth to suppress a scream. *No, Lord. Not this.* She pushed Daniel behind her and stepped farther back into the darkness where they would not be seen.

Blackthorn, Weller, and Luke faced their enemy, their faces pale.

Noah slowly turned around. He dropped the raft to the deck with a clunk.

"I'll have you all court-martialed and put to death for this." Lieutenant Garrick's chuckle bubbled over the deck, so at odds with his grim statement. "Were you all to fit on that?" He picked up the raft and examined it. Then setting it on the deck, he stomped it with his boot, breaking it in half.

The crunch and snap of the wood skewered any hope left within Marianne.

"Odious cur," Weller mumbled.

"What did you say?" Garrick peered around Noah toward the three men at the railing.

"He said you are an odious cur, sir." Luke grinned, not an ounce of fear on his face.

Garrick's eyes narrowed, and he started toward Luke. Noah stepped in the way and pushed the man back.

The insolence fled the lieutenant's face, replaced by fear. "Guards!" His smirk returned but fell when no footsteps answered his call.

Luke barreled forward. As did Blackthorn and Weller.

Garrick drew his sword and leveled it at Noah's chest. "Not another step or I'll run him through. Guards!"

A red spot blossomed on Noah's shirt beneath the point.

Marianne's stomach collapsed. Daniel gripped her hand from behind. His whispered prayers rose on the wind.

Luke and Blackthorn charged Garrick. Noah ducked and rammed his body into the Lieutenant's torso. Marianne stopped breathing. Garrick toppled to the deck with a thump. His sword flew into the air, struck the binnacle, and toppled to the waist of the ship with a *clank*. His bicorn landed beside him.

Before the man could recover, Noah, his face a mass of rage, lifted Garrick up by the lapels of his dark coat and slugged him across the jaw.

Garrick stumbled backward, terror screaming from his pointy face. "Guards!"

This time, grumbling sounded from the foredeck. The dark mass of the watchman struggled to his feet and peered in their direction.

"Time to go." Luke urged.

"It's certain death now if we don't." Blackthorn peered into the darkness. "Come along, son." Slipping from behind Marianne, Daniel darted toward his father and the two of them started over the railing.

Noah released Garrick and shoved him aside.

"You'll never get away." Garrick straightened his coat, his voice quavering. "I'll have the marines after you in moments."

"Only if you're able to tell them where we are." Noah slammed his fist across the lieutenant's jaw once again. Garrick's head snapped backward, and he fell to the deck in a heap.

Noah turned to Marianne. "Let's go." He grabbed her hand and tugged her to the railing. Luke dove into the water. Blackthorn and Daniel clambered down the rope to the black sea below. Weller straddled the bulwarks and gave Marianne one last look of concern before he held his nose and dropped over the side. *Splash.*

The watchman tumbled down the foredeck ladder and made his way across the main deck.

Noah swung over the gunwale then reached back for Marianne. "Hold on to me. I'll help you down."

Terror clamped her every muscle, nerve, and fiber. "I can't, Noah. There is no raft."

"I'm a strong swimmer. You can hang onto my back." His eyes, brimming with concern, pleaded with her. He nodded as if to reinforce his statement. As if that would somehow dissipate all her fears.

She wished with all her heart that it would.

The watchman's heavy steps sounded on the quarterdeck ladder.

"I can't." She stepped back, knowing all too well the hopeless life she chose. But better to be alive and a prisoner than dead at the bottom of the sea. "Go without me."

Noah's jaw tightened. "No. Come." He held out his hand. "Please trust me, Marianne."

She couldn't. She couldn't trust him. Not him, not anyone, not even God. "The captain's orders are to rendezvous with the HMS *Guerriére* in the north and find and destroy the USS *Constitution*."

"Why are you telling me this now?" Noah huffed. "Come!" He held out his hand.

"It's too late. The marine will see us." She glanced over her shoulder. "Go. I'll divert his attention."

"Who goes there?" the watchman's slurred voice shot over them.

Tears burned in her eyes. She stepped back again. "I'm sorry, Noah."

The watchman's boots thumped upon the quarterdeck. "What's this about?"

Pain, desperation screamed from Noah's eyes. "I'll come back for you." He glanced at the guard then below at the water, then back at her. "Do you hear me? I will come back for you."

But Marianne dared not hope. Promises made were promises broken. She longed to run into his arms, if only to feel his strength surround her one last time. A tear slipped down her cheek.

Then he disappeared over the side.

A splash bellowed hollow and empty.

Swiping her moist cheeks, Marianne turned to face the marine.

"Oh, it's you, Miss Denton. I thought I heard voices." He lowered his musket and swayed on his feet.

"My apologies, Mr. Jameson. I couldn't sleep." Marianne hoped he didn't hear the quaver in her voice nor see Lieutenant Garrick's unconscious form lying in the shadows by the railing.

"Very well." He swung about and stumbled on his way.

Releasing a sigh of relief, Marianne turned and loosened the rope from the bulwarks. The thick hemp dropped to the bay with a hollow swish. She gripped the railing and peered into the thick darkness. Not a trace of the five men, not a shimmer, splash, or flicker marked their passage.

Her legs crumpled like loose ropes and she fell to the deck. They had left her.

Noah had left her.

❖ CHAPTER 22 ❖

Noah dragged his drenched body onto shore and dropped onto the sand. His heart felt as heavy and saturated as his clothes—as empty as his lungs as he gulped to fill them.

He could not shake the look on Marianne's face right before he dropped into the sea—the look of pure terror and desperation. And it had taken every ounce of his strength to leave her.

But he had no choice.

Or did he? During the long, arduous swim ashore, he'd had plenty of time to replay every painful detail in his mind. Should he have grabbed her and forced her to go? But how could he swim with a hysterical woman clawing at him? Both of them would have drowned. Then there was the problem of the approaching watchman. Marianne had been right. They wouldn't have made it very far if he had seen them and alerted the ship. He wondered what had become of Garrick. Had he awoken? He assumed not.

Noah could still hear Marianne's soft voice as she mollified the watchman's suspicions. Protecting them. So they could get away.

While they left her behind.

His gut churned. Waves washed over his legs, trying to drag him back into the sea. Which was what he deserved or worse.

Weller crawled up beside him. Followed by Luke and Blackthorn with Daniel clinging to his back. Their heavy breaths sounded like a flock of birds frightened into flight.

Digging his hands into the sand, Noah lifted himself to his knees. No time to rest. They had chosen a spot far away from the lights of town, but that didn't mean they were safe. "Follow me," he whispered, struggling to his feet.

Trudging through the sand, he made out a clump of shadowy vegetation in the darkness. His gut roiled. If he had stayed with Marianne, he would have been court-martialed and hanged. What good would he be to her dead? Noah was sure Lieutenant Garrick had not seen her in the shadows. Therefore, she could not be implicated in their escape. She would survive.

She must survive.

Self-loathing rose like bile in his throat. What sort of man left the woman he loved in such a dangerous place? *Woman he loved*. The truth struck him like the sharp wind that now blasted over him.

Shivering, he batted away the leaves of a nearby tree and plunged into the jungle. The smell of earth and life saturated his nose. If they could make their way to a less inhabited side of the island, stay hidden, and avoid British authorities, Noah hoped to be able to spot the *Fortune*. He had a feeling Matthew would be searching for them. He knew because that was exactly what Noah would do.

The twigs and leaves of the forest crunched beneath his bare feet, biting into his skin. Noah fisted his hands and tromped through the underbrush, one thought, one purpose driving him forward. Once he got off this island, he would rescue Marianne from that British frigate. Even if he died trying.

Marianne stared at the deckhead above her bed. Since dawn had broken and dared to force its light upon the callous darkness of her cabin, she had occupied her time counting every divot and scratch in the fine oak. What else could she do? Her body, numb from shock and agony, refused to move from the supine position it had assumed upon her mattress after she'd spilled every last tear onto the coverlet. Nor did she want to move. If she were forced to get up and greet the day, she'd be forced to accept that she was all alone, without a friend, without any help, without hope aboard an enemy frigate. And that reality would surely crush her beneath its massive weight.

"Miss Denton!" the captain's growl blared down the passageway and screeched beneath her door. Either he wanted his breakfast or he'd discovered her friends' escape. She supposed she should be frightened that he'd also discovered she'd given rum to the guards, but she could find no fear within the numbness that consumed her. Unless she'd be punished for the offense or hanged, the day loomed before her with endless scrubbing, buffing, polishing, rinsing, and cleaning. Not to mention listening for hours to the captain's rumblings and bracing herself to endure his rapid shifts from madness to complacency.

As far as Marianne could see, an endless, pointless future extended out before her like a dark tunnel that sped to hell but never quite arrived.

Closing her eyes against the pounding in her head, she struggled to sit. Daniel had told her God had a great purpose for everyone. If this was hers, she wondered if she could politely decline.

"Miss Denton!"

Rising, she ran her fingers through her hair—still damp from the thousand tears she'd shed—and tried to pin it up. Then attempting to press the wrinkles from her skirts, she took a deep breath and gathered the resolve she needed to face her bleak future. God had a destiny for her all right. It just wasn't a very pleasant or important one.

Opening her door, she headed toward the captain's cabin. Nodding at the marine guard, she stepped into the lion's den.

Where vile curses curled her ears.

"Where have you been, Miss Denton?" Slouching in one of his chairs, the captain lifted a hand to squeeze the bridge of his nose.

"Lieutenant Garrick has disturbed my sleep with some rather unsettling news."

Marianne felt the blood race from her heart. She stepped forward and followed the captain's gaze to see Lieutenant Garrick standing behind the open door.

Instead of the usual smirk on his mouth, a red gash slashed across his swollen bottom lip while a dark purple blotch marred his left jaw and spread upward to cover his bloated cheek.

Marianne suppressed a smile. "What news, Captain?"

Garrick shifted his weight, his eyes fuming. "Do you see that? She smiles."

"Perhaps she finds amusement in your clownish appearance." Captain Milford released a long sigh and rubbed his temples. No doubt he suffered from his overindulgence in drink last night. "How ridiculous you appear, sir. A lieutenant in His Majesty's Navy allowing himself to be assaulted by ignorant Americans—and on board a warship. Absurd!"

Garrick's chest heaved. His face reddened.

"Captain, allow me to fetch your breakfast," Marianne offered. "You don't look well."

"I don't feel well either!" Grunting, he inched to the edge of his chair and rose. "Miss Denton, it appears some of the crew escaped last night."

"Oh?" She forced innocence into her tone despite the angst churning in her gut.

"Lieutenant Garrick believes you were complicit in their plans. . . may have even aided them?" The captain's stern voice held a hint of disbelief as he ambled to the center of the cabin.

Garrick fumbled with the bicorn in his hand. He glared her way.

"Me?" Marianne swallowed. "That's absurd. Who escaped?"

"The men from your merchant ship and a few others of my crew."

Marianne twisted the ring on her finger. "Indeed?" She feigned shortness of breath and clutched a hand to her chest. "They left me." Yet she didn't have to feign the pain burning in her heart.

The captain pressed a hand to his side. "Those loathsome rebels! I'll have them all hanged when I find them!"

Marianne looked down, holding her breath.

"It's the treasonous wench you should hang, Captain." Garrick gestured toward her. "She assisted them."

"Me?" Marianne clutched her throat. "How could I have helped them? I was tucked in my bed all night." She cringed at the lie, but it couldn't be helped.

Garrick's jaw stiffened. "Captain, I implore you. Lock her up at once."

"Preposterous!" Captain Milford gave an incredulous snort. "She's but a silly woman and certainly incapable of such treachery. I'll hear no more of it." He studied Garrick. "But you!" He crooked a thick finger toward the lieutenant. "Allowing ill-bred Yankees to beat you and then escape beneath your nose. Shame on you, sir!"

Lieutenant Garrick looked as though he would explode. Even his red hair seemed aflame atop his head. "Four against one, Captain."

"Fully armed, you couldn't subdue a cow." The captain huffed. "If it weren't for the money your father pays me to keep you here—or should I say to keep you away from home—I'd have tossed you back to Portsmouth long ago."

Marianne blinked at the news, amazed that such arrangements were made. However, it did offer an explanation as to why the captain tolerated a rogue like Lieutenant Garrick.

Garrick's eyes simmered. "But I *am* here, Captain. And you do accept the payment."

"Do not test me, sir." Captain Milford seethed. "Or I may find the extra coins have lost their luster."

A moment of silence passed between them before the captain waved a hand in dismissal. "Send in the watchmen who were on deck last night. Drunk on duty. I'll have them all flogged!"

Marianne's stomach curdled. *Flogged?* Because of her. Because she'd tempted them with rum. Maybe she should confess—tell the captain it was her fault. Perhaps he'd lessen their punishment.

Or perhaps he'd have her flogged right alongside them. Or worse. Perhaps he'd realize her complicity in the escape and have her hanged. She bit her lip. *Lord, please do not let him punish those men.*

Grinding his teeth together, Mr. Garrick turned to leave, then stopped. "What of the deserters, Captain?"

"I have no time to search for them now." Swerving about, the captain stared out the stern windows where the first rays of the sun seemed to hesitate, cowering, outside the panes. "We must get underway. As soon as the supplies arrive, prepare the ship to sail. I'll be on deck shortly. And you, Miss Denton, bring me my blasted tea and biscuit!"

Lieutenant Garrick donned his hat and knuckled a salute before he stormed from the room. Marianne followed him out and shut the door before she realized her error. Halfway down the passageway, the lieutenant turned on her. His eyes boiled like lava. "I know you helped them," he spat out through his swollen lips.

Marianne cleared the tremble from her voice. "You know no such thing, Mr. Garrick."

He snorted and a sultry grin formed on his lips. "Your fiancé left you, eh? No one around to stand up for you anymore." He ran a finger over her cheek and she stepped back.

"I'll find proof that you helped your friends escape and when I do, you'll have to choose between me and the noose."

Marianne shuddered. The noose would win. But she dared not anger him further by telling him so.

With a coarse chuckle, he turned and marched away.

Marianne released the breath that had stuck in her throat. Her future looked bleak. Bleak indeed.

From her position at the stern, Marianne gazed at the island of Antigua as it faded to gray in the distance. Somewhere on that island were Noah, Luke, and the others. At least she hoped they had made it safely to shore.

And weren't locked in some horrid British prison.

A shiver coursed through her, and she gripped her belly. Daniel's sweet face filled her mind, and she chided herself for thinking only of her own poor predicament. Thank God he and his father were finally off this ship. And Weller and Luke. And of course Noah. He had been brutalized aboard this ship because of her. Now he was free. For that she was grateful.

Oh, why hadn't she simply jumped overboard? Wouldn't it have been better to drown than suffer her present fate? She had wanted to. Had desperately wanted to trust Noah.

I am a coward. A coward who trusts no one.

The ship bucked and she braced her feet against the deck. A gust of brine-scented wind whipped her hair and cooled the perspiration on her neck. Above her, the sun inched toward its high command for the day. The captain would be wanting his noon meal soon. His commands blared across the ship from his position on the quarterdeck. No doubt he was still furious about the escape.

She couldn't help but smile. But it quickly faded as a vision of the pleading look on Noah's face crossed her mind. He said he'd come back for her.

But as the island sunk below the horizon and dropped out of sight—just as Noah had done over the railing—she knew that would not be possible. Even if he connected with his merchant ship, even if he could convince his men to pursue the HMS *Undefeatable*, Noah's ship was no match for a British frigate. That much she had learned.

Besides, who would try to defeat a ship named *Undefeatable*?

Especially to free an ordinary woman like her.

No. There would be no rescue party coming to save her. She was destined to serve Captain Milford aboard this ship of horrors for as long as God determined. And from the looks of things, that may be a long time indeed.

Unless, of course, she was hanged for aiding in the men's desertion.

Lieutenant Garrick's threat reignited her fear. She would do her best to avoid being alone with him, but eventually he would trap her. That, too, she must accept.

The captain barked at her and headed down the quarterdeck stairs. Releasing the mast, Marianne turned, all life and hope draining out of her feet onto the deck as she followed him below.

Noah clutched Matthew's hand and swung over the bulwarks. Planting his sandy feet on the deck—his deck, the deck of the *Fortune*—he embraced his friend. "I knew I could count on you."

The man's bald head gleamed in the morning sun nearly as bright as his smile. "Alls we had to do was follow you. I knew ye'd find a way to escape sooner or later."

"How did you find us?" Noah and his men had been hiding in a clump of trees on the southwest side of Antigua, living off coconut milk and crabs for three days.

Luke clambered over the railing, followed by Weller, Blackthorn, and Daniel.

"I figured if you escaped when the ship anchored, you'd be somewhere away from the Brits hiding amongst the trees. All I had to do was sail real slow-like around the island till I spotted your signal fire." He winked.

Noah stretched his back, still raw from the flogging.

Daniel's eyes lit up. "So this is your ship, Mr. Noah?"

"Yes, it is." He tousled the boy's hair and scanned the deck as his crew swamped him with greetings.

"We thought you was gone for sure, Cap'n," Mr. Rupert said.

"Good to have you back, sir," Mr. Pike shouted.

"What's it like on one of them British frigates?" another sailor asked.

"Thank you all." Noah scanned his men. "Not a pleasant experience, I assure you."

Blackthorn eased beside Noah and shook the water from his hair, reminding Noah of a wet bear. "Nice ship, Brenin."

Noah smiled.

"Weller made it back without losing any more of his fingers!" Mr.

Rupert said, and they all chuckled.

Agnes emerged from the crowd and absorbed Noah in her fleshy arms, nearly squeezing the life from him. "I was so worried about you, son." She held him back and took a good look at him. Noah felt a blush rising up his neck.

"A bit skinny, but you look well." She slapped his belly then glanced over at Luke and the others. "Where's Miss Denton?"

Noah opened his mouth to tell her, but the words withered on his lips.

"We had to leave her behind." Luke frowned.

"You what?" Her face grew puffy and her eyes sharp. She faced Noah. "You did what?"

"It couldn't be helped, Agnes." The breeze tore his words away as if they bore no weight.

Her eyes filled with tears. "That poor dear. All alone on that enemy ship."

"Don't worry, ma'am." Daniel sidled up to the large woman. "We're going to go rescue her, aren't we, Mr. Noah?"

"That we are." Noah said with as much conviction as he could muster. Problem was, he didn't know how.

"And who might this be?" Agnes drew Daniel into the folds of her skirt.

"My son, Daniel." Blackthorn ran a sleeve over his forehead and stood tall. He exchanged a look with Noah and Luke. "Feels good to be able to claim the lad as my own."

Agnes pushed Daniel's hair from his face. "Why, you sweet boy. What were you doin' on that ship?"

"God's work, ma'am." Daniel smiled up at her.

"An' I'd say he fared better than the rest o' us because of it." Weller tugged at the scarf around his neck and laughed—the first laugh Noah had heard the man utter since they'd been impressed by the British.

"Indeed." Daniel's prophesy of rescue leapt into Noah's mind, and he eyed the boy curiously. Coincidence? Or did the lad truly hear from God? But he didn't have time to ponder it now. Marianne was in trouble. "Haul in the boat!" he ordered. "We set sail immediately."

Luke began braying orders to the crew, sending them scampering across the deck.

Noah turned to his boatswain. "What is the status of the ship, Matthew?"

Matthew scratched his bald head. "We dumped all the rice and flour that got wet, Cap'n. Still got the cloth we can sell. But as far as sailin' goes, she's fit as a fiddle."

"Good." Noah nodded and glanced at the glistening shores of Antigua a mile off their larboard side then shifted his gaze to the endless turquoise sea. His gut twisted in a knot. Agnes's sorrowful eyes met his, and he knew her thoughts must also be of Marianne.

"Never fear, Agnes, I'll get her back."

She pursed her lips. "I'll hold you to that, Noah." Then with a swipe to rid her face of tears, she gathered Daniel close and led him away. "I bet you're a might starved, too, little man."

Later, in his cabin, with his belly full, Noah leaned back on his desk and faced a line of his men. Luke, Matthew, Mr. Weller, Mr. Pike, Mr. Boone, Blackthorn, and Daniel.

Mr. Pike shuffled his feet. "This is self-destruction, Cap'n." He kneaded the hat in his hands. "The crew ain't sure they want to be a part of it."

Noah shifted his back, glad to be out of the filthy garb the British had given him to wear and back into his own clothes. Rays of morning sun angled in through the stern windows, creating spears of glittering dust through the air.

"We can still make some money with the goods left in the hold." Mr. Boone's voice lifted in enthusiasm. "The trip won't be a complete loss."

Seafoam arched her back and rubbed against Noah's side. He picked her up and scratched her head, surprised that he'd actually missed the cat.

Matthew shook his head. "I like Miss Denton, too, Noah, but chasin' after a British frigate with no plan as to how to rescue the lady, why it be sheer madness."

"You'll get us all killed." Weller scratched the scar on his face and muttered to himself. "Or worse, impressed again."

Blackthorn nodded. "I know I'm not a part of this crew, but I've been on that frigate long enough to know there's no way to get close enough to get Miss Denton off without waking their broadside."

Setting the cat down, Noah folded his hands over his chest, fighting back a wave of frustration. "Yet *we* got off."

"Aye, in a British port." Blackthorn scratched the hair sprouting from the collar of his shirt. "It's the only time the frigate won't be guarded so heavily. Now, that we're at war, we won't be able to get within a stone's throw of a British port should the HMS *Undefeatable* anchor in one again."

Seafoam sauntered over to Daniel.

Noah gripped the edge of his desk until his fingers hurt. Blackthorn was right. They were all right. Then why did everything within him scream in defiance. He gazed at Luke, who stood eyeing them all, unusually silent. The bruises on his face had faded to yellow.

" 'Sides," Mr. Boone joined in. "I hear the lady won't go in the water. How are we to rescue her? Sprout wings?"

"Impossible." Blackthorn shook his head and gave Noah a sympathetic look.

Daniel picked up Seafoam and gazed up at his father. "But, Pa, nothing's impossible with God."

"Hush, lad." Blackthorn put a hand atop Daniel's head. "And from what I've seen, Noah, you don't have more than eight guns onboard. Four pounders at that."

Frustration bubbled in Noah's stomach. "What do you say, Mr. Heaton?"

Luke grinned, then shrugged one shoulder. "I say we have a lady to rescue."

"That's the spirit, Mr. Luke!" Daniel cuddled the cat to his chest, and Noah could hear the deep rumble of her purrs from where he sat.

Well, at least Noah had one man and a boy on his side. And a cat.

"Have the both of you gone mad?" Matthew shifted his wide eyes between Noah and Luke.

Noah held up a hand, silencing him. "Gentleman, there is a fully armed British ship of war sailing up the coast of America—the coast of our great nation, *our* coast. She intends to do us harm. She intends to sink our ships, impress our men, and steal from us the freedoms we fought so hard to gain. On that ship is a young American girl held against her will."

Noah took up a pace before the men, examining each one in turn. A surge of strength, of purpose, billowed within him. "We know where this frigate is going. She and her companion hope to engage the USS *Constitution* and sink her to the depths. How can we go about our way and ignore our duty? How can we close our eyes and concern ourselves with money when the very future of our nation hangs in the balance?"

He stopped, blood surging to his fists. "We are Americans. We are a people who stand up for what is right, who do not tolerate injustice, who will do anything for the cause of liberty. Even risk our own lives."

The men remained still, their eyes riveted on him.

"How can we do anything but follow our enemy and do everything we can to thwart her evil plans *and* rescue Miss Denton?"

Matthew's expression twisted. "You've changed, Noah."

"Spend some time on a British warship and see if it doesn't inspire your patriotism." Noah snorted.

A tiny grin played at the corner of Blackthorn's lips. Matthew gave Noah a knowing look while Mr. Boone and Mr. Pike stared out the stern windows.

"But what can we do?" The glee in Mr. Weller's eyes, present since their rescue, had dissipated, and Noah hated himself for it.

"I don't know." He lengthened his stance. "Gentlemen, let us follow this ship the British call the *Undefeatable* and find out if she lives up to her name." He scanned his men, searching their eyes for compliance. "Who's with me?"

"Aye." Luke smiled.

"I am," Mr. Pike and Mr. Boone said simultaneously.

"We are!" Daniel burst out, then tugged on his father's sleeve. "Aren't we, Pa?"

Blackthorn gave a reluctant nod.

Noah glanced at Matthew. The old man shrugged. "You know I'll sail wit' you where'er you go."

"And what is your decision, Mr. Weller?" Noah asked. "I will put ashore all those not wishing to join us. No one would fault you for it."

Weller grunted, then shook his head. "You promised to get me off that British frigate, Cap'n, an' you stuck to your word. Nay, I'm goin' wit' you. Even though I still don't think it's a good idea."

"Thank you, Mr. Weller." Emotion clogged Noah's throat at his men's loyalty, especially since most of them knew the price they would pay if the British caught them again.

"Very well." Noah planted his fists at his waist and cleared his throat. "Luke, inform the rest of the crew of our mission. Those who do not wish to join us will be dropped off at Charleston on the way north."

Ignoring the fear that most of his men would abandon him, Noah dismissed his friends and watched as they slowly marched from the cabin. His friends, indeed. For he doubted he'd find a more loyal bunch.

And he hoped to God he wasn't leading them all to their deaths.

❖ CHAPTER 23 ❖

Marianne set the captain's polished boots beside his bed and examined the black leather gleaming in the lantern light. Perfect. Tucking the rag into the pocket of her skirt, she turned to face the captain, hoping he wouldn't overindulge in drink tonight.

Her hopes faded when she saw him pouring yet another glass of brandy. She studied him as he stood alone with his thoughts, unaware of her censure. Dark circles tugged his eyes downward. The lines on his faced etched a sad tale. He sipped his brandy and stared into the darkness beyond the stern windows as if he wished he were somewhere else. Anywhere else. The light from lanterns swaying overhead sent the buttons lining his lapel shimmering like gold, but their luster fell flat when reflected off his haggard face.

Marianne's heart sank for this man.

It had been two weeks since they'd left Antigua. Two miserably long weeks in which Marianne's agitated emotions had gone from despondency to anger to sorrow and finally to a benumbed acceptance of her fate. If God wanted her to be a slave on board an enemy ship, if He wanted her mother and sister to go uncared for, then so be it.

She would accept her destiny. Accept it, yes, but not without feeding a growing anger toward a God who was supposed to care for and love her.

But as John Milton said his poem, "Comus," *"A sable cloud turns forth its silver lining on the night,"* such a silver lining had shone on Marianne's recent storms. For Lieutenant Garrick had not followed through with his threat to prove her involvement in her friends' escape. Nor had he made any advances toward her. In addition, the drunken watchmen made no mention of her actions and had only received a dozen lashes each.

Gazing back at Captain Milford, she cringed in shame at her self-pity, for he was just as much a prisoner as she. Possibly more so. She headed toward his desk to clear off the dishes from his supper and hopefully make a quick exit, but his eyes latched on her as if he just remembered he was not alone.

Marianne picked up the tray. "Is there anything else I can get for you, sir?"

He tossed the remaining brandy into his mouth, then poured himself another glass. "What do you think of your friends leaving you, Miss Denton?" His jaw tightened. "Egad, your fiancé!" He shook his head and stared out the window. "My wealth for a loyal, honorable man. Are there any left in the world, do you suppose?"

Must he remind her? Must he rub salt in the wound when it was still so fresh? Marianne's hands began to shake. The dishes clanked, and she set down the tray. "He really wasn't my fiancé." She hoped the truth of the statement would soothe the ache in her heart, if only a little. It didn't.

The captain let out a "humph," then eyed her, his eyes misty. "Do you think me a monster, Miss Denton, for keeping you on this ship?"

Marianne flinched. She wrung her hands, wondering how to respond so as not to set this volatile man into another one of his tirades. Yet what difference would it make? What could he do to her that could make her situation any worse? Lock her in the hold? She would welcome the change of pace. Hang her from the yardarm? Then she would be free at last. Finally she said, "I think you are a man who has missed his destiny."

One gray eyebrow arched incredulously. "Indeed?" He snorted. "You amaze me, Miss Denton. Pray tell, what destiny have I missed?"

Marianne swallowed against her rising fear. "Though you are a great captain, sir, I don't believe you were meant to be in His Majesty's service. Clearly, you are not happy. You are not fulfilled." Her gaze took in his row of plants on the stern ledge. *No doubt, you should have been a farmer.*

His face grew red and puffy as his eyes skittered over the cabin. "Preposterous!" He shifted his stance then downed his drink. After pouring another, he sauntered to the windows. "What do you know of such things? I have made a distinguished name for myself in the king's navy. While you are nothing but a silly woman."

Marianne hung her head. He was right. What did she know about destiny? If there was such a thing. Either she had missed hers, too, or she was not significant enough to be assigned one. Or worse, *this* was her destiny. "You are correct, Captain. I am nothing but a silly woman." A silly woman to believe in destiny at all. Hers or anyone else's. A silly woman to believe a man like Noah Brenin could ever love her.

He shot a glance at her over his shoulder. "Dash it all, don't cry. I have no tolerance for women's tears."

Marianne drew in a deep breath and pursed her lips. The captain hovered somewhere between Captain Maniacal and Captain Tolerable—a dangerous spot if he continued in his cups. She must urge him to cease drinking and go to bed before he became too morose.

She took a tentative step toward him. "What made you join the navy, Captain?"

Still facing the window, he sipped his brandy and let out a bitter chuckle. "A woman, if you must know."

"Elizabeth?"

He spun about, his eyes snapping to hers. "How do you know of her?"

"You mentioned her before."

He looked perplexed for a moment then sadness shadowed his face. Drink in hand, he circled his desk and fell into a chair.

Marianne eyed the open bottle of brandy on the desk. Perhaps if she put it away. . .

The captain fingered the gold buttons on his waistcoat. "Ah she loved the sea. Loved a man in uniform." He chuckled and sipped his brandy, his eyes alight with happier memories. "And since I had nothing else to recommend me, I joined the navy, promising her I'd make captain and give her a good life."

Marianne corked the bottle and replaced it in the cabinet. "What happened?"

"I married her."

"Indeed?" The news startled her for the captain did not seem the marrying type. She returned to stand before him. The light in his eyes faded to a dull gray.

He waved his glass through the air, sloshing brandy over the side. "But I was never home. I hardly saw her."

Sorrow burned in Marianne's throat, knowing whatever transpired couldn't have been good.

"She was accosted on the streets of Pembroke," he said.

Marianne raised a hand to her mouth.

"A common thief after the coins in her reticule and the gold locket I gave her for our first anniversary. He killed her."

Moving to him, Marianne knelt by his feet and reached for his hand.

He waved her away. "If I had been there, I could have prevented it. She would be with me now."

"You do not know that, sir." Tears pooled in Marianne's eyes. So much pain. So much anguish in the world.

"She never saw me promoted to captain," he added in a nonchalant tone.

She studied him as he stared off into the cabin, his eyes glazed with drink and sorrow. His loss had turned him into a bitter old man. Would Marianne's tragedies do the same to her? Or did she have a choice? "Why do you stay in the navy?"

"I was in line for commander. What was I to do"—he lifted one shoulder—"start over on land with nothing to my name? No one to go home to?" He pressed a hand to his side and winced.

"What a sad tale, Captain." Marianne flattened her lips. "I'm sorry. I'm so sorry."

He shifted moist eyes her way. "Humph. I believe you are, Miss Denton." He leaned his head back and closed his eyes. "Yes, I do believe you are. Sweet, sweet Miss Denton."

"Sweet and silly." Marianne attempted to lighten the conversation.

He laughed. "Perhaps simply sweet."

Marianne smiled at the compliment then eased the glass from his hand and placed it on his desk. "Let me help you to bed."

"Leave me be, Miss Denton." He growled as if suddenly embarrassed of their conversation. "I have no need of a nursemaid."

Since when? But Marianne didn't need to be told twice. Swerving about, she quietly left the room without saying a word and made her way down the passageway. Against her better judgment, she passed her cabin and instead took the few steps to the quarterdeck above. She needed air. She needed to clear her head. The night breeze cooled the tears on her cheeks, and she batted them away. Slipping into the shadows, she leaned against the mizzenmast and gazed off the stern of the ship. A moonless night afforded her no glorious view save that of a dark mass of seething water that extended forever. She fought back the tears that kept filling her eyes. Where did they come from? She had forbidden herself to spend any more time in useless weeping for something that could never be changed.

"You should not be up here alone, Miss Denton." The low voice startled Marianne, and she jumped.

Lieutenant Reed stepped into the light from the stern lantern and faced her, a look of censure on his stiff features.

Marianne's heart returned to its normal pace at the sight of him. "I needed some air."

He glanced over the ship. "It is not safe."

Two bells rang from the foredeck, announcing the passage of a half hour. "Thank you for your concern, Mr. Reed, but am I really safe anywhere aboard this ship?"

"Some places more than others, Miss Denton."

She studied him. His tight expression refused to give her a hint of his emotions. Nor did the stiffness of his spine or the slight tilt of his chin. Yet out of all the officers on board, he had been the most kind to her. Perhaps not all British were cruel beasts, after all. No, she could see now that they were just men like any other men—some bad and some good.

The ship rose over a swell, and Marianne leaned against the mast. A gust tore at Lieutenant Reed's bicorn, and he shoved it down on his head.

Her curiosity rose regarding this officer who seemed to be a conflicting bundle of arrogance and kindness. "Forgive my boldness, Mr. Reed, but why did you join the Royal Navy?"

"I serve because my father procured a commission for me."

"But what of your wishes?"

"The youngest son in my family always serves in the navy." He shifted his feet.

"And your father?"

"He chose Parliament."

A sail snapped above her. The mast behind her vibrated. "Would you have joined the navy if you had no family name to uphold, if your father had not required it of you?"

His face scrunched as if she'd struck him. "Your point is moot, miss. For I do have family expectations to honor. It is my duty."

The lantern light rolled over him with the swaying of the ship. One second she could make out his sour expression, the next it was lost to her in the shadows. "Surely you have your own dreams."

His glance took in the deck before he gazed out to sea. "I had not considered any other endeavor."

Marianne thought of Noah. Even away from the strictures of British hierarchy, Noah's father had enacted the same pressure of familial duty upon him. And both men suffered for it.

Thoughts of Noah scraped across the fresh wound on her heart. A gust of chilled wind swept over her, thankfully drying the tears that formed in her eyes. She must stop thinking of him. She must accept her fate.

Reed cleared his throat and adjusted his neck cloth. "I am sorry your friends deserted you."

Marianne looked down, hoping he wouldn't see the tears fill her eyes.

"If it is any consolation, I've seen the captain release female prisoners before. Two French noblewomen taken off a supply ship." Mr. Reed gazed to the west, in the direction Marianne assumed was her home. Her country. "He set them ashore in France."

"I am no noblewoman, sir, as you can well see for yourself."

"But the captain likes you."

"Indeed?" Marianne chuckled at the absurdity of the statement, though at times she guessed it was true. "Thank you, Mr. Reed, but I'm finding hope to be a fickle friend. I prefer not to consider any other possibility but the station in which I find myself."

"Humph. A coward's declaration." His lips flattened in disdain.

Yet Marianne felt no anger at his insult. He simply did not understand. "No. A realist, sir. I am a realist."

"Even a realist leaves the possibility open for a miracle."

A miracle? Did he mean from God? She wanted to tell him she didn't believe in miracles—not anymore, but she simply gazed out to sea, too numb to argue.

He took a step toward her. "Allow me to escort you to your cabin, miss."

The statement seemed more of an order than a request. "Very well." She followed the tall man across the quarterdeck and down to her cabin where he left her with a nod and a "Good evening."

Closing the door, she leaned against it and peered into the shadows. With the marine stationed at the captain's cabin not ten feet away, this was the safest place on the ship, aside from standing right beside the captain himself.

Inching forward, she knelt before her bed. The ship creaked. The sea rushed against the hull in a continuous thrum as they sped north on their way to sink a ship of the fledgling United States navy.

And there wasn't a thing Marianne could do about it. Nor about her imprisonment, nor about the impending attack.

"I am alone."

"You are never alone."

A voice, loving and soft, heard, yet not heard, rang clear in Marianne's head. She glanced over the cabin, her heart lifting. "Everyone has left me."

"I have never left you."

"Oh Lord." She dropped her head into her hands. "Are You truly there?"

No answer came. Just a sensation of love, of peace, that whirled around her like a warm summer breeze. "Where have You been? Why have You allowed this to happen? Why am I here, Lord?"

A sail snapped above, and the ship canted. Marianne's knees shifted on the hard deck. An ache shot up her thigh. But no answer came.

Had she heard from God at all, or had she simply imagined it?

After several minutes, she crawled atop her bed, plopped down on the hard mattress, and forced her eyes shut. Better to drift asleep into sweet oblivion than to spend another night awake, haunted by her fears.

But sweet oblivion never came. Instead, Marianne wrestled with her coverlet for hours in a semiconscious dream state. Blurred images swept through her mind: Her father's bloated, white face staring up at her, his typical expression of bored despondency present even in death; the sea raging all around her, reaching liquid tentacles up to grab her; her mother, standing on their front porch, calling Marianne's name in despair; Lizzie, gaunt and thin from lack of food; and the agonized look on Noah's face before he leapt over the side of the ship—and abandoned her.

Marianne snapped her eyes open. She sat up, trembling, and wiped the perspiration from her forehead and neck. "Just a dream. Only a dream." She hugged herself.

Light from a late-rising moon entered the window in ghost-like streams of wispy milk, trickling upon her desk, the door, and bulkhead.

She lowered her chin, forcing down her loneliness and fear. Beside her on the bed, a black book glistened, drawing her gaze. A Bible—the Bible Daniel had given her. How had it gotten there? She'd been so mad at God last week, she'd stuffed it into the small trunk at the foot of her bed.

Grabbing it, she flipped it open and moved into the moonlight. She fingered the pages with reverence. The precious Word of God. How often had she read from it with zeal and anticipation? But that was a long time ago. When she believed the words. Before her father died and her world fell apart. "Where have You been?"

"I never left."

That voice again. So soft. So loving. And coming from deep within her. "Perhaps it was I who left You, Lord." She glanced over the room. "But how could I believe Your Word was true after Father died. No. Not died. Left." She wiped a tear spilling down her cheek. "Betrayed us. Abandoned us. If I couldn't trust him, how can I trust You?"

"I never change."

The unassuming statement settled in her mind, joining together abstract events from her past. If that was true, then God had known about—even allowed—all her tragedies. "Why has this happened to me?" Marianne flipped through the pages of the Bible with no destination in mind. The words grew blurry. Her finger brushed over the book of Esther, chapter four. Her mother's favorite book. Marianne could still picture her mother reading the story to her when she was a little girl. The way her face shone with excitement and her voice nearly sang as she relayed the romantic, adventurous story. The kind of adventure Marianne had come to believe only happened to beautiful, talented ladies. Not someone like her.

She skimmed over the tale, refreshing her memory. Esther, a

common but beautiful girl, became queen of all Persia. But an evil plot had been hatched to annihilate Esther's people, the Jews. When her uncle begged her to go speak to the king on their behalf, Esther refused. To enter the king's presence without an invitation meant certain death. Marianne read down to her favorite part, Esther's uncle's reply, " 'Who knoweth whether thou art come to the kingdom for such a time as this?' "

The words seemed to fly off the page and circle her cabin, proclaiming their truth and dispelling the shadows. Marianne's eyes burned. She gazed at the words once more. A tear spilled onto the Bible—right in the center of the phrase.

Her throat went dry. "Is this for me, Lord? Is this a message?"

No answer came.

She kept reading, skipping down to Esther's last declaration. She would do as her uncle asked. She would do the right thing. She would approach the king. Marianne read her final words out loud. " 'If I perish, I perish.' "

Such faith. Such trust. She closed the book and laid it aside, wiping the tears from her cheeks. "Esther risked her life, believing You'd be with her, Lord. And she had an opportunity to save an entire race of people. What a destiny."

She lay back down on her mattress and listened to the pounding of the sea against the hull. But she was no queen. She couldn't save a nation. She couldn't even save herself.

❖ CHAPTER 24 ❖

Noah stood before the helm of his ship on the quarterdeck, boots spread apart, arms folded over his chest. A blast of hot summer wind punched him, clawed at his hair, and tried to shove him backward. But he stood his ground. He would surrender neither to the relentless wind nor to the dread churning in his gut.

He rubbed the sweat from the back of his neck, then raked his hair aside. It had grown long during the past month. What would his father think of Noah's shabby appearance? He snorted. Better yet, what would he think of Noah losing half his cargo and sailing his precious ship on its way to engage in a battle they were sure to lose? Noah chuckled as he pictured the expression on his father's face in light of such news, then surprised himself when he realized he no longer cared.

Marianne had changed all that. She had shown him that some things were more precious than wealth, than pleasing his father, than even his own life. In her, Noah had found the heart of an angel encased in a woman he would have shunned. But a heart that made her the most beautiful woman in the world to him. A heart loyal to country and family, an honorable heart, a loving heart—a heart he could only hope he was worthy to possess.

Shaking his head, Noah squinted against the bright sun as it began its trek back down to the sea. Ribbons of sparkling waves reflected a clear blue sky. If the wind continued blowing strong, Noah would make up the time he had lost when he had stopped in Charleston two days ago to send ashore those of his crew with enough sense to escape while they could.

Half his crew, to be exact. Leaving him with only twenty men, only five of whom had prior fighting experience. Mr. Weller, among them. Noah still couldn't believe the man had stayed and risked impressment again—or worse, death.

A gleam struck Noah's eye, and he squinted toward a swivel gun mounted on the foredeck. Cloth in hand, Daniel buffed the brass-capped barrel while Weller and Matthew hovered around the lad, pointing out different sections of the gun. Daniel nodded and listened intently, his expression beaming with eagerness to learn. Noah smiled. The boy added a spirit of innocent hope to the ship. A hope they desperately needed.

Eight guns lined his deck—eight four pounders against the frigate's thirty-two eighteen pounders and four twelve pounders. Not to mention that during battle, the crew of the frigate operated like a war machine, not like his bunch of shoddy, disorganized sailors.

He glanced at Luke who stood beside him. His jaw firm, his black hair blowing in the wind. The scar on his ear stood out in the afternoon sun. Noah had always wondered how Luke got the scar, but he assumed his first mate would tell him if he wanted to. The man had the morals of a rabbit, but the heart of a lion. He had no emotional investment in seeing that Marianne was safe. No loyalty for his country drove him to risk his life. He stood by Noah simply because they were friends.

Luke turned and gave him a knowing look.

"Unfurl the topgallants, Mr. Heaton. Set the stuns'ls. Let's bring her to a swift sail."

With a nod, Luke brayed commands over the ship, sending the men aloft as Daniel and Matthew leapt onto the quarterdeck.

The boy ran up to Noah, his eyes sparkling with excitement. "Mr. Hobbs and Mr. Weller showed me how to load, run out, and prime the gun, Mr. Noah."

Noah smiled at the boy. "Excellent." He may need the lad's help when the time came. Shielding his eyes from the sun, Noah found the boy's father up in the yards, unfurling sail. He, too, had stayed, despite the overwhelming odds against them. Despite the danger to his son.

"And a quick learner he be." Matthew patted Daniel on the back.

"Do you think we'll catch up with them?" Luke's blue eyes stood stark against the fading bruises on his cheeks.

Noah inhaled a deep breath of the sea air. "We have no choice."

"Of course we will." Daniel's voice carried not a shred of doubt as he leaned over the railing and closed his eyes to the wind.

"It's not the catchin' up that bothers me." Matthew doffed his hat and wiped the sweat from his brow. The afternoon sun gleamed off his bald head. "It's what happens when we do find them."

The sails caught the wind in a deafening snap, and the ship canted, picking up speed. The men grew somber, all save Daniel. He clung to the railing and smiled as if he hadn't a care in the world. Perhaps the boy knew something they didn't. If only Noah could know the future. If only he could know whether he led his men to their deaths.

"Daniel." Noah drew the boy's gaze his way. "Have you a word from God on our fate?"

"It doesn't work like that, Mr. Noah." Daniel shoved hair from his eyes and squinted into the sun. "If God has something He wants me to know, He tells me. If not, He don't."

The ship pitched over a wave, sending spray upon the bow. Noah spread his boots on the deck and huffed. "Then how is one supposed to trust Him without any direction?"

Daniel gazed at Noah as if he were the child. "God wants you to trust Him no matter if He tells you things ahead of time or not. Like it says in Romans. 'All things work together for good to them that love God, to them who are the called according to his purpose.'"

Luke snorted and took a step away, as if wanting to get out of ear-shot of the sermon.

Noah wished he could do the same. "Nice words, but I fear they don't apply to me."

Daniel shrugged. "You don't know the end yet."

"What's that, boy?" Luke inched closer, a frown on his face.

Daniel gestured toward Noah. "He doesn't know how the story ends. None of us do. Not until the day we die."

"Which may be sooner than we hope." Matthew chortled.

Daniel tugged up his oversized breeches—the only pair Noah had found onboard to fit the lad. "How do you know everything in your life is going to turn out for good if you're not at the end of everything in your life?"

Matthew's eyes flashed. "The lad makes a good amount o' sense."

"So, I must wait until my death to verify what God says is true?" The sarcasm in Noah's voice surprised even him.

"Or you can just trust Him now and be done with it." Daniel smiled. "Seems to me, He knows a lot more about our lives than we do. 'Sides, He loves us."

Noah flexed his jaw and he steadied himself as the ship bolted again. The faith of a foolish child. A foolish child who knew nothing of life.

Daniel's eyes twinkled. "What if God put together all the things that happened: me and my pa gettin' impressed, then you and your lady friend and crew bein' impressed, the escape, even leaving Miss Marianne behind"—the twinkle faded from his eyes for a moment—"all of it for this moment when a simple merchantman takes on a British warship." He grinned. "It could be your destiny."

"I don't believe in destiny," Noah growled, trying to ignore the lad, trying to ignore the longing buried deep within him—a longing for some meaning to his life.

Daniel frowned and lowered his chin. "It don't matter if you don't believe. You have a destiny just the same. But you have to surrender to God to find it." He shrugged. "An' then you have to do it."

Noah clenched his jaw. He patted his pocket where Jacob's bloody handkerchief lay. He knew the boy meant well, but Noah refused to believe destiny had led his brother to his death. Refused to believe in a God who allowed such a destiny. No, it was far easier to believe there was no such thing. That God was aloof and distant and kept His hand off the affairs of men.

"I feel God telling me that you do have a destiny, Mr. Noah," Daniel said. "Yes, a great purpose."

Noah pressed down upon the boy's shoulder, hoping to silence him. "I'm afraid God takes no note of me or my life."

"God takes note of everyone," Matthew added.

"I'll have no more talk of God or destiny!" Noah barked, instantly regretting his tone. "If the Almighty has been orchestrating my life, then He is nothing but a cruel taskmaster—one I will never be able to please."

"He's not anything like that, Mr. Noah." Daniel's voice weighed heavy with sorrow.

Luke excused himself and leapt onto the main deck. Noah couldn't blame him.

"If I didn't know better," Matthew said to Noah, "I'd think you were describin' your father." He gave Noah a look of disapproval before hobbling away.

Noah flinched. Was he mistaking God for his father? Hadn't Luke told him the same thing back on the frigate? But God had not proven himself to be any different from Noah's father. Both had far too many rules. And all it took was one mistake to invoke their disapproval.

A mistake like Noah's jealousy of his brother—a mistake that had sent Jacob to his death.

He wanted no part of a God like that.

The sun descended farther toward the horizon off the port side. He glanced aloft. Mountains of bloated canvas crowded the masts. Salty mist sprayed over his face as the ship rippled through the sparkling sea on a north by northeast course. If the weather and wind held, they would catch the HMS *Undefeatable* in no time.

"I'm coming, Marianne," he whispered into the wind. "Be strong, princess."

He drew in a deep breath and gripped the railing. Strength and an unusual, if not misplaced, confidence surged through him. Nothing could stop him now.

"A sail! A sail!" someone shouted from above. "Four points off the starboard beam."

Below, on the main deck, Luke darted to the railing and peered at the horizon.

Daniel stood at attention as Noah drew his scope to his eye. A two-masted sloop came into sharp view, the Union Jack flapping from her mainmast. He lowered the glass. Luke scrambled up the stairs and marched toward him.

"It's a British war sloop," Noah stated.

Luke nodded. "And she's bearing down on us fast."

Gripping the broom, Marianne swept the painted canvas that served as a rug in the center of the captain's cabin and gathered the dust into a pile by the door. She had already scrubbed the deck, served the captain two meals, brought his clothes down to the laundry, and polished five lanterns that now hung in various spots on the bulkhead. Her back ached. Her feet hurt. And her stomach growled.

Sweep. Sweep. Dust flew through the air, transforming into tiny pieces of glitter that danced in the afternoon sunlight. Amazing how something so base and dirty could become so beautiful when exposed to the light. She pondered that thought as she watched the thin line of the distant horizon fill the stern windows, then fall out of view, then rise again, then fall. She barely noticed the sway of the ship anymore, barely had any trouble remaining upright. Another month out to sea, and she would forget what it felt like to walk on something that wasn't heaving to and fro.

She continued her sweeping. Ten days had passed since she'd read Esther. Ten days had passed since she thought she'd heard God's voice in her cabin telling her He loved her and was with her.

And nothing had happened.

If she was here for a purpose, other than cleaning and scrubbing and serving, she had no idea what it could be.

She sneezed and dabbed at the perspiration on her neck. It had been a little over three weeks since Noah had dropped over the bulwarks and disappeared into the sea. Since then, each day had slipped by, snatching a bit more of her hope in passing. If Noah had found his ship and intended to come after her, surely he would have arrived by now. She swept more dust into her growing pile. But why would he? What could he and his merchant ship hope to accomplish against such a formidable foe?

She was on her own.

"I am with you, beloved."

She sighed and gazed around the cabin. "Lord, where have You been?" She leaned on the tip of the broom. "I need You. I need to know what You want me to do."

"Trust Me."

Shouts filtered down from above, followed by the pounding of feet on the deckhead. Within minutes the snap of sails thundered, and the captain's booming voice rang through the timbers. Marianne stared above, wondering what caused all the commotion.

The sighting of another ship, perhaps? Her heart froze. The frigate jolted and the purl of the water against the hull grew louder. She listened for any further clues, but only the muffled voices of the crew and the chime of a bell drifted over her ears.

She pondered going aloft to see what was happening when the door swung open, crashing against the bulkhead. Marianne jumped, then moved out of the way as the captain charged into the cabin. Lieutenants Garrick, Reed, and Jones followed on his heels.

The stomp of their boots hefted her pile of dust into the blast of wind that entered behind them, scattering it across the cabin.

She blew out a sigh and laid a hand on her hip. Lieutenant Garrick's gaze slithered over her, and she resisted the urge to swat him with her broom.

Captain Milford circled his desk, dropped his spectacles onto his nose, and leaned over a chart.

The three lieutenants doffed their hats, stuffed them between their right arms and bodies, and lined up before him.

"Here we are." The captain's finger stopped on the chart. "And here is where we spotted her."

Lieutenant Reed leaned on the desk and peered at the chart. "I'd say not more than eight miles northeast of us."

The captain studied Mr. Jones. "Are you sure of what you saw?"

The thin, nervous man nodded. "Yes. American. I'd swear by it, Captain."

American. Marianne's ears perked up.

"If the admiral's information is correct, it must be the USS *Constitution*. We could be upon her tomorrow." Garrick's voice dripped with greed.

"Yes, my thoughts exactly, Mr. Garrick." The captain lengthened his stance and grabbed his chin. "Yet we were told to rendezvous with the *Guerriére* at this location." He pointed at the chart.

"Perhaps they spotted the enemy and took pursuit, Captain," Mr. Jones offered.

The captain's eyes twinkled. "And if so, I believe they would appreciate our help." He rubbed his hands together. Then grabbing four glasses from his cabinet, he lined them on his desk and poured brandy into each one. "We are at war, gentlemen. At war with a bunch of quarrelsome, jingle-headed farmers who have more backbone than brains!" He chuckled and grabbed his glass.

More backbone than brains, indeed. Marianne feigned disinterest as she kept sweeping.

Garrick stiffened his back and grabbed one of the glasses. "There's nothing like the pounding of the guns to get your blood pumping."

"The Americans don't stand a chance, sir." Reed took another glass. "Didn't the admiral say this laughable rebel navy only possessed six frigates, three sloops, and a few smaller vessels?"

Garrick's malicious laugher filled the cabin. "Compared to our six hundred warships, one hundred and twenty ships of the line, and one hundred and twenty frigates. Egad, are they mad?"

Marianne felt his eyes on her, no doubt hoping to gloat her into a reaction, but she kept her gaze on the deck. When he faced forward again, she swept dust onto his boots.

"It will be good to put these rebels in their place." Mr. Reed nodded.

Sweep. Dust showered over Mr. Reed's boots.

"And restore order to the colonies," Captain Milford said. "To the war, gentlemen." He lifted his glass.

Mr. Jones grabbed his.

"To victory!" Garrick said, and all four men raised their glasses together.

A sour taste rose in Marianne's mouth at their pompous display. The sharp scent of brandy filled the room.

"Besides, I hear their land is rich and free for the taking." Mr. Jones sipped his drink.

Marianne ground her teeth together and swept dust onto Mr. Jones's boots.

The captain gazed out the window. "Ah, a nice piece of land to call my own." He seemed to drift to another place as the men stood savoring their drinks.

"Blast it all!" The captain growled so loud even the lieutenants flinched. "Unfortunate that night falls within an hour."

"We shall catch them at first light, Captain," Reed said with confidence.

"If they have not outwitted us." The captain's weary eyes surveyed the chart. "We shall see." He raised a gaze to Garrick. "Maintain our present heading and place extra men in the masthead to keep a weather eye out for her." He slammed his glass down on the desk. "Let us find this American rebel and give her a hearty British welcome."

They all chuckled and tossed the brandy to the back of their throats.

Fire burned in Marianne's belly. Of all the impertinent, bombastic, audacious…who did they think they were? Congratulating themselves on a victory not yet won.

The captain grinned. "Who knows if we aren't here for such a time as this?"

Marianne froze. She lifted wide eyes to the captain, fully expecting to see his taunting smile directed toward her. But he paid her no mind and began pouring the men another drink.

"For such a time as this."

Marianne's heart sped to a rapid pace.

What are You trying to tell me, Lord?

"For such a time as this."

Yes, they were chasing an American warship, intent on destroying her. But what could Marianne do? She was a nobody. A prisoner. A servant. Was she supposed to take on an entire ship full of British sailors and soldiers?

She gripped the handle of the broom until her fingers reddened. Yet hadn't she done something similar on Noah's ship? Disabled the entire ship all by herself? She sighed and continued sweeping. There was no cargo to ruin on board this ship. What else could she do? She searched her mind for her conversations with Weller about accidents aboard a ship. What else had he said would disable a ship?

The tiller. Blood rushed to her head.

"Look what you've done, you insufferable woman." Lieutenant Jones stared down aghast at his dusty boots. The other men followed his gaze.

"Egad!" Mr. Reed lifted one foot up to examine the damage as Garrick's curse raked over Marianne's ears.

All eyes shot to her.

She shrugged. "My apologies, gentlemen. How careless of me." Forcing down a smile, she swept the broom over each of their boots, scattering the dust into a cloud.

The captain cleared his throat and gave her a look of reprimand that held a promise of punishment. But that didn't matter anymore. Marianne had a plan. And she knew exactly what she needed to do.

❖ CHAPTER 25 ❖

Noah studied the oncoming sloop. His gut wrenched. From what he could tell, she carried fifteen thirty-two pounders on her main deck, six twelve pounders on her quarterdeck, and two carronades mounted on her forecastle. Twenty-three guns in all and probably more that he couldn't see. He snapped his long glass shut. The *Fortune* pitched over a roller, and Noah gripped the railing. Salty mist stung his eyes. He gazed above where every inch of bloated canvas was set to the gusty breeze.

And still the sloop gained.

"Bring her as close to the wind as you can, Mr. Pike," Noah ordered the helmsman.

"Aye, aye, Cap'n."

The sails snapped. The ship canted to larboard as blue squalls swept over her deck. Noah balanced himself and stared at the oncoming ship. With the confidence of a mighty predator, she dashed after her prey, white spray foaming at her bow.

"What does she want?" Matthew staggered to Noah's side.

"We are at war. She intends to take us as a prize." Noah's voice gave no indication of the fear gnawing at his gut.

Weller mumbled beside him. A glaze of terror covered his eyes as he clutched the two fingers remaining on his right hand. "Not again."

Noah laid a hand on his shoulder, but the comforting words he intended to say withered on his lips.

The *Fortune* crested a wave, creaking and groaning under the strain.

"It'll be worse this time." Blackthorn shifted his large frame. "Especially if they discover we escaped from the *Undefeatable*. We'll be hanged or sent to a prison hulk to rot until the war is over."

Noah shook the words from his ears. He would accept neither option. For both prevented him from rescuing Marianne and stopping the *Undefeatable* in its mission against the United States navy. His country's navy.

He surprised himself at the patriotism welling inside him.

"She's gaining, Captain," Luke shouted from the main deck below.

Noah squinted toward the sun, which sat a handbreadth over the horizon. He must stay outside the range of the British sloop's guns until nightfall. It was the only way. "Blackthorn, take Daniel and gather some men. Go below and find anything we can throw overboard, even our food if we have to, and bring it aloft."

Blackthorn nodded, cuffed Daniel on the back of the neck, and dragged him along. The boy laughed at his father's antics. Noah shook his head. Did nothing bother the young lad? Was his faith so strong that it pushed back all fear, even fear of death?

Two hours passed. The slowest two hours of Noah's life. An hour in which Noah's crew proceeded to toss bars of iron, bolts of cloth, sacks of flour, and kegs of water over the side. The *Fortune* picked up speed. But was it enough?

Relieving Mr. Pike at the helm, Noah took the wheel himself. He was desperate to keep busy—do anything besides standing and watching the sloop advance upon them. Weller paced the quarterdeck. Matthew dropped below to douse the fire in the stove and settle

Agnes somewhere safe should a battle ensue. Luke stood like a stone sentinel at the stern railing, arms folded over his chest, staring at the oncoming ship.

A blast of salt-tainted wind tore at Noah's hair and shirt, bringing with it a hint of cool evening air. Darkness would be upon them soon.

"Mr. Weller." Noah stopped the man from his nervous pacing. "Gather the men and ready the guns, if you please." Not that the action would matter. The sloop's guns outranged Noah's and could easily hit their target before Noah would have any hope of striking in return.

Beneath the wild black hair lashing about his head, Weller's dark eyes found Noah's and a look of understanding passed between them. With a nod, he leapt down the quarterdeck ladder. Daniel dashed across the deck to join him, excitement in his every step, making Noah wonder whether the boy's father would want his son assigned to such a dangerous post. But Blackthorn had jumped below again, searching for more things to toss overboard.

"She fired a gun!" Luke bellowed.

The lack of fear in his first mate's voice kept Noah steady on his feet. He'd barely swerved around when a resonant *Boom!* cracked the air. Gray smoke curled up like a charmed snake from the sloop's bow. The ball splashed impotently into the sea twenty yards off their stern.

Twenty yards too close.

"A warning shot." Mr. Pike offered as he approached Noah. "If ye don't mind, Cap'n, can I take back the helm? If I'm goin' t' die, I'd rather die at me post."

A weight seemed to fall on Noah at Mr. Pike's lack of confidence. But how could he blame the man? Noah had never engaged in battle before. He pried his fingers from the wood, not realizing until then how tight his grip had been, then stretched the kinks from his hand.

Luke sauntered toward him. "I believe they want us to stop, Captain."

Noah glanced at the sun barely touching the horizon. It would be at least an hour before the darkness would hide them. A very long hour. He snapped the hair from his face. "To the devil with what they want. Have the men go aloft and trim the sails to the wind again."

Luke gave an approving nod and shouted orders across the ship. Taking a spot at the stern, Noah raised the long glass to his eye but immediately lowered it. The sloop was so close he no longer needed it to make out the details of the ship. At least a hundred men crowded her decks. Crews hovered around the guns, petting and coaxing the iron beasts as they awaited their captain's command to fire. The captain stood on the quarterdeck. The gold buttons on his coat winked at Noah in the setting sun, taunting him to fight, challenging him just like his brother had done when they were younger.

Noah's nerves burned. His blood pounded in his head. "Another hour, Lord. Just give me another hour." He surprised himself with the prayer, but the harrowing situation called for desperate measures. If a miracle did not occur before the day was spent, Noah and his crew would be killed or captured. And Marianne would be doomed.

With her ears tuned to the snoring that emanated from the captain's sleeping chamber, Marianne slid open one of the drawers in the massive oak desk.

It squeaked. The snoring stopped. She froze and listened for any movement. But only the creak of timber and slosh of water met her ears.

The captain resumed his snoring.

Drawing the lantern near, she sifted through the contents of the drawer: a quill pen, a bottle of ink, foolscap, the ship's log, a locket, and. . .there it was. A key. She gripped the cold metal and drew it to her bosom. Not just any key. The key to the cabinet full of weapons in the wardroom.

Where she planned on stealing a knife.

It had been a fairly easy task to draw the location of the key from the captain, especially after several more brandies and a spoonful of laudanum. Assured of his victory tomorrow over the American warship, he had been in a most jovial humor all night long—right up to the moment he'd dropped unconscious onto his bed.

Then she had only to wait a few minutes until his deep breathing confirmed that he was fast asleep.

Clutching the key in one hand and the lantern in the other, Marianne tiptoed out the door, down the passageway, then descended the ladder to the lower deck. Turning a corner, she pressed a hand to her chest to still her frantic heart. The dash of water against the hull joined the pounding of blood in her ears.

The ship groaned.

Footsteps sounded.

Marianne halted and backed against the bulkhead. Perhaps it was just the ship's timbers complaining as usual. She started again, this time more slowly. A light shone from the distance. Another lantern, a candle? But then it went out. Had she imagined it? Whispers curled around her ears. Or was it the purl of the water?

She should go back to her cabin.

But she couldn't. Tomorrow they planned on attacking an American ship—possibly the USS *Constitution*. She couldn't let that happen. Pressing forward, she entered the wardroom. The smell of whale oil and smoke and the dried beef the officers had for dinner whirled about her nose. Lifting her lantern, she scanned the shadows. No movement came from the officer's canvas cabins that lined both sides of the larger room. She prayed they were all fast asleep. The light reflected off the cabinet's glass doors. She squinted. Setting the lantern down on the table, she inserted the key and turned the latch. The door swung open with an aged squeak.

Marianne held her breath. She listened for footsteps, voices, but only the familiar hum of the ship and the snores of the officers met her ears. She perused the knives. Any one of them would do. She plucked a particularly long blade with a sharp point and lifted it toward the light to examine it. The wooden handle felt smooth in her fingers as the steel blade gleamed in the lantern light. Sliding it into her pocket, she closed the cabinet, grabbed the lantern, and dashed out the door.

Now to find the tiller.

She descended another level to the orlop deck. The smell of tar and human sweat burned her nostrils. Her hand trembled, and the lantern clanked. The flame sputtered then steadied. She wished her heart would do the same. With most of the crew asleep, this late hour afforded her the best possibility of completing her mission without drawing unwanted attention. But that didn't mean she wouldn't cross paths with one of them. Her lantern light skimmed over barrels, tackles, spare canvas, and ropes. Nothing that looked like a tiller.

The ship canted, creaking and moaning. She pressed onward. Sweat beaded on the back of her neck. Rats scattered before her arc of light, darting for the cover of the shadows. She shivered at the sight of them then entered a small space that, by her best calculation, should be directly below the wheel. She lifted the lantern to examine the room. Empty save for a stack of crates in the corner and a pile of cordage hanging from a nail in the bulkhead. She started to leave when something above her caught her eye. Two thick hemp ropes dropped down from holes in the deckhead. Strung through iron loops, they extended out along two sweeps of wood.

The tiller!

Reaching up, she brushed her fingers over the itchy, rough hemp. It scraped her skin. The lines were strong and sturdy and at least two inches thick.

But still possible to cut through with a knife.

But not yet. Since the tiller ropes could be repaired within a few days, she must wait until the *Undefeatable* engaged the USS *Constitution* in battle. And not a moment before.

Thank You, Lord. But now, I will need Your help when the time comes. She bit her lip. Would God use her to do this important task? A task that could change the course of history? Or was she only deceiving herself?

Time would tell.

Turning, Marianne hurried back the way she'd come.

And ran straight into Lieutenant Garrick.

Noah spotted a yellow flame burst from the British sloop's hull. "All hands down!" He dove to the hard wood.

Boom! Cannon shot thundered across the sky. Tar and oakum filled his nostrils. He lifted his head. His crew lay scattered across the deck. Water splashed like a geyser not two feet off their starboard quarter.

He leapt to his feet. "Clear the deck! Lay aloft and ease the topgallants!" His gaze met Luke's as his first mate wasted no time in ordering the men to their tasks.

The pursuing sloop crashed through the waves a mile astern. A few more minutes and they'd be within firing range. "Man the guns! Load the chain shot," Noah commanded. At least they'd put up a fight before they'd all be killed. He fisted his hands until they ached. Confound it all. Blasted British.

The remainder of his crew who weren't in the shrouds or at the helm, swarmed the eight guns. With Noah's depleted crew, two men would be forced to do the jobs of three as they took their positions. Daniel and Blackthorn took one cannon at the stern, while Noah joined Weller at the other. A bucket filled with bags of powder sat on the deck along with a pile of shot. Mr. Lothar dashed across the ship, distributing red-hot cotton wicks soaked in lye to each team.

A gust of wind needled over Noah, carrying with it the sting of gunpowder. Off their starboard quarter, the British sloop shouldered the sea, foam cresting her bow. The Union Jack flapped at her mainmast, taunting Noah with the power and audacity of a nation who believed they ruled the seas.

His stomach crumpled. Thoughts of Marianne drifted through his mind. His heart ached. Would he ever see her again or would she be forever doomed to a life of slavery?

Noah gazed across his crew. All good sailors. But they weren't soldiers. Yet despite the terror screaming from their eyes, they manned their posts with bravado. "Good job, men," Noah said. "Steady there. Wait for my order." Noah tried to encourage them with a tone of assurance, yet it sounded flat coming from his lips.

A streak of bloodred sky spread across the horizon as the arc of the sun sank out of sight. A portent of their fate? Noah hoped not. He glanced above. Already the black sky descended, swallowing up any remaining light in its path. "I just need a few more minutes," he whispered again to no one in particular. Deep down he hoped the Almighty would hear and take pity on him. At least for Marianne's sake. And the sake of his crew. Men he was responsible for.

The *Fortune* flew through the sea with everything she could set to the breeze, plunging into the rollers and sending spray back over the deck.

One man at each gun held the burning wick, awaiting Noah's command. He studied their enemy. Not in range yet.

Darkness tumbled upon them. Noah peered toward Daniel and Blackthorn who manned the gun beside him. The red glow of the wick shook in Blackthorn's hands as the giant bear of a man hovered protectively over his son. Daniel stood his ground beside the carronade—the sturdy form of a boy with more courage and faith than Noah had ever seen.

Noah's throat went dry. Though only a shapeless gray mass, he could still make out the sloop as she swept alongside them, a half mile off their beam. The black mouths of ten guns on her larboard side gaped tauntingly at him. His nerves clamped.

They intended to fire a broadside.

"Hard to starboard, Mr. Pike!" Noah shouted. He'd cut them off and try to get close enough to cripple their rigging.

The ship groaned and heaved as the deck canted high in the air. Noah clung to the railing, Weller at his side. "On my order, Mr. Weller."

His gunner nodded.

Yellow flames burst from the British sloop.

"Fire!" Noah yelled. The boom of his guns merged with the simultaneous blasts of the sloop's ten cannons resulting in a thunderous volcano.

Shot whizzed by Noah's ears. He dropped to the deck. The crunch and snap of wood filled the air. A scream of agony. The *Fortune* jolted. Black soot settled on him like a death shroud. He coughed.

The beat of his heart drummed a funeral march in Noah's head. He shook the fog from his brain and struggled to his knees. Agonizing screams and harried shouts fired over the deck. Noah stood. Batting away the smoke, he eyed the sloop, her sails full, her rigging tight. His shots had not met their mark.

And still they came, veering to follow him.

The sound of coughing drew his gaze to Blackthorn and Daniel. They staggered to their feet, but they appeared unharmed.

Luke darted to his side, a bloody gash across his cheek.

"Damage?" Noah asked.

"Grainger is dead. Two others injured. Three of our guns were blown to bits, and they punched a hole in our forward hull. We're taking on water." Luke wiped the blood from his cheek with his sleeve.

Grainger dead. Noah lowered his chin. What had he done? But he couldn't think of it now.

"Put Mr. Lothar and Mr. Boone on the pumps at once. Have Matthew attend to the injured." Noah glanced at the sky, dark enough to see stars flickering back at him, and then at the sloop. Only the foam lining her gray hull gave away her position.

Which meant she could barely see the *Fortune* as well.

Luke brayed orders across the deck then returned to Noah's side.

"Relentless," Noah spat as he watched the sloop tack to starboard, no doubt in an effort to offer him another broadside. "She's like a mad demon."

Luke gripped the railing, his eyes narrowed on their enemy. A slow smile spread over his lips. "Even a demon can't see in the dark."

Noah nodded at his first mate. "Douse all lights. Every light." He directed Luke, then he turned toward Mr. Pike—ever faithful at the helm. "Three points to larboard, Mr. Pike." He faced Luke again. "Have the men lower topsails. Let's alter our position and see if we can't lose them in this darkness."

"Aye, Captain." Luke's approval beamed in his gaze as he turned and left.

Noah stared out upon the choppy waves of the ebony sea. He patted the stained handkerchief in his pocket. "I may be joining you soon, my brother."

With all lanterns snuffed, darkness hungrily consumed the ship, swallowing both sight and sound in every crack, plank, and timber. Only the wash of the sea against the hull and the occasional snap of sail as they tacked to starboard marked their position.

A yellow jet of flame burst in the darkness off their starboard beam, followed by an ominous boom. Noah's spine tightened. Could they see him? Was the *Fortune* outside their range? Seconds ticked by as long as minutes. Visions of his own splintered, crushed body flashed across his mind. But then a splash sounded off their starboard quarter, and he released a ragged sigh.

Matthew joined him. The metallic smell of blood filled the air. "Praise be to God, they can't see us."

"What of the injured?" Noah prepared himself for the answer.

"Mason and Crenshaw? They'll live." Matthew's normally cheery voice sounded as thick as molasses.

Blackthorn slipped beside Noah. "I'll bet on me mother's grave, those Brits'll be there in the morning. Sink me, I've served long enough wit' the likes o' them to know they never give up. They'll follow any spark of light, any sound, and be right on us at first light."

Noah frowned. The tiny thread of hope he'd been clinging to slipped through his fingers at Blackthorn's morbid declaration.

"He's right." Luke sighed.

"At the rate we're taking on water, it won't matter," Noah said. "We'll sink before dawn."

Despite her trembling legs, Marianne squared her shoulders and gave Lieutenant Garrick her most defiant look. It did not, however, wipe the odious grin off his face or make him disappear. Instead, it emboldened him to take a step toward her and finger a strand of her hair. She batted his hand away and tried to skirt around him.

He blocked her exit. "What have we here? Come looking for me, perhaps?"

"Don't be absurd, Mr. Garrick." Marianne tried to shove past him, but he remained as immovable as a brick wall. She pursed her lips and dared a glance into his icy blue eyes. "If you don't mind, I shall be on my way."

"But I do mind, Miss Denton." He scratched the well-groomed whiskers on his jaw. "Your absence above deck these past weeks has left me pining for a moment alone with you. Then what do I hear in the middle of the night, but you fumbling about the wardroom? Fortunate, indeed."

"Fortune has nothing to do with this." Marianne stepped backward. Her foot thumped against a barrel. A dull ache formed at her ankle.

Mr. Garrick's gaze leeched over her, sucking in every detail. "Whatever are you doing down here, Miss Denton? I perceive you are up to no good."

"I. . .I. . ." Marianne's knees began to quake. "I was searching for the surgeon. I do not feel well." Which was no lie as nausea began to brew in her stomach.

"Hmm. I am sorry to hear it." But his nasally voice indicated more disbelief than concern. "But you are nowhere near sick bay."

"I got lost."

He studied her. The lantern light accentuated the malevolence in his eyes. "Have you given much thought to my offer, Miss Denton?"

Marianne raised her nose. "Not a second's worth, Mr. Garrick."

"Hmm. Most unfortunate." He grinned and leaned toward her. "Most unfortunate for you, that is."

His hot breath, tainted with rum, wrinkled her nose. Marianne slipped her hand into the pocket of her skirt and searched for her knife. The thought of stabbing a man horrified her.

Mr. Garrick loosened the cravat around his neck. "Quite unsafe for a woman to wander around the ship at night."

"Pray don't trouble yourself, Mr. Garrick." She laid a hand on his arm to push him back. "I shall remedy the situation immediately."

Lieutenant Garrick clutched her shoulders.

Jerking from his grasp, Marianne stepped backward. The hard wood of the bulkhead blocked her retreat. "I implore you, sir, to behave with the propriety of an officer and a gentleman in the Royal Navy."

He chuckled. "A gentleman's chivalry extends only to ladies, not rebel wenches."

Indignation stiffened her jaw. "I am no wench, sir. I am a respectable lady."

"Upon my word, Miss Denton, what do you expect me to believe when I find you skulking around a place only meant for officers? No doubt you hoped to awaken me so I would follow you here. Ah, such sweet encouragement."

"I have given you no such encouragement, sir!" Marianne's throat closed. Her sweaty hands slid over the knife handle. She was beginning to think she could indeed stab a man—especially this particular man.

He extended his hand. "Give me the knife, Miss Denton."

So he had seen her. "I'll give you the knife." Marianne's tone held the sarcasm she intended. *Right through your black heart.*

In one swift movement, she tried to draw the knife from her skirts. The handle became entangled in the fabric. Her breath halted in her throat as she struggled to extricate the blade. Finally, she freed it. It slipped from her sweaty grip and clanked to the deck.

"Pathetic display, my dear." Garrick snickered as he kicked the blade out of her reach.

Any hope Marianne had fostered that she would escape this monster smothered beneath a wave of dread. *Lord, please help me.*

Garrick took the lantern from her grip and placed it atop a barrel.

"I'll scream." Her voice quavered.

"No, you won't." He slammed his hand over her mouth.

❖ CHAPTER 26 ❖

E ase her down slowly, Matthew," Noah whispered, not daring to use his normal voice lest the sound alert their enemies. He glanced up into the night sky lightly dusted with stars then over the ebony sea.

Matthew directed the two men holding the tackle ropes on either side of the cockboat. They released the lines inch by inch, and the boat slowly lowered over the side of the ship. As soon as they heard the craft strike water, Luke tossed a rope ladder over the edge. Blackthorn, unlit lantern in hand and rope tied about his thick waist, straddled the bulwarks and nodded toward Noah.

"Are you sure?" Noah asked him once more, barely making out his bulky form in the darkness.

"Aye. You got me off that British frigate. I owe you. 'Sides, I'm the strongest swimmer." He looked over the edge and shrugged. "I'll see you soon." His affectionate gaze took in Daniel before he dropped over the side and eased himself down into the rocking vessel.

"Be careful," Agnes called after him, drawing Daniel close to her.

"Pa can do this. He used to be a pirate," the boy whispered with glee.

Boom! A shot thundered in the distance, cracking through the nighttime silence and drawing each man's attention over their larboard quarter. The remnants of a flame drifted away in a tawny haze. The splash came, crisp and foreboding, just yards off their hull. Like all the other shots the sloop had fired that night.

Noah cringed. One more hit to their hull and they'd sink for sure. His crew had done their best to plug the hole with sailcloth, yet some seawater still seeped in through the canvas barrier.

Mr. Weller tugged at the scarf around his neck. "They ain't givin' up."

"So it would seem." Noah ran a hand over the back of his neck, moist with sweat, though the air was cool. Indeed, it appeared the sloop intended to keep firing their guns all night until they struck their target.

And Noah intended to grant them their wish.

"Mr. Heaton," he said. "Inform Mr. Pike to bring her hard to starboard on my signal. He glanced aloft but could not make out the men he'd stationed in the yards ready to adjust sail. Good. The moon had not yet made an appearance. He hoped it would sleep a little longer.

"Yes, Captain." Luke leapt up to the quarterdeck.

His men removed the tackles and handed Noah the other end of the rope attached to Blackthorn. He tied it to the bulwarks, then glanced over the railing. Too dark to see the boat below although he heard it slap against the hull.

"God be with you, Blackthorn," Noah whispered. He didn't know if the man heard him or not, but the rope grew taut in his hand, and he slowly released it bit by bit over the side.

Matthew took his place beside Agnes and Daniel. Weller leaned on the railing and peered into the darkness. Several minutes passed. The rope tightened with a *twang* and tugged at the knot tied around the bulwarks.

Blackthorn could go no farther. Silence settled on the ship as every crewman gaped into the black bowl surrounding them. A pinprick of light formed in the darkness. It blossomed into a small circle. A circle that wobbled with each passing wave.

Hurry, Blackthorn. The rope slackened then tightened again. A distant splash sounded.

Daniel shot Noah an excited glance. Clutching the rope attached to Blackthorn, Noah began pulling it over the railing, handing portions to Matthew and Weller beside him. Together the men groaned in silence as they heaved on the line.

Minutes passed. Noah listened for the sound of splashing.

A flash of yellow off their stern. *Boom!*

Resisting the urge to hit the deck, Noah hauled the rope. The muscles in his arms screamed. A splash echoed off the waves, not the one he hoped to hear, but one that, from its distance, told him the sloop had taken the bait.

Yet the light remained.

"Ahoy aloft!" Blackthorn's muffled voice rose from the sea.

"Papa!" Daniel peered over the side.

The rope slackened and Blackthorn stumbled over the rail, his chest heaving and his body dripping like a fish.

Noah clapped him on the back.

Daniel embraced him. "I knew you could do it."

Another gun blast thundered. Noah signaled the helm. The ship swerved to starboard, sails snapping in the wind. Noah and his men steadied themselves on the deck as Matthew supported his wife. A spray of white foam spit from their larboard point as the *Fortune* tacked away from the decoy they had planted.

The air went aquiver with the roar of guns. Leaping on the gunwale, Noah grabbed a backstay and stared behind them. The bobbing lantern exploded. Shards of wood and glass shot through the air. Then all went black.

Whispered huzzahs sprang from his crew.

Gesturing for them to be silent, Noah sprang into the ratlines and scrambled above to order his top men to furl sail. The slower the ship sailed, the less noise they would make. A gust of wind tugged at his hair and shirt and flapped his breeches. He'd made it to the lower yard before he noted an absence of fear—at least a fear of falling.

His top crew gathered around him to hear his orders, then went about their tasks. Sliding down the backstay, Noah landed with a thud then stared into the darkness behind him.

Hope caused his breath to quicken. Had they lost their pernicious pursuer in the darkness?

Boom! A yellow jet spiked upward, smoke curling in its wake.

Seconds crept by as Noah and his crew held their breath and waited for the ominous splash, the location of which would tell them if their ploy had worked.

Instead of a distant splash, the eerie whine of speeding shot followed by the snap and crack of wood filled the air around Noah.

Marianne struggled against Lieutenant Garrick's grip. Pinned between the bulkhead and his fleshy body, she gulped for air beneath his sweaty hand.

Her attempts at screaming withered into moans.

Terror turned her blood to ice. She kicked him, clawed at him, but to no avail.

Please, Lord. But even as she said the prayer she knew it would take a miracle to save her. Noah was gone. There was no one on this ship to save her now.

His hands groped over her. He gave a heated groan. Nausea curdled her belly. He fumbled with the hooks on her gown.

"Unhand her at once, Mr. Garrick." The strength of the commanding voice left no room for argument.

Withdrawing from her lips, Garrick froze, his eyes simmering. A spark of fear skittered across them.

"I said unhand her."

Garrick took a step back. Marianne's head grew light, and she leaned against the bulkhead to keep from tumbling to the deck.

Garrick slowly turned to face Lieutenant Reed who stood as prim and proper as ever, a look of abject revulsion on his face.

"This is none of your affair, Reed." Garrick sneered. "Go back to your bed and leave us be."

"The captain ordered you to stay away from Miss Denton, I believe, which makes it every bit my business."

Marianne's breath returned to normal as she studied the two men. They stood sizing each other up like lions battling over prey.

Garrick snorted. "And of course you will run and tell the captain like the bootlicking lackey you are."

Mr. Reed lifted a haughty brow. "Since you are assured of my actions, you must know the outcome does not bode favorable for you."

"That is where you are wrong, sir." Garrick gave a pompous snort. "The captain and I have an arrangement."

"Yes, I know of your arrangement. And it stretches only as far as the captain's patience. Which as we both know is as fickle as an ocean squall."

A spark of fear crossed Garrick's eyes, but he stood his ground.

"And you do know the punishment for ravishing a woman is death, do you not?" Mr. Reed raised his brows.

"Not for me, it won't be." Garrick snorted. "Besides, she's the enemy. No one would fault me for putting her in her place."

"Enemy or not, you know the captain favors her." Mr. Reed shrugged. "I wouldn't risk it if I were you."

Garrick wiped the spit from his lips and fingered the service sword hanging at his side. "What's to stop me from killing you and throwing your carcass to the sharks?"

"Perhaps the fact that I won the Royal Naval College swordsmanship competition the year I graduated." An arrogant smile danced over Mr. Reed's lips as his hand crept down to the hilt of his sword.

Lieutenant Garrick narrowed his eyes. His breathing grew rapid. "Madness." Casting Marianne a look of disgust, he shoved past Mr. Reed. At the foot of the ladder, he faced them. "You will regret this. Both of you."

"I never regret, Mr. Garrick. Good evening to you." Mr. Reed's calm voice soothed over Marianne. Grumbling under his breath, Garrick leapt up the ladder and disappeared.

"How can I thank you, Mr. Reed?" She released a heavy sigh and took a step toward him.

"What, pray tell, are you doing down here in the middle of the night?" Anger shot from his hazel eyes. "I cannot help you if you put yourself in such compromising positions. Now, come along and I'll escort you to your cabin."

Marianne dropped her gaze to the knife lying on the deck by the barrel. She must retrieve it without Mr. Reed's notice. She must have that knife or all would be lost. If she didn't pick it up now, someone would, no doubt, find it tomorrow. She kicked off one of her shoes.

"Forgive me, I behaved foolishly." She laid a hand over her heart and leaned on the barrel, feigning a loss of breath. She must delay him. "How did you know we were here?"

The harsh look on Mr. Reed's face faded. "I heard Garrick rise from his bed and leave. Something told me to follow him." His brow wrinkled. "I am sorry for your distress."

Marianne gazed up at him. "You are an honorable man for an Englishman."

"We are not all like Mr. Garrick." He chuckled then proffered an elbow. "Shall we?"

Marianne pressed a hand to her back and started to rise, then she glanced at her feet. "Oh, my shoe. Please forgive me, Mr. Reed." She knelt. Fluttering her skirts around her as cover, she grabbed a shoe in one hand and the knife in the other. Slowly, she rose to her feet, tucking the blade within the folds of her skirt while she eased her foot into her shoe. The knife once again became entangled in the fabric. She could feel the tip tugging at the folds. She only prayed it wouldn't tear her gown. Her heart took up a rapid beat as she smiled at Mr. Reed and placed her other hand on his arm.

The curious look on his face made her blood run cold. "Egad, Miss Denton, what is that in your hand?"

Noah gripped the ledge until his knuckles grew red and gazed out the stern windows of his cabin. A streak of orange flame lit the horizon. He froze in the dark, awaiting the explosion. The menacing splash grated over his tight nerves. Close. Too close. This British captain was savvy. Not a single lantern or candle was lit on the *Fortune*, and still he seemed to know where they were. The last strike had taken a chunk out of their capstan. Noah feared much worse the next time they came within range.

The savage dash of water against the hull told him the *Fortune* sailed only as swiftly through the dark seas as the rent in her hull allowed. Not an altogether safe thing to do when they couldn't see two feet off their bow, but Noah had deemed the fate that followed them to be far worse than the risk of striking a reef or another ship.

Confound it all! Noah fisted his hands across his chest and squinted into the darkness. Nothing but black as dark as coal met his gaze. Only the few stars twinkling overhead separated sky from sea. Like Noah, the British commander had extinguished all lights on board his ship. Only the occasional flashes from the sloop's guns gave away their position. A position that seemed to be forever in Noah's wake.

If he could not evade this monster by daybreak, all would be lost.

The anxious gazes and fainthearted groans of his crew had forced Noah below where he could steal a moment alone and try to formulate a plan of escape. But after an hour, none had come to mind. None but pleading with God for their salvation. And that plan offered no more hope than any other.

I have led these men to their deaths. Noah swallowed down the burning in his throat. Just as he had caused his brother's death. Was this to be his legacy? Not only a failure, but also a murderer?

His thoughts swarmed around Marianne, another of his victims. With Noah killed or captured, she was as good as dead. *"I'll come back for you, I promise."* His last words to her chanted a woeful melody in his mind. Another promise he could not keep. And for Marianne, another person she could not trust.

Noah's heart felt as heavy as a thirty-two pounder and just as deadly. Because of him, everyone he cared about was in harm's way. Everyone he cared about would soon be dead. He was nothing but a disappointment, just as his father had always declared.

The man's rage-filled face bloated in Noah's mind. "You'll never live up to your brother. Never," he spat in disgust then wiped his mouth with his sleeve.

And Noah hadn't. Not only had he not lived up to Jacob's legacy, but with this last venture, Noah had far exceeded his own record of shortcomings.

Boom! The thunder of another cannon pounded the air. Noah gazed at the smoke spiraling upward in the distance, no longer bracing himself for the blast. What would it matter? Perhaps it would be better to get it over with.

The splash crackled the air as if laughing at him. Much closer this time.

"I could never please you, Father." Noah leaned back on the edge of his desk and hung his head.

"You please Me."

Noah's heart picked up a beat. He glanced over the dark cabin. The terror of his impending death had no doubt befuddled his mind. Withdrawing the stained handkerchief from his pocket, Noah placed it over his heart. "If I make it to heaven, brother, I hope you won't be angry at me."

If *I make it to heaven.* But why would God let him through those holy gates? He'd been nothing but incompetent his entire life. Even in his death, Noah would fail. God would no doubt raise His voice in indignation, spout a litany of Noah's failures and cast him from His sight.

"I am not like your father."

That voice again, soft, confident, coming from within him. Emotion clogged Noah's throat. He had called both God and his earthly father cruel taskmasters. Was it possible, as both Matthew and Luke had said, that Noah confused the two?

The blast of a cannon roared.

"I love you. I am proud of you."

Proud of me? Noah rose and took up a pace before the windows. Nothing but his warped imagination turned the creak and groan of the ship into words he longed to hear.

Splash. Closer still.

Yet the promise imbedded within that gentle voice was too much to ignore.

"If that's You, God, where have You been?"

"I have never left."

The gentle words floated around Noah, penetrating his heart with their truth. He was the one who had left God. But who could blame him? After God allowed Jacob to fall to his death? After He allowed Noah to carry the guilt for all those years?

"Why, God, why?"

"You do not know the end yet." Daniel's ponderous words echoed through the darkness. Noah pivoted and headed back the other direction. But what happy ending could such a tragedy produce?

"Trust Me."

A cannon thundered. Noah halted his pacing and stared out the window. Yellow smoke dissipated into the darkness just like his faith had done so many years ago. "Trust You with an ending when the beginning has been so horrid?" Noah shook his head and balled the handkerchief in his hand.

No answer came save the moan of the ship and the rush of water. He wanted to trust God. He wanted to believe there was some purpose to this madness. Some reason for the tragedies. Someone who truly loved him.

But would a God who loved him do the things He...

"Trust Me."

His brother's smiling face formed out of the darkness. He winked at Noah and flashed a challenge from his blue eyes so full of life and adventure. Guilt pressed heavy on Noah, forcing him to his knees.

"Give Me your guilt, son. I will take it from you."

He squeezed his eyes shut. "I don't know how." A sense welled up in his belly. A strong sense that Jacob's death happened for a reason, that there was nothing Noah could have done to prevent it. Nothing would have changed an outcome predestined from before time.

"But why make me a part of it?"

"Give Me the guilt."

"Please tell Jacob I'm sorry."

"He knows."

A cannon thundered as if affirming the statement.

Noah squeezed the handkerchief to his chest. "God, can you ever forgive me? For turning away from you? For my anger toward you?"

"I already have."

Wiping the moisture from his eyes, Noah shifted his shoulders. He felt as if a massive weight had been torn from his back. He drew in a deep breath and his lungs, his very spirit, filled with such a strong sense of love it threatened to knock him over.

He rose, feeling light as a topsail fluttering in the wind. "I've been such a fool, Lord. My anger kept me separated from You—from this." A love so consuming, so pure, it filled every crack and crevice in his heart. He bowed his head. "My God and my King."

Boom!

He lifted his gaze to the flash in the distance. His predicament had not changed. "Lord, if You could, please save us so we can go save Marianne. But if not, if that is not Your will, please save her and bring her home."

Boom!

Wood snapped. Glass flew through the air in an ear-piercing shatter. The last thing Noah remembered was his face hitting the deck.

❖ CHAPTER 27 ❖

Marianne bit her lip. Her legs wobbled. "To what are you referring, sir?"

Mr. Reed gave her a caustic look. "I am referring to the long knife you are hiding in your skirts, miss."

"Oh, that." Her heart sank. Freeing the blade from the folds of her gown, Marianne lifted it, point forward.

Without warning, the lieutenant grabbed her wrist, plucked the knife from her grasp, and released her hand.

Marianne rubbed the mark he left on her skin.

Mr. Reed studied her. "Where did you get this?"

She glanced at the knife Mr. Reed so casually held in his hand. She must get it back. Without it, she would be helpless to assist her country. But surely this officer would never allow someone who was, for all practicality, a prisoner on board this ship, to have a weapon. Unless...

"Mr. Reed, I beg you. Allow me to keep it. I only intended to borrow it for a time. To ward off Lieutenant Garrick. Surely you won't deny an innocent woman the protection she needs against such a lecherous villain." She drew her lips into a pleading pout that she feared made her look ridiculous.

But Mr. Reed did not laugh. Instead, he fingered his chin, his gaze flickering from the knife in his grip to her eyes and back again.

His hesitation gave her hope. "Even if I promise to avoid Mr. Garrick, you know as well as I there is no guarantee of my safety," she added.

"If you aspire to avoid Mr. Garrick, miss, might I suggest you avoid wandering about the bowels of the ship alone at night." He spit out the last word with sarcasm.

Marianne looked down so he couldn't discern the lie in her eyes. "It couldn't be helped. I was not well and needed the surgeon."

He released a sigh of frustration. "Could it not wait until morning? When you could have the captain summon him for you?"

"I'm afraid not, sir."

"Very well, let me show you the way."

She saw his boots turn and his elbow came into her view. She lifted her gaze and offered him a sweet smile. "No need. It seems I have recovered."

"Just like that."

"I believe Mr. Garrick frightened my illness away."

"Perhaps we should employ him as surgeon instead of first lieutenant. Then he could go about scaring everyone into perfect health." He cocked a brow.

A giggle rose to Marianne's lips, but she held it back. "May I have the knife, Mr. Reed?"

"I could be court-martialed."

"No one need know." Marianne saw the tight muscles in his face loosen. "Please, sir. It is bad enough I am a slave aboard this ship, but must I suffer ravishment as well?"

His hazel eyes darkened. Releasing a sigh, he flipped the knife and handed it to her, handle first. Grabbing it before he changed his mind, Marianne slipped it into her pocket.

He offered her his elbow. "What knife?" His lips curved in a rare smile that made him appear quite handsome.

Taking his arm, Marianne allowed him to lead her back to her cabin. Every step heightened her fear that the lieutenant would come to his senses and take back the blade. Perspiration trickled down her back as they navigated the dark companionway. Finally at her cabin, she opened the door and spun around to thank him, but he had already disappeared into the shadows.

Closing her door, Marianne took a deep breath to steady the thrash of her heart. *Thank You, Lord.* Plucking the knife from her pocket, she held it up to the moonlight, its blade a silver slice in the darkness. *Perhaps You are on my side, after all. Perhaps You do have a task for me to accomplish.* For tomorrow, if they came across the USS *Constitution*, Marianne would be ready.

"Captain, Captain." The word tugged on Noah's consciousness, dragging him back to the living.

"Captain." Arms lifted him from behind. Gunpowder and smoke filled his lungs. He coughed and struggled to rise, struggled for a breath, struggled to open his eyes, yet deep down within him, afraid to struggle for anything.

"Captain, we're hit, and the sloop is fast on our wake." The urgency in Luke's voice slapped Noah like a wall of icy water.

Batting Luke's hands aside, Noah rose to his feet and opened his eyes to what was left of his cabin. Wind blasted in through the broken windows. The scent of the sea joined the smoke and the smell of charred wood. Half his desk was missing, leaving nothing but wooden spikes and burnt shavings. Shards of glass littered the deck, and all that remained of one of his chairs was a pile of splinters. A jagged hole pierced his canvas rug. Leaning over, he peered through it to the deck below. Nothing but darkness. At least the shot had not started a fire.

Matthew flung a strip of cloth around his head and began tying it in place. Only then did Noah notice the blood trickling into his eyes.

Wiping it away, he pushed the men aside and barreled for the door. "Status," he barked to Luke.

"Just the one hit to your cabin, Captain." Luke's voice trailed him. "And we are still taking on water."

"The pumps aren't working?"

"The water is leaking in too quickly."

Noah leapt on deck and then up on the quarterdeck. The nervous whispers of his crew joined the creaks and rush of water. Off their stern, their enemy lurked, cloaked in the invisible shroud of darkness.

"Two points to starboard," Noah whispered to Mr. Pike. "Slow and easy."

Sails snapped in the night breeze. The ship's tilt to starboard was barely discernable.

Noah took up a position at the stern railing, Luke by his side. Tension stalked the decks like a nefarious demon. But despite their dire predicament, Noah felt no fear. Renewed faith surged through him. He was no longer alone. Almighty God was with him, and He had all things in His hands. Noah bowed his head. *My life is Yours, Lord. Let Thy will be done.*

A jet of bright yellow in the distance followed by a threatening boom seemed to seal their fate.

Yet...

The splash landed several yards off their larboard quarter.

Minutes passed. Weller, Blackthorn, and Daniel joined Noah and Luke. All five men formed a staunch line of defense across the stern railing.

Another thunderous blast cracked the silence.

Yet no one spoke.

Not even when the next roar came from even farther away.

No huzzahs. No yells of triumph. Just the silence of men who had let go of hope and who didn't want to cling to its fickleness so soon again.

Noah continued praying silently.

He was still praying an hour later when a thin strip of gray lined the horizon.

With cautious hope, he scanned the sea surrounding the ship.

Nothing. Yet still too dark to tell.

Weller coughed.

Daniel began humming a tune.

Minutes passed. The gray strip transformed to saffron and began pushing back the darkness.

Noah swallowed. He gazed over the calm sea, his heart in his throat. Nothing in sight but cobalt blue, furrowed with creamy ribbons. Slowly turning, he took in the entire panorama. Not a hint of sail or mast marred the golden horizon.

"Masthead, what do you see?" Noah yelled to the lookout above.

"I see nothing, Captain. Not a thing!"

The sun peeked over the horizon. Wave crests glittered with golden light.

Huzzahs rang through the ship, pushing the tension overboard to the depths.

Thank You, Lord.

Luke slapped Noah on the back and nodded his approval.

Weller's shoulders lowered, and he released the loudest sigh Noah had ever heard.

"God protected us." Daniel's voice sounded like an angel's. He gazed up at Noah with sparkling brown eyes.

"Yes, He did." Noah drew the boy to himself and gripped his shoulder.

Luke crossed his arms over his chest. "God? Humph."

Blackthorn scratched his head. Morning sunlight turned his tan face to bronze and accentuated his two missing teeth. "Sink me. I'm startin' t' believe that as well."

"I told you, Pa, I told you." Daniel smiled up at his father.

Luke rolled his eyes and turned away. "Where should we point her, Captain?"

"North by northwest. I still intend on overtaking the frigate."

"With a rent in our hold?" A breeze whipped Luke's hair about his head.

Noah furrowed his brow. "Very well, furl sail and send a crew down to patch the hole as best they can and pump out the remaining water. Then we must be on our way."

Every minute they delayed meant another minute Marianne must suffer aboard that British frigate.

"We've lost three guns, Cap'n." Weller gaped at Noah as though Noah's mind had also been a casualty of the battle.

"Aye, but we have five left, do we not?" Noah forced confidence into this tone, but Mr. Weller simply frowned.

Daniel, however, beamed a hearty grin. "That's the way, Mr. Noah!"

Blackthorn gazed out to sea then drew Daniel close. "Ye know my thoughts on the matter. Pure foolery."

Noah chuckled. "And it wasn't pure foolery when we had all eight guns?"

Blackthorn nodded and joined in his laughter.

With a smile, Luke turned and began shouting orders to furl sail.

Noah touched his shoulder. "Wait, let me speak to the men first."

Luke nodded then cupped his hands around his mouth. "Belay that. All hands, assemble amidships!"

Taking a position at the quarterdeck railing, Noah gazed at his measly crew as slowly one by one, his men mustered on the main deck, their curious gazes filtering upward. A surge of pride rose within him at their loyalty and courage.

Taking a deep breath, he said a silent prayer for the right words. Something had changed during the long night, during the fear, during the thunderous blasts, during the heartache. Noah had not only renewed his relationship with God, but the Lord had forgiven him and filled him with such love he'd never known.

And now he knew what he was supposed to do.

"We are no longer a private merchantman." He began, ignoring the quizzical groans. "As of today, we are no longer the *Fortune*." The groans silenced and a sea of wrinkled brows stared back at him. "Today, gentlemen, we are the *Defender*." Noah raised his hand. "I deem this ship a privateer for the United States of America. Let us defend the freedom we have come to love. Let us defend our homes, our families, our cities from the pompous tyranny that is trying to crush us."

The men stared agape at him. Seconds passed. Would they join him? Or would they think him mad?

"But don't we need a letter of marque or somethin'?" Mr. Simon said.

"And more guns?" Mr. Boone chuckled and his fellow sailors joined him.

"Yes, we do." Noah's shout silenced the laughter. "Items I intend to procure next time we make port. But for now, we haven't the time to follow proper procedure. We must help defend the USS *Constitution*."

"An' risk bein' hanged as a pirate?" Mr. Lothar spit to the side.

"Some things are worth the risk, Mr. Lothar." Noah gazed across the grimy faces of his crew. Exhaustion tugged on their haggard skin. "Are you with me?"

The wind blasted over them. A snap sounded from above, and all eyes shot to the American flag flapping on the gaff of their foremast, its red and white stripes waving proudly in the breeze. Each man seemed mesmerized by its beauty.

One by one they dropped their gazes as shouts sprang from their midst.

"For America!"

"We are wit' you, Cap'n!"

"For freedom!"

"For the prize money!" one man yelled, eliciting chuckles from the others.

The men pumped fists into the air.

Luke gave Noah a slanted grin and shook his head. He faced the crew. "Let's be about it, men. Rupert, aloft to furl sail! Mr. Boone, fetch planks and nails to repair the hole!"

The men scattered to their duties.

"Pa, you get to be a pirate again." Daniel snapped hair from his face.

Blackthorn grinned, revealing the black holes of his two missing teeth. "Aye, but not for treasure this time, son. For something far more valuable: honor and country and the life of an innocent woman."

Patting the handkerchief in his pocket, Noah leapt on the gunwale. He grabbed a line and leaned over the churning waters. A crisp morning breeze played with his hair and filled his nostrils with the briny smell of the sea. Blood pumped through his veins, heightening his senses, strengthening his resolve. A sense of purpose filled him. And for the first time in his life, he felt as though he had finally come home.

Perhaps he did have a destiny after all.

Perhaps this had been his destiny all along.

Marianne hefted the sack of laundry in her arms and trudged down the ladder. She blew a breath toward her forehead, sending her hair fluttering and cooling the perspiration on her brow. The smell of rot and sweat and bilge assailed her. Would she ever get used to the foul stench of a ship below deck? Or the heat?

Eight days had passed since she'd hidden the knife in her cabin. Eight days and they'd not come across a single ship, American or otherwise. Eight days in which she'd been forced to endure the captain's furious grumblings as he pored over his charts and snapped at anyone who dared enter his cabin. Marianne was beginning to think she'd risked Mr. Garrick's ravishment to steal a blade she would never need.

Sorrow tightened her throat. Perhaps she had not heard from God. Perhaps she had no destiny at all.

Making her way to the laundry, she lowered the stuffed bag and tossed it beside the others. Griffin, the sailor who cleaned the captain's clothes, looked up from the huge water-filled barrel he stirred and gave her his usual scowl. Black soot blotched his face and his muscled bare arms. Marianne resisted the urge to suggest he dunk himself in the barrel along with the clothes.

Turning, she withdrew her handkerchief and dabbed at the perspiration on her neck and face. The day, like all the others before it, had slogged by with a legion of chores and errands until the ache in her feet matched the one in her back. Possessed by one of his foul moods, the captain had spent the day in his cabin ordering her about and criticizing everything she did. She had not laid his tooth powder and cloth out properly. The water in his basin wasn't warm enough. She'd forgotten his morning sip of brandy. She'd missed a few specks of dust on his boots. After a while Marianne had drowned out his incessant whining and simply nodded and went about her tasks— tasks that had become so routine to her, her mind could be occupied elsewhere with thoughts of distant lands and magical places where she was free and happy and not a prisoner aboard a British warship.

But much to her dismay, Noah always appeared in those distant lands. It had been a little over a month since he'd dropped over the side and left her. Why couldn't she get him out of her mind? Instead of dwelling on what could never be, she'd resorted to praying for him and for Luke, Weller, Blackthorn, and precious Daniel. Praying they were all safe somewhere.

She pressed a hand on her back and started on her way back to the captain's cabin when a burst of muffled thunder echoed through the timbers of the ship. A storm? *Lord, not another storm.* Memories of the last storm she had endured pushed themselves forward in her mind. And there she found Noah again, coming to her cabin to comfort her.

"You enchant me." The memory of his soft words lit a dark place in her heart. She could still see the look of adoration in his blue eyes, so clear and bright against his tawny skin. She could feel his gentle embrace, could sense his warm breath on her neck and his lips on hers. Heat swept over her as she ascended the ladder.

Did he love her? Or was it just the allure of the moment? Regardless, he had not come back for her. He had left her a prisoner both of this ship and of her memories. Memories of being loved and cherished by an honorable man—if only for a moment.

Boot steps pounded on the deck above as she made her way upward. Shouts flew like pistol shot through the air, the captain's authoritative voice chief among them.

Thunder bellowed again in the distance.

All this commotion for a storm?

Curiosity drove Marianne farther above where she halted at the head of the companionway and stared at the flurry of sailors dashing about the deck. A brisk wind wafted around her, playing with the hem of her skirt and fluttering her wayward strands of hair. The captain and his officers stood at the quarterdeck stanchions, taking their posts as masters of the sea, their jaws tight and their eyes focused straight ahead.

The ship bolted. Bracing her feet, Marianne wove through a mob of sailors to the railing. Following the gazes of the officers, she squinted against a setting sun to see the faint tips of masts, crowded with snowy sail, poking above the horizon.

Gray smoke puffed and the thunder bellowed again. That was no storm. It was *cannon fire*. Her heart clamped. Had they found the *Constitution*? Too far away to tell.

And who was firing at whom?

As the frigate sped toward the battling ship, Marianne's gaze distinguished the masts as two sets from two different ships. A cloud of smoke filled the gap between them.

She glanced aloft. With all sails crowding the masts and bursting with wind, the *Undefeatable* flew through the water like an angry demon out for blood. The ship pitched over a rising swell. Salty spray showered over Marianne, threatening to loosen her firm grip on the railing. Her stomach flipped and nausea boiled within. Fear of the sea, fear of death, fear of living out her days on board this ship caused the blood to swell in her head until it throbbed.

Though longing to go below to the false safety of her cabin, Marianne kept her feet in place. At least until she discovered the identity of the ships.

French, British, or American? She shifted her gaze between Captain Milford, his officers, and the ships, knowing one or all of them would soon answer her questions.

Above her, top men scurried across lines to adjust and tighten the canvas to the wind. Thank God Noah was not among them anymore.

Another thunderous boom echoed across the graying sky. "Bear off, haul your braces, ease sheets!" Mr. Garrick shouted.

Minutes passed as the *Undefeatable* plunged through roller after roller, riding the sea high and wide, foam spraying over the deck.

Marianne craned her neck and she squinted toward the ships, but she couldn't make out their ensigns.

"It's the HMS *Guerriére*!" Captain Milford barked, lowering his spyglass.

As the ships closed in on one another, the sky exploded in a barrage of cannon fire and the *pop pop pop* of musket shot. A thick cloud of smoke consumed the two ships. When it cleared, one of the vessels veered toward the setting sun, bringing its flag into full view. The red and white stripes and star-studded blue flapped proudly in the evening breeze.

The USS *Constitution*. And she seemed to be holding her own against the British warship. Marianne's heart swelled with pride, then shrank in fear.

The *Constitution* was no match for *two* British warships.

"Clear for battle!" Lieutenant Garrick bellowed. "Starboard guns stand by!"

The fife and drum played the "Heart of Oak," signaling the call to quarters. A shrill whistle sent sailors scrambling over the deck, removing all obstructions and sprinkling sand across the planks. Some landed on her shoes. Crewmen rigged nets over the deck to protect those below from falling blocks and other tackle. Gun crews mobbed the guns as powder boys leapt above from the hatches carrying the powder bags, wads, and shot. Marianne thought of Daniel and thanked God he wasn't here as well.

But she was. And she had to do something.

Boom boom boom boom boom, the blast of a broadside drew her gaze back to the battling ships, not more than fifty yards away now. When the smoke cleared, the *Guerriére's* main yard hung shattered and lifeless.

She resisted the urge to raise a huzzah in the air. Excitement charged through her as the *Constitution* bore around the British ship yet again. The air thundered with another broadside. Marianne held her breath until the sooty smoke cleared. The mizzenmast of the *Guerriére* dragged lifeless in the water. *Thank You, Lord.* The *Constitution* was winning!

Could the ship also beat the *Undefeatable* and rescue Marianne? Dare she hope?

"Run out the guns!" Mr. Reed's deep voice bounced over the deck.

The *Undefeatable* would be upon the ships within minutes. Marianne faced the battling duo again just in time to see the two ships ram into each other and the *Guerriére*'s bowsprit become tangled in the *Constitution*'s fallen lines. Musket and pistol shot popped through the air. Along with the screams of men.

A gust of wind struck her, bringing with it the sting of gunpowder.

"We've got her now!" Captain Milford shouted.

He was right. Entangled as she was and unable to maneuver, the *Constitution* would have no defense against the *Undefeatable*'s broadside.

Panic iced through Marianne. She must do something. Perhaps this was her time. Perhaps she'd been placed here for such a time as this.

❖ CHAPTER 28 ❖

S ail-ho!" A shout bellowed from the masthead.

"Where away, Mr. Crenshaw?" Noah scanned the surrounding sea.

"Off our starboard bow, Cap'n."

Plucking his scope from his belt, Noah jumped onto the main deck and raised it to his eye. Steadying it against the rise and fall of the ship, he focused on the fading horizon.

"Two sets of sail!" the shout spiraled down from above just as the billowing canvas came into view.

Noah lowered the scope. "Four points to starboard, Mr. Pike," he yelled over his shoulder. "All hands on deck. Let go the topgallants!"

Behind him, Luke repeated orders that sent his meager crew scurrying into the shrouds.

Noah braced his boots over the hard planks as the ship veered to starboard. Wind whipped his hair, tossing it in his face. He snapped it away and raised his glass again.

They'd not spotted a sail since their encounter with the British war sloop. And now two sails appeared near the area Marianne had said the *Undefeatable* was to join the *Guerriére*.

Marianne. His heart jumped at the thought that she was near. *Oh Lord, let it be her.*

Under a full press of canvas, the newly christened *Defender* sped through the choppy seas. But not fast enough. Though his men had plugged the hole with canvas and tar and boarded it up with wood, seawater seeped in to join the waterlogged hold, weighing them down.

Luke appeared beside him, his stubbled jaw stiffening. They shared a knowing glance.

"Make that three sets of sail!" Mr. Crenshaw's excited voice once again showered over them from above.

Noah raised his scope. Three distinct hulls settled on the horizon. And if his eyes weren't playing tricks on him, a cloud of smoke drifted between them.

Cannon shot thundered, confirming his suspicions.

"Seems we're intruding on someone's battle." Luke rubbed the scar on his ear.

"But 'Whose battle?' is the question. Only one interests me."

Scratching his chin, Matthew took a spot on the other side of Noah. Behind them, the setting sun tossed golden spires across the foam-capped waves and reflected on the ships beyond.

Another burst of cannon cracked the air. Noah leapt up the foredeck ladder and dashed to the bow for a better view. He studied the ships through his glass but still could not make out their ensigns.

The *Defender* plunged down a massive swell, and Noah gripped the railing as salty spray stung his face.

More cannon shot exploded.

He focused his scope on the ship closest to him. His heart skipped a beat. He'd know that ship anywhere. The *Undefeatable*. Spinning on his heel, he approached the foredeck railing and spotted Weller and Blackthorn below. "Ready the guns!"

With a shake of his head and a look of disbelief, Weller swerved about and called for the men to assemble. Blackthorn and Daniel scrambled to their positions at one of the stern guns.

Noah patted his pocket, seeking comfort from his brother's handkerchief, but nothing but fabric and air met his touch. It was gone. He'd had it in his hand when the shot crashed into his cabin. Panic seized him. But then he realized something anew—he had another comfort, one that went far deeper than a piece of fabric, a comfort that didn't fade. An odd peace settled on him. He no longer needed the token. His brother was in heaven, and Noah had been forgiven. His guilt was gone. His debt was paid.

Not by a bloody handkerchief, but by the blood of the Son of God.

Noah smiled and turned to Agnes and Matthew who stood arm in arm gazing at the battling ships. The woman's normally ruddy cheeks had turned as white as sea foam.

Even Luke's blue eyes held a hint of foreboding.

Noah swallowed. Was he leading his men to their deaths? *Oh Lord, please be with us.* Turning, he stared at the *Undefeatable.*

Undefeatable, indeed.

Yes, his ship was half its size. Yes, he was taking on water. Yes, he had only twenty crewmen compared to the frigate's two hundred and fifty. Yes, he only had five guns compared to the frigate's thirty-two.

But he had something far more powerful than anything they possessed.

He had God on his side.

Gripping the handle of the knife through the fabric of her skirt, Marianne squeezed past throngs of sailors as they dashed through the companionway. The pounding of her heart joined the pulsing cadence of the crew's boots thumping over the wooden planks as they bumped and shoved her with barely a pardon tossed her way.

She gazed over the harried scene. With most of the bulkheads removed to clear the area for battle, the lower deck had transformed into a large open space that reminded Marianne of a dreary tavern where she'd once found her inebriated father. Only the occasional furniture or crate marked where the walls once stood. The crew's anxious muttering tied her nerves in knots. Though no doubt accustomed to battle, the men's heightened intensity told her that familiarity with war did not lessen their terror. She pressed a hand over her stomach in an attempt to quell her own fear. They intended to do battle against the USS *Constitution*—against her country's ship. And in the *Constitution*'s present situation, entwined with the *Guerriére*, they would win.

But Marianne could not let that happen.

Thankfully, no one noticed her as she slipped down the ladder farther below decks. The mad dash of water against the ship muffled both the shouts above and distant cannon fire, offering a surreal peace—a peace that could be obliterated at any moment with a puncture to the hull.

Allowing the sea's mighty fingers to pour in, grab her, and drag her to the depths.

Marianne trembled. She could not think of that now.

The rotting smell drenched her heaving lungs as she made her way to the tiller. Without a lantern, darkness created ghostly shadows on the bulkhead. Shadows that loomed above her on both sides as though they intended to pounce on her and stop her from completing her mission. Sweat crept down her back and chest, molding the fabric of her gown to her body. The knife slipped from her moist hand. She fumbled for it in her pocket and gained the handle once again.

Voices grew louder. Light poured down the ladder.

Drat. Marianne shrank into a dark corner. Crewmen descended like a waterfall, shouting and cursing. Footsteps tromped over the wooden deck.

Blood raced through Marianne's veins. Her head grew light. She closed her eyes and stiffened against the wood.

Groans screeched through the dank air as if the men lifted something heavy. More footsteps. More cursing. And then they were gone.

Marianne melted against the rough wood. She caught her breath, then inched forward, feeling her way as she went.

The ship pitched. She stumbled to the deck. A splinter pierced her hand. Her knees ached. But she barely felt the pain above the numbing terror that gripped her heart.

If she accomplished this. If she disabled the ship and Captain Milford discovered her treachery, what would he do to her? Did the Royal Navy punish women in the same way they did men? Would she be flogged? Or worse. . .

Executed?

Her knees transformed to custard. She couldn't find the strength to rise.

Bowing her head, her vision blurred with tears. *Lord, help me. I'm a coward. I need Your courage.*

She sat for a moment, searching for the voice of God amidst the distant gunfire, the creak and groan of the ship, the boot steps pounding like hail above her.

But no voice came.

Yet. . .

Strength returned to her legs. Bracing herself against the deck, she rose to her feet, and once again grabbed the knife in her pocket.

She took a step forward.

For such a time as this, for such a time as this. Whispery words formed from the water crashing against the hull.

"So be it, Lord," Marianne said. "Whatever comes of this, let it come, but I will obey You. I will fulfill my destiny."

Armed with a courage that was not her own, she entered the tiller room. She withdrew the knife from her pocket then brushed her fingers over the deckhead above her. There. The rough hemp scratched her skin. Gripping the ropes with one hand and the knife in the other, she began sawing through the tight threads.

Minutes that seemed like hours passed. Sweat moistened her face. Blisters formed on her palms. Fear threatened to force her to her knees. But finally, she sliced through the final twine. With a snap and an eerie whine, the ropes split.

Zip. Twang.

Clank! The sound of iron and crashing wood echoed through the hull.

Marianne jumped back. The knife slipped from her hand.

No time to retrieve it. She dashed toward the ladder. Her knee hit a crate. Pain shot into her thigh. Grabbing her skirts, she leapt to the deck above faster than she thought possible.

Joining a line of sailors rushing down the companionway, she followed them up another ladder. Better to be found above than suspiciously hiding in her cabin. She emerged onto the main deck to a wall of smoke-laden wind and a man at the helm shouting, "We've lost steering, Captain."

Curses, followed by commands flew from Captain Milford's mouth. "Send men down to check on the tiller ropes at once, Mr. Reed! Mr. Blake, have the top men adjust sail. We must maintain our course!"

An unavoidable smile toyed upon Marianne's lips as she pressed through the crush of sailors and made her way to the railing. She gazed toward the *Constitution*, still entwined in the *Guerriére's* lines. Swords drawn, men from both crews scrambled back and forth between the ships. The yellow spark of pistol and musket fire flashed from the top yards.

Wind snapped in the sails above her. The *Undefeatable* yawed widely to starboard.

Away from the battling ships!

A river of foul words spewed from the captain's lips, confirming Marianne's assessment.

"Blast it all!" He pounded a trail across the quarterdeck. "We'll have to come around again."

Lieutenant Reed and a horde of men jumped up from below and approached the captain. Reed caught his breath. "The tiller ropes have been cut through, Captain."

"Cut through?" Red blotches exploded on the captain's face.

"Yes, Captain."

"Who would do such a thing?" Spit flew from the captain's mouth.

Heart clawing at her throat, Marianne swerved around and gazed down at the trail of foam bubbling off the side of the ship. The wind blasted over her, stealing what was left of her breath. Her knuckles whitened on the railing.

She lifted her gaze and saw a two-masted merchantman heading straight for them.

She closed her eyes against the deceptive vision, no doubt a fabrication of her overwrought nerves. Clearly she'd gone mad with fear. As she sought her mind for an ounce of reason, she listened to the sounds surrounding her: the distant crack of gunfire, the rush of water against the hull, the whine of strained wood, the curses and commands of the ship's officers.

Nothing had changed.

"A sail! Bearing fast, Captain, off our stern!" The call from the tops bounced off the deck. She forced her eyes open.

The *Fortune* stormed toward them, foam cresting her bow.

And there perched on the gunwale, gripping a stay and leaning over the edge of the ship, stood Noah, hair flapping in the wind, looking more like a pirate than a merchantman.

Noah's heart soared. Marianne. She stood at the railing, her maroon gown fluttering in the breeze. Wayward strands of her brown hair blew about her face. She was alive. He wished he could see her expression. Wished he knew whether she saw him, and if so, what was she thinking?

"What ails the frigate?" Luke approached the bow railing.

With a frown, Noah's gaze took in the ship once again. At first sight, he'd seen nothing but Marianne. But now he noticed that the frigate veered away from the battle. But why? One glance at her stern and then at her sails brought a chuckle to his lips.

"She's lost steerage."

Luke gave a disbelieving snort. "You don't say?"

Noah dropped from the gunwale to the deck, spouting a string of rapid-fire orders that sent some of his crew up into the shrouds and others to the remaining guns.

"She's lost her steering, my friend," he repeated, slapping a stunned Luke on the back.

Matthew approached, shaking his head. "How?"

"I haven't time to ponder it." Noah could hardly believe it himself. "But let us not miss the opportunity it affords." He found his gunner down on the main deck. "Weller, load the chain shot. We'll go for her masts."

"Aye, aye, Cap'n." The stout man grinned, his single gold tooth twinkling in the setting sun.

"They may not be able to steer, but they've still got their guns." Matthew's voice carried a hint of fear.

Noah gave him a reassuring look. "Then we shall have to stay out of their path, shan't we?"

"What luck," Luke exclaimed with a huff.

"Not luck." Noah's gaze shot beyond the *Undefeatable* to the two warships stuck together in the distance. "Whoever or whatever destroyed the frigate's tiller saved the *Constitution*. Until she frees herself, any enemy that comes along could blast her into splinters within minutes." Noah rubbed the back of his neck. No, not luck at all. *Thank You, Lord.*

A sly grin formed on Luke's lips. "Luck or not, I say we make it so the *Undefeatable* never has that chance."

"Aye, and then we'll go after the *Guerriére*." Blackthorn joined the conversation, rubbing his thick hands together.

Noah flinched. "What, pray tell, has sparked such fervency, Blackthorn? I seem to remember hesitancy on your part in joining this venture."

From his six foot two frame, Blackthorn gazed at Noah, his black hair flailing in the wind. "Sink me, but too much has happened for me to deny that God is with us." He shook his head. "My pretty wife was right all along. About God, about our special son." His gaze took in the ship until he found Daniel at the stern. "An' about God bein' real an' powerful an' active in people's lives."

Despite the chill of the approaching night, Noah felt warmth down to his toes. He grinned and slapped the man on the back. "I couldn't have said it better."

Noah gazed at the *Undefeatable*. He hoped—no, he prayed—that today would be the day the mighty ship would not live up to its name. He needed her to be not only defeatable but also willing to surrender her precious cargo into Noah's hands. Even as his thoughts drifted to Marianne, he could no longer see her on deck.

Good. She'd be out of the line of fire. But Noah still had no idea how to rescue her from the frigate. How did one board a man-of-war, saunter through two hundred armed sailors and fifty marines and beg the captain's pardon while he stole the man's steward? An impossible task, to be sure.

"Nothing is impossible with Me." Noah started beneath the inner voice. "Okay, Lord. Then You're going to have to show me what to do," he whispered. "I'm putting my trust in You."

Crossing the main deck, he leapt to the helm to assist Mr. Pike with the wheel. While Luke handled the sails, Noah gently coaxed the *Defender* to within forty yards of the drifting *Undefeatable*, just off her larboard quarter. So close he could hear the anguish and fury searing in Captain Milford's voice as he stood at the railing, raising his fist in Noah's direction.

The red coats of the marines lining the deck of the *Undefeatable* darkened to maroon in the deepening shadows. Drums thrummed a war song as sailors dashed across her deck. Men crowded the yards, adjusting sail to push the ship in the right direction. Others hovered around guns.

"Steady as she goes," Noah ordered Mr. Pike as he released the wheel and dropped on the main deck.

Luke and Matthew joined him.

"Are you sure they can't hit us?" Matthew's brow lowered beneath fearful gray eyes.

Noah tightened his jaw. "Yes." He hoped. He prayed.

Matthew swallowed hard. He must have sensed Noah's hesitation. He glanced down a nearby hatch, and Noah knew he thought of his wife. If either were hurt, Noah would never forgive himself.

If *any* of his crew were injured, he would never forgive himself.

"Get below, Matthew, and attend to Agnes," he ordered.

With an appreciative nod, the older man rushed away.

Noah snapped the hair from his eyes. "We are out of range of the swivels on their stern, and they can't maneuver their broadside in our direction," he said more to comfort himself than his first mate. At least by his best calculations—the calculations of a man who'd never faced battle before.

As if in defiance of his words, the muzzles of twelve guns thrust through their ports on the main deck. Noah's stomach dropped.

The sky exploded with a thunderous boom.

Marianne paced before the stern windows in the captain's cabin. She wrung her hands together and released a sigh.

Noah had come for her.

The thought swirled around in her mind, making her dizzy, and finding no solid place to land. Her toe banged into the bulkhead. Spinning on her heel, she headed the other direction.

He had come for her. Just as he'd promised. For her? Plain, ordinary Marianne.

Just after Captain Milford spotted the *Fortune*, he'd also spotted her standing at the railing. Immediately, he ordered two marines to escort her below and lock her in his cabin. Why? Did he think she'd jump overboard? If so, he didn't know her too well.

Distant gunfire tapped the gray sky. Boot steps pounded above her. She fisted her hands at her side. She must know what was happening. Was Noah all right?

She glanced at the battle raging outside and realized his predicament. Was he mad?

Single-handedly taking on a British frigate? Albeit, a frigate that had gone on a wayward stroll, but a fully armed and functional frigate, nonetheless.

What was his plan? Did he think he would saunter on deck and steal her away beneath the British officer's blue-blooded noses?

What did it matter? He'd come for her. Her heart swelled.

She'd completed her destiny, and the man she loved had come to her rescue.

She would die happy with that knowledge.

And die she might.

Halting, she leaned her hands on the ledge and plastered her face against the cold, salt-encrusted glass. At the right corner of the window, the edge of the *Fortune*'s stern drifted in the sea just thirty yards away.

Too close.

Weren't they too close?

Her answer came in an enormous roar that jerked the frigate to starboard and sent a quiver through her timbers.

The deafening blasts echoed across the water and pounded in Noah's ears. His crew froze as if time stood still. No doubt they all knew that dropping to the deck would make no difference if one of the shots struck them at this range.

Splash after splash chimed a sweet melody in the sea just off their bow.

"When that cap'n gives a warnin' shot, he gives a warnin' shot." Weller chuckled though his laugh came out tense.

Noah gathered his breath. "Indeed. Aim our guns at their rigging, if you please, Mr. Weller."

"Aye, aye, Cap'n." Weller turned and brayed orders to the gun crew.

Luke's blue eyes, wild with the thrill of battle, flickered over Noah before he leapt into the shrouds to direct the men aloft.

Blackthorn and Daniel hovered around one of the guns on the starboard side. Blackthorn, his stance tight and his dark eyes burning with zeal, stood before Daniel like an iron shield of protection. But as Noah approached, Daniel didn't appear to need protecting. The boy glanced up at him, a mischievous look in his eyes, a grin that reflected no fear, and a lit slow match in his hand.

"I'll allow you the first shot, Blackthorn," Noah said. "I assume you'd want the honors."

A wide grin, devoid of two teeth split the man's face. "Me pleasure, Cap'n."

The honor the title bestowed caused Noah's throat to close. He turned away.

Commotion on the *Undefeatable* drew his gaze to a gun crew preparing one of the swivel guns on their stern.

Luke dropped to the deck with a thud. "The men are ready, Captain."

Noah glanced aloft where his crew awaited orders to unfurl sail. Mr. Pike, ever vigilant at the helm, gripped the wheel in preparation to bring the ship across the frigate's bow.

Within reach of her swivel guns.

In order so that Noah could rake her and cripple her rigging, then be off in the wind's eye before she could respond.

At least that was the plan.

"On my mark, gentleman!" he bellowed.

Sails flapped and thundered. Then *whoomp*, the canvas caught the wind and billowed above them like bulging muscles. The ship jerked, then veered to starboard, picking up speed.

Bracing his boots on the deck, Noah took his position at one of the guns beside Weller. The *Defender* swept forward, crashing into rollers and sweeping spray onto her deck. Before them, the *Undefeatable* rose like a massive whale emerging from the sea.

"Fire!" Noah yelled.

Weller applied the red-hot end of the wick to the gun's touchhole.

Five guns exploded in a deafening chorus. The ship quivered under the blast, then groaned in protest.

Black smoke slapped Noah in the face.

Coughing, he batted it away, gulping for air. "Hard to larboard!" he shouted.

With straining lines and creaking blocks, the *Defender* lurched and swung away from the *Undefeatable*.

Yellow flames shot through the haze in the distance. The air burst with thunderous *boom* after thunderous boom as the *Undefeatable* gave her reply.

Clutching the railing, Noah shook the salty spray from his face and peered through the dissipating smoke. No eerie whine of speeding shot sped past his ears, no strike jolted the ship, no screams of agony, only the splash of cannon balls sounded as they struck the sea.

But then, in the distance, the ominous snap of a mighty piece of wood crackled the air.

"Move aside! Get out of the way!" followed by various expletives shot toward Noah through the fog.

A thunderous boom echoed. Not the boom of a cannon. But the sound of sweet carnage.

As the last vestiges of sooty mist cleared, Noah's eyes confirmed what his ears had already told him. The top half of the mainmast of the *Undefeatable* had toppled to the deck and now hung over the side in a tangle of halyards, cordage, and sailcloth.

Huzzahs filled his ship like bubbles in champagne.

Noah released a breath. His crew swamped him with congratulations.

Without their mainmast, without their steering, the *Undefeatable* was nothing but a crippled hulk.

"Bring us athwart her bow, Mr. Pike. We'll give her another raking." Noah scanned the deck. "Mr. Boone, go below and check for damage. Matthew, retrieve my weapons."

His old friend gave Noah a curious look before disappearing down a hatch.

Off Noah's starboard side, another snapping sound, followed by cheers, drew his gaze. Released from the maze of tangled lines, the *Constitution* eased away from her enemy. Free at last, she appeared in far better condition than the *Guerriére*, whose main- and foremasts toppled to her deck in a snarled heap of lines and canvas. At least now the *Constitution* could defend herself.

Behind the two ships, the last traces of sunlight spilled over the horizon. In minutes, it would be too dark to see anything.

The *Defender* spun around and came in across the drifting *Undefeatable*'s bow. Noah grabbed his spyglass and searched her decks for any sign of Marianne. He saw nothing but the frenzied efforts of the crew as they chopped away the broken mast before it dragged the ship onto her side. Captain Milford stood at the head of the quarterdeck, flanked by his officers, his head bowed and his hands gripping the railing.

Marianne must still be below.

Short of pummeling the *Undefeatable* into surrender with broadside after broadside, and risk injuring Marianne in the process, Noah had no idea how he was going to get her off that ship.

❖ CHAPTER 29 ❖

The pulse of guns throbbed in Marianne's ears. She darted to the cabin door and swung it open. The red blur of a marine uniform jumped in her vision. A musket crossed the doorframe, barring her passage.

"Allow me to pass at once!" She stomped her foot.

The man's face was a mask of control. "My orders are to keep you within, miss."

"Blast your orders, sir. Can you not tell we have been fired upon?"

An ear-piercing snap split the air, followed by an ominous groan, screams and shouts, then a *boom* that shook Marianne straight down to her bones.

A flicker of alarm crossed the marine's stiff features.

Just before the ship jerked to larboard.

Arms flailing, Marianne toppled over the deck and struck the captain's cabinet. Pain flared up her arm and into her shoulder. Shaking the fog from her head, she leaned forward and inched over the tilted deck, back to the open door. Surely the marine would have left his post for more important tasks.

But there he stood, rigid as a wooden soldier.

She slammed the door on him and stumbled to the stern windows. Squeezing onto the ledge, she peered out at the chaotic scene. Turbulent seas churned beneath a smoke-filled darkening sky. Who had struck them? The *Constitution*?

Or, as unimaginable as the thought could be, Noah?

Oh Lord, keep him safe.

Before she finished her prayer, the *Fortune* swung into view, riding high and wide on a valiant steed of foamy white.

Her heart stopped beating as she pressed her forehead to the glass, seeking its captain.

There. On the foredeck, feet spread apart, spyglass to his eye, Noah stood—in defiance of his lack of battle experience—with the confidence of a hardened warrior.

But he wasn't a warrior. He was a merchantman. And by all appearances, a merchantman who had lost his good sense.

"I'm here! I'm here!" Marianne waved her arms in desperation but soon dropped them to her lap. He could not see her.

But she must get his attention.

Why? Even if she did, how could he rescue her? The frigate was disabled, but not the men aboard her. She could hear all two hundred and fifty of them buzzing above her like a swarm of angry bees.

Lord, what do I do?

A undeniable pain lanced her heart as she gazed at the man she loved. He was so close. So very close. So close she could almost see the resolution on his face, could almost hear his deep, courageous voice.

But they might as well be oceans apart.

Withdrawing from the glass, she brushed her frantic fingers over the edges of the window, searching for a latch, a lever, something that might open them. She pounded on the panes. Her palms ached as tears streamed down her cheeks.

She searched again. A latch. There *was* a latch. She unhooked it and shoved open the window. A blast of chilled air shoved her backward. She barreled forward and poked her head through the opening. Wind, stained with gunpowder and smoke, whipped over her face from all sides, tearing her hair from its pins and nearly forcing her to retreat.

She dared to glance below at the foaming, angry waves. Her throat closed, and a shudder ran through her. Tearing her gaze from the sight, she peered toward Noah's ship.

"Noah!" She tried to yell but the heavy breeze stole her words and swept them away.

"There she is!" Noah lowered his scope and handed it to Luke. The *Defender* had tacked around the bow of the *Undefeatable* and now sailed off her larboard quarter. He pointed at the stern of the frigate where two arms waved frantically amidst a wild array of wind-thrashed brown hair.

Luke chuckled. "Quite a woman you have there."

Have? Noah was surprised at the sudden joy that flared within him at his friend's statement. Was Marianne his? Did she forgive him for leaving her? "Sink me, she's broke through the captain's cabin!" Blackthorn's roaring voice ended in a hearty chuckle.

"Miss Marianne, Miss Marianne!" Daniel jumped on the gunwale and flung his arms through the air.

Noah swerved on his heel, forcing the command from his mouth before he allowed reason to strangle it. "Lower the cockboat!"

"Are you daft, Cap'n?" Blackthorn grabbed his arm, stopping him. "You won't get within twenty yards o' that ship before their swivels blast you from the sea."

Noah glanced at the two guns fastened to the *Undefeatable's* stern railing. Already gun crews hovered busily around them. "Perhaps. But have you any other ideas how to save the lady?"

"We've done our duty, Cap'n." Weller ran the two remaining fingers on his right hand over the scars on his face. "We saved the *Constitution*. But to try and rescue Miss Denton. Why that's sheer foolery."

Noah knew he was right. He also knew he couldn't expect his men to risk their lives any further for him or for Marianne.

Luke gripped Noah's shoulders. "Yet to not try would be even more foolish."

Noah's throat burned at the man's loyalty as Luke cocked a brow, then turned and barked orders to the men to lower the tackles and attach the lines to the boat.

Daniel fed his hand into his father's and gazed up at Noah.

"Do you have a word for me?" Noah hoped to hear something positive from God, anything that would give him a hint that they might succeed.

But the boy lifted clear eyes and shrugged. "Sometimes you just have to trust Him."

With a nod, Noah swung about to watch the narrow vessel dip over the side. Trust was one thing when life was ordinary. But Noah faced impossible odds. He prayed he wouldn't take a shot through his head or a sword through his gut.

Mr. Rupert leapt up from below and approached Noah, a look of concern wrinkling his face. "We're taking in more water."

"How bad is it?"

He shook his head. "We'll probably sink within the hour."

Impossible odds that had just become more impossible.

Noah faced Matthew. "If things go awry, head for the *Constitution*."

"I won't leave you, Cap'n." The old man's voice brooked no argument.

Mr. Lothar approached, holding out Noah's weapons. Grabbing a pistol, Noah primed it and then stuffed it into his belt and sighed. "Do as I say." Turning, he laid a hand on Matthew's shoulder and gave him a knowing look.

The man snorted in return.

Plucking Noah's sword from Mr. Lothar's grasp, Luke strapped it on his own waist. "I'm going with you."

"And me," Blackthorn said.

Though moved by their loyalty, Noah could not allow it. "This is my fight, gentlemen. I can't ask you to join me. It's too dangerous."

"I didn't hear you ask." Blackthorn kissed his son on the forehead then leapt on the bulwarks.

"There is a good chance we will all be killed." Noah gave Blackthorn and Luke a stern look.

Luke grinned. "Some things are worth dying for."

Yanking her head back into the cabin, Marianne heaved to catch her breath. They'd seen her. A vision of Daniel waving with enthusiasm brought a smile to her lips. And Noah. As soon as he'd spotted her, he fell into deep conversation with Luke and Blackthorn.

About how to rescue her?

But what did it matter? There was nothing they could do to help her.

She twisted the ring on her finger and gazed back out the window. They were lowering a boat. A boat?

No! They'd be blown from the water.

Was Noah mad?

Thrusting her face into the buffeting wind, she waved her arms. "No! No!" But when she retreated, she found her warning had gone unheeded. The boat struck the water, and Luke and Blackthorn flung themselves over the bulwarks and ambled down a rope ladder. Noah dropped into the vessel and took his spot at the bow.

A wave of terror swept through her as they shoved off from the *Fortune* and dipped their oars in the water.

Her heart froze.

Footsteps pounded above her. The eerie squeal and crank of the swivel gun being maneuvered into position sent a shiver down her back.

She must do something.

Dashing to the door, she opened it to the red-coated back of the marine still in position. She slammed it and toured the cabin, seeking anything—anything she could use.

For what purpose, she didn't know.

She slid open drawers, flung open cabinets. Her fingers trembled.

Boom! The gun fired. The ship quivered.

She raced to the window.

The shot splashed harmlessly into the sea not ten feet from the boat.

Still they came.

Noah, no! What are you doing?

She flung open the armoire doors. Her eyes landed on a coiled rope tucked at the bottom next to the captain's dress boots. Grabbing it, she returned to the window.

She tied one end of the rope to the captain's desk and flung the rest out the window.

If they insisted on coming for her, if by the grace of God they made it to the ship, the least she could do would be to meet them halfway down the stern.

Even though the thought of dangling in midair over the raging sea sent blood pounding in her head.

Even though the thought of sitting in that tiny boat—with only a few planks of wood between her and the sea—made her shake uncontrollably.

Even though she wasn't altogether sure she could even do either of those things.

Still if they intended to kill themselves, maybe God would allow her a few minutes in Noah's arms before they were all blasted to heaven.

She poked her head out the window and glanced down. Claws of angry foam reached up to grab her. She jerked back inside—to the safety of the ship. She grabbed her throat. Her rapid pulse thrummed against her fingers.

Boom! Another shot fired.

She peered again at the darkening sea. The splash sent a frothy geyser into the air just a few feet before the bow of Noah's boat.

Barely flinching, he continued rowing.

She could make out his face now, could even see the firm lines of determination that etched his bronzed skin whenever he'd made up his mind to do something.

Stubborn fool.

Yet. . . She bit her lip. If he could risk his life for her, surely she could face her deepest fears.

Crawling up on the ledge, she clutched the rope and swung one leg over the side. Taking a deep breath, she swung the other leg over.

Close your eyes. Don't look down. Don't look down.

Salty mist struck her face. The wind whipped her skirts. She gripped the rope and slowly lowered herself over the side.

Her feet dangled like bait over the ravenous sea, and she tapped them against the hull until she found a foothold.

Her sweaty hands slipped on the rope.

Boom! Another shot fired above her. The rope quivered like the string of a fiddle.

She opened her eyes to see the shot strike Noah's boat and blow it to pieces.

"Jump!" Noah shouted then dove over the side into the raging sea. Cold water enveloped him. The roar of the blast filled his ears. A liquid wall struck him. Spikes of wood shot through the sea. One pierced his leg. Pain burned up his thigh. The screams of his men, the cannon blasts, the lap of waves, all combined in a muted symphony beneath the gurgling water.

His lungs ached. He righted himself and kicked his feet. His head popped above the surface to see nothing but planks of charred wood where his boat had been. Swirling around, he searched for his friends. Luke's head bobbed in the distance. Blackthorn appeared beside him.

"Go back!" Noah shouted their way.

"What about you?" Water dripped from Blackthorn's dark hair.

Noah glanced toward his ship. In the encroaching darkness, nothing but a gray shape loomed where he'd left the *Defender*. Even so, he could tell her hull sat lower in the water.

"I order you to go back. Sail to the *Constitution*."

He gazed at the stern of the *Undefeatable* and was shocked to see Marianne hanging onto a rope, dangling midair.

Foolish, brave, *wonderful* girl!

He couldn't leave her. He wouldn't leave her. Even if it meant he became a prisoner of the British navy once again. Even if it meant his death.

"You're mad!" Luke shouted over the waves. He spit out a mouthful of water. Concern shone from his eyes. "Come back with us."

Noah shook his head.

Luke groaned, but finally nodded and turned toward the *Defender*. Blackthorn followed him.

Blue waters transformed to ebony as the last traces of light escaped below the horizon. Gathering a huge breath, Noah dove beneath the murky waters and swam toward the monstrous shadow of the frigate. A monster holding his princess captive.

Marianne listened to the cheers and howls blaring down from above as the men manning the gun congratulated themselves on their good aim.

Holding her breath, she searched the waves. *No, Lord, no.* Her heart felt as though it would explode in her chest. She squinted into the darkness, refusing to tear her gaze away, refusing to admit they were gone. Then slowly, one by one, three heads surfaced, barely discernable in the darkness. She released a heavy breath. They were alive!

But the boat was gone. Obliterated.

Her only way to be rescued swallowed up by the ravenous waves.

Did the crew above see that Noah and his men had survived? She listened for their excited chatter and for the sounds of the gun being reloaded, but only the slosh of the sea against the hull and the pop of distant musket fire swept past her ears.

She leaned her head against the stern. It was cold and wet against her cheek. Her lungs filled with the smell of wood and tar. It was over. Noah had tried.

She would forever be grateful to him for that.

Anguish squeezed every nerve and fiber, threatening to crush her heart. Perhaps getting off this ship was not part of her destiny. *Oh Lord, I don't think I can bear it.* She would miss Noah terribly. And what would become of her mother and sister? Tears barely left her eyes before the breeze batted them away. The cruel wind allowed her no time to mourn.

Yet hadn't she surrendered all to God, no matter His will?

Or was it only when things happened the way she desired that she would give herself freely to Him?

I am sorry, Lord. If I am to stay on this ship, then I will stay.

Her hands burned against the rope's rough fibers.

Bracing her feet on the hull, she slowly pulled herself up. Better to face whatever punishment the captain would wield upon her for breaking his window than drown all alone. That was, if he didn't also discover she'd cut the tiller. Who knew what hideous fate awaited her then.

One final glance over the sea told her Noah and his men must have swum back to the *Fortune*. Good. They were safe.

Then a faint splashing from below caressed her ears. Looking down, she squinted. Tingles ran across her arms. Noah's head popped from beneath the choppy waves. He reached the tip of the lame rudder and gazed up.

"Go back, you fool!" she shouted.

He snapped wet strands of his hair from his face and grinned. "I come to rescue you and you call me a fool?"

Marianne inched down the rope closer to him. "Yes! When that is how you are behaving. What do you think you are doing?"

"I have already told you."

"Are you mad?"

"Definitely." He smiled again.

Marianne huffed. Part of her screamed in fear for Noah's life while another part of her screamed in ecstasy at his chivalrous action.

"Go away before they see you!" She waved him off.

A swell splashed over him and he shook the water from his face. "I'm not leaving without you."

"You have no boat."

"I have my back."

Marianne's fingers grew numb. They slipped on the rope. "Are you daft? I can't come down there."

"Yes you can."

"You know we are both already dead."

"Probably."

His nonchalant tone jarred Marianne. She searched for a glimpse of his expression, to know if he smiled or if fear tightened his features, but the descending shadows stole his visage from her.

"Jump, Marianne. If we are to die, I would rather die in your arms."

Her heart melted as tears filled her eyes. "Don't be such a romantic goose."

A sound came from the captain's cabin. Marianne's mouth went dry. "Leave! I beg you before they discover you." Her voice broke in a sob. "I will not have your death on my hands."

"I will not leave you."

"But I'm asking you to. Please? For me?"

Marianne glanced toward the *Fortune*, but the ship had moved. A nebulous shadow skating on an eerie mist drifted toward them.

"It's time, princess. Jump!"

She shook her head. Her blood turned to ice. "I can't. You know I can't."

"Ah, but you can. You have only to trust me." He clung to the rudder chain with one hand as he held up the other. "I'll catch you, and you can hold onto my back while I swim."

"We'll sink." Pictures of her father's bloated white body swelled in her vision. She gazed down. Below the surface of the murky sea, nothing but cold and dark extended to a bottomless pit.

"We won't sink. I'm a strong swimmer." Noah's confident tone held a hint of panic.

Terror clogged in her throat. She couldn't speak.

"Trust me." He waved her on with his hand. "Come, we haven't much time."

Trust. She'd sworn never to trust anyone again.

"Marianne, I promise I'll catch you." Urgency and conviction fired from his voice.

"Trust Me." The words rose from deep within her, strong and convicting and filled with promise.

"Lord, You want me to jump?" she whispered.

"Yes. Trust Me, beloved. I'll always be there to catch you."

Marianne's eyes burned with tears.

The rope tugged in her hand.

"Ah, here you are." A familiar voice dribbled down upon her.

Marianne slowly raised her gaze to the stern windows where the dark barrel of a pistol hovered over her forehead.

❖ CHAPTER 30 ❖

"L ieutenant Reed." All hope fled Marianne, turning her muscles into mush.

He leaned over the window frame, a pistol in one hand, a knife in the other. "Look what I found lying beside the slashed tiller ropes."

Marianne's head grew light. Her fingers slipped on the rough hemp.

"Come up here, Miss Denton at once, or I'll be forced to shoot you."

She studied his face, but it was too dark to see his expression. "Please, Mr. Reed, let us go."

"Lieutenant, I beg you!" Noah shouted from below.

"Beg all you want, Mr. Brenin." Mr. Reed's voice held the pompous ring of the London ton. "But you and this lady are enemies of England. Together you have disabled a British frigate, and you must pay the consequences."

"Take me instead!" Noah yelled.

"No, Noah!" The ship hefted over a swell, sending the rope swinging. Marianne's stomach tightened. Her fingers ached. Pain burned across her palms. Bracing her feet on the stern, she settled the line.

"Let her go and take me," Noah shouted louder this time. "She's a lady and should not be entangled in the wars of men."

"Very heroic, Mr. Brenin." Mr. Reed's voice carried none of the expected sarcasm. "But my life and my career are on the line. I've too much at risk to care about the lives of two Yankee rebels."

A heaviness settled on Marianne. All was lost. With one last glance at Noah, she inched her way up the rope. "Go back, Noah. He can't shoot us both."

"I told you, I'm not leaving you."

Tears spilled down her cheeks, cooled by the night breeze. "Noah, please." She continued climbing. Nearly at the ledge, she halted and glanced up. The knife in Mr. Reed's hand blurred into a silver streak. *The knife.* Of course. "Mr. Reed, if memory serves me well, it was you who allowed me to keep that knife." Threads of strength wove through her trembling voice.

"For protection only."

"But you *did* allow me to keep it."

"Yes."

"And I did slash the tiller ropes with it."

Nothing but the creak of the ship responded.

Marianne gathered her resolve and said a silent prayer. "If I stay on this ship, I will inform the captain of such. And from what little I know of your precious Articles of War, I would say that information will not bode well for your naval career."

The shadow that was Mr. Reed remained frozen in place.

"However, if you grant Noah and me our freedom, Captain Milford need never find out."

Voices barreled down from above. "There's a man on our rudder chain!"

Mr. Reed withdrew the pistol. She heard him sigh. His shadow shifted. Boot steps thundered.

Reed gazed down at her. "Jump and be quick about it."

Marianne glanced at the dark water gurgling beneath her feet.

More boot steps. More voices shouting.

"Do it now!" Mr. Reed hissed, then he disappeared from the window.

"Trust me, Marianne." Noah's voice of assurance wrapped around her from below.

But she couldn't see him in the darkness. Would he catch her?

A light appeared in the captain's cabin, spilling over the ledge like a glittering waterfall.

Trust Me.

"There's a woman out here!"

Words from the book of Esther drifted through Marianne's mind—words Esther said after she had decided to follow God and trust Him.

"If I perish, I perish."

Marianne let go of the rope.

If not for Marianne's scream and the shadow of her falling body blocking the light streaming from the stern windows, Noah wouldn't have been ready to catch her.

But catch her, he did.

She barely hit the surface of the sea before he reached out and grabbed her waist. Together they plunged under the water.

Zip zip. Bullets sped by his ears. Grabbing the thrashing woman, Noah dove deeper into the cold, wet void. Darkness surrounded him. The sounds of shouting and the tap of musket fire combined in a muted undersea chorus.

Lord, please save us.

His lungs ached. He dragged a squirming Marianne to the surface.

With effort, he held her face above water. She heaved and spewed up the sea, then screamed.

He covered her mouth and dove again just as the air filled with musket shot.

She writhed in his grasp, kicking her legs. She struck him in the groin. Agony burned down his thighs. He surfaced, biting back a wail of pain. The sea slapped his face. Marianne gasped for air.

One glance over the choppy black waves told him Matthew had not obeyed his last command. The *Defender* slid through the ebony waters just twenty yards away and began to slow.

Too close. The *Undefeatable* could reach his ship with their swivel guns.

"It will be all right, Marianne." He whispered between breaths what he no longer believed then wiped a strand of hair from her eyes. "Hang onto my back and hold your breath."

She nodded. A burst of light came from the *Undefeatable's* stern, highlighting the terror on her face.

Boom! He pushed her below the surface then dove beside her. The shot struck only a few feet to their right. A wall of water crashed into them, shoving them through the sea.

Noah broke through the waves again. "Hold on." He placed her hands on his shoulders then plunged through the frothing waves. She groped frantically at his shirt, her legs flailing. She clutched his neck. Pain shot through his shoulders. His throat constricted. But she held on.

Tap tap tap. More musket fire sped around them, peppering the sea.

Every muscle in Noah's body screamed in agony. His lungs throbbed. Marianne's weight felt like an anchor on his back, threatening to sink them both.

Lord, help.

Noah's head grew light. He began to sink.

Cold water closed in on him from all around. His mind went numb. It was all over. He had failed.

A strong hand grabbed his arm.

His head popped above the surface. He heaved for air, but Marianne's tight grip on his throat barely allowed a breath to enter his lungs.

"Hold on to me." Blackthorn's voice, thick with effort and concern, sounded like heavenly music in Noah's ears.

Behind him, Marianne gasped. Her hot breath fanned his shoulder. He felt himself being dragged through the water.

The smell of wood filled his nose. His hand struck the moist hull. His ship.

Blackthorn placed Noah's hand on the rope ladder. "Can you climb?"

Unable to speak, Noah nodded. Grabbing the rope with one hand, he tried to pry Marianne's hands off of his neck with the other.

Her firm grip told him she was alive. But he needed to see her. To make sure she wasn't injured.

Blackthorn assisted him in loosening her grip.

Gulping air, Noah swung around. He couldn't make out her face in the darkness. "Are you all right?"

She leaned on his shoulder, her chest heaving.

Grasping her waist, Noah tightened his grip on the rope and glanced aloft.

"Ahoy up," he commanded as loud as he dared. Groans filtered down as the ladder rose along the side of the hull. Or what remained of the hull still above water.

Matthew clutched Noah's arm and helped him and Marianne over the bulwarks. Blackthorn thumped onto the deck behind them.

Marianne's brown hair hung to her waist in saturated strands. She let out a shuttering sob and started to topple. Noah grabbed her and drew her close. Her cold, wet body trembled against his.

"You came for me," she whispered, her voice raspy and filled with wonder.

Noah embraced her and kissed her forehead as the shadows of his crew surrounded them, muttering congratulations and patting him on the back.

"I can't believe you did that, Cap'n," Mr. Rupert exclaimed.

"Ain't never seen anything like it," another sailor added.

"We thought you was sunk for sure." Mr. Boone chortled.

In the distance, the stern lights of the *Undefeatable* winked at them as the mighty frigate drifted listlessly out of sight.

And out of gun range.

Huzzahs rang from his crew.

Emerging from the shadows, Daniel dashed to Marianne's side. "I told you God had a plan."

"Yes, you did." She pressed the boy close. "Yes, you did."

Noah still clung to Marianne, refusing to release her, too afraid she'd disappear. Her face was just inches from his. Her sweet breath wafted over him. He peered through the darkness for a glimpse into those lustrous brown eyes where he hoped to find appreciation, admiration, and perhaps even—love.

But they were lost to him in the shadows.

Agnes dashed toward Marianne. "Oh, you poor dear."

Reluctantly releasing her to the older woman, Noah gazed in the distance where he could still make out the lights from the *Constitution*.

"All hands aloft! Unfurl all sail!" He faced the helm. "Head for the *Constitution*, Mr. Pike."

"Aye, aye, Cap'n." Yet absent was the usual confidence in the helmsman's voice.

Luke brayed the orders, sending the men aloft, then took his spot beside Noah. He huffed and shifted his stance.

But Noah knew what troubled the man before he opened his mouth. He knew because as the sails filled with wind, the ship barely moved. Hull down, she slogged forward like an anchor dragging over the bottom of the sea.

"We will sink before we reach them. *If* we reach them." Luke's words of defeat landed like grapeshot on Noah's open wounds.

But he could not accept them. Not after all he'd endured.

Noah paced across the deck. "Light every lantern, Mr. Weller. Light every candle, every wick. And load one gun for a signal shot!" He glanced aloft where the American flag flapped from their foremast. Surely, with all lanterns blazing, the *Constitution* would spot the ensign and come to their rescue.

Oh Lord, open their eyes.

They had to see it. He stopped and clenched his fists. He had not risked his life and the lives of his entire crew just to see them all drowned.

Marianne could not stop trembling. And not because her gown was wet. They were sinking. And once again she would be thrust into the merciless sea.

Blackthorn called for Daniel. The lad squeezed her hand then darted to his father.

"Come below, dear. Let's get you into some dry attire." Agnes tugged on her wet sleeve but Marianne remained firm.

"Please, I don't want to go below if we are to sink." Her lips quivered making her words come out harsh.

"No, of course, dear." Despite her calm tone, Agnes trembled when she wrapped an arm around Marianne's shoulder. "What a horrible ordeal you've been through. Just horrible. I prayed for you every night."

Turning, Marianne hugged the woman, taking comfort from her warm embrace. "Thank you, Agnes. God answered your prayers."

Agnes withdrew and stared across the sea. "I hope the Almighty answers the prayer I'm makin' now." She sighed and forced a smile. "Well, the least I can do is get you a blanket. That is, if the water has not reached my cabin yet." She buzzed away and dropped below deck.

Hugging herself, Marianne slipped into the shadows. Her eyes latched on Noah. He marched confidently across the ship issuing orders and encouragements to his men. His brown hair dripped onto his collar. His white shirt clung to a muscled torso still heaving from exertion.

He had come for her.

He had risked his life for her. And now faced with another crisis, he handled himself with such assurance, such wisdom, such bravery.

Marianne swallowed the burning in her throat. Because of her, his ship was sinking. Because of her, he would lose everything. . .possibly even his life.

But God had been faithful thus far.

Lord, I trusted You. I dove into the waters. And You didn't let me drown.

Now, please don't allow us to sink.

With lanterns hanging on every mast hook and railing, the ship lit up like a tree at Christmas.

Sails snapped overhead, bursting with wind like bloated specters. Yet the vessel slogged through the water as if pushing through black molasses. Trembling, Marianne inched her way to the railing. If they were going to sink, she would face the waters with the same bravery Noah displayed.

The ravenous waves slapped the hull just a few feet below her. Yet strangely, she felt no fear. She thought of the frightful dream she'd had not long ago where she'd been aboard a sinking ship while all her friends sailed away leaving her alone. Now she realized it was a trick of the enemy to discourage her. She was indeed aboard a sinking ship, but she was not alone. No one had left her, especially not God. She leaned over and examined the waves again. The sea gurgled and spit and carried on like an insolent child. She laughed. Why had she ever been afraid of it? With God's help and Noah's strong back, she had crossed these waters and survived. If she sank in them now, God would bring her home to heaven. The sea would not hold her captive for long. In fact, as she watched the foam-capped ebony waves, she saw them as nothing but slippery fingers always reaching, grabbing, threatening, but ultimately powerless.

The musky scent of Noah surrounded her. Her heart leapt. He stood beside her, his hair and breeches still dripping. Lantern light glimmered in his eyes as they soaked her in from head to toe.

She wanted to throw herself into his arms. To thank him. To tell him she loved him. But before she could, he pressed her head to his chest and covered her other ear with his hand.

The *boom* of a single gun thundered through the ship. Timbers shook and creaked. Marianne felt the reverberations through Noah's strong arms. Strong arms that seemed to filter out the fear. She wished he'd never let go.

The sting of gunpowder burned her nose as smoke enveloped them.

Batting it away, Noah released her. She grew cold again.

Both gazed toward the *Constitution*.

The entire crew gazed toward the *Constitution*.

Waiting. . .waiting. . . The sea laughed at them as it broke against their hull.

Had the men aboard heard them? Did they see them? Did they care?

A jet of orange light came in reply, followed by a *boom* that cracked the night sky.

"They've spotted us. We are saved!"

❖ CHAPTER 31 ❖

With Seafoam nestled in her arms, Marianne followed the tall, lithe lieutenant down the passageway. Below deck, the *Constitution* was not much different from the *Undefeatable*. Narrow, dank hallways lit by intermittent lanterns stretched into the murky shadows. Small, cluttered cabins lined the hull, and the smell of bilge and unwashed men permeated every plank and timber.

But there *was* one glorious difference.

The *Constitution* was an American ship, not an enemy. And here, Marianne was a guest, not a prisoner. For she'd been treated with nothing but courtesy since she had boarded last night.

In fact, within minutes of spotting them, the *Constitution* had come alongside and quickly dispatched two boats to deliver Noah and his crew from the sinking ship. But no sooner had Marianne's feet hit the deck than she and Agnes were rushed below to the cabin normally occupied by the ship's master, John Alwyn, who'd been wounded during the battle. There, the two ladies were given hammocks to sleep in, basins of water for washing, and hot tea to soothe their nerves.

Though the hammock was comfortable, Marianne found no sleep

during the long night. Her mind kept replaying the harrowing events of the past few days. Stealing the knife, cutting the tiller ropes, crawling out the stern windows, Noah risking his life for her, her dive into the sea, and their ultimate rescue. She thanked the Lord over and over for His faithfulness until tears of joy streamed down her cheeks onto the coverlet.

God had told her to trust Him. He had told her to jump. And even though everything within her screamed in protest, she had obeyed. And God had saved her—saved her straight into Noah's arms.

Yet she'd not seen Noah since. Or any of his crew. In fact, she'd hardly spoken a word to Noah since she dove into the sea. How she longed to feel his arms around her again, to look into his eyes…to find out whether he had come back for her out of a sense of duty, honor, or because of something deeper—something that made her heart leap for joy.

Agnes's heavy footsteps thudded behind her, bringing her back to the present. Marianne glanced over her shoulder. A huge smile broke the elderly woman's face even as her puffy cheeks pinked. She appeared as flustered as Marianne felt. For neither woman knew why they had been summoned to the captain's cabin so early in the morning.

Marianne's stomach tightened around the biscuit she'd eaten for breakfast. She scratched Seafoam beneath her chin. Had something else gone wrong? But when they reached the end of the passageway, deep voices and laughter echoed through the bulkhead, settling her nerves.

Especially since one of the voices was Noah's.

Nodding toward the marine who stood guard outside the captain's cabin, the lieutenant knocked. Upon hearing the captain's "enter," he swung open the door, ducked beneath the frame, and beckoned the ladies forward.

Marianne took a step inside and swept the room with her gaze. A blast of wind swirled around her from the broken stern windows. The scent of scorched wood burned her nose. Black soot and ashes covered the deck and the charred remains of what looked like a cabinet; two chairs and a mahogany desk had been shoved into the corner. Everything else, however, appeared intact. In addition to a few placards, lanterns, and a row of swords, only a single painting of George Washington decorated the bulkheads.

Noah, Luke, and Weller stood at attention before a tall, portly man dressed in white breeches and a dark blue jacket, crowned at the shoulders with gold-fringed epaulets. Matthew, Daniel, and Blackthorn stood behind them while a row of officers lined the aft bulkhead.

Agnes darted to her husband. Wrapping an arm around her, Matthew drew her close.

Seafoam leapt from Marianne's arms and sprang toward Noah.

"Ah, there is the lady of honor." The tall man Marianne assumed to be the captain approached her.

Halting, Marianne watched as he bowed slightly and offered her his elbow.

"Captain," Noah's voice sent a warm tremble through her. "May I present, Miss Marianne Denton. Miss Denton, Captain Isaac Hull."

"Miss Denton." Stylish brown hair curled around his forehead as his dark, intelligent eyes found hers.

"Captain." She smiled, placed her hand in the crook of his elbow, and allowed him to lead her forward.

Luke winked at her as they passed.

"Hi, Miss Marianne." Daniel waved.

She smiled at the lad.

Noah's gaze met hers. A mischievous twinkle flickered across his blue eyes. Aside from a few bruises on his face and the dark circles of exhaustion beneath his eyes, he looked well, commanding—handsome.

"I see your cabin suffered during the battle," Marianne said.

"You see correctly, Miss Denton." The captain released her arm and surveyed the damage. "The *Guerriére's* bow guns played havoc with my new desk. Alas, but Mr. Hoffmann"—he gestured toward the man who had led her and Agnes here, and who now stood at attention by the door—"saved the day and put out the fire."

The man smiled at Marianne.

"However, Miss Denton." Captain Hull faced her. "It is my

understanding that I have you to thank for disabling the HMS *Undefeatable.*" He laughed. "*Undefeatable.* I believe they should rename their ship."

One of the officers chuckled.

"I did nothing, really," Marianne said.

"Did you or did you not cut the ship's tiller cables?"

"I did, sir."

"Then you are a heroine."

Marianne flinched. "Me? I believe it was Mr. Brenin who shot out her mast."

Noah smiled, saying, "A feat I was only able to perform due to your action, Miss Denton." Seafoam circled his legs, rubbing against them.

So it was Miss Denton again. Marianne twisted the ring on her finger. "I was happy to do my part, Captain."

"Your part?" He chuckled, sending the golden fringe on his epaulets shaking. "Egad, she is a treasure." He shared a look with Noah. "You disabled a British frigate, miss. A feat many a man has never achieved, yet you are a lone woman. I find your humility refreshing."

Marianne felt a blush rising and lowered her gaze. "God was with me."

"Ah yes. God was with us all." The captain adjusted his coat "Those redcoats would have blasted us from the sea, entangled as we were with that infernal *Guerriére.*"

"I love my country, sir. I could do no less." Marianne lifted her gaze to Daniel. "It was my destiny."

Daniel beamed. His father patted him on the back.

"Destiny." The captain cocked his head, then paced before Noah and his crew. "I like the sound of that. I like the sound of that, indeed." He halted and adjusted his white cravat around his fleshy chin. Despite the long pointed nose that reminded Marianne of a cannon, the captain possessed a friendly face that seemed at odds with his commanding position.

He squared his shoulders. "Then it was God's destiny that we are the first American ship to defeat a British man-of-war. And those pompous redcoats thought they ruled the seas. Egad." He fisted his hand in the air. "We taught them a lesson." He took up pacing again.

His officers murmured their agreement from behind Noah and his men.

"Humph. And to think they were saying in Washington and all up and down our coastline that our amateur navy did not stand a chance against the expertise, the experience, and sheer power of the British Royal Navy." He chuckled, his eyes sparkling. He stopped again. "Do you know what this will do?" He asked no one in particular. "This will give great encouragement to our fleet! We have proven that the British navy is not invincible. Not only that, this victory will no doubt prompt Madison to increase our funding for more ships and weaponry. Aye, this is good news. This battle may turn the tide of the war before it has barely begun."

As Marianne listened to the captain's speech, she couldn't help but feel a sense of pride in her part of the battle. If what Captain Hull said was true and this defeat would lead to more victories at sea, then God had used her for something truly important. Little, ordinary Marianne from Baltimore.

Reaching down, Daniel picked up Seafoam and began petting her.

"How many men did you lose, Captain?" Noah asked.

A fresh breeze whirled in through the broken window, stirring flakes of charred wood across the deck. Captain Hull released a sigh, heavy with sorrow. "Seven. One marine, five seamen, and Lieutenant William Bush. All good men." He glanced over his officers who stood at attention in the back of the cabin. "Heroes."

They nodded in agreement.

"You are all heroes," the captain continued, and Marianne got the impression he loved to hear himself talk. "And you." He stopped and pointed at Noah. "You would make a great officer in the U.S. navy. I shall be happy to write a letter of recommendation to Madison and request a commission for you."

An officer in the navy? Marianne eyed Noah. Now that his merchant business had sunk—thanks to her—would he take the man up on his offer?

But he seemed unaffected. "Thank you, Captain. I am honored to have one so distinguished as yourself willing to stand up for me. Allow me some time to consider it."

"Very well. Take your time, Mr. Brenin. I am in your debt."

"And what of you?" The captain narrowed his eyes on Luke.

Luke's lips slanted. "Me? In the navy?" He raised his hand to cover a cough that Marianne could tell was more of a laugh.

Noah smiled.

Weller chuckled.

Luke shifted his stance. "I fear I am not a man who thrives under authority."

Captain Hull studied him. He let out a disgruntled moan. "Regardless, I am in your debt as well."

"If I may call on that debt, Captain," Noah said, drawing the captain's gaze. "My crew and I would be most grateful if you could deliver us to Baltimore at your earliest convenience."

"Can we go see Mother?" Daniel tugged on his father's torn, stained shirt.

Noah glanced at them, then back at the captain. "By way of Savannah, perhaps?"

The captain fingered his chin.

Marianne's heart skipped at the possibility of seeing her mother and sister again soon.

A uniformed man tapped on the doorframe. "Captain, they are signaling from the *Guerriére* that they're ready to bring the remainder of the prisoners aboard."

"Thank you, Lowe." Captain Hull studied Noah, then released a heavy sigh. "Jones's locker be cursed. I think we can manage it. Perhaps"—he chuckled—"God will find it in His destiny to send us another British warship to defeat along the way."

Daniel nestled Seafoam against his cheek and smiled up at his father. The look on Blackthorn's face slowly melted into one of joy. His eyes moistened, and Marianne swallowed the emotion burning in her throat. Finally, after two years, the man would be reunited with his wife.

Agnes kissed her husband's cheek, and Luke and Weller smiled at Noah.

"Excellent." The captain slapped his hands together. "Gentlemen." He glanced over Marianne and Agnes. "Ladies, if you'll excuse me."

And he marched from the cabin.

Marianne stood at the bow of the USS *Constitution*, away from the hustle of the crew, and gazed at the crippled *Guerriére* listing to larboard several yards ahead of them. After their meeting in the captain's cabin, Agnes retired to her cabin with a headache, and Noah and his men darted off to assist Captain Hull in retrieving the remaining British sailors from the defeated ship.

One casual glance and a smile was all Noah had offered Marianne as he left the cabin. Not much to go on. Not much of an indication of where his heart lay. She longed to know what he was thinking. She longed to thank him for risking his life for her, for keeping his word. And deep down, she longed to know if he cared for her as much as she did him.

Shielding her eyes from the afternoon sun, she scanned the horizon. No sign of the HMS *Undefeatable*. No doubt she drifted away during the night at the mercy of wind and tide and would continue to do so until the crew repaired the tiller and the mast. Thoughts of Captain Milford saddened her. She had come to care for the old curmudgeon, who despite his foul moods and maniacal episodes, had been kind to Marianne—even complimentary. She hoped, no she prayed, he would find his way to land and live out his days as a farmer.

A gust of wind danced through her hair and brought with it the smell of gunpowder, the sea, and charred wood. Leaning over the railing, she glanced at the blue waves frolicking against the hull. She chuckled. She was no longer frightened of the water. No longer frightened of anything.

Except spending her life without Noah.

Would they simply return to Baltimore, end their engagement, and go their separate ways? Without a ship, without a merchant business to fund, Noah had no reason to please his father with a forced marriage, especially since he now knew the true state of the Denton fortune. After Noah explained it to his father, the man would no doubt agree to call off the marriage. Then Marianne would have to find another way to care for her sick mother and her sister.

Yet that pain was nothing compared to the gnawing ache of losing Noah.

A light touch on the small of her back caused a flutter in her belly. Noah's warm breath fanned her neck. "Marianne." Shivers tingled down her back.

She turned her head. His blue eyes caressed her face. His lips lingered just inches from hers. She swallowed and faced forward, her heart in her throat.

He slipped beside her, keeping his hand on her back. "You are no longer afraid of the sea?"

His brown hair whipped behind him. She longed to run her fingers over the stubble on his firm jaw.

"No. I believe the Lord has cured me." She gave a little laugh.

"Would that He had done so before you nearly drowned us both." He huffed, his voice ringing with playful annoyance.

Marianne's face grew hot. She pushed his hand away. "Noah Brenin, I was terrified out of my mind. I thought I was drowning. I wasn't myself."

He grinned.

"You taunt me." She lowered her shoulders. "I'm sorry. You are right. I could have drowned us both."

"I shouldn't tease you." He raised her hand to his lips and kissed it. Her body warmed. "Thank you for coming back for me."

"I said I would."

"You risked everything. Your ship, your men, your life."

"Did you doubt that I would try?" He frowned.

Of course she did. "Few people keep their word under such dire circumstances."

MaryLu Tyndall

The afternoon sun painted his hair with streaks of gold. He leaned toward her. "It depends on the value of the prize."

Marianne's breath halted. Did he mean her, or saving the *Constitution*? She wished she had more experience with courting. If that was even what this was. She wished her heart didn't twist in a knot whenever Noah was near. She wished she believed that a man like him could love a woman like her. "Yes, Captain Hull seems quite taken with your performance," she said.

"And yours." He frowned again. Shifting his boots over the planks, he gazed at the sparkling azure waves spreading to the horizon. "Destiny. There's something wonderful about knowing you belong to an Almighty God who loves you. A God who has a purpose for your life. Makes the fear of dying fade by comparison."

Marianne could relate. She, too, had found her destiny aboard the *Undefeatable*. But Noah's words stunned her. "Did I hear you correctly, Mr. Brenin? You speak of God and destiny as though you now believe in both."

He smiled. "I was wrong about both. I was wrong about many things." He brushed a strand of hair from her face. "I have discovered God's nothing like my father. I don't have to perform to win His love."

Marianne smiled, her heart bursting with joy. "What of Jacob's death?"

"Part of God's plan." He shrugged. "I may never know His reasons until I die."

"I'm so happy, Noah." She laid a hand on his arm. "I, too, have begun to trust God again." She shook her head. "I am still shocked that He used me, a plain, ordinary woman with no special talents to win a major victory in a war for our country's freedom."

"Plain? Ordinary?" Noah took her hand in his. "Woman, you are the most extraordinary creature I have ever met."

Tears filled her eyes. She gazed out to sea, overcome with emotion. Extraordinary? She flattened her lips. If that were true, why did her father leave her?

"*Precious child.*" God's voice filled her spirit.

And the answer came to her. Her father's problems had nothing to do with her, nor did his death bear any reflection on her value. She twisted the ring on her finger. A ray of sunlight caught the ruby and set it aflame. She had intended to sell it once. For to her, it represented the extent of her father's opinion of her worth. But now she knew her worth. She was a child of God. Precious and beloved. No, she would not sell it. She would cherish this ring as the last memento she had from her earthly father.

She gazed up at Noah and found him looking at her, concern filling his brow.

"You don't believe that I find you extraordinary?" he asked.

"I've never received such flattery."

"Not flattery, my love." He toyed with a strand of her hair, his gaze hovering over her lips.

She laid a hand on her chest to still her beating heart, beating in the hope that the love she saw in his eyes sprang from his heart. "So, it was destiny that brought you back to me?"

"Aye." Wind blasted over them, lifting the hair at his collar. He stared at the *Guerrière*, her masts nothing but shattered twigs, her decks littered with tangled lines and canvas. She listed heavily to larboard, groaning in despair of her ultimate demise. One final cockboat pushed off from her hull and headed back to the *Constitution*. Blackthorn and Daniel waved at them from the stern.

Noah waved back.

"And what does destiny prompt you to do next?" Marianne pressed him. He squared his shoulders. "I believe I shall become a privateer."

Daft man. Ignoring her disappointment, Marianne gave him a coy smile. "Privateering? Why, Noah Brenin, if I didn't know better I'd say you've turned into a patriot."

He gave a jaunty huff. "A few months aboard a British frigate would change even the staunchest renegade." He grew serious. "I've been selfish, thinking only of my father's business, only of our family...only of myself. America is a great country. And I sense God leading me to defend her." He faced her, his eyes glittering. "For the first time in my life, I feel as though I have a purpose."

Marianne nodded, admiring his zeal.

"To defend our nation is a privilege worth fighting for—even dying for," he added.

"Dying? I cannot risk losing you again, Noah Brenin." The words came out before Marianne had a chance to check them.

His expression softened, and he ran a thumb over her cheek. "You'll never lose me."

Marianne searched those words for the meaning she longed to hear.

He cupped her chin, and then slowly lowered his lips to hers.

An explosion broke the peaceful afternoon. Jerking away from Noah, Marianne swept her gaze toward the sound. Yellow and orange flames, littered with chunks of wood shot high into the air above the *Guerriére*.

"What happened?" she asked.

"Captain Hull ordered the ship destroyed." Noah gazed solemnly at the scene.

Cheers and howls and huzzahs blared from the crew of the *Constitution,* then all grew quiet as they watched the British ship shudder. Streams of light ran along her hull. The quarterdeck lifted in the air. With an ominous boom, it exploded into fragments that flew in every direction. The hull split in two then reeled and staggered like a drunken man before plunging forward and sinking beneath the sea.

Until nothing but a swirl of foam-capped waves marked the spot where once she stood.

Marianne felt an emptiness in her gut at the sight of the mighty warship sinking to the cold depths—never to sail the majestic seas again.

Yet she supposed that was its destiny.

Noah's jaw tightened as he continued to gaze at the sight.

Had he been about to kiss her? Her heart raced.

He faced her, a mischievous gleam in his eye. "Now, where were we?" He leaned toward her.

Against every urge within her, she held up a hand to stay his advance. "Regardless of what you think, I do not allow just any man to kiss me."

His brow furrowed. "Just any man? Have I been reduced to standing in a line of common suitors vying for your affections?"

Marianne huffed. As if she'd ever had such a line. "Last I heard,

Noah Brenin, you had no interest in marrying me."

"And you said you'd never marry me." He gazed at her mouth and began his descent again. "Much has happened since then."

She placed a finger on his lips. They were warm and moist and made her hand tingle. "Enlighten me as to exactly what has happened?"

His eyes lifted to hers, then he backed away, a playful smirk on his face. "For one thing, we have not called off the engagement. Hence, I am still your fiancé and have every right to kiss you." He pressed in again.

Her finger rose. "Then you wish to marry me?"

He straightened his stance. The adoration in his eyes threatened to turn her legs to jelly. His warm fingers pressed on her neck as his thumb caressed her jaw. "Woman, I will die if you don't marry me." He laid his forehead against hers. "I love you with all my heart."

Now Marianne's knees became custard. His words sailed through her, squelching all her insecurities and fears. She clung to him and tilted her head up to receive his kiss.

Warm and hungry, his mouth devoured hers, seeking, caressing, enjoying. He tasted of salt and coffee and. . .Noah. A wave of passion swept through her, tingling her toes.

Whistles and howls from the crew pulled them apart. Marianne's face grew hot.

She smiled. "I love you, too, Noah." She rubbed a finger over his stubbled jaw. "I can't wait to become your wife."

His breathing came hard and rapid. He drew her to his chest. "Me either, princess. Me either."

As commands to get the ship underway shot across the deck, Noah and Marianne stood arm in arm, and stared over the wide expanse of glistening sea that seemed to spread out before them with endless possibilities.

The snap of a sail sounded above them.

The ship jerked forward as the purl of the water played against the bow.

"Do you think God has more for us to do?" Marianne looked up at Noah.

He smiled. "I think God has only just begun."

ABOUT THE AUTHOR

MaryLu Tyndall

MaryLu Tyndall dreamed of pirates and seafaring adventures during her childhood days on Florida's coast. She holds a degree in math and worked as a software engineer for fifteen years before testing the waters as a writer. Her love of history and passion for storytelling drew her to create the Legacy of the King's Pirates series. MaryLu now writes full-time and makes her home with her husband, six children, and four cats on California's coast, where her imagination still surges with the sea. Her passion is to write page-turning, romantic adventures that not only entertain but expose Christians to their full potential in Christ. For more information on MaryLu and her upcoming releases, please visit her Web site at www.mltyndall.com or her blog at crossandcutlass. blogspot.com.